THE STORM
BEYOND
THE TIDES

JONATHAN CULLEN

This is a work of fiction. Any resemblance to actual persons, living or dead, or actual events is purely coincidental.

"Leaves that made last year beautiful, still strewn

Even as they fell, unchanged, beneath the changing moon…"

—Alan Seeger

1939

Ellie Ames stood at the edge of the dock, a crate of tools beside her, while her father worked on the motor, his forearms red and streaked with grease. Jack cared for the twenty-foot sloop like it was his, but he was only captaining it for a commercial outfit in Portland, getting paid a percentage of the catch, beholden to an owner he never met. He once had his own boat, before Mary got sick, and Ellie knew that working for someone else hurt his pride, tore at his soul, made every day a living penance for his past mistakes.

"Wrench," he said.

She got one from the box and handed it to him. Standing at the helm behind her, dressed in a smock and cap, was Benjamin Frazier, a family friend who had been working with Jack for several seasons.

"Hammer."

Ellie gave him one and Jack reached back without looking. As he crouched, his shirt lifted and she saw the scars on his back, as hideous in appearance as they were for the injury they represented. Ellie still cringed at the sight of it, as did Mary, although the disfigurement had always been there and was as much a part of him as his dark beard and his slight limp.

Finally, Jack sat up and sighed. Squinting in the morning sun, he held out the broken rubber belt like it was evidence from a crime scene, then looked at Ellie.

"Go to Lavery's," he said. "Get a new one."

She nodded and waved to Mary, who was leaning over the dock on her crutches, searching for minnows and jellyfish.

They walked up the gangway and when they came to the pier, Monk Island was bustling for the Fourth of July. Throngs of people—locals, vacationers, and day-trippers—crowded the small waterfront and village, browsing the shops and lingering on the sidewalks. American flags hung from every lamppost, in every shop window, and on the grassy slope overlooking the docks, people were already claiming spots for the evening fireworks over Portland Harbor. Young boys hawked souvenir brass lobster trinkets, and an old man dressed like Uncle Sam was selling maps for a nickel. There were vendor carts with roasted peanuts, cotton candy, and frankfurters, and the small port had the festive air of an outdoor carnival.

They passed the terminal, where a ferry had just arrived and passengers were streaming off with suitcases and bags, beach chairs and umbrellas. As they merged with the crowd and headed up towards the village, something caught Ellie's attention and she was distracted. It was a boy, or young man—much like herself, he was in that period of life that skirted the line between youth and adulthood. He was tall and thin, with short-cropped hair and a linen shirt, and he walked alongside his parents, pulling two suitcases. His father limped with a cane, a cigar in hand and scarf around his neck— unusual attire for summer—and his mother was a petite brunette with a flowered dress and pearls around her neck. Monk Island drew visitors from everywhere, but there was something mysterious about the family and Ellie couldn't stop staring.

"What are you looking at?"

Ellie turned to Mary, who looked up with a toothy grin.

"Um, nothing. Thought I recognized someone."

......

The "village" on Monk Island was little more than a small intersection with a grocer, butchery, ice cream parlor, and some tourist shops which sold souvenirs, hats, and postcards. But as the only commercial area, people spoke of it like it was a metropolis. On one corner was The Devonshire, an inn and wedding hall that had once been the summer estate of a nineteenth-century oil baron. Behind it, on the dirt road leading up the hill, was the American Legion, opened after the First World War when the Portland post became full. Farther down Gull Avenue was the Bowladrome, a twelve-lane bowling alley that was once a fish salting facility. With its big neon sign, it was the closest thing to glamor on the Island, and young people, both locals and tourists, flocked there on summer nights.

Lavery's Delicatessen was a combination hardware store and bait & tackle shop that catered to the Island's fishermen. On an island with such sparse commerce, every business had to maximize what it offered. Once an actual delicatessen, Lavery's was owned by their neighbor, Joe Mallet Jr., who bought it cheap during the Depression and never changed the sign.

When Ellie opened the door, a bell overhead jingled. Inside, the shop was dry and dusty, with wide-plank floors whose nails were worn shiny from boots. The walls had bins filled with galvanized fasteners, brown paper bags, and a chain-scale hung from the ceiling. The shelves were stocked with gallons of deck paint, spar-varnish, pine buoys, coils of line. In one corner was a stack of slat & leather-hinged lobster pots; in the other, the more modern wire traps. There were wooden oars of all lengths, cotton cordage, toggle buoys, and gaff hooks. Combined with all the bait in the storeroom, Lavery's had everything a fisherman would want and Jack once remarked that there was enough equipment to outfit the Phoenicians.

Ellie walked towards the counter and Mary wandered over to look at things. The smell of pine-tar oakum caulk, turpentine and kerosene was awful and Ellie had to hold her breath. She tried not to wince, but when Kate looked up from behind the register, it was obvious she could tell.

"Ellie, are you alright?"

"It's hot as toast out there," she said. "I need one of these."

Kate took the part and examined it. Although motorized sloops arrived in the early '30s, mechanization was still a fascination on an island where half the boats used sails.

"Daddy!" she called out.

Kate was the only girl Ellie knew who still called her father *Daddy*. They had been friends since either of them could remember, and Kate lived just down the hill from her in a cottage by Drake's Cove. Jack grew up with her father and uncles, and the Ames and Mallet families had been close for generations. Kate was pretty in a plain way, with sandy-colored hair and blue eyes that she inherited from an Irish great-grandfather.

Moments later, Joe Mallet came out from the storeroom, his shirtsleeves rolled up, glasses tilted, sweating.

"Afternoon, Ellie."

"Good afternoon, Mr. Mallet."

He approached the counter, wiping his hands with a rag, and when his daughter held up the belt, he squinted.

"Lemme check."

While he went out back to look, Ellie and Kate waited and, for the first time in their lives, they had nothing to talk about. With Kate's acceptance to nursing school in Lewiston, something had changed between them and Ellie didn't know if what she felt was sadness or envy. They had just graduated in May from Portland High, where for four years they took the ferry together every day. Some of the local boys in their class returned to work in fishing, but with the lobster industry still in a slump, many young people left Monk Island, finding jobs in the factories in Portland, or moving out of Maine altogether.

"So? When do you leave?"

Before Kate could answer, something rattled and they both looked over.

"Mary!" Ellie snapped. "leave that be!"

Leaning on her crutches, Mary stood beside a sloop motor, up on blocks and waiting to be repaired. Like everything related to fishing, it was rusted and covered in barnacles.

"It's no bother, Ellie, really. Let her look."

Ellie consented, but only because Kate didn't mind and, a moment later, Joe Mallet came out shaking his head.

"I'll have to order it. I could maybe have it before the weekend."

He seemed as disappointed at not having the part in stock as Jack would be when he found out, and Ellie dreaded having to tell him. Her father wouldn't blame her directly, but he would grumble, hiss, curse—throw a quiet tantrum that would make her feel somehow partly responsible.

"I'll let Father know. Thank you."

Joe Mallet returned to the backroom and Ellie called for Mary, who pried herself away from the motor, positioned her crutches, and headed for the door.

"Ellie," Kate said. "I'm off Saturday if you wanna go to the beach?"

When she hesitated, it wasn't because she couldn't decide, but that she might have to work on the boat.

"I'll have to see."

"Okay," Kate said. "Let me know."

Ellie held the door for Mary and they walked out. Going from the dim shop to outside was a shock to the eyes and, for a few seconds, she was blinded.

"Pardon?"

She heard a voice and, as the sunspots cleared, saw the young man from the ferry standing beside his parents in the street. She acknowledged him with a courteous smile and he walked over with his hands in his pockets.

"Would you happen to know where Thrush Lane is?"

The first thing she noticed was a foreign accent, and she wasn't surprised because Monk Island got visitors from everywhere. The second was that he was taller than her father by at least three inches. His eyes were crystal-blue, his face smooth in a way that was handsome but not unmasculine. In a place where every male seemed to have a pug-nose and a scowl, he was almost debonair, and she felt self-conscious in her dirty dress and work shoes.

"Oh, yes, Thrush Lane," she said, stumbling. "Go up that road there, past the American Legion, to the top of the hill, then turn left."

As he repeated the directions, the young man looked at her and Ellie felt herself start to blush.

"Thank you," he said, with a slight bow.

"My pleasure."

He backed away like he was retreating from a stage, his expression gracious yet somehow strained, and returned to his parents, who stood weary in the heat, their clothes wrinkled, shoulders slumped.

"He talks funny."

Ellie turned abruptly to Mary like she forgot she was beside her.

"They're from another country."

"What country?"

Ellie mumbled something, but it wasn't an answer because she didn't know. Instead, she watched as the family picked up their suitcases and began to walk. Just as they turned the corner onto Gull Avenue, the young man looked over and Ellie responded with a faint smile, but by then he was out of sight.

......

The cottage on Thrush Lane was a small clapboard house with a front porch and gabled windows. It was set back off the street, nestled among a scattering of birch trees and spruce, and an old stone wall ran along one side, a Colonial remnant from the days when Monk Island was farmland and pastures.

By the time the Brinks arrived, it was noon and the interior was stifling. Karl brought the luggage in and they wandered through the rooms, separately and with a silent fascination, as if exploring an ancient tomb. Like any summer cottage, it was dank and drafty and smelled like must. The furniture was clean but shabby, a mismatch of wooden chairs, wicker couch, handmade coffee table, and floral curtains which appeared to be made from bedsheets or a tablecloth. On the walls were some old oil paintings—a seascape and picture of a man on a bicycle—and coral shells were stacked above the windows. As Karl peered into the pantry, he heard his mother in the next room say, "So simple."

He went out the back door to a small porch with three Adirondack chairs, a pedestal ashtray, and an empty beehive birdcage. The yard was overgrown with crabgrass and dandelions and, in the distance, he could see the next cottage through the trees. Standing at the threshold, Karl breathed in the salt air, smelled the wildflowers, listened to the low and constant hum of bees, and other insects. The sensations of nature brought back fond memories when he was just a boy and they vacationed at the seaside town of Lübeck.

"Karl!"

Karl ran back inside and up the stairs and when he got to his parents' bedroom, his father was bent over the luggage, panting and frustrated.

"Father?"

"Help me with this."

Karl lifted the suitcase and put it on the bed. As he went to undo the straps, Mr. Brink held out his hand.

"That's enough."

Karl flinched and stepped back, offended by the outburst but in no mood to argue. He stormed out of the room, down the narrow staircase, and into the kitchen, where his mother was going through the cabinet. She turned to him slowly, almost like she was in a trance, and held up a coffee can.

"The previous tenants left this. Can you believe it?"

"I'm sure they intended to."

She smelled inside, shook her head.

"At least half a pound."

Like anyone who lived through the scarcity of the Weimar years, she hated wastefulness, but Karl knew that wasn't the only reason she was in a stupor.

"Come," Karl said, putting his arm around her. "You rest. I'll put these away."

"But I must organize things."

She tried to resist, but Karl urged her into the parlor and onto the couch, where he told her to lie down then put a pillow under her head. Her hairline was damp, her cheeks flush, and she was lethargic from the heat. Although they had opened some windows, Mr. Brink insisted the curtains remain closed and Karl could tell it was trapping the warm air.

He grabbed her pocketbook from the table and, as he reached in for a napkin, his hand brushed her pills. They had been prescribed in Germany by a doctor who told her to take one whenever she was "feeling gloomy." But the drugs had become more than an occasional comfort—she couldn't go a day without them—and Karl feared they were the cause of her problems and not the cure.

"What is this?"

He let go of the vial, shut the pocketbook, and turned to see his father in the doorway, dressed in his shirtsleeves, suspenders loose over his shoulders. Without a suit, Mr. Brink looked like a skeleton under a sheet and Karl was surprised by how much weight he had lost.

"Mother is tired. She needs rest."

Mr. Brink nodded, then reached in his pocket and took out his wallet. As he opened it, Karl saw a thin stack of bills, mostly small denominations, their weekly allotment, the rest being in a bank in Portland. With restrictions on currency leaving Germany, they brought as much as they could, but it wasn't enough.

"Go to the butcher. Get some ham, cured if possible—"

"And beef," Mrs. Brink said, her voice shaky. "I can make a stew."

He gazed at his wife with a tender smile, then handed Karl a five.

"Get as much as possible. Bargain, if you can."

Karl scoffed to himself, knowing that prices in America were fixed and not open to negotiation like some Arab bazaar. His father was a sophisticated man, he thought, but as the son of a cobbler from Munich, the naivety of his rural upbringing sometimes showed.

"I will try."

"You must do more than try."

"Would someone please get me some water?" Mrs. Brink said, and they both looked over.

As Karl went to go in the kitchen, his father sidestepped and blocked his way.

"I'll get water—you get the food. And don't talk to anyone."

Their eyes locked in a quiet standoff that was cordial but no less tense. For Karl, every conversation with his father seemed confrontational, every interaction a competition of wills. He conceded for his mother's sake only and turned to leave when suddenly—boom!

They all jumped and Mr. Brink stood panicked, his eyes darting and arms out, prepared for something much worse than what it was.

"What in God's name was that?!"

For a man who was a committed atheist, he blasphemed more than anybody Karl knew.

"Fireworks, Father. It's American Independence Day."

Mr. Brink swallowed and nodded, looking away as if embarrassed, and Karl went towards the door.

"Son," his father said and he stopped. "Talk to no one."

2

Ellie lay on the sand, eyes closed, the hot sun against her back. In the backdrop, she could hear the steady whoosh of the waves, children laughing, seagulls. Beyond that, the low hum of trawlers going through Taylor Passage and the gong of a channel marker.

"Can you believe those louses?"

She lifted one eye and saw Kate leaning on her elbows, staring at the spot where only a few minutes before a family had been. All that remained was an empty milk carton, cookie boxes, cigarette butts, and a dirty diaper.

"Maybe they'll be back?" Ellie said.

But she didn't believe it, knowing it was the main reason locals hated tourists—they treated Monk Island like their own playground, renting cottages and leaving them in shambles, crowding the ferries and sidewalks.

"That's why I can't wait to leave this place."

"It that so," Ellie said, with obvious bitterness.

"I don't mean it like that," Kate said, glancing back. "But wouldn't you like to see the world?"

Ellie thought back to high school when all they talked about was leaving Monk Island, going so far as to get maps from the library, books on travel, employment guides for major cities. But those dreams of youth were soon tempered by the reality of circumstances, and although Kate's parents could afford to send her to college, Ellie's could not.

"I've been applying for jobs in Portland."

"Would you really move?"

"If the right opportunity came along."

Something caught Kate's attention and she paused, squinting towards the water.

"And maybe this is him."

When Ellie looked, she saw a young man strolling down the beach alone, arms at his side and looking around with shy curiosity. He was tall and lean, and with the glare of the sun, it took her a moment to realize it was the foreigner she had met in front of Lavery's.

"He asked me for directions a couple days ago."

"Did he?" Kate said, but she was more interested in gawking.

"He's from another country."

"Where?"

"Not sure."

"Maybe he's a prince," she went on. "I'd be his princess."

"Stop with such nonsense."

Ellie was just ready to lie back down when she heard, "we have a raft!" and turned to see Mary and June "Junebug" Mallet, Kate's sister, coming over the dunes. They looked like two waifs, windswept and sunburnt, with hand-me-down dresses and bare feet. Junebug was dragging something with a rope and Mary struggled to keep up with her crutches sinking in the sand.

"Where'd you get that?" Kate said.

"Somebody threw it out."

Ellie stood up and saw an inflated contraption with faded numbers on one side, German words she didn't understand. The rubber was split in places, but it was sturdy enough to hold air and she was sure it was an old military raft. Twenty years on and keepsakes from the Great War were still emerging from the sheds and barns of Monk Island.

13

"Can we go to the sandbar?"

Mary glimpsed up pleading, her face scrunched, her tangled hair glistening. Ellie's first instinct was to say no, but she knew that Mary had to take some risks if she was ever going to be independent.

"Okay. Just to the sandbar."

Mary turned to Junebug and their faces beamed. They pulled the raft down to the water and Mary got in, putting her crutches over her lap. Junebug pushed them into the waves then hung onto the side kicking, and Ellie watched as they drifted towards the sandbar. Satisfied that they were safe, she leaned back, closed her eyes and, with the soothing sounds of the shore whirling around, sank into a drowsy semi-sleep.

Sometime later—a scream.

Realizing she had dozed, Ellie leaned up and scanned the water and saw splashing a hundred yards out.

"My God, Mary?!"

She ran down to the shore, with Kate close behind, but stopped at the waterline because, like everyone in her family, she couldn't swim. People got up from their lounge chairs and towels, gravitated towards her, unsure what was happening.

"What's wrong, Dear?" one woman asked.

"Is everything alright?" said another.

The questions came fast and frantically and Ellie was too panicked to answer. Kate threw down her hat and was just ready to go in when, from out of nowhere, the foreigner came sprinting down the beach. He splashed into the water, pointed his arms and dove in, and Ellie's chest pounded as she watched, quietly praying, terrified beyond words. He swam towards the scene faster than she had ever seen anyone swim before and within seconds, he was halfway to the girls and closing in.

"He's got them," Kate said, gripping Ellie's arm.

The entire beach watched anxiously as the young man took the girls in his arms and the limp raft drifted away. With a slow and graceful backstroke, he returned to shore and Ellie met him in the shallows to the applause of dozens of onlookers.

"This one's okay," he said, panting.

Junebug leaped out of his arms and plopped through the water to dry land.

"Mary," Ellie cried, pushing the wet bangs from her sister's face.

"She swallowed some water, I think."

The young man rushed Mary up to the beach and people gathered around. He flipped her over, tapped her a couple of times on the back, and she began to spit up seawater. Once she was empty, she coughed and took a few deep breaths, then looked up.

"My crutches sank."

There was nervous laughter all around and the young man grinned. Bystanders patted him on the back, praised him for his quick response—someone even used the word "hero." Ellie wiped a tear from her eye, put her arm around her sister, and they were both trembling.

Finally, she turned to the young man and their eyes met.

"Thank you so much. That was awful brave."

"It was nothing, really," he said with genuine modesty. "She's the brave one. But next time have a sturdier boat."

Hearing his accent again, she wondered where he was from, but before she could ask, a man came over and said, "Where'd you learn to swim like that, Son?"

"Back home, I used to swim, competitively."

"And where's that?"

He wavered, glanced around uncomfortably.

"Um, I am from...Germany."

......

As Ellie and Mary walked up the hill, Ellie saw her father standing in the shadow of the porch, his arms crossed, glaring. She could always feel his presence, whether he was a mile out at sea or at the far end of the beach, and she could tell his mood simply by his posture. On an island where everyone knew everybody else, news spread quickly and she was prepared to get scolded even before coming in the yard.

"Mary should NOT have been out there alone!"

Ellie stopped short on the walkway.

"Alone?" she said coldly. "She wasn't alone. She was with June."

Their mother burst out the front door, her hands waving, flustered.

"Darling. Are you alright?"

She met Mary on the steps and felt her forehead, looking her up and down, as fraught as any mother would be.

"She's fine, Mother. She swallowed some seawater is all."

Vera put her arm around her daughter and brought her inside. Before the door shut, Mary glanced back with a long face, as if to apologize, and Ellie smiled to let her know it wasn't her fault. And it wasn't. The differences between Ellie and her father were deeper than what happened at the beach, and her mother said they fought like Cain and Abel. Ellie knew he always wanted a son and, in some ways, Jack found an adoptive heir in Ben Frazier, whom he mentored closely, teaching him all the fine points of lobstering. But it wasn't the same and she often wondered if he resented her for being a woman.

They faced each other from a distance, Ellie in the yard and Jack on the porch. She hoped the silence would calm him, but the longer it went, the angrier he looked. With his boat still out of order, he hadn't worked since Tuesday and she knew the idle time made him irritable.

"Mary shouldn't be in the water. She can't swim."

"Neither can you!"

Ellie could feel the tension rise like a change in atmospheric pressure. When she was a girl, one look from her father was enough to make her cower, shiver, repent. But she was an adult now and wouldn't be blamed when she hadn't done anything wrong. They all talked about giving Mary more freedom, but Jack seemed unwilling to let either of his daughters out from under his protective grasp. He was *damn domineering*, as Kate once said and, although Ellie was offended at the time, she realized later that she was right.

"Go down to Lavery's," he said, finally. "See if that belt came in."

Ellie consented with a quick, stubborn nod and her father went back in the house, leaving her alone and fuming. She walked to the top of the street and turned onto Gull Avenue, a wide thoroughfare lined with ancient trees that curved down to the waterfront and into the village. In the cool of the shade, the effects of the argument faded and, as her mind wandered, Ellie thought about the young man who had saved Mary.

There was something different about the German family—she felt it the moment she saw them. All her life, she had watched tourists come off the ferry, wide-eyed and bursting with excitement, their hectic city lives behind them for a few weeks. But this family seemed much more somber, like they had just come from a funeral, and in their eyes, she saw a deep exhaustion that no amount of work or travel could produce.

By the time Ellie got to Lavery's, the shop was closed but the door was still open. She walked in and Joe Mallet was in the corner, hunched over a crate, unpacking supplies from Portland. He always seemed to be at work, whether it was before dawn or late at night, and he tended to the shop like it was his child. Jack grumbled that Lavery's was a *license to print money*, and he always envied the Mallet's for having a business.

"Ellie," Joe Mallet said. "Kate told me what happened. How's Mary?"

When he stood up, she heard his knees creak.

"She swallowed some seawater is all. She'll be fine."

It was a response that, by now, was well-rehearsed and she would have to repeat it until people stopped asking.

"Well, I'm glad to hear it. The belt arrived."

While he went in the back room, she stood quietly and looked around. She remembered when Kate's father bought the place before Mary and Junebug were born, and Jack helped install the original shelves, built the plywood counter. As young girls, she and Kate would spend hours in the shop on hot days, watching men come in with soiled bibs, wet boots, their faces crisp from the sun. Lavery's then was the center of the world, and Ellie once had the same fascination with boats, bobs, and buoys as Mary. But that was long ago when the freshness of youth made everything seem new and important, even the day-to-day drudgery of lobstering.

"Ellie?"

She came out of the daydream and Joe was in front of her, holding out the belt.

"Yes, terrific, looks fine," she said, although she didn't know much about motors. "Would you please put it on his tab?"

He hesitated, squinting through his glasses, his expression strained but kind. Ellie never asked her father about money, but the lobster industry had been struggling for almost a decade and many men had gone out of business.

"Sure, Ellie, sure."

She thanked him with an awkward smile, then took the belt and went to leave.

"Say, Ellie?..."

She stopped and turned around in dread, fearing that he was going to mention the tab. Even with no one else around, it was a humiliating topic.

"...with Kate leaving, I'll be looking for help if you're interested?"

The relief she felt was bittersweet because, like many locals, Joe Mallet knew that she had graduated in May and still didn't have a job.

"I'd have to check with Father...it being the busy season and all."

"Well, let me know."

"I will. Thank you," she said and walked out.

Somedays Ellie felt like the entire community was waiting to see what she would do with her life. She had applied for several positions in Portland, mostly bookkeeping and secretarial work, but she had yet to receive a single offer. Her father always claimed that mainlanders were prejudiced against Islanders, a myth that everyone in his generation clung to. Like any two places so closely linked by culture and economics, there was a long history of tension, disputes, suspicion, and one-upmanship. But the world had changed since Jack was a boy and the Great War did much to upend the Yankee tribalism of the past. Ellie found it hard to believe that anyone in the City cared enough about Monk Islanders to despise them.

Outside the wind had shifted to the east and the sun was almost down, immersing the village in a dusky twilight. By now, the crowds had dwindled to a few random couples browsing the windows of the closed shops, relaxing on benches. Down at the terminal, a ferry was idling and passengers were lined up at the gate, waiting for the deckhands to finish unloading the cargo so they could board.

As Ellie crossed the street, she heard a loud rumble and saw two Army trucks roll off the ramp and come towards her up the hill. It was an unusual sight in peacetime, but Monk Island was no stranger to the military and, because of its location, had always been part of the Portland Harbor defense system. During the Great War, the Army built a bunker and generator building on the eastern side of the Island where, as a child, Ellie and her friends played among its abandoned ramparts.

The trucks stopped at the intersection and a young soldier looked over, his helmet low, his expression stern. They locked eyes for a moment, then the driver put it in gear, cut right, and sped off down Gull Avenue, and Ellie watched as they went around the bend and vanished in the shadows.

Everyone knew about the political troubles around the world, and, in high school, Ellie's class had followed events in real-time, from the war in Spain to the Japanese invasion of China to the rise of Adolph Hitler. For most of her peers, the chaos beyond was as significant as the stars, astonishing but of no consequence on the remote shores of Maine. The older generation that lived through the First World War was more leery, however, and people grumbled about how, if America got pulled into another one, it might not have the luxury of fighting it somewhere else. Jack had mentioned the possibility of America being attacked—although never in front of Mary—and Joe Mallet too. As Ellie stood thinking, the stench of the truck exhaust still in the air, she realized that the world was changing fast, and for the first time she was worried about the future.

3

Karl and his father walked in the front door, as weary from disappointment as they were from travel. Karl loosened his tie and took off his jacket and hat to hang them. When he looked around and couldn't find a coatrack, he just tossed them on the chair and, although his father gave him a scolding look, he had more immediate concerns.

"Hilde?"

Mr. Brink went over to the windows, whose curtains were wide open, and he drew them with such force that one of the decorative seashells fell and broke. His wife crept into the parlor, timidly and with her eyes averted, like a child who is called to the headmaster's office. She had a wooden spoon in one hand and she was wearing the apron she had sewed from his old shirts.

"These must remain closed!"

She flinched—looked down at the floor.

"I dusted the room. I thought it would be nice to have some sunlight."

Seeing that his mother was frightened, Karl couldn't stay quiet.

"Father, it was a minor oversight. The curtains are closed now."

The way his father stood, leaning forward with his chin out, was almost a fighting stance, and Karl braced for an argument. But instead, Mr. Brink shook his head and hissed in exasperation. He reached for his cane, grabbed his bag, and hobbled upstairs to the bedroom, slamming the door behind him. Karl sighed, but the relief was only temporary because his father's temper was becoming more and more unpredictable. With Mrs. Brink in such a fragile state, Karl did everything he could to protect her, but he knew that sometimes it wasn't enough.

"I cleaned the house. I just wanted—"

"Shh, Mother," Karl said, holding his finger to his lips. "The matter is settled."

She nodded nervously, touching her chin, her hand fidgety. Karl looked down into her eyes and they had a glassy emptiness that he knew wasn't from pollen or fatigue. As she went to get his coat and hat from the chair, Karl stopped her.

"I'll put those away. You finish dinner."

......

The Brink family sat around the table under a tense silence. The only time anyone spoke was when Mr. Brink asked for the salt, which he was supposed to limit because he was on blood pressure medication. The temperature outside had cooled to a tolerable eighty degrees, but the air in the house was still hot and heavy. After all the outrage over the curtains, Mr. Brink was the first to lift the shades in the kitchen, which he assured everyone was safe because *the darkness conceals.*

"So how did things go today?"

Karl and his father looked up at the same time. Mr. Brink went to speak but Karl beat him to it.

"Not very well, Mother."

"Not well?"

Mr. Brink put down his spoon in a way that suggested he had to restrain himself from slamming it. When he looked across to his wife, his glasses were fogged, his neck damp with sweat.

"Of course it didn't go well."

She dropped her head and stared down at the bowl. Knowing how his father's words could hurt, Karl quickly intervened.

"Mother, you must make the trip."

"But I signed the document—"

"Hilde," Mr. Brink interrupted. "Each party must sign in the presence of an official. I told you as much."

"I will try—"

"There is no try!" He pounded his fist on the table and all the glasses shook. "Either we go or we do not."

Reaching over, Karl touched his mother's hand and she was trembling.

"Father, please, enough."

Mr. Brink calmly wiped his mouth with a napkin and stood up. He walked over to the cabinet, got his brandy and a glass, then proceeded towards the back door. Before he stepped out to the porch, he stopped and looked over, spoke in a low and somber tone.

"If you are unable to make the trip, we are certainly doomed."

Mrs. Brink put her head in her hands and burst into tears. Karl jumped up from the table and went to comfort her, rubbing her back.

"It's alright, Mother," he said, glaring at his father.

Without the slightest change of expression, Mr. Brink turned and walked out.

......

It was close to midnight when Karl peered out the kitchen window and, in the darkness, saw the silhouette of his father, slumped in the Adirondack chair, a cigar in one hand and drink in the other. Throughout his life, his father always seemed to be facing away from him in some tragic pose. Like most professors, Mr. Brink was a serious man, yet Karl remembered a time when that seriousness was tempered by the softer sentiments of life, when he would occasionally smile, sometimes even laugh. The last few years had sapped all the joy from his spirit, leaving him cold, cynical, suspicious.

Karl opened the door and stepped out into the humid night, where mosquitos buzzed unseen in the darkness and crickets chirped in the grass. He sat in a flimsy chair and his father acknowledged him with a slight turn of the head—nothing more. For the first few minutes, they were silent, as still as two shadows. Somewhere a fire was burning and the smell reminded Karl of camping trips to the Black Forest as a boy.

"Where's your mother?"

Karl saw the outline of his arm as he took a sip of brandy.

"She is sleeping."

"That's good news. She needs to rest."

"Father, I worry about her medication."

When his father hesitated, Karl knew that he was thinking—he could tell by the way he breathed.

"In these times," he said, flicking an ash, "there is much to worry about."

Karl waited for more but there was no more, and he knew his father would never talk about things he didn't wish to discuss—he only ever spoke on his own terms. Karl was just about to get up and go in when Mr. Brink blurted, "White-throated Sparrow."

"Pardon?"

"That sound. It's a White-throated Sparrow. Do you hear it?"

Karl leaned forward in the chair, his head tilted, listening. Somewhere he could hear a high-pitched tweet that was strangely familiar, the melody repeating itself twice, stopping, resuming.

"I think so. Is that?—"

"Yes!" Mr. Brink said, and Karl smiled. "I remember that beautiful voice, before the War, when your mother and I first came here. There's nothing like it back home."

"Father, what was Monk Island like back then?"

His mood changed suddenly, he sank deeper into the chair.

"Back then? A different place. But the world was different."

At home, they never talked about the past. Born after the Armistice, Karl had no memory of the War, but he experienced the consequences, the ragged veterans begging in the streets, the unemployed dockworkers standing in breadlines. Throughout his youth, there were union strikes, fuel shortages, food riots, and political demonstrations, rowdy and often violent. One of his earliest memories was hearing gunfire from a street battle between Communists and police. When Karl was five years old, they left Hamburg for the country to get away from the madness and, although he resented his parents at the time, he later understood why they did it.

"You met Mother here? Am I right?"

Mr. Brink took another sip of brandy, savoring the taste before answering.

"I met her…" he said, rubbing his chin, distracted. "…here, yes. On this Island."

"This is where you fell in love, is it not?"

Startled by the question, Mr. Brink stretched his neck, turned back squinting.

"Love?" he said as if he did not understand the word.

Karl smiled to himself, feeling suddenly mischievous. His father was confident about many things, but romance was not one of them, and Karl liked to see him fret.

"With Mother," Karl said, pressing him. "It was here. She told me so."

Mr. Brink looked away and Karl heard him sigh.

"If she says it's so, then it's so."

4.

The four university students stood on the top deck of the ferry as it approached the pier. In the distance, the homes and cottages of Monk Island were partially obscured by vegetation, creating the impression of a remote and thinly settled land. The tallest structure was the steeple of the Congregational Church, which pierced the tree line like a landlocked lighthouse. A single osprey moved in wide circles above the shore—sandpipers nibbled at things along the rocky cove.

As the boat turned around to back in, the paddle wheel spun and black coal smoke engulfed the entire top deck. Passengers were appalled, including John Hatch, who winced and waved his hand in front of his face.

"No worse than your hideous cigars."

Leaning against the railing, Nik Brink glanced over with a wry smile. Normally, he wouldn't respond to derision in public, but he knew Americans had different standards of propriety.

"And no worse than the smoke from your family's sweatshop."

Hatch looked at his girlfriend Julia and raised his eyebrows—he always liked a good retort. While everyone else was sober, he had been drinking all day and his face was patchy red from the heat, sun, and alcohol.

"Touché," Hatch said.

Hilde Volk, who had been silent for most of the trip, turned to Julia.

"What means *sweatshop*?" she said in broken English.

"A place where people work but aren't paid enough."

Hatch scoffed and spoke under his breath.

"More like a place where people get paid but don't work enough."

Hilde smiled to be polite, but Nik could tell she really didn't understand. So he leaned towards her and said something in German which he knew would make her laugh.

"A translation or a ribald joke?" Hatch said.

"A bit of both."

Nik and Hilde had met only a week before when Hatch, who knew her from working part-time in the Office for Foreign Students, introduced them. She was smart *and* pretty, a rare combination for any woman in academia. As it turned out, Hilde got along with Julia as much as with Nik, and at the University of Maine, they were two out of only ten females in a post-graduate population of over 200 students. Hilde was getting her Ph.D. in chemistry—Julia was studying art. However divergent their fields, they had the same rebellious attitude towards life, wearing flared skirts, bobbing their hair. They talked of politics, literature, and sex—they drank hard liquor and smoked cigarettes. The two women were moderns in every sense of the word.

When the ferry bumped against the wharf, Hatch almost lost his balance but caught the handrail just in time. A single deckhand, no more than fifteen years old, tied off and the Captain hollered from the wheelhouse for everyone to disembark. The four students picked up their suitcases and bags and walked down to the aft deck, where they joined the line of exiting passengers. Squinting in the sun, Nik adjusted his glasses as they stepped off the gangway onto the pier.

"So this is Monk Island?"

"The very same," John Hatch said.

Before they went any farther, Hatch reached in his leather bag and pulled out a flask. After a quick look around, he took a swig and put it away. Then he waved to the group and they started up the hill, coming to a small crossroads with a livery, grocer, post office, and blacksmith. On the far corner, Nik saw a grand inn, The Devonshire, surrounded by lavish gardens, enclosed with a white picket fence. A few horse-drawn buggies went by, but there were no automobiles and people walked openly in the streets.

They followed Hatch up a dirt lane with some scattered homes, open fields, woods. Nik marveled at it all, remembering his childhood in Bavaria, when he would roam the hills behind his village, searching for wild mushrooms, chasing rabbits and butterflies. Since leaving home, he had only lived in big cities, which for a young man from the countryside was the hallmark of achievement and respectability. But something about Monk Island—the scents, sounds, or colors—had triggered some lost feeling, some primal urge, and Nik was once again entranced by the mysteries of nature. In the sunny haze of the dusty backroad, he was so relaxed he couldn't help but yawn.

"Stay awake, Dutch. Almost there."

Nik cringed. He hated being called Dutch because it was boorish and sounded too American. Hatch started using the nickname shortly after they met, when their graduate adviser, in a feeble attempt to speak German, asked if he was *Deutsch*. As an idealistic young student from Munich, Nik never could have imagined that his best friend in college would be someone like Hatch. Loud, crass, and shamelessly elitist, he

30

was a conservative Yankee from Tewksbury, Massachusetts whose family owned woolen mills on the banks of the Merrimack River. Unlike Nik, Hatch took nothing seriously and he referred to alcohol as his "poison," which was no small irony because it was killing him.

Despite Hatch's reckless spirit, Nik found him interesting and, in some ways, liberating. Nik's father had struggled for years so his only son could go to university and, as a result, Nik's every move in life had been careful, calculated. He was driven as much by a desire to improve the world as he was by the need to escape his modest roots, and there had never been much time for fun—until he met Hatch.

"Here we are."

When Nik looked up, he saw a ramshackle cottage, overgrown with weeds and covered in moss.

"I thought you were rich," Julia remarked.

"Welcome to my castle, m'lady."

Hatch lifted the latch on a rickety gate and pushed it open.

"It's been a while. Now let's go see what's for dinner."

They plodded through the overgrowth, thorns, and burrs clinging to their clothing, and while Julia looked disgusted, Hilde maintained a polite but skeptical smile. When they reached the front porch, Hatch wiped away some cobwebs, opened the door, and there was a burst of musty air.

"Not so bad," Nik said, as they stepped in.

"Not so good either," Julia muttered.

The first floor was sparse, with a wooden bench, a rocker, an empty china cabinet, and, oddly, a grandfather clock.

"Now," Hatch said. "Let me show you to your room."

The women looked at each other and then everyone followed him up a tiny staircase. When they were halfway,

31

Hatch stumbled and almost fell, a mishap he attributed to the uneven steps and not his drunkenness. At the top, there was a short hallway with a room off to each side. Hatch pushed open the first door and turned to Nik and Hilde.

"This is your room. We're in the next."

Nik and Hilde glanced at each other and, noticing their apprehension, Hatch added, "…there are two beds, of course."

The arrangement was more proper but no less awkward and Nik was uncomfortable. Nevertheless, when Hilde thanked their host and went in, he felt obliged to follow her.

"See you in an hour for dinner," Hatch said.

The beds were on opposite sides of the room, one next to the window and one beside the wall. As Hilde fixed her sheets, Nik lay his suitcase on an old bureau and started to unpack. His every movement was magnified by a nagging self-consciousness—he had never slept in the same room with a woman. And as much as he liked Hilde, it was more an inconvenience than a thrill because he didn't want the distractions of romance in his life.

"You don't snore, do you?" Hilde said in German.

"Nein—"

"Because I do."

Nik turned slowly around and their eyes met. As he stood flustered, she stared back with a cute smile, her head slanted, hands on her hips. Looking around the small room, they both acknowledged the peculiarity of their circumstances. Then they burst into laughter.

......

The four friends sat on the beach, huddled around a campfire, the remnants of their makeshift dinner in a basket—cold chicken, hard cheese, some biscuits. The sky was clear, a tapestry of stars, infinite and wondrous, and with the tide out, the sea was calm and the waves lapped against the shore with low, hypnotic persistence.

John Hatch leaned forward and used a branch to stir the logs, sending hot embers into the air. The temperature had dropped and Julia snuggled beside him under a blanket they brought from the cottage. Nik sat opposite Hilde, his arms wrapped around his knees, puffing a cigar and staring into the fire. With his tie loose around his neck, his shoes off and bare feet in the sand, he experienced a warm contentment he hadn't known in years.

"So," Hatch said, pouring another glass of Merlot. "What are our plans for after graduation?"

"I'm going to open an art studio in Kennebunk," Julia said.

John turned towards her with a frown.

"I know *that*. I mean our foreign friends."

Nik flicked an ash, cleared his throat.

"Who knows? Teaching, perhaps."

"Why not business?"

"Your idea of business and my idea of business are quite different."

Julia adjusted the blanket, looked curiously up to John.

"You see," he explained. "Nik believes in spreading the wealth—"

"What I believe," Nik interrupted. "Is that all citizens—all people—should share in a nation's prosperity."

"In this country, we call that communism."

Hilde, who had been struggling to follow the conversation, suddenly looked up.

"Well," Nik said, choosing his words carefully. "I call it common humanity."

John took another sip and pulled his girlfriend closer. Even for graduate students, the conversation was unnecessarily serious and the beach was no place for debate.

"Don't worry," Hatch said. "Dutch and I argue about this stuff constantly." He looked over to Nik, who responded with a sour smile. "He's a bit of a radical and I'm...how should I say?...a bit of a slacker."

Hatch laughed out loud and raised his glass.

"A toast," he said and the others raised their glasses as well. "to friends...and slackers!"

Nik held his glass even higher.

"...and radicals!"

For the first time that night, they all laughed together, their voices echoing down the long and desolate beach. Hatch opened another bottle of wine and passed it around. Through the glow of the fire, Nik could see him and Julia giggling and flirting, and he was sure that Hatch was rubbing her breasts under the blanket. Nik glanced across to Hilde, who sat still, a sweater around her shoulders. When she peered up, he quickly turned away. He gazed out at the water, where the lights of a merchant ship shimmered on the horizon, and fell into a dreamy stupor. Moments later, he felt movement and was startled to see Hilde right beside him. Nik glanced at her nervously and she smiled but said nothing.

It was past midnight when the four roused themselves from the comfort of the beach and got ready to go. The tide was coming in and with the fire fading, the mosquitos were starting to bite. John Hatch was too drunk to do anything, so Nik offered to take the basket and the last bottle of wine. Julia and Hilde got the blankets and wrapped them around themselves like shawls. Everyone kicked sand over the ashes, although there was nothing flammable in sight, and they trudged back up to the road.

After a long day of travel, everyone was exhausted and the journey back to the cottage was long. Hatch sang a few bars of Pennies From Heaven and then tried to make a joke about walking nude in the dark. But everything he said was a stuttering slur and finally, he just shut up. Nik never drank much, but seeing how it could silence someone as boisterous as John Hatch, he realized its usefulness.

"You're always thinking," Hilde said to Nik in German.

Julia glanced back at them with an encouraging smile.

"A head full of cabbage, as my mother used to say."

Hilde chuckled and came closer and he could smell her perfume. They were the least drunk, but they lagged behind and Nik blamed it on the fact that he had to carry everything.

"Should we send you two a taxi?" John yelled from the top of the street.

Julia swatted him playfully and they vanished around the corner.

Walking alone with Hilde, Nik was suddenly at a loss for words. He had always found it difficult to speak with women and as a boy, he was terribly shy. But as an adult, it was more a feeling of personal alienation. As Hilde said, he was *always thinking*, and it was hard to share those thoughts with another person.

"You know," Hilde said. "I believe what you believe."

"And what do I believe?"

"I saw the books on your table…Campanella, Fournier, Marx, Proudhon."

Nik looked around, worried someone might hear, knowing that ideas were dangerous things.

"Those are for study, nothing more."

"But you believe in a world without want."

Nik stopped and turned slowly to her. The darkness was complete, but somehow he could see her face and she was beautiful.

"I believe," he said, "in a just world."

"And this world isn't just?" she asked, taunting him with a smile.

Nik thought for a moment and then glanced down at the basket in his arms. Other than the wine, some plates, and a jar of relish, it was empty and yet was beginning to feel heavy.

"Not when one man is made to bear the burden of another."

They both laughed and Nik was filled with a happy confidence.

"Come," he said, shifting from German to English. "Let's get home."

When Nik and Hilde got back to the cottage, Hatch was passed out on the couch, his tie over his face, bare feet hanging over the side, sand-covered and dirty. His flask was on the floor, a half-empty bottle of bourbon on the table. It was a pathetic sight, but one that Nik was used to because every time they went out together Hatch got blind drunk.

Above they heard Julia moving around and getting ready for bed. Nik put the basket in the kitchen and he and Hilde tiptoed up to the bedroom. While she had a dressing screen, he had nowhere to change so he decided to use the washroom.

"I'm...going...to the lavatory," he said, uncomfortably.

When Nik looked over to Hilde, she was standing with her arms crossed, a sultry smile on her face. Considering that he had terrible night vision, he assumed he was imagining it.

"Carry on," she answered in English.

He got his clothes and toothbrush from the bag and went downstairs, where Hatch's snoring reverberated through the first floor like the gasps of a dying whale. He hurried out of disgust, maneuvering in the cramped space, pulling on his pajamas and socks, and when he came back up to the room, he walked in and froze.

"Pardon me."

There stood Hilde, completely nude, her nightgown draped over the dressing screen behind her. The glow of the lamp accentuated her body in ways that daylight could not, her pointed shoulders and hips contrasting sensuously with the curves of her breasts and thighs. Even in a moment of seduction, Nik watched with an academic wonder, her figure reminding him of a painting he had once seen before, a Rembrandt or was it Gustav Klimt? He knew he should have looked away, but he was too shocked to move.

While Nik stood trembling, Hilde stepped out of the shadow and walked over. With their eyes locked, she took one of his hands and placed it on her breast. Nik's heart pounded—sweat rolled down his neck. He had never had sex with a woman and the prospect was almost too exhilarating to bear. Instead of panicking, however, he dropped his things and took her in his arms, slowly pressing his lips to her, yielding to the instincts of desire, a deep and awkward bliss.

. . . . . .

The next morning, Nik awoke with Hilde beside him, her face buried in the pillow, her back half-exposed in the tangled sheets. He lay still for a moment, admiring her naked body in the soft haze of the morning light. But he didn't stare for long because he was overcome by a quiet guilt, knowing it was improper to watch a woman unawares.

Hearing some movement downstairs, Nik pried himself away from Hilde and put on his robe. He crept out of the bedroom and pulled the door closed behind him. He had only gone halfway down the stairs when he heard a blood-curdling scream. He ran to the bottom and into the front parlor, where he found Julia leaning over Hatch.

"What's wrong?"

It took a few seconds before he noticed that there was blood all over the couch and floor. Nik rushed over and helped Julia sit him up on the couch. Hatch looked around stunned, blinking from either pain or disorientation, shaking all over.

"What is it, Darling?" Julia said, tears in her eyes.

When Hilde came in in her nightgown, Nik glanced back to her and spoke in German.

"Some water, please."

Moments later, she returned with a full glass and Nik held it up while Hatch drank. Although he kept some of it down, most spilled back in a chalky mixture of blood, water, and saliva.

"I'm sorry," Hatch said, finally able to speak.

"You'll be alright," Julia said, rubbing his back.

When Hatch tried to lie down, Nik stopped him, worried he could choke on his own blood. Nik then motioned to Julia and Hilde and they all met in the kitchen. Leaning against the counter, he stared at the floor, analyzing the situation like it was an economic theorem. His eyes swept Hilde's feet and he was momentarily distracted by thoughts of the previous night. But he shook them off, ashamed for being so crude, and looked up.

"We need to get him to the hospital."

"Is it tuberculosis?" Julia said.

"It's hard to know."

"The ferry doesn't run on Sundays."

Nik shook his head, acknowledging the fact, but no less determined.

"Stay with him," he said, and they both nodded. "I'll go for help."

......

The morning seas were calm as they cruised across the open bay in the white Hampton sloop. With no one else around, Nik had found two young crabbers who were willing to take them into the City. The boat was cramped, with a one-cylinder engine in the center and stacks of lobster pots at the bow and stern. Everyone squeezed along two short benches and Julie stayed beside Hatch, running her hands through his hair, speaking softly in his ear. Nik stayed calm, but he worried that whatever caused Hatch to bleed internally would rupture again and he would die before they reached Portland.

"What happened?" one of the crabbers said to Nik.

"We don't know. He woke up covered in blood."

The young man leaned in closer.

"Consumption?"

"Let us hope not."

As the boat approached the wharf, Nik, Julia, and Hilde leaned up and looked around, eager to assist but not sure how. The port was crowded with steamers, schooners, trawlers, and barges, and their small sloop seemed minuscule among so many giants. One of the crabbers stood up and yelled to some men, who quickly ran down the gangway to meet them.

"I feel like such a nuisance."

Nik looked over to Hatch, relieved to hear him speak.

"Darling, don't," Julia said, patting his forehead with a handkerchief that was red with blood.

The dockworkers helped the ladies out of the boat, then Nik and the others lifted Hatch. He didn't have to be carried, but he was very unsteady and almost tripped over the edge. While everyone started up the ramp, Nik stopped and turned to the young men who had ferried them over.

"Thank you," he said, lifting his hat. "You've been too kind."

When one of them extended his hand, Nik at first hesitated, unaccustomed to shaking without first being formally introduced.

"Niklaus Brink," he said.

"Jack Ames."

Nik hurried to catch up with the others, who were making their way down the wharf as fast as they could considering Hatch's condition. When they came out to Commercial Street, most of the shops were closed because Sundays were for church and relaxation. People strolled lazily along the waterfront, men in top hats and women with parasols, and the traffic was a mix of buggies, bicycles, and automobiles.

Somebody whistled and they looked over to see one of the dockworkers standing beside a taxi. They stepped off the curb and headed towards him, people stopping to let them cross, and Hatch even found the strength to wave. On the far corner, a newsboy was calling out the day's stories, but everyone was too distracted to listen until they got closer and the words were unavoidable.

"Germany declares war on Russia!"

"Did he say Germany and Russia?" Hilde said quietly in German.

Nik nodded because he was too stunned to speak. Like most people, he had been following events in Europe all summer, from the assassination of the Archduke to the riots in Sarajevo. Austria-Hungary had declared war on Serbia, and Russia was mobilizing its massive army. In the warm tranquility of the summer morning, it was hard to imagine that the world was about to ignite. Nik gazed at Hilde, trying to contain his own dread, and saw tears in her eyes.

"Sir?"

Startled, he turned and the driver was holding the door open.

"Yes, of course," Nik said, clumsily.

He put his arm around Hatch and led him over to the taxi. Before Hatch got in, he hesitated, speaking in a voice that was both tense and whimsical.

"A war on a scale unlike any before? What a dreadful time to be dying, Dutch."

"You are not dying."

Nik nudged him into the back seat and Hatch went willingly.

"Well, if I do, consider me the first casualty."

5.

Ellie stood atop the stool on the back porch while her mother made the pots, planting the lilacs and peonies she had picked that morning from the garden. Vera's hands were stiff and gnarled and, although she winced once or twice, she never complained. She was still able to work, but arthritis made every task harder, and some days Ellie watched her struggle just to get the laundry off the line.

"Mother, did you take your aspirin?"

"I take any more aspirin, I'll be numb."

Vera held up another pot and as Ellie hung it, she glanced into the yard and saw Mary on the grass, her legs tucked beneath her, blowing petals off dandelions. Her auburn hair glistened like trillium in the sun, a color so unlike the rest of the family's that they had been asked if she was adopted. With her new crutches hidden in the weeds, she looked like a normal girl her age, but Ellie never thought of her as crippled anyway.

"Where's Mary?!"

Startled, Ellie fumbled with the hook and her finger hit a nail. She let go of the pot and it fell and smashed.

"Oh, for heaven's sake, Jack!" Vera cried, bending over to clean up the mess. "Mary's in the yard. Do you always have to be so abrupt?"

He ignored the remark and stepped out onto the porch. Dressed in a work bib, his shirt filthy and damp, he looked like a lagoon creature that had washed ashore, and Ellie was repulsed as much by his appearance as she was by the stench of fish, kelp, and salt water. Jack looked over the railing and, satisfied that Mary was safe, he turned to Ellie.

"Why weren't you at the dock this morning?"

Standing on the stool, she gave him a cold stare.

"I had things to do."

He looked at the mess on the deck, his wrinkled and sunburnt face forming a slight smirk, and she knew he was about to say something sarcastic.

"I asked her to help me," Vera said, speaking before he could. She got up, put the broken shards in a box, and dusted off her hands. "Besides, no girl her age should be hauling traps."

Jack's face got tense, his dark eyes narrowed. Ellie knew that if anyone else had criticized his occupation—be it a man, woman or child—they would have experienced his fury. But things were different between him and his wife and, although they often bickered, they never fought. Joe Mallet once said that Vera was the only woman who could tame Jack and, for that reason, he was always deferential towards her.

Jack stood facing out from the porch, chewing his lip, thinking. At first, Ellie thought he was watching Mary until she followed his gaze and realized he was looking out to sea. In moments like this, when she was most infuriated, he seemed to reveal some softer, more introspective side that made up for his harshness—but it never lasted.

"Help your mother clean this up," he barked and he walked in the house.

. . . . . .

There were times Ellie was sure she had consumed more fish than a humpback whale would in the course of its life.

Some nights they had seabass, haddock, hake, or flounder; on others, shrimp, clams, mussels, scallops. They only ate meat on holidays—turkey for Thanksgiving and a ham for Christmas—but it was always accompanied by chowder, raw oysters, sea urchin.

The only thing the Ameses didn't eat was lobster, a poignant irony for a family that relied on it for its survival. Jack said he hated the taste, that it was foul, that the crustacean was a bottom feeder and thereby had no self-respect. But Ellie knew the fish had a deeper significance, being as much an indication of social class as it was a source of income. Lobstering had once been an honorable profession, but as the country became more industrialized, the men who hauled traps were viewed at best as quaint throwbacks to a simpler time, at worst as the peasants of the sea. At Portland High, Ellie knew girls who threw out the lobster salad sandwiches their parents made, ashamed to be seen with them.

Ellie sat picking at the remnants of her dinner, some fish bones, potato skins, carrots. Mary was beside her and her mother was at the sink, up to her elbows in soapsuds. Jack sat across the table with the newspaper open wide, the only thing visible his knuckles, the top of his head.

"Look here," he said. "Jews can no longer buy lottery tickets in Germany."

"I'm sure it's the least of their worries."

"Hitler seems bent on another war."

"Mrs. Halstead said the military was looking at some land on the backshore."

"I saw two Army trucks last week," Ellie said.

The only one who acknowledged the comment was Mary, who looked at her sister and smiled.

"If Europe goes to the dogs again," Jack said, "Roosevelt better keep us the hell out of it."

Vera shut off the sink and turned around, finished with the dishes and ready to make a point.

"If there's another war, Jack, we may not have a choice."

He shook his head, turned the page.

"Damn Krauts."

Mary giggled and Vera gave her husband a sharp look.

"It was a German who saved Mary," Ellie said, speaking up again.

Her father slowly lowered the paper until they were eye-to-eye. She didn't mean it as a criticism, but she could tell he didn't like the idea of another man rescuing his daughter, especially a foreigner.

"Well, he mightn't've had to if she was watched properly."

A quiet tension filled the room and even Scuttles, who had been under the table looking for scraps, seemed to sense it because he left. Inside Ellie was fuming, but she kept a straight face and didn't react, knowing that nothing frustrated her father more than when his words had no effect. She put down her fork and wiped her mouth with a napkin.

"May I be excused?"

Her mother looked over.

"But won't you have some fresh strawberries?"

Ellie shook her head and got up. She walked out of the kitchen and by the time she reached the stairs, she could no longer hold back the tears. She stormed up to the bedroom, where she opened the drawer of the desk, an old roll-top an aunt had given them years before. Everything the girls ever received, whether it was a birthday gift or a hand-me-down, seemed to be "for the two of them," like they were separate halves of the same person. They had shared a bedroom since Mary was in a crib and Ellie could barely remember sleeping alone. She didn't resent her sister, who was so much younger and needed help with things, but combined with their father's constant oversight, it made for a life with little privacy.

Ellie reached in the desk and took out the letter she had written almost two weeks before.

Dear Sir or Madam,

I am writing in response to the advertisement for the position of secretary, which I read in the Herald. I am a recent graduate of Portland High School with qualifications in typing and bookkeeping...

She read it over and over, checking for mistakes, knowing how the errors of grammar had a mysterious way of reappearing. She had written it after an argument with her father, a silent threat that was directed as much to herself as to him. She told Kate she was looking for a job and it wasn't a lie because for weeks she had been scouring the classifieds of Jack's discarded newspapers. But each time she found a position she was qualified for, she would craft a query letter and never send it. She blamed her reluctance on everything from the high cost of stamps to the fact that there was only one mailbox on the Island.

"Going somewhere?"

Ellie closed the note and spun around to see Mary standing in the shadow of the doorway, her long hair hanging down over her face. Ellie didn't like being sneaked up on, but she couldn't fault her sister because it was her room too.

"I have to mail this."

"Can I go?"

"Not tonight."

Ellie got her handbag from the dresser and when she went towards the door, Mary moved aside, but not completely.

"I don't like the way he talks to you."

Ellie turned to her sister with a warm smile.

"Thanks."

She continued out to the hallway and when she reached the stairs, she heard, "Momma says the catch has been slow all summer."

Ellie stopped for a moment, but she didn't look back. It was like a compliment wrapped in an insult, but Mary was too young to see the contradiction. They all defended Jack in their own ways, and for different reasons. As his wife, Vera understood more about his past, more about the things that haunted him, than anybody, and she treated him like someone who needed to be cared for rather than contended with. Mary had the natural admiration any girl would have for her father, and being at an age where she couldn't see the faults in others, she couldn't see them in him. For Ellie, it was more complicated, but she knew that, beyond loving or hating him, she mostly felt sorry for him.

......

Karl lay in the cramped metal-framed bed, his neck turned and knees bent to accommodate the angle of the roof. In his hands was a novel, a Hardy Boys' mystery, which he had found in the cabinet downstairs, left behind by another tenant. The book was childish but easy to follow and Karl didn't read English as well as he spoke it. Still, he found himself going over each paragraph twice, distracted by every small noise—birds, insects, a barking dog. When he observed a spider climbing up the wall to the ceiling, he quietly cheered it on, relating, in some way, to the challenge it faced.

"Dinner!"

Karl closed the book and got up, leaning over to put on his only shoes, a pair of brown loafers with mismatched laces and worn-out soles. They had been living meagerly long before coming to America, but now they were close to destitute. Mrs. Brink made bread stretch a week and she mended garments that, in the past, they would have thrown out.

Karl came downstairs and the smell of sausages and fried potatoes made his mouth water. He walked into the kitchen and his mother was at the stove.

"Sit," she said.

"Where's Father?"

When she nodded, Karl looked in the front parlor and Mr. Brink was hunched over the coffee table, a pile of documents spread out before him. There was a newspaper on the floor and a cigar smoldering in an ashtray.

"Will he be joining us?"

"He is not hungry."

A few minutes later, Mrs. Brink came over and put down a plate of hot food. As Karl reached for his fork, he felt a looming presence in the room.

"There are some things to discuss."

He looked up and his father was in the doorway. Neither of them had heard him approach because he didn't use his cane

49

indoors, insisting that pressure and movement would heal his ankle quicker than convalescence. He had on tweed pants, suspenders and a white undershirt that was stained at the armpits. For a man who only ever wore a conservative suit, he was dressed like a pauper.

"May I eat first?"

"You eat. I'll talk," Mr. Brink said coldly. "We leave for our appointment first thing tomorrow morning. Wear your best clothing, bring something to eat."

He waited a few seconds and no one responded.

"Is that agreed?"

Karl glanced over to his mother, who looked afraid to say anything.

"Of course, Father."

Mr. Brink nodded and turned to go back to the parlor.

"What time precisely?" Karl said and his father stopped.

"Why? Have you plans?"

"I may want to swim in the morning."

"The first ferry departs at 7," Mr. Brink said.

"Perhaps, I'll swim tonight then."

After a short, stubborn pause, his father said, "Very well then, but be discreet. Don't make a spectacle."

"Father, all this secrecy is—"

"It's a small island. People talk."

Even as he spoke, Karl knew he should have kept quiet, but the hours of boredom had made him irritable, and he could no longer restrain his frustration.

"This is absurd. We might as well be in Timbuktu. No one cares. And we've every right to be here."

"The same was said in Germany!" Mr. Brink shouted.

Karl flinched and not because he was intimidated. His father was always at the edge of losing his temper, always one small remark away from a full-blown argument.

"You were a child when the nightmare began," Mr. Brink went on, his tone firm but more conciliatory. "You don't remember—"

"I DO remember, Father. I remember everything. And that has nothing to do with now!"

Karl abruptly turned to his mother, as if for an ally.

"Mother, don't you agree?"

Mrs. Brink stood by the sink, her head down, clutching a wet rag like a scullery maid.

"I abide your father," was all she said.

Karl jumped up from the table and faced his father across the room, the only thing separating them the simmering tension of their mutual rage. In the past, Mrs. Brink would have tried to calm them down, but she was too clouded to reason, too docile to intercede. Karl clenched his fists, grunted in exasperation, and when he went to leave, Mr. Brink stepped aside, the first time he ever conceded. As Karl passed by, their shoulders almost brushed and, knowing his father would try to get the last word in, he was ready for it.

"Don't be late."

"I'll do as I goddamn please."

. . . . . .

Karl walked swiftly in the darkness, his mind racing, sweating in the humid air. As he went through the maze of backroads, he could hear movement in the woods, the crack of twigs, the crunch of leaves. He knew it was only small creatures but, much like his father, he had become suspicious of everything. Back home, they had lived in constant mistrust of the society around them, and his parents had stopped socializing altogether. The only friends Karl had were acquaintances, men from the aquatics club in Hamburg and some neighbors from their village. But it wasn't just his family—all throughout Germany people seemed to have retreated into their most private lives.

As Karl came down the hill, the woods yielded to an open sky, the stars so vast and so bright they took his breath away. A salty breeze came off the harbor, soothing his body and his mind, and by the time he reached the village, he realized that he was no longer angry.

The restaurant at the Inn was open, its shaded lamps visible through the windows, but everything else was closed. Karl continued towards the pier with some vague intention of jumping in—he could never go long without swimming—but he didn't have his trunks and had to wear the same clothes the next day. He came down the slope and followed the boardwalk, gazing out at the water, the lights of Portland shining in the distance.

Karl passed a man playing harmonica, an elderly couple, a stray dog. Farther down, he heard rowdy laughter and saw a group of locals fishing off the dock, cans of beer in their hands. They were only in their early twenties, a couple of years older than Karl, but had the hardened faces of men much older. Some had no shirts on and their backs and arms were brown from working in the sun. They reminded Karl of the dockworkers he would see around Hamburg, working-class men whom his educated parents would glorify but never interact with.

Karl nodded with a nervous smile and one of them took a long drag on his cigarette and nodded back. He continued on, walking faster, and although he didn't look back, he sensed that the men were watching. Since coming to America, he never felt unwelcome, but they hadn't talked with anyone long enough to know if they were prejudiced or not. Karl wasn't naïve and he knew that even though the Great War had been over for twenty years, Germans were still the enemy in the minds of many.

As he came to the end of the dock, he saw the silhouette of a person staring out to sea. He took a few more steps and realized it was a young woman. She was thin, with long dark hair and a plain dress, and something about her posture suggested deep contemplation. Not wanting to disturb her, he started to turn around when, suddenly, she glanced back and he was surprised to see who it was.

"Oh, hello."

"Hello."

If it had been any darker, Karl wouldn't have recognized the sister of the girl he had rescued at the beach.

"How's our little captain?"

"Mary is fine. Thank you again."

"Karl Brink," he said.

"Eleanor Ames—Ellie."

She looked up with a slight modesty, and Karl could see that her eyes were red.

"Is...is something wrong?"

"My father and I, we don't always get along."

"That makes two of us," Karl said, "Perhaps this is the waiting room for stubborn children."

His English didn't always translate the way he intended it and, even as he spoke, he knew the remark was corny. But she smiled nonetheless, which told him that charm meant more than cleverness.

"How long are you here?"

Karl paused because he didn't know how to answer. So much of their lives, both here and back home, was constrained by secrecy, bound by deceit, that sometimes he couldn't keep track of what was true and what was not.

"Six weeks."

"How on earth did you find Monk Island?"

"My father taught at the University of Maine for several summers. This year he decided to bring us."

"He's a professor?"

"Of economics," Karl said, with a hint of sarcasm.

"In Germany?"

"Yes. Hamburg."

All the questions caught him off guard—he wasn't used to women being so direct.

"What brought your father here to teach?"

"He studied at the University," Karl said, then added, "before the—"

When the ferry horn blasted, the interruption was a relief because it saved him the awkwardness of mentioning the War.

"The last boat," she said.

"It's getting late."

"I should be going."

"As should I."

They began to drift down the dock, almost subconsciously, in a way that Karl found easy and not forced. Because of his family's situation, he had less interaction with women than most men his age and it was just nice to be in the presence of a female.

Ellie looked ahead as they walked, her arms crossed and chin up, moving with a confident strut that was no less feminine. With her wispy hair, dark skin and chipped fingernails, she had a rugged beauty that was much like the island itself, Karl thought, and inside he experienced a warm elation, some tender feeling that had long ago vanished, making him, for a moment, sad for having lost it.

"So you're a swimmer?"

"I..I was," he said, stumbling.

"No one stops being a swimmer."

Karl raised his eyebrows, acknowledging the truth of the statement.

"Thank you."

"I should like to learn someday."

"You don't swim?"

She shook her head.

"Father or Mother neither. Mary could once, but not anymore."

Thinking about her crippled sister, Karl realized that all families had their troubles.

"Do you work on the Island?"

"I help Father with the boat sometimes."

"He's a fisherman?"

"A lobsterman."

"Does that make you a lobsterwoman?"

Ellie glanced over, made a cute smirk.

"I guess it would—"

They heard voices and looked up, and ahead Karl saw the men he passed by earlier, congregated on the dock with their bait boxes, tackle, lures. Most were still standing in the same positions and the only difference was that they looked drunker. The closer they got, the more nervous Karl became, and he had never felt more like a foreigner.

"Evening, Ellie," one of the men said.

"Hi, Ben."

They might have been glaring but Karl couldn't tell because he stared straight ahead. And although he continued at an easy pace, he wanted to break into a sprint.

"Are you okay?"

"Pardon?" he said, distracted. "Yes, of course."

They went by the terminal, where the remaining few passengers were coming off the ramp. As they continued up the hill towards the village, Karl kept his hands in his pockets, stared at the ground, nodded and smiled, spoke in fractured sentences. He stumbled more from lack of practice than from shyness, and, considering how secluded his life had been, it was like talking to a girl for the first time again.

Karl was no prude, however, and he had many girlfriends throughout his adolescence. The first time he had sex was under the stands after a soccer match. She was a student at the sister school to his all-boys Catholic academy, and the next time he saw her, she had joined the League of German Girls and somehow regained her virginity. Karl's last relationship was with a girl named Hannah who was the daughter of one of Mr. Brink's colleagues. On the weekends when he didn't have a swim meet, they would go to the cinema, have sodas, explore the streets of Hamburg. He thought they might even marry someday, until, without warning, her father whisked the family away to French Indochina and he never heard from her again. In the chaos of Nazi Germany, nothing seemed permanent, nothing was sacred.

Before Karl knew it, he and Ellie were at the corner by Lavery's, the shop where he first saw her. As they faced each other under the streetlamp, he had the urge to explain everything, to confess it all. It was less for her to understand, relate or sympathize, and more out of some primal need to purge from his soul all the anguish of their troubled lives. As a schoolboy, Karl went to confession twice a month, and although uncomfortable at times, the experience always left him feeling freed from the burden of his secrets.

"So."

"So," Ellie said.

But now was not the time, and Karl knew that telling her anything would be as selfish as it was irresponsible.

"I enjoyed our chat."

"As did I."

"Okay, then."

"Have a good night."

"You, as well."

The exchange was brief, light, even clumsy, and Karl always hated to say goodbye—even to people he hardly knew. But when Ellie turned to go, he sensed a momentary pause, some slight hesitation that gave him the confidence to take a risk.

"Ellie?"

She spun around, her eyes wide, lashes fluttering.

"I'd be happy to teach you to swim."

"I should like to learn," she said, almost before he could finish.

Karl exhaled, as much from joy as from relief because for the first time in months, possibly years, he had something, and someone, to look forward to.

"How's Saturday? At the beach?"

She made a quick, girlish nod.

"Saturday, at the beach."

6.

"Achtung!"

Karl stood at the edge of the pool, his knees bent and arms pointed. His cap was on tight and his goggles were secure. Beside him were eight other swimmers—four to his left, four to his right—but he was so focused he felt like the only person in the universe.

"Set!"

Above, ceiling lamps hung from the cracked ceiling of the old aquatics club, their white glare giving Karl the added alertness he needed to perform. His body was energized, but he was mentally fatigued, having stayed up all night with his mother because his father didn't come home. When Mr. Brink finally showed up just before dawn, Karl didn't have time to berate him because he had to catch the first train to Hamburg.

"Go!"

In a single burst, he jumped in a perfect arc and slipped into the water with the grace of a dolphin. He swam with all his strength, thrusting his arms and kicking his legs, propelling himself forward with a savage intensity. He looked ahead squinting and the far edge of the pool emerged in the hazy froth. He tapped it once, pushed off the wall, and all his momentum shifted in the opposite direction. Like clockwork, he turned his head every few seconds for air. The two laps passed in a flash and when he glimpsed up, he saw Coach Lang and his assistant on the pool deck. Moments later, Karl touched the side and it was over.

"Gut gemacht!" the coach yelled.

Karl tore off his goggles, panting heavily, tingling all over from adrenaline. He looked up to Coach Lang, who stood marking the clipboard with his pen. Karl searched for signs of satisfaction or disappointment, but like most men of his generation, the coach showed no emotion. Those few seconds it took to tally his time felt like eternity and Karl could barely contain himself. With the National Championships the following month, he had to beat his previous time in order to qualify.

Finally, the coach nodded to the assistant and glanced down at Karl, who waited with his arms crossed on the pool edge. Their eyes met and Karl's heart pounded as he braced to hear the results.

"Coffee or tea?"

Karl blinked, frowned in confusion. Everything got suddenly blurry and the sounds of the pool were replaced by a slow and steady thumping. Standing before him was a pretty stewardess, dressed in a navy uniform, smiling. Karl shifted in his seat, as startled as he was embarrassed, and the dream faded to the present.

"Um, no, thank you," he said.

The stewardess continued down the aisle and Karl looked beside to see his mother, her eyes closed, her face serene. He made a loving smile and patted her hand, but she was out cold. With her sateen hat and gold earrings, she had a quiet dignity that seemed to belie all the troubles within, and Karl watched her with a mix of sympathy and sadness. She had taken more than her regular dose, and although Karl had been opposed to it, he finally agreed with his father because he knew it was the only way she could make the trip.

The train began to slow and Karl glanced out to see the tall buildings of Boston. As they pulled into North Station, the car jerked and Mrs. Brink awoke with a gasp.

"Mother, it's okay," he said in German.

A couple of passengers looked over, and Mr. Brink, who was in the row in front of them, peered between the seats with a sharp expression. Soon the train came to a full stop and passengers started to rise and collect their things. Huddled together, Karl and his parents followed the crowd down the platform and into the station, where people rushed by in all directions and schedule boards flickered with arrival and departure times. Karl could tell the noise and activity made his mother anxious, but she nevertheless arched her back, held her chin up, and continued on. As they went, they all locked arms like families did back in Germany, until they realized no one else was and that it only attracted attention.

"Are we almost there?"

"Very close, Mother."

They came out to the street and the commotion was even worse. Trolleys passed on the overhead rail, automobiles and buses zoomed by, jackhammers rattled at a nearby construction site. When someone hit their horn, Mrs. Brink jumped and Karl took her by the arm to both stabilize and comfort her.

"Don't worry, Mother. We're safe here."

While Karl walked with her, Mr. Brink waited impatiently at the curb, leaning on his cane. They waited for the light to change and proceeded across with a stream of pedestrians. The moment they reached the other side, Mrs. Brink stopped suddenly, her mouth fell open, and her handbag began to slide off her arm until Karl caught it. He at first thought she was having a seizure, perhaps from the drugs, until he followed her gaze to the window of a small ethnic diner.

NO GERMAN CUSTOMERS WANTED
HITLER RETURN CZECHOSLOVAKIA

Karl glanced over to his father, who responded with a grim look. Europe was far away, but its immigrants and their descendants were everywhere in America and, for the first time since arriving, Karl didn't want anyone to know he was German. As he and his mother stared at the sign, Mr. Brink came over and leaned in, speaking with a firm but hushed urgency.

"Come. There's no time to waste."

......

Four hours passed and they still hadn't been called. The waiting area was jam-packed with people, squished into benches, squatting on the floor, lined up against the walls. Those who couldn't find space waited in the corridor, and families sat huddled together like refugees, babies crying, children restless. With no windows and poor ventilation, the room was stifling and it reeked of sweat, perfume, snack foods, and cigarette smoke.

While his mother slept on his shoulder, Karl looked around at the great cross-section of humanity, soft voices speaking in Italian, Yiddish, Polish, Greek and more. With the situation in Europe deteriorating, visa quotas for each country were running low and people were desperate to help friends and relatives escape. Karl knew that, as the son of university-educated parents, these day laborers, shopkeepers, street vendors, and dockworkers would never view him as an equal, but he understood their struggle and felt some quiet solidarity with them.

"Nik Brink?!"

An official stood at the doorway, a file in hand, and the moment the Brinks got up, their seats were taken by another family. They followed the man down a hallway, past offices bustling with secretaries and administrators, into a small office that was even hotter than the lobby. Karl tried to take off his jacket, but his father stopped him, insisting that it was vulgar. Mrs. Brink maintained her composure, which Karl attributed to the drugs, and sat still between her husband and son, her pocketbook on her lap. For the next twenty minutes, they waited in complete silence for the clerk assigned to their case.

Finally, the door opened and in walked a middle-aged man, his white shirtsleeves rolled up. With his yellow teeth, bald crown and thick glasses, he looked like every government official and, in those short seconds, Karl searched his face for any signs of compassion or empathy. But he greeted them with a formal salutation, not making eye contact, and sat behind the desk. After confirming some basic information, he thumbed through the case file, scanning each page.

"Madam," he said, pushing a document across the desk to Mrs. Brink. "Your signature please."

Pointing out the location, he handed her a pen and she took it with a trembling hand. She hesitated at first, looking beside to her husband, who reassured her with a nod. Then she leaned forward in the chair, pressed the ballpoint against the paper and scribbled her name. That simple act seemed like the culmination of months of planning and preparation and Karl experienced tremendous relief. When he glimpsed over, his father looked back with a faint smile that, considering his seriousness, was almost jubilation.

The man went through the application with a mechanical precision, and Karl watched him closely, wondering if his coldness was from the monotony of his job or because he didn't like Germans.

"When did you arrive?" he asked, not looking up.

"July 4th."

The clerk acknowledged the irony of the date with a dry smirk.

"And the purpose of your visit?"

"I am teaching a course," Mr. Brink said, "at the University of Maine."

Karl blinked in surprise, a tingle went up his back. The remark caught him off guard, but he looked ahead and didn't react.

"It says here you come every year?"

"That is correct, since '33," Mr. Brink said.

"Lucky for you."

Mr. Brink raised his eyebrows and leaned forward.

"Pardon?"

"You wouldn't have gotten a tourist visa this year…impossible. But you had a prior travel history, which is probably why it was approved."

Mr. Brink's moved his lips, but he didn't respond, and the man returned to the form.

Karl hadn't eaten since morning and the acid in his stomach made him restless and irritable. He took small comfort in knowing that each page the clerk turned over was another hurdle in a process that was over a year in the making. More daunting than the time it took, however, were the things it required; five copies of the visa application, two copies of their birth certificates, a *Certificate of Good Conduct* from the German Police, and, finally, an American citizen who would legally vouch for their good character.

"I'm afraid there's a problem."

They all looked up at the same time.

"Your sponsor didn't check out."

"Check out?" Mr. Brink, wincing in confusion. "What means this, *check out?*"

"It means he wasn't approved, Father," Karl said.

"But why? Dr. Grayson is perfectly respected. He's in good standing at the college."

The clerk shrugged his shoulders, shook his head, indifferent to the point of seeming annoyed.

"Any number of reasons. Financial troubles."

"Impossible."

"Let's see," the man said, and he went back to the report. "*...A history of insubordinate activity of a political nature.*"

Mr. Brink averted his eyes, fumbled with his fingers, shifted uneasily in the chair. He was a master at concealing his emotions, but the statement was a bombshell and everyone could tell that he was flustered.

"I see," was all he said.

"Where does this leave us?" Karl asked.

"You still need to get an approved sponsor."

Mr. Brink looked at his son, then to the clerk.

"And if we find someone?"

"The same process as before—six copies of the Affidavit of Support and Sponsorship form...all notarized."

"And then?"

"It has to get processed by security."

When a secretary knocked and opened the door, the man held up his finger. In the background, Karl heard the clamor of telephones, typewriters, footsteps, and chatter. He knew they were just one small family among the desperate masses, and he had never felt more insignificant in his life.

"All this to be accomplished in three weeks..." Mr. Brink muttered.

Karl glimpsed over and his father looked almost shrunken with his back curled, his chin in his chest. He had never seen him so defeated, and, for once, he was glad for his mother's psychosis because it meant she was less aware.

The man closed the folder, pushed it aside, and looked up.

"In America, anything is possible."

7

"I told him I wanted to learn to swim."

"That's no way to start a relationship. Admitting your weaknesses?"

Standing in a tide pool in her black one-piece bathing suit, Ellie glanced back to Kate with a frown.

"Who's to say it's a relationship?"

"I found one!"

They looked over and Mary and Junebug were waving in the distance. With the tide out, they had all been searching for life in the fissures of the rocks, a stretch of jagged granite that, according to a teacher, was deposited by glaciers during the last Ice Age. Situated at one end of the beach, the formation acted as a breakwater against the strong currents flowing into Taylor Passage, trapping fish, crustaceans, and things lost at sea. Throughout their lives, the girls found everything from oyster pearls to anchor arms, and it was rumored that Blackbeard had once even buried treasure there.

"What time did he say?"

"Saturday," Ellie joked, walking towards the girls.

"When will you realize not everyone is on island time?"

Ellie ignored the remark and kept going, leaping from rock to rock on her bare feet, watching out for sharp edges. She extended her arms for balance, moved with the grace of a nymph, and even though Kate tried to catch up, Ellie was too quick. Kate had always been the better athlete—she played tennis and ran track in high school—but Ellie had a natural gift for navigating the contours of the wild.

"Slow down, Ellie!"

When they got down to where the rocks merged with the sea, Mary and Junebug were gazing into a wide gulf, their dresses damp.

"What is it?" Ellie said.

"Starfish."

The tide had already started to turn and water rushed in and out, creating a small fjord that was deep and getting deeper.

"Where?" Ellie said

When Junebug pointed, Ellie peered over and saw the most magnificent starfish, it's green tentacles visible against a bed of coral-colored sand. The water was as clear as glass, marred only by blades of eelgrass that swayed with the current. Ellie crouched down and began to descend, and although the barnacles hurt her feet, she was determined to get the creature.

"Almost!" Mary said.

As she went to take the final step, her foot touched wet moss. Suddenly, the earth dropped out from under her and she tumbled into the pool, her fall broken by the sand. When she stood up, the water was above her waist and she was drenched from head to toe.

"Eleanor?"

Ellie wiped her eyes and looked up to see, towering at the edge of the rocks, Karl.

"Are you alright, Ellie?" Kate said.

"Fine."

As she started to climb, Karl reached down and she took his hand. He pulled her up with a single tug and she landed on the dry surface. She pushed back her wet hair, fixed her bathing suit, relieved that she didn't get scraped up, but embarrassed nonetheless.

"You always seem to show up at the right time."

"Perhaps I should be a lifeguard."

"This is Kate," Ellie said and Karl bowed. "You're already acquainted with Mary and Junebug."

When he turned and greeted the girls, they didn't respond but instead watched him with a gaping wonder. Ellie and Kate smiled at each other, remembering what it was like to be on the verge of adolescence, when boys were like exotic animals, fearsome yet captivating.

"I see you started without me?" Karl said.

Ellie crossed her arms, looked up with a pretty smile.

"That was unintentional."

"Are you ready to swim?" he said, then he looked over to Kate. "Won't you join us?"

Kate shook her head with a sheepish grin, mumbled some excuse about the time, or chores, or having to stop by the shop—all of which Ellie knew were untrue. Ellie glanced back and the girls had already wandered off, exploring the nooks and crevices of the rocks before they all became submerged by the sea. When she turned to Karl, she shivered slightly, as much from nerves as from exhilaration.

"Sure, let's swim."

. . . . . .

With the tide in transition, it was low enough to walk beyond the shallows and Ellie followed Karl out, the water getting higher and colder as she went. She had never been out this far, and even though she could still touch the ground, she felt vulnerable amid the vast ocean. The currents knocked her around and she even swallowed a little seawater, but she was too proud to complain or make a fuss.

Standing on her tiptoes, the water up to her neck, Ellie was just ready to ask for help when Karl swam over and got behind her.

"Lean back."

At first, she hesitated, but when he came closer, she felt his presence and her fear was lessened. Taking a deep breath, she allowed herself to fall back and Karl took her under the arms.

"Now kick," he said softly, his mouth only inches from her ear.

Secure in his embrace, Ellie pointed her toes, moved her legs up and down, and began to feel the effects of her own propulsion. They swam backward together in a wide semicircle and drifted farther into the channel.

"So easy," she said.

"You're a natural."

They continued swimming and Karl kept them stable, turning into the waves, going with the currents. She was so comfortable that she closed her eyes for moments at a time, suspecting but not certain that the way she felt had something to do with him.

"What is it? What?..."

Feeling herself being raised up, Ellie started to flail and, before she knew it, they were coming out of the water.

"Sandbar," he said. "Go ahead, stand."

She lowered her legs, timidly at first, then her feet touched the gravelly bottom and Karl let go. The water was only a few feet deep, barely to her chest, and she stood in the middle of the strait and looked around amazed. All her life, the sandbar marked the halfway point between Monk and Holyhead Islands, an eternal barrier that vanished and reappeared each day with the tides. She had come close to it by boat, and once on a small skiff, but she never actually stood on it.

Ellie moved her arms, circling around, as giddy as a child who, upon learning to walk, discovers grass. The elation didn't last, however, because once her eyes swept Frazier Point, she saw the green hull of her father's boat and froze.

"What's wrong?"

Karl stood beside her, hands on his hips, squinting in the sun. As Ellie watched the small sloop tack, she could see her father at the helm and Ben at the transom. They were only hauling traps, but it seemed more intrusive and, throughout her life, Ellie felt like she never had privacy.

"It's nothing," she said, spinning around to face him. "Shall we swim some more?"

"Now I'll show you the crawl."

......

By the time they came out of the water, it was late afternoon and the sun was beginning to set over Portland, casting a dusky light across Taylor Passage. They walked up the beach, their hair wet and skin crisp, and Ellie shook her head to clear her ears. Most people had gone home and all that remained were a few scattered families. They found their shoes and clothes where they had left them hours before, at the foot of a large rock and safe from the tide, then collapsed on the sand beside some bushes. Many minutes passed before either said a word.

"You're burnt."

When Ellie touched his shoulder, Karl turned and looked her up and down.

"As are you."

"Not as burnt as you."

"I don't get much sun back home."

"What's Germany like?"

Karl's expression changed and he looked away, his arms around his knees.

"Not the best place to be right now."

The moment she asked, she wished she hadn't, and she bit her lip with a quiet regret. The unrest in Germany was distant but real and she was sure he had seen terrible things. Everyone was talking about the prospect of another war in Europe, and the question no longer seemed to be *if* but *when*. Ellie remembered seeing photographs of the last conflict; the devastated towns and villages, the corpses tangled in barbed wire, the dead animals upended in muddy battlefields. And although she had never gone farther than Bangor or Boston, she understood the brutality of war because she saw what it did to her father.

"We might very well stay here," Karl said.

Ellie blushed—it seemed like he had read her thoughts.

"Here?"

"In America."

"Won't you miss home?"

"My father has some difficulties, unfortunately. It's not safe."

"What sort of difficulties?"

"I'd rather not—"

"Because I'd understand."

Before she could finish, he leaned over and brought his lips to her. Surprised by his kiss, it took her a moment to react, then she wrapped her arms around his shoulders, responded with equal passion. They fell slowly back against the sand, their mouths enjoined and bodies writhing and, for those few seconds, the world and all its troubles went away.

8

When Ellie walked in the kitchen, Mary was at the table stirring a bowl of frosting while their mother rushed to prepare dinner. The counter was covered with carrot and onion peels, the floor dusted with flour. It was Mary's eleventh birthday and Vera acted like she was cooking for her daughter's wedding. They seldom used the oven in summer—almost everything they ate was boiled or pan-fried—but she was making a cake and the fire was on, increasing the temperature on an already scorching day.

"Get the pans for me, would you Ellie?"

Ellie went in the pantry, where, standing on her tiptoes, she reached for the two cast-iron skillets a relative in Bangor had given them years before. As she handed them to her mother, she heard the front door open. Moments later, her father came in with a letter in one hand, a paper bag in the other, the newspaper under his arm. His forehead was red from the sun—a dark stubble covered his cheeks and neck. When Ellie noticed grease marks on his arms, she knew the motor was having problems again and may have even broken down.

He dropped the letter on the table and when Ellie saw that the return address was Portland Library, she was overcome by nervous anticipation. Jack smiled at Mary and gave Ellie a wry look that had all the undertones of ridicule. Everyone in the family knew she was looking for a job, but no one seemed to take it seriously.

Jack put the bag down on the counter and when Vera peered in, she took a second look and frowned.

"Pollock?"

"Cod is 10 cents a pound."

"Jack, this is baitfish."

Ellie and Mary looked at each with a silent dread, knowing their father didn't like being challenged about the food he brought home.

"At least it ain't lobster."

"It's not swordfish either."

"Dammit Vera, I do what I can do!"

"There's no need to shout," she said, nodding at the window, suggesting that people might hear. "I just thought with Ben coming over—"

"Ben would eat scup."

"It wouldn't be far from different."

Jack stood fuming while his wife worked calmly at the sink with her back to him. She could stump him with a single remark—outwit him with the raise of an eyebrow. All her life, Ellie had watched this arthritic housewife dominate a man who was twice her size and as tough as a gad.

Jack turned around and stormed out of the room. The ceiling shook as he went up the stairs, and Ellie and Mary sat uncomfortably in the aftermath of the spat.

"Ben is eating with us?"

"Your father invited him," Vera said, sliding the baking pans in the oven. "Why? Is there someone else you'd prefer?"

Ellie couldn't see her face, but she heard the irony in her tone and was struck by a numb astonishment, a feeling of mild embarrassment, unjustified shame. She had known Karl for two weeks and hadn't told her mother or anyone else, but the insinuation, as subtle as it was, suggested she knew. Ellie never intended to keep it a secret, but knowing how her father felt about outsiders, especially Germans, she didn't want the relationship ruined before it began. In moments like this, when Ellie felt threatened and exposed, she hated Monk Island and all the pettiness of Down East life.

"I have to go and get ready."

She grabbed the letter, got up and went upstairs. As she passed her parents' bedroom, the door was open and she peered in to see her father sitting at the edge of the bed, facing the window. With his boots off and suspenders unstrapped, he rubbed his legs with both hands, and she wondered how he felt after a long day, whether he ached all over or just in certain places. She knew it was difficult work—she had threaded bait needles, spliced rope, repaired mesh, painted buoys—but aside from the day-to-day drudgery, it was an industry that was volatile and unpredictable, and everyone struggled to get by. For a man who only ever wanted to fish, Ellie knew it must have been discouraging and she sometimes wished her mother wasn't so hard on him.

When Jack suddenly looked over, Ellie was caught by surprise. She continued into her bedroom, closed the door and turned on the table lamp. Lying on the bed, she opened the letter and began to read.

"Dear Miss *Amis*," it said, and she was appalled that they misspelled her name. "We appreciate your interest in the position of secretary, but regret…"

Ellie stopped at *regret*, knowing that nothing good or consequential came after that word. She crinkled the note in her hand and tossed it on the floor, and went to the closet for a clean dress.

. . . . . .

Ellie and Mary had known Benjamin Frazier all their lives. Jack grew up with his father, who only a month before Ben was born was killed during the Meuse-Argonne Offensive in the First World War. He lived with his mother on the north side of the Island, in an area that was mostly swampland and shanties, where the roads were unpaved and many residents still survived off the land, raising pigs and sheep, hunting fowl, growing vegetables. Mrs. Frazier was an eccentric woman who ran a small flower nursery and seldom left her property. She never recovered from the death of her husband and some said she was still waiting for him to come back.

Ben starting working with Jack four years before when the outfit he was with went bankrupt. For a man who could be as callous as a clam, Jack was particularly kind to Ben and Ellie saw a tenderness in her father that she never experienced at home. There was a time before the girls were born when Jack watched over him like a son and they were together so much that little Ben started to believe it. But it all ended once Ellie was born and Jack had to attend to his own family.

Ben was shorter than Jack, but heavier set, with a full head of hair that covered his ears and hung over his forehead, frizzy from the sun and salt air. He had a scar above his eye from an old swimming accident, and on his left arm was a tattoo of the State of Maine. Although a Monk Islander to the core, Ben was gentler than his peers, which Ellie attributed to the fact that he was raised by a woman. When he spoke, he squinted between sentences and sometimes stuttered, more personal tics than signs of shyness because he would talk to anyone. Ellie and Kate both had crushes on him at different times during their childhood, mainly because he was three years older and always around.

"Ellie?"

She looked up from her plate and her mother was talking to her.

"Ben asked you a question."

"Sorry," she said, flustered.

"I hear Kate's going off to college?"

"Yes, nursing school. She leaves in August."

"Good. We could use another nurse. Ms. Reynolds is getting old."

Ellie nodded to be polite, not because she agreed, and only a local would presume that any personal accomplishment was made for the benefit of Monk Island—that Kate's only reason for getting an education was to come back and give children flu shots. But she didn't blame Ben for the way he thought, knowing they had all been shaped by the same narrow attitudes, the same small-town conceits.

Ben went to speak again but was interrupted when Vera got up to collect the dishes. He and Ellie both offered to help, and Jack grumbled something about letting him *take care of it later*. She ignored them all and carried what she could, hobbling into the kitchen and coming out, moments later, with a cake, two chocolate layers with white frosting. The candle that burned on top was the same one they had used for months, and with the cost of wax, it would last many more.

As Mary sat with a bashful smile, everyone sang happy birthday and, after pausing to make a wish, she blew out the flame. Vera cut the cake and Jack reached down for a box, sliding it across to his daughter.

"Go 'head, open it."

Mary took off the cover and when she reached in, it was a pair of binoculars. The black finish was heavily faded, the rubber eye caps brittle, but the lenses were intact.

"Where'd you get those?" Ellie asked.

"Came up with one of the traps," Jack said, snickering. "Most we caught all week."

Mary held them to her eyes and pointed towards the window.

"It's blurry."

"Turn the wheel to focus it."

"Jack, those are...lovely," Vera said.

As she passed out slices, her expression was wistful, almost sad, and Ellie understood why. With the exception of Christmas, gifts were a rare luxury in the Ames family, even before the Depression, and their mother always stressed that possessions were unimportant.

"Maybe I can spot a seal," Mary said.

"Maybe you can spot a U-boat."

She put down the binoculars, looked at her father with a comical frown. Instead of explaining, Jack glimpsed over to Ben in what Ellie knew was a subtle moment of shared bitterness. Both were victims of the last War, although in very different ways.

"Are there really U-boats?"

"That was a long, long time ago, Dear," Vera said, looking around uncomfortably.

Even Jack wasn't one to dwell on the past for too long, so he opened the newspaper and skimmed the headlines.

"They've forced Roosevelt to hold the line on neutrality, that's one step in the right direction."

"The Germans foiled a Communist plot in Danzig," Ben said.

"Where on earth is Danzig?" Vera wondered.

"France, I think," Jack said, appearing confused. "No, Denmark?"

"Poland," Mary said, and everyone was impressed.

"Hitler's got everyone on the edge of their seats."

"Damn Krauts."

Krauts. The word was like a jolt to Ellie's ears and she was suddenly uneasy. While her father and Ben talked, she got up and started to clear the table. She put the dishes on the counter and went up to the bedroom to get her purse. When she came down, she smelled cigarette smoke and could hear her father and Ben on the back porch.

"Ellie?"

Standing at the door, Ellie turned around and saw her mother, a soapy sponge in hand, an expression of mild concern.

"Where are you off to?"

"Just to meet a friend."

As she said it, she knew it sounded elusive because Monk Island was a small place, and of the few friends she had, her parents knew them all.

"Be mindful who you associate with," Vera said.

Ellie's face dropped, and she stood aghast, hoping but doubtful that she had misunderstood her.

"Mother?"

"You know what I mean."

Ellie always saw her mother as a bulwark against the unreasonableness of her father, someone who understood the nuances of life in ways that most men didn't. But she never felt like she could confide in her because her mother was loving without being warm, a difference that Ellie finally came to understand in adolescence. The only advice Vera had about menstruation was *not to get it everywhere*—all she said about sex was *once it stops hurting, it's not all that bad.*

"I'm a grown woman," Ellie said, and she walked out the door.

9

Karl came downstairs for dinner with a towel around his neck, his shoulders and arms deep bronze, eyebrows bleached white from the sun. His swim trunks were still damp from the night before when he and Ellie met at the beach at dusk and swam for hours in the dark as the last few trawlers trickled into port. At times Karl would hold her close, but she was getting stronger and could wade for several minutes, swim for yards unaided. Eventually, they collapsed on the sand, their bodies close together and although thoroughly exhausted, they still found the strength to kiss. The sound of her breathing, the expansion of her warm back against his chest, lulled him into a quiet bliss, and for moments at a time, he felt like he was sleeping with his eyes open. Karl had never felt so content, and the evenings alone with her somehow made up for all the years of isolation and loneliness.

"Guten tag, Mutter!"

Karl walked in the kitchen and could smell the salty aroma of the shoulder of ham they had been eating all week.

"Going swimming again?"

"What more to life than swimming?"

While she looked at him amused, he took the wooden spoon from her hand and reached in the pot for a taste.

"Deeeeelicious," he said.

Karl turned on the faucet, got a glass from the cupboard and filled it up. The water was salty, but he forced it down and had a second, all the while his mother watching suspiciously.

"I know this look."

"What look, Mother?"

"You've met someone," she said flatly.

All at once the mood in the kitchen went from lighthearted to serious.

"And what if I have?"

"Karl," she said, stepping closer and speaking with the pleading timidity of someone begging for his or her own life. "Please, this is not a good idea."

"What if I am happy."

"There's more at stake than happiness."

Karl looked down into her hollow eyes, as tired as they were troubled, and was overcome by tremendous sadness. He had always understood in some abstract way what his parents had given up for their beliefs, but only now did he realize that they had sacrificed joy, love, and all the tender sentiments which made life worth living.

"I've not chosen this," he said, swallowing with emotion.

"You can choose to avoid it."

"Mother, I'm not—"

"It's not just about you."

As Karl went to speak, the front door opened and the interruption was timely because he really had no good response. They immediately stopped talking and, seconds later, Mr. Brink hobbled in holding his hat. His suit was wrinkled, but nothing was out of place, and his handkerchief was folded in his breast pocket, his cufflinks perfectly set. In an age where propriety was on the wane, he looked almost old-fashioned, and Karl always wondered why, despite his forward-thinking, his father's style and manners were very much rooted in the past.

"How was Portland, Father?"

"The good news is we still have $117 dollars."

Karl glanced at his mother in confusion.

"Father, that's not much."

"Of course it's not much," he said.

"What's the bad news?"

"Frank Merrill won't help us."

"Why not?"

"Because he's dead!" Mr. Brink barked, tossing a letter on the table. "His widow wrote me back."

His father's voice was always grave, but it had reached a new level of frustration. As Karl and his mother stood watching, he went to the cabinet, got his brandy and a glass. Karl never saw him drink before dinner and he was as unsettled by the change in habit as he was by the disappointing news—above all, they relied on him for consistency.

"Won't you eat with us, Father?"

Mr. Brink stopped but didn't look over, his lips pressed together, his expression tense. Then he walked out to the porch and the door closed behind him.

......

Karl and his mother ate alone, sipping watery ham soup, chewing crusty bread. Facing her across the table, he tried to make conversation, but she would only respond with halfhearted nods, one-word answers. After dinner, Mrs. Brink cleaned up and Karl stepped out back, where his father had been sitting for over an hour. Although still light out, the yard and woods were dappled with the shadows of the encroaching dusk. The air was hot, but not as sticky, and Karl took a seat in the shade of the porch. For the first few minutes, he didn't speak, knowing how his father appreciated the etiquette of silence prior to deliberation.

"Father, I'd like to talk about the—"

"Shh," he said.

Mr. Brink gestured to the next cottage, thirty yards distant through thicket and birch trees, as dense as a jungle and no more conductive of sound than a wall. What had once been sensible caution was now paranoia and Karl worried that his father, like his mother, was becoming delusional. Nevertheless, he honored the request and lowered his voice.

"What are we to do?"

Mr. Brink sighed and took a puff of his cigar.

"What can we do?"

"Even if we don't find a sponsor, we will stay. Right?"

"Son, we are not scofflaws. We're permitted to be here for sixty days. Once our travel permits expire, we are expected to leave."

"But Father it's too dangerous."

"Life is dangerous!" Mr. Brink hissed, then quickly composed himself. "I've tried my damnedest. Once we get home, I will reapply."

"Is everything alright?"

Startled, Karl glanced back, while his father made no effort to look, and his mother was in the doorway.

"All is well, Hilde," Mr. Brink said.

"My pills," she said. "I can't find my pills."

"They're on the table beside the bed."

Mrs. Brink withdrew back into the kitchen like a ghost, and Karl listened to her footsteps, steady and plodding, as she made her way up the stairs.

"Father," he continued. "We can tell the Consulate she's too unwell to travel."

"I'll not lie. I've spent my life fighting the lies of these Nazi monsters. I will not stoop to their level."

Their whispering was quiet but strained, like two soldiers arguing in a foxhole on a tense night.

"You lied to the INS. You weren't invited to teach this year."

Mr. Brink reached for his brandy and Karl noticed that his hand was shaking.

"That was administrative expediency, nothing more."

He leaned forward, closer to his father, who sat slumped in the chair, staring out blankly.

"Niklaus? Where?"

His mother was now calling from the second-floor window, her voice faint and pleading.

"Check the bag on the bureau," Mr. Brink yelled up, then muttered. "Helpless."

Karl's mouth dropped open and the blood rushed to his face. All the resentment he ever had towards his father coalesced in one blinding burst of rage and, at that moment, he understood how delicate was the separation between love and hatred. Fearing he might do something rash, he immediately got up to leave.

"If she is helpless, it was you who made her so!"

He went for the door and was just ready to go in, when Mr. Brink mumbled, "You are right."

Karl stopped and a chill went up his back—it was the first time he ever heard his father admit he was wrong. He stood still, his hand gripping the doorknob, and felt his eyes begin to well up.

"Please, Son. Sit."

Karl slowly turned around and sat back down, as limp as a glove, all his anger gone. His father took a sip of his drink, cleared his throat, and spoke.

"I always meant to protect you from the madness. When I was your age, I was far too serious—a head full of cabbage, as your grandmother used to say. At University, I learned about all the suffering in the world and wanted to do something about it. Your mother was an idealist too…in some ways more than me. When we lived in Africa, she brought fresh water to the entire village. Not alone, of course, but she drafted the project plan, secured the funding. I was so proud of her." He took another sip and continued. "When the Nazi's came to power, we had no idea a civilized nation like ours could spawn such savagery. We watched a century of progress disintegrate in just a few years. Some days it seemed like the whole damn country had gone mad." He took a drag on his cigar, blew out the smoke, and turned to look Karl in the eye. "So I fought against it…with all my will. An Army of one. It wasn't much, but it was something…"

When his father paused, Karl waited half a minute to be sure he was finished.

"Father, you've persevered through all this, we can't give up now."

Mr. Brink looked away, nodding, and Karl sensed he was too emotional to speak.

"You'll find a sponsor. I know you will," Karl said.

He patted his father's hand and then, without a word, got up and went towards the door.

"Son, where are you going at this hour?"

"Swimming."

10

The night sky was clear and the moon full as Ellie walked to meet Karl. When she reached the village, all the stores were closed except the ice cream shop and Lavery's, which stayed open late in the high season for boats that came in after dark and needed bait for morning. With time to spare, she crossed over and went inside, where she saw Mr. Mallet standing at the counter, measuring and cutting lengths of rope.

"Kate's already gone home," he said before she could ask.

As she turned to go, he cleared his throat to get her attention.

"Say, Ellie. How's your German friend?"

The question stumped her but she tried not to act surprised.

"He's…he's well, thank you."

Since she started seeing Karl, they always met at night, spending their time in the shadows, evening swims and long walks on the beach, an occasional ice cream cone or an hour spent on a public bench. It seemed so secretive but was mostly out of convenience because Ellie worked down the docks most days, and Karl couldn't leave his mother alone if his father was out. Yet she couldn't deny there was comfort in their discreetness, knowing how, on a small island, gossip was a curse that could kill.

Joe Mallet put down what he was doing and came around the counter.

"I'm not one to give advice unsolicited," he said, lowering his voice. "But try to be careful."

"I will."

"Not for yourself, for your friend. Folks can be awful strange about foreigners, especially Germans."

Ellie made an emotional smile, touched by his concern, thinking how he always had been the kind and sensible counterweight to her father's cynicism. As one of the few men on Monk Island who hadn't fought in the Great War, Joe Mallet seemed less damaged, less hung up on the past, and Ellie admired him for it.

"One more thing," he added. "Kate tells me you're looking for a job in the City?"

Ellie blushed, overcome by a mild embarrassment, and not because she didn't feel worthy of working on the mainland. But life on Monk Island had always been so fragile that the subject of leaving was controversial, especially for older members of the community who saw it as betrayal.

"I've applied for a few positions."

"I'm still gonna need some help around here. So the offer still stands."

"Thank you, Mr. Mallet."

"Only if you don't find anything in the City."

......

Ellie stood under the oak tree at the corner of Gull Avenue. Across the street, a brass band was playing in the ballroom at the Inn and some guests lingered under the portico drinking wine, smoking cigarettes. The air was warm and humid, but already Ellie could detect a change, some faint scent or atmospheric quirk which hinted that, although it was only the first week of August, autumn was fast approaching.

"Ellie?"

When she spun around, it was Karl, dressed in his swim trunks, a loose white shirt with the top buttons undone. She put her hand to her heart, winded and wondering why she startled more easily than she used to.

"You scared the Dickens—"

Before she could finish, he brought his hand from behind his back and held out a flower. At first, she thought it was a peony, which grew everywhere on the Island, then she took it and realized it was a small rose.

"It's lovely."

She stuck it in her hair between two pins, raised her eyebrows, tilted her head and made a cute smile. Whenever they met, the first few moments were always disjointed, hesitant, but never awkward. Ellie felt that more was communicated between them through silence than through words, something she had experienced to a lesser degree with only a handful of other people, namely Kate and Mary.

"Did you see the moon?"

Ellie looked across the harbor, where the giant orb glowed high above the City, its surface a haze of whites and yellows so vibrant they seemed fluid. Without a word, they started towards it, down the hill, Ellie reaching for Karl's hand as they went.

"Your Father went to Portland today?"

"He did."

"How'd it go?"

"Not so good."

"Why?"

"He found out his colleague he hoped would help us died."

"I'm so sorry."

"Don't be, he was ninety-five," Karl said, and they both grinned. "Some days, I feel like we're destined to go back."

"Don't say that."

"It's just that…"

She squeezed his hand tighter, spoke more firmly.

"Don't say that."

Karl gave a conciliatory nod and they continued in silence. The short, two-sentence exchange was the closest thing they had ever had to a disagreement or spat, and for Ellie, there was something satisfying in the tension because it meant what they had was real. Nevertheless, she felt bad for snapping and would have apologized except she didn't want him to think she wasn't serious.

As they approached the pier, some men were fishing off the side, surrounded by the accouterments of their pastime, buckets of bait, toolboxes of line and lures, bottles of beer and hard liquor. Loud and rowdy, they wore the drab colors of local lobstermen, their red faces and beards visible in the half-light of the moon. Ellie had hoped to walk to the end of the dock with Karl, but as they got closer, she felt his hand grow tense, sensed a rising reluctance. Soon his uneasiness became hers and she was suddenly uncomfortable as if all of Monk Island was watching and didn't approve.

When a couple of the men looked over, Ellie let go of Karl's hand and he seemed relieved.

"Come," he said, stopping before they went any further. "Let's go to the beach instead."

"That's a better idea."

11

Ellie arrived home just after midnight, opening the door slowly so it wouldn't creak, knowing that everyone was asleep except Scuttles, who roamed the house at night looking for mice. She never worried about getting in late because their house had no locks, and with Jack normally the first one in bed, she had always been able to sneak out when she wanted. Sometimes he knew, but even then he didn't scold her because neither of the girls was ever really given a curfew. For a man who sought to control every part of his daughters' lives, he was oddly lenient on their whereabouts, which Ellie attributed to the fact that he saw Monk Island as an extension of his own domain. But the moment she stepped inside, she knew that had all changed.

"Where the hell were you?!"

She turned around, her back against the door, and standing in the shadow of the parlor was her father. He was shirtless and barefoot, dressed only in the linen shorts he always wore on hot summer nights.

"Down at the beach," she said.

"Were you with that boy?"

Ellie paused before answering, sensing that he wasn't the only one awake, and as her eyes adjusted to the dark, she could see her mother standing behind him. There was someone else too, and when she looked over Mary was crouched at the top of the stairs, eyes wide and clinging to the banister.

"What's this all about?" Ellie said

Feeling cornered, she had the urge to turn around and run, but there was nowhere to go. And she could only watch as Jack came towards her, his gnarly finger pointed.

"You need to stay away from him."

"But why?—"

"Never mind why!" he shouted.

Ellie startled and began to cower into the door, its knob pressing into her spine.

"Those people are animals," he went on, *those people* meaning Germans in general. "I know from experience."

Ellie stopped, glanced at her mother and her sister, panting from emotion. Her father never talked much about the War, other than to say it was *loud and bloody*, but they all knew he was haunted by it. Either way, she wouldn't let Karl and his family be vilified for the prejudices of the past.

"They aren't animals, his father is a professor."

Even as she said it, she knew it was a mistake because Jack despised intellectuals, academics, and professionals—anyone who did "clean work."

"That don't impress me."

"Father," she said, starting to cry. "You don't even know him."

"And I don't intend to. But stop seeing him or he'll know me!"

The threat filled Ellie with a sudden rage that was almost beyond her power to control. She stood up straight, leaned forward and shrieked, "I'm an adult! I'll see who I want!"

Smack! He slapped her across the face so hard she lost her balance. Instantly, Ellie put her hand to her cheek and it was hot.

"Enough, Jack!" Vera said.

She pulled him away, but he wasn't finished.

"Be down the docks first thing tomorrow morning!"

Stunned and silent, Ellie watched as he turned and marched back up to bed, the scars on his lower back made visible by the moonlight through the window.

......

As Ben steered the boat, Ellie stood quietly in the wheelhouse beside him. She didn't usually come out to haul traps, and she could only guess it was her father's way of trying to keep her occupied so she couldn't be with Karl. Her cheek was still sore, but the anger from what happened the night before had subsided, leaving her with a dull sadness. Her father hadn't hit her since she was a girl and those times were mostly justified.

"Everything alright, Ellie?" Ben said.

Before she could answer, the boat lurched to one side and they all braced themselves.

"I'm fine."

"Back it up," Jack said, leaning over the side with a gaff, trying to hitch a buoy that bounced in the surf.

Fishing was rough on the eastern side of Monk Island, where the shoreline was exposed to the open Atlantic. But Jack was never afraid to take risks, and with the lagging industry threatening to do him in, he had even talked about going out to the Shoals, one of the most dangerous areas in Casco Bay, a jagged minefield near Beacon Light that could cut a ship in two.

"A little to port," Jack called out.

Ben pulled the throttle back, black smoke puffed from the exhaust, and they started to reverse.

"A little more."

As Ellie watched, he leaned against the gunwale and reached out. The hook missed by a fraction of an inch and, before he could try again, the stern drifted and the buoy went under it.

"Jesus, Ben!"

Jack dropped the gaff and ran over to take control and, in an instant, the two swapped places.

"If we hit that line," he shouted over the wind. "that prop's a goner."

As Ben stood ready, Jack jerked the throttle, cut the wheel and they swung around in a wide loop, approaching the trap from the other side.

"Now!"

Ben lunged and hooked the buoy with so much momentum he almost went over.

Jack turned to Ellie and said, "Take the helm."

"What?"

"Take it, dammit."

Ellie grabbed the wheel and he rushed over to help pull in the line, which was black and slick with algae. They hoisted the trap over the edge, opened the door, and lobsters poured out, squirming across the deck, their antennas going wild.

"Now that's what I call a catch!"

Squatting down, he collected the hens and tossed them to Ben, who put them in the crates and covered them with wet burlap. There was a time when they would be measured and checked for eggs too, but the industry had been in a slump for so long that no one bothered with the rules.

"See what man's work looks like?" Jack said, standing up, wiping his hands.

Ellie knew the remark was meant as a dig to Karl and his family, but she hadn't spoken to her father all morning and wasn't about to acknowledge it.

"What've we got here?"

When Jack walked over to the side, Ellie looked and saw an Army truck parked beside the marsh on Passamaquoddy Way—*The Pass*, as locals called it—a long and meandering road that ran along the eastern side of the Island. A group of men, some in combat fatigues and some in civilian clothing, stood in a circle talking.

"I heard something about a new base," Ben said.

"I heard the very same."

"Think they're scouting out land?"

"Yeah," Jack said, rubbing his chin, thinking. "Must be the Army Corp of Engineers."

"Do you really think there'll be a War?" Ellie said, abruptly, almost like she was thinking out loud.

They looked over to her at the same time, but only Jack spoke.

"You just keep the boat steady."

......

The afternoon winds had shifted to the southeast as they headed to Portland, the sloop sluggish with three people, twenty traps, a few hundred pounds of lobster. As they went through Taylor Passage, the beach was a thin strip of beige in the distance, dotted with colored umbrellas and towels. The tide was high and the sandbar submerged, but Ellie knew the exact spot where Karl first taught her how to swim. She thought about that day and all the days between, the pleasure of small moments, when they cuddled in the shade of the dunes, walked the path to Drake's Cove, the scent of the lavender and beach rose in the air.

As they chugged into port, the wharf was crowded with trawlers and small sloops, docked end-to-end in the Friday afternoon rush. Jack backed into a tight spot and Ben tied the lines and they got to work. Ellie felt obliged to help, but when her father took her out to haul, it was to learn the finer points of fishing and not to do the dirty work.

Getting the lobster to the pound had all the efficiency of an assembly line and, with more boats waiting to come in, dockworkers scrambled up and down the pier, shouting, pointing, and waving. Two men came over to assist and Jack and Ben lifted the first crate, a rickety box that dripped seawater. Jack made all his own crates—most lobstermen did—from knotted pine and tap nails, and between the slats, Ellie could see snapping and wriggling within. She pitied the small creatures, confined in the darkness and out of their natural habitat, and although her mother always said they were God's bounty, she wondered what god would want that.

As Jack and Ben went to pass a crate over the side, Ben wasn't paying attention and his corner hit the dock.

"Watch it!"

Ben was flustered, but he quickly rallied and lifted the crate higher. Ellie despised how her father talked to him because it reminded her of how he spoke to her, with a cold condescension. People knew how Jack treated Ben when he was a boy, watching over him like the father he never met, but as Ellie saw it, kindness in the past didn't make up for cruelty in the present.

Jack was always irritable at the pound when the week's catch was tallied and he went to see the foreman to get paid.

He never met the actual owner, an investor from Camden who had a fleet of small craft, but that didn't stop Jack from ridiculing him. He said the man probably couldn't tell a lobster from a rock crab; didn't know a pintle from a gudgeon. It was obvious how much he resented working for someone else, and Ellie remembered a time, before he lost his boat, when he was not so bitter.

With the crates unloaded, the men put them on dollies and Jack followed them to the pound so the fish could be weighed and inspected. Ellie noticed another crate wedged between two stacks of traps and covered with a tarp.

"You forgot one," she said.

Leaning back with his arms on the gunwale, Ben turned to her with a vague but mischievous grin.

"I guess we did."

Ellie looked at the crate, then looked away, overcome by a creepy, suspicious feeling. The lobster business had always been shady, and in an industry where production and profits were dependent on the whims of nature, there was bound to be corruption. One of the most common was "shacking," selling part of the catch without the owner knowing, usually to restaurants, fish markets, and even other boats. As theft, it was technically a felony, but few would pursue it in criminal court because local judges, many whose own fathers worked the sea, could be sympathetic to defendants. Still, Jack had lost his first boat through deceit, an incident that changed all their lives, and Ellie would be outraged if he hadn't learned his lesson.

"Is that to meant to go?" she said, nodding towards the crate, prodding him a little.

"That's for all of us, for chowders and such."

"We don't eat lobster."

When a ferry horn blew, they were interrupted, and Ellie decided it was probably better because, if her father was shacking, she'd rather not know. She scanned the decks as the boat pulled out and saw some local women, neighbors, and parents of friends, loaded with bags after shopping in town. Just as she turned away, someone caught her eye and she looked back. It was an older gentleman with a gray suit and hat, leaning against the top railing alone, smoking a cigar. She couldn't quite see his expression, but something in his posture suggested a deep and troubled contemplation. Only when Ellie noticed a cane did she realize that it was Karl's father.

12

Ellie walked with Karl down Gull Ave in the pleasant evening air, their hands clasped, two figures in the dark. As the weeks passed, Ellie could sense a growing disapproval, some subtle yet stubborn force that aimed to keep them apart. First, it was her mother's remarks, then Joe Mallet's advice, then the confrontation with her father. Beyond that, there were the furtive glances in the street, regardless of whether she was with him or not, and some days she felt like everyone was watching. Ellie knew much of it was her imagination because in the summer the crowds made it easy to blend in and they were hardly a spectacle. All that would change soon, however, when the tourists were gone and the cottages shuttered, and that was why she and Karl decided they would leave Monk Island.

"How about New York City?" Karl said.

"Too big."

"Florida?"

"Too hot."

They had discussed moving away, but this was the first time they talked about where. Much of it was playful banter because, in truth, Karl couldn't leave his parents and Ellie would have to be near her mother and Mary. But they could go to Portland, or somewhere up the coast, starting a new life together far from the watching eyes of her father.

Everything now was dependent on the visas, and although Ellie knew Mr. Brink had some setbacks, Karl assured her he would find a sponsor. His father was a respected academic, with many friends and colleagues in America, and someone was bound to help. Still, she knew their deadline was approaching, and it was hard to enjoy the small moments with the future so uncertain. Over the past week, he had stopped talking about the visas altogether so Ellie stopped asking, and they both maintained a quiet, but anxious optimism.

Soon they approached the Bowladrome and music was thumping within. A group of teenagers stood smoking out front and when Karl stopped, they stared at him.

"It's like a nightclub?" he said to Ellie, both curious and amused.

"Bowling."

"The building is so old."

"They used to salt fish here when I was a girl."

The neon sign which hung from its façade was strangely out-of-place, but there was a time when Monk Island was a booming vacation spot, with a theater, photo shop, two hotels, and an arcade. The theater burned down, taking with it two other buildings, and by the time the Depression came around, most of the seasonal businesses had closed. Jack said the decline was caused by politicians in Portland who, after years of disputes with Island leaders, had stopped promoting tourism. Whether it was true or not, Ellie didn't know—Jack seemed to blame everything on mainlanders—but there was no doubt that the waterfront was a shadow of what it once was.

"Shall we go bowling?" Karl said, finally turning to her.

Ellie hesitated, if only because she preferred their time alone, and the place was swarming with locals. But knowing they couldn't avoid people forever, she said, "Sure, why not?"

When Karl held the door for her, she stepped inside and it was dark and crowded, the cigarette smoke as thick as fog.

They pushed through to the counter and the owner came over, sweating and in a rush. With his thinning hair and mustache, Paul Schofield always reminded Ellie of a heavier version of Groucho Marx. He grew up with her father and started out as a lobsterman before purchasing the Bowladrome at auction in the Twenties after the original owner fled to Florida.

"What'll it be, Ellie?" he said, wiping his forehead with a napkin.

"Two pairs."

He knew her size, but not Karl's so he looked over the counter to see his feet. He got the shoes and Karl gave him a dollar and they walked over to the lane. Karl handed Ellie a ball and it was heavier than she remembered—she hadn't been to the Bowladrome since sophomore year. Taking one step back, she swung her arm, let it go, and the ball bounced off the floor and rolled down the center before banking right into the gutter.

"Oh my," Karl said, clenching his fists.

Ellie rolled her eyes in embarrassment and reached for another. On her second try, it clipped two pins and the last shot was much the same.

"Humiliating!" she said, stepping aside to let him go.

Karl arched his back and bent his knees and, in a single motion, lunged forward and sent the ball flying. It went straight down the middle and hit the pins so hard that one of them flipped into the next lane. The pinboy looked back with his hands raised and Karl waved in apology.

He went twice more, each time getting a strike, and after a few more rounds, Ellie trailed him by forty points and was getting frustrated.

"Here," Karl said, calling her over. "Let me help."

He got a ball and put her hand in his.

"Bend your knees. Look straight—not to the side. You must focus."

With Karl close, Ellie felt as secure as when he first showed her how to swim and her confidence grew. She stepped forward, released the ball and, although it went slower than before, it didn't veer and she held her breath as it rolled steadily on.

Smash! It hit dead center and every pin went down.

"Guter schuss!"

She spun around, her face beaming and, for a moment, she thought they might embrace. But then they heard a voice, a cutting comment, a snide remark, nearby and no doubt directed at them. Ellie turned first, followed by Karl and in the next lane they saw four men glaring. With their scuffed shoes and greased back hair, she knew they were from the north side of the Island, a year or two younger than her, familiar by sight although she didn't know their names.

"I'm sorry? Is there a problem?" Karl said.

One of them stepped forward, nodded at Karl.

"Are you German?"

"What should it matter?"

"Maybe we don't like Krauts."

"I advise you not to insult me."

When his friends jeered, the young man put down his bottle and walked over. He and Karl stood face-to-face, their eyes locked, and Ellie came to Karl's side and took his arm. People in other lanes stopped to watch and the whole place seemed to go quiet. The young man glanced back to his friends, gritted his teeth and took one step closer.

"Kraut."

"I said, *I'd advise you not to insult me.*"

"Fucking Nazi—"

Karl lunged and grabbed his collar. The young man swung, but Karl had a longer reach and instead of striking back, he tried to pull him to the ground. Instantly, the others dropped their bottles and ran over and Ellie jumped in their way.

"Stop!" she screamed.

Karl and the young man wrestled for a few seconds, knocking over glasses and bowling balls. There were cheers in the background, hoots and hollers from rowdy locals, and Ellie feared it would turn into a melee.

"What the hell's going on here?!"

From out of nowhere, Paul Schofield appeared, shoving the men away and getting between Karl and his opponent. He circled around like a drill instructor, staring everyone in the eye—including Karl and Ellie—making no judgments or distinctions, challenging anyone to defy him. The troublemakers all stepped back and Ellie wasn't surprised because Monk Island, for all its faults, was a place where the young still respected their elders.

"This man," Karl said, struggling to catch his breath, "insulted me."

His shirt buttons were broken, there were red marks on his neck, but Ellie could tell he was more shaken up than hurt. Schofield looked the four young men up and down, a slight disgust in his expression.

"You boys. Outta here!"

As outraged as she was, Ellie had some vague pity for them, knowing how residents from the north side of the island were always looked down upon.

"What? You gonna believe a Kraut?"

"You heard what I said," Schofield shouted, and he pointed at the door.

To Ellie, however, it made no sense to bully the bullies and all her life she had watched one group disparage another. People in Portland were prejudiced against Islanders, locals were prejudiced against tourists, lobstermen were prejudiced against anglers, Congregationalists were prejudiced against Baptists. The whole world was an endless torrent of squabbling and mistrust, and Ellie knew that, whether you won or lost, acknowledging it only made you part of it. Just because Schofield told the others to leave and not them, didn't mean people would hate Karl any less for being German.

"No," she said. "Let them stay. We'll go."

. . . . . .

Karl and Ellie sat between a rock and some beach grass, looking out across the strand, empty and desolate, the waves lapping. On the other side of Taylor Passage, Holyhead Island loomed like a great shadow, black and mysterious, a phantom landmass. With one knee bent, Karl grabbed handfuls of sand and let the grains fall through his fingers, over and over again, like a slow meditation. Ellie was more ashamed than angry at what happened, and she only wished she could tell her father because he would have set the local boys straight. But Karl was a tourist and a foreigner—an outsider in every sense—and the fact that he was a German only made him more suspect.

"I understand why they said it," he said.

"You do?"

"In their minds, Germany is Adolph Hitler."

"Then they have small minds."

"If only they knew how much we hate Hitler too. What we went through."

After a short silence, Ellie said, "Karl, what happened back home?"

"I told you, my father fell out of favor with the Nazis."

She accepted the answer with a slow nod and not because she was satisfied with it. In their time together, she had learned a lot about his past, stories of beach vacations in Lübeck, ice swimming with his uncle in Bavaria, a crazy aunt from Dusseldorf who kept cats—all the quaint recollections of childhood whimsy, light and inconsequential. But whenever she tried to get to the heart of exactly why they had come to America and why they were trying to stay, he resorted to vague generalities, repeated things she already knew, sometimes changed the subject entirely.

"No," she said, firmly. "What *happened* back home?"

"I don't want to frighten you."

"I want to know."

"You don't—"

"I do."

Karl sighed, staring ahead, thinking, and although it hurt Ellie to see his distress, she had to know. Finally, he turned to her and when their eyes met, she shuddered and didn't know why.

"It all started when I was thirteen…"

13.

Karl saw himself walking with his father through the busy streets of Hamburg at rush hour. With his school bag over his shoulder, the back of his coat was damp from the wet trunks and cap he brought for swim practice each day. The sky was steel gray—to Karl the City always seemed gray in winter—and he sensed a coldness that went beyond mere temperature. People looked ahead and not at each other, moved with a restrained urgency, spoke in whispers.

As Karl and his father came around the corner onto the Neuer Steinweg, Mr. Brink stopped. Karl looked ahead and saw a group of men in brown uniforms in front of a department store. They were loud and rowdy, harassing passers-by and waving signs that read "Germans! Don't Buy From Jew!" and "Zionist Bloodsuckers." A few people walked away appalled, but far more remained, watching with the amused delight of seeing a juggler in a park.

Karl stood frozen, his heart racing. He had heard about violence in the cities, but never saw it firsthand. When he turned to his father for an explanation, Mr. Brink just stared ahead with a long and simmering revulsion. Then he calmly put down his briefcase, remarked, "wait here," and marched over. Karl was too frightened to try to stop him, and he could only watch as his father went up to a man with a bullhorn, pointed his finger, and began to berate him. It happened in an instant—the group encircled him, some of them shouting, others laughing. Suddenly, one of the men belted Mr. Brink in the face and he fell back on the pavement, losing his hat and glasses. Karl sprinted towards him, but by the time he got there, his father was on his feet.

"No, Son."

He grabbed Karl firmly by the arm and they headed in the other direction. They had only taken a few steps when Karl heard a noise and looked back to see the men shattering all the shop windows. He realized then that something about his father's defiance had piqued their rage because they began pulling out mannequins and merchandise, hurling it all onto the sidewalk like marauders. He followed his father through the crowded streets, tears streaming down his face, and neither spoke a word until they were on the train. He had never been so relieved to get out of Hamburg.

Karl's eyes flickered and he came out of a drowsy stupor that was somewhere between sleep and wakefulness. The bedroom was beyond stifling and he lay half-naked on the mattress, covered in sweat, a book on his chest. The days were like a long prison sentence and the summer heat only added to the tension of the boredom, anxiety, anticipation. While his father traveled to the mainland to do their business, Karl stayed at home to look after his mother, and his only respite was evenings with Ellie. Mr. Brink had stopped asking where he was going, satisfied that his son would draw less attention at night.

But as Karl sat up on the bed and felt his swollen cheek, he knew it was too late for anonymity. If the whole Island didn't know Eleanor Ames was seeing a German, they soon would. He told his parents he had collided with a lobster buoy while swimming, but that didn't explain why his shirt was missing buttons. The incident at the Bowladrome had stolen from him any innocence he had left about their situation and seemed to vindicate all his father's secrecy and stealth. Vulnerable back in Germany and not trusted in America,

Karl felt like he was floating in space, alone and untethered, without neither a home nor a purpose.

When he came down to the kitchen, a pot was on the stove and his mother was on her knees, scrubbing the floor with an old brush, its bristles worn and frayed.

"Mother, what are you doing?"

She sat up, wiped her brow.

"Washing up."

"Where's Father?"

She gestured towards the door and Karl looked out to see him standing in the high grass, a cigar in his mouth, playing horseshoes alone with the rusted equipment a renter had left behind. In his fedora and wrinkled shirt, he looked like an impoverished country gentleman.

"I thought he wasn't expected home until late?"

She gave him a blank stare, as if she didn't understand the question, then continued cleaning.

"Would you get his blood pressure medication?" she said, not looking up. "It's on the nightstand."

Karl nodded to himself and stood watching her—her dirty forearms, brittle hair, faded day dress—realizing, as if for the first time, how desperate their lives had become. Seeing her stoop made him upset and when he spoke his voice quivered.

"Mother, it's really too hot to be—"

"I should like to be of use!"

Karl flinched, but he wasn't offended because her response told him that, despite her condition, she still had dignity. He turned around and rushed upstairs, stopping when he got to the bedroom door. Even at nineteen-years-old, there was something sneaky about entering his parents' quarters. Nevertheless, he went in and walked over to the nightstand, where he found the medicine between a box of tissues and his father's wallet. As he reached for it, he also noticed a brown Western Union envelop.

Karl glanced back at the door. His mother was in the kitchen and he knew his father was still outside because he could hear the clank of the horseshoes. The envelope was unsealed and when he opened it, he found a telegram inside.

Compagnie Générale Transatlantique confirms
three passengers for SS Normandie.
Departing August 26th. New York To Hamburg.

Karl stared at the document with his mouth agape, feelings of anger, shock, confusion, and disbelief rippling through his body and mind. He had the urge to scream, but remained calm and put the telegram away. He went to his room to dress for dinner and when he came down, his mother was setting the table and his father was washing his hands in the sink.

"What a game."

"I imagine it was," Karl said coldly.

He slapped the medicine bottle on the table and took a seat. Mrs. Brink spooned soup into the bowls and put out a loaf of crusty bread.

"How was your day, Father?" Karl asked as they ate.

"As good as can be expected."

"You went to Dartmouth College to see Dr. Rutledge, did you not?"

"Indeed."

"So, will he sponsor us?"

"He said he would consider it."

Karl didn't know if he was lying, but he was sure he wasn't telling the whole truth, and his father seemed remarkably calm about a situation that was urgent.

"Tell me," Karl said, and his father peered up. "When we do get the visas, what should become of the steamship tickets?"

All at once the room got tense, and when Mr. Brink glanced over at his wife, Karl suspected that she knew as well.

"Listen here, my boy—"

"Why would you buy tickets if we still have a chance to stay?"

"A precaution, nothing more."

"But that's nearly all our money!"

Mr. Brink put down his spoon, cleared his throat.

"The fact is, Son," he said. "Dr. Rutledge is no longer at Dartmouth. Dr. Ferris is on sabbatical in Ecuador. Dr. Peterson retired from Tufts last year. Many of these men I haven't see in two decades. I can't just expect to show up and have them commit their reputations for—"

"For what's right!" Karl shouted and he stood up. "Like you risked your reputation for what is right."

"To oppose a bloody dictator!"

Mr. Brink pounded his fist on the table and got up too. They faced each other in fury across the small table while Mrs. Brink looked on, her eyes dilated, her expression blank.

"You intellectuals are all the same. You'll die for your principles, but you won't live for them!"

Karl thought his father would strike back, and he hoped for it because sometimes antagonism was the only way to get him to talk. Instead, Mr. Brink sighed and Karl watched as the anger left him like the soul leaving the body. He sat back down with a sullen composure that, for Karl, was an indication of his surrender to their fate.

"You are young and foolish. You are blinded by love."

Karl gave his mother a sharp look. He knew she suspected he was seeing someone, but he didn't think she would tell her husband, and he now felt betrayed. He shook his head, as disappointed with his mother as he was outraged by his father, then stormed out of the room.

"Karl!"

When his mother shrieked, he cringed with guilt, but he was already out the door and couldn't go back.

......

Karl walked with a light rain in his face through the dark and unpaved roads. After a day indoors, it was a relief to be outside and he felt like he could finally breathe again. As he came down the hill, the American Legion was busy, and he could hear music and voices within. People were congregated out front, spilling into the street, drinking and smoking in the dim light of early evening. Karl couldn't see any faces, but he felt a thousand eyes, and as he got closer, he was overcome by a sudden and mind-numbing panic. He stopped almost subconsciously and stood frozen in the middle of the road, his heart pounding and hands tingling. Then he turned and took off in the other direction, away from the locals and away from civilization, towards the one place where he knew he would find solace.

When Karl came out to the beach, the moon was glistening over Holyhead Island. Taylor Passage was flat and quiet, with only a single boat passing through, the ripples of its wake long and undisturbed.

Karl walked down to the shoreline and tossed off his shoes, unbuttoned his shirt, undid his belt and threw off his trousers. He splashed through the shallows, dove in and, moments later, surfaced twenty yards out, where he pushed his hair back, blew water from his nose. As he looked around, the sea was perfectly calm while inside a storm raged.

I've spent my life fighting the lies of these Nazi monsters...

He leaped forward and swam off.

Karl thought of all the nights his father came home from work visibly shaken. Maybe someone slipped a threatening letter under his office door, or his teaching schedule had been rearranged for no good reason. On one occasion Gestapo officers came to the University and threatened him in front of his class; on another, several colleagues petitioned the administration to have him removed from his post. Mr. Brink was a minor economics professor, and Karl knew he was no more influential, no more a danger, than the many other middle-class professionals who opposed the Nazis, both publicly and in private. But in a society caught up in the fever of National Socialism, his opinions made him a pariah and the whole family suffered. The more Karl thought about how his father was treated, the harder he swam.

Won't you miss home?...

He explained to Ellie that he loved his country, but hated what it had become, a conflict that ran deep in his soul. Karl had trained for the '36 Olympics out of pride and patriotism and when he got cut from the team, he was devastated but accepted the loss as fair play. The harassment of his father, however, was an outrage and an injustice, and although Karl at first had been against going to America, he came to realize Germany was no longer their home.

He went faster, kicking furiously.

Fucking Nazi...

But how could he live in America with the inherited guilt of things he and his family had no part in? In Germany, his father was despised for standing up for human rights; here they would be despised for spurning them. Karl now had the same paranoia he chided his father for and wherever he walked he felt like people were watching. He knew they could always move to another city or state, but they would still be Germans, and if there was another war, they might find themselves exiled once again.

As he shot through the water, Karl experienced a terrifying alienation that took his breath away. Panting and exhausted, he paddled towards shore and collapsed on the beach.

......

Sometime later, he opened his eyes, heard the whoosh of the surf, felt the sand against his back. Under the momentary fog of sleep, he imagined that he was in Lübeck, the place where he had first learned to swim. But the dream faded fast and he leaned forward on his elbows, squinting in the sun. It was early morning and fishing boats were cruising through Taylor Passage, headed to sea. With the tide out, seagulls descended like dive bombers, plucking things from the muck before quickly flying off.

Karl stood up, looked around groggily, and although he didn't remember falling asleep, he had somehow ended up fully dressed. As he knelt to put on his shoes, he heard a sound and turned to see a fishing boat in the cove, backing up slowly, one man at the helm, another leaning over the side with a gaff. Karl watched in a daze, as much out of curiosity as from surprise—he was always fascinated by the ancient profession. Suddenly, the man at the back looked up and Karl flinched. His face was dry and sunburnt, his chin covered by a scruff or beard—Karl couldn't tell—and he had a hostile glare that went beyond the mere coldness of two strangers. With his dark eyes and quiet sternness, he looked like every other lobsterman, but somehow Karl knew that it was Jack Ames.

Karl averted his eyes, breaking their stare, an act of deferential humility. Even if Mr. Ames detested him, he was determined to show him respect, if only because he was the father of the girl he loved. Karl turned around and started to walk, glancing back only when he reached the rocks, but by then the boat was gone. He climbed up the bluff, found the path through the woods, and ran all the way home.

By the time he got back to the cottage, he was covered in sweat and his clothes were soaked. Nevertheless, he walked up the front steps, fixing his hair and smoothing out his shirt, ashamed for being out all night. He opened the door quietly, hoping that by some miracle his parents were still asleep.

"Son?"

Sitting in the front parlor, Mr. Brink looked up from his chair. There was a smoldering cigar in the ashtray, documents spread across the table.

"Father…" he said and his mother burst into the room.

"Karl!" she cried. "Thank God."

She ran over and put her hand to his forehead, looking him up and down, examining him like a found dog.

"Are you okay?"

"I'm fine, Mother," he said, gently pushing her away. "I fell asleep at the beach."

As his mother stood in a quiet panic, Karl faced his father.

"I am sorry about last night. I am willing to return home...if it's necessary."

Mr. Brink acknowledged the apology and took a puff of his cigar.

"It may not be so necessary," he said and Karl winced. "There may be someone."

"Someone?"

Karl looked at his mother and she had an excited smile.

"Someone to sponsor us. An old friend."

14.

The sky was gray all the way to the horizon, Taylor Passage blanketed by a hazy mist, as Kate and Ellie walked barefoot over the rocks. Kate was leaving in a week, and they would be separated for the first time in their lives. The envy Ellie felt towards her earlier in the summer had been replaced by a sad but heartfelt encouragement, knowing that Kate always wanted something beyond Monk Island. They had always relied on each other, from the time Ellie fractured her ankle in the woods and Kate ran for help, to when Kate broke up with her first boyfriend. While Kate was feisty, outgoing, and more emotional, Ellie was quiet and sometimes too serious. Nevertheless, their differences created a natural symmetry, and they offset each other's strengths and weaknesses in a way that Ellie could only understand after falling in love with Karl. More than companionship, Ellie would miss Kate's spunk because she was always on her side.

"Those bastards. Is he okay?"

"Karl's fine," Ellie said. "He's just a little shaken up."

They stopped at the end of the rocks, where in the distance Junebug and Mary stood ankle-deep in the water, staring out the binoculars and looking for seals.

"Who were they?"

"I don't know, I mean, it was dark. North-siders, for sure."

"Have your parents said anything?"

"No. I'm sure Father knows...and is glad."

"Don't say that."

"The saddest thing is that his father was attacked too, back in Germany, at a rally. That's why he has the cane. Now it's happening again."

"What a horrid way to live."

"Karl said it started when he was thirteen and got worse every year. His father spoke out against the Nazis. He got demoted, they got death threats, the police harassed them. Their friends turned their backs on them, his mother had a nervous breakdown…"

Ellie recounted all he had told her, not only imagining the horror but feeling it too. But as she gazed out at the sea, she was surprisingly unafraid and wanted to believe that the fate of her and Karl was in the hands of something bigger. When it came to matters of God and religion, she had always been a lost soul, and yet growing up on Monk Island made her particularly aware of the mysterious forces behind nature. Lightning storms, squalls, nor'easters, and blizzards— the only thing they didn't have was earthquakes, but some storms were so fierce the ground shook. The harsh Atlantic climate, with all its noise and intensity, made it hard to deny that someone or something was trying to get the attention of humanity.

"They can't go back to that," Kate said.

"Without the visas, they have to."

"Will they get them?"

"Karl says yes, but they can't find a sponsor."

"Surely, you could sponsor them?"

Ellie made a sarcastic smirk, thinking that, for a girl who was going off to nursing school, Kate could be incredibly naïve. But if she was, then Ellie was no less so because she had considered it too, until she learned that an immigration sponsor had to provide certified copies of their federal tax returns as well as a letter from an employer, requirements that only added to her shame of not having a real job.

"And wouldn't Father love that?" Ellie said.

Then she took off down the rocks and Kate rushed to catch up. The mist had turned to a light fog, creeping in from the sea, obscuring the channel and islands like a leaden sheet. When Ellie reached the girls, their shoulders were together and they each had an eyepiece. They were perfectly still, Mary balancing on her crutches while Junebug adjusted the lens.

"What do you see?"

"A battleship."

"Battleship?" Ellie said, dipping her feet in the water and coming toward them.

Mary handed Ellie the binoculars and she held them up. Beyond Holyhead Island, about three miles offshore, was a small ship, cruising along the coast and leaving a wide wake. Ellie knew it was no battleship, but with a gun turret at the stern and military markings on the hull, it was no doubt Navy or Coast Guard. With the Portland Harbor Defenses, military vessels were always in an around Casco Bay, but there was something ominous about the boat and Ellie felt a creeping dread.

"Is that in case of war?"

She turned to Mary and shoved the binoculars back in her hands.

"There's not gonna be a war. C'mon, let's get home."

. . . . . .

Ellie stared at her plate, pushing the food around, eating without enthusiasm. Ben was over again and they sat crowded around the kitchen table, nearly elbow to elbow. He had come to dinner more in the past few weeks than in the entire year previous, and it was obvious to Ellie, and probably everyone else, that her father was trying to increase Ben's exposure so his daughter would come to her senses and get romantically involved with a local. As a man who saw all human affairs in nautical terms, Jack had set a good bait, but Ellie wasn't biting.

"Red Sox are on a streak."

"10 out of the last 14," Ben said, shaking his head.

"They won the first game yesterday against the Senators."

"That Fritz Ostermueller has quite an arm."

Ben looked over to Ellie and she responded with a faint smile.

"He's no Lefty Grove," Jack said.

"But he's not bad for a southpaw."

"Not bad for a Kraut."

As her father said it, Ellie saw his eyes flash by her, a quick but deliberate glance that had all sharpness of sarcasm. Ben continued talking, oblivious to the insinuation, although Ellie was sure that by now he knew about Karl. Somedays she felt sorry for Ben, following her father around like a hapless puppy, eager to please but never appreciated, and the only time he wasn't with him was when he was at home or at the American Legion drinking.

When Vera got up and started to collect the dishes, it gave Ellie a reason to be excused from the table. She went upstairs to brush her hair and put on a sweater—evenings were starting to get cool—and when she came down, her father and Ben were still talking, the conversation having moved on from the Red Sox to bait prices. Ellie wanted to slip out unnoticed, but as she went for the door, her mother came in the parlor.

"Going somewhere?"

120

"To meet Kate. She leaves next week."

Vera stopped and they locked eyes, a polite yet persistent stare. Ellie hated to lie, but sometimes it was easier than an unwanted truth, and she didn't want to provoke her father.

"Vera, make us some coffee," Jack called out.

Ellie could tell her mother was disappointed, troubled even, but she didn't know if it was in her or in herself, some deeper regret for the risks she never took when she was young. Vera had known her husband since they were kids and they married as soon as they could, which was age sixteen at the time. While Jack's view of the world was as a firm and settled as the seabed, she had always tried to be more open, encouraging her daughters to think beyond the shores of Monk Island. But as a woman who never went further than the 8th grade, it was hard to give what she didn't have. As they faced each other, Ellie got tearful in knowing that, despite their silence, it might have been the most profound moment they ever shared.

"Vera!" Jack called again.

She turned her head, yelled back, and Ellie was glad to know she hadn't lost her mettle.

"Tell Kate I say hello."

......

The night air was damp and the mist hung suspended in the twilight. The days were getting shorter and Ellie could sense autumn like the approach of a far-off storm. Even with two weeks left until Labor Day, things were beginning to wind down, and as she neared the village, the Bowladrome was quiet and the Inn was dark.

Ellie waited in the shadow of the oak tree, looking up and down Gull Avenue for the tall silhouette of Karl. The seconds turned to minutes, the minutes to an hour, and soon she was overcome by an unforeseen panic. She thought about how she didn't even know where Karl and his family were staying, other than that it was *a little cottage in the woods*. Early on she was content with the mystery of it all, but the closer the deadline for the visas, the more tenuous their plans for the future seemed, and she feared he could vanish as quickly as he had appeared. Even his name, *Karl Brink*, was as generic as John Smith and she doubted she could track him down if she tried.

The longer Ellie waited, the more she obsessed on these things, wavering between sadness, anger and worry, feeling a fool for loving a man whose life was so upended, whose past was so unknown. The winds kicked up, mimicking the storm she felt inside, and suddenly it began to drizzle. Her tears mixed with rain, and as much as she dreaded walking home alone, she knew she couldn't wait all night.

"Ellie?"

She looked up, so startled she lost her breath.

"Karl?"

"I've got good news."

15

"It all seems so secretive, Father."

Mr. Brink turned to Karl, squinting through his glasses.

"In those days it was, especially in America. Ideas can be dangerous things."

They sat in the last row of the last car, on a midmorning train that was half-empty. The nearest passenger was beyond earshot, but they still spoke in whispers, using English so they wouldn't draw attention. It was their third trip to Boston and, although they had traveled alone many times together, Mr. Brink talked about things he never had before.

"When I got to the University of Maine," he continued, "I was young and passionate. Naturally, I found colleagues who shared my views."

"Such as John Hatch?"

Mr. Brink laughed then put his head back against the headrest.

"It's true, Hatch was an exception. But we don't choose our friends by their ideology. It's the differences that make human relationships special. I was a serious young man back then, overly so. He made me...how do Americans say?...*lighten up*."

Karl smiled to himself and glanced out the window as coastal New England flashed by in a hazy repetition of church steeples, town commons, pastures. He fell into a daydream, thinking about what his father told him, all the pieces that filled-in the gaps of a past which, for much of Karl's life, had been a mystery. He learned that his grandfather committed suicide with a shotgun while Mr. Brink was away at college; that the long scar on his father's left arm was from trying to stop a Nazi book burning in Berlin; that Mr. Brink once ate a poisonous mushroom while hiking in the Pyrenees and spent a month in the hospital; that his brother, Karl's uncle, received the Iron Cross for bravery in the First World War; that his father had considered the priesthood; and, finally, Mr. Brink's years as a renegade professor. Karl didn't understand much about politics, but he knew that, in Nazi Germany, Communists were reviled as traitors to the Fatherland.

"Did you ever consider how your work affected us?"

Mr. Brink took a long pause before replying.

"Every minute of every day."

Staring out the window, Karl accepted the answer with a nod and not because he was bitter. There was no time for blame or accusations—this was their last chance to stay in America. He appreciated his father's candor, however, and for a man who had always been so stoic, it was like a sobbing confession. Karl wondered why he chose now to open up, and he couldn't tell if it was a belated reckoning between father and son, or some deeper sign of resignation. Mr. Brink was more than physically weary, his soul looked tired, and Karl knew the conversation had drained him because when he looked over again, his father was asleep.

An hour later, the conductor announced their arrival and the train came to a long, steady stop. Mr. Brink got his cane and briefcase and they exited and went down the platform. When they came out of the station, the first thing he did was light a cigar; the second was to pull out a map. Concerned about his father's ankle, Karl suggested taking a taxi, but Mr. Brink was too stubborn to drive when he could walk.

They headed into the bustling city streets and crossed an intersection with billboard signs for Coca Cola and Camel Cigarettes. Standing on the corner, Mr. Brink took out the map again and pointed to a neighborhood of Georgian row houses. They turned up the first cobblestone street, walked half a block and stopped. Mr. Brink proceeded up the stairs, rang the knocker and, moments later, the door creaked open and an old man in a burgundy robe peered out squinting.

"May I help you?"

"John?"

The man's dour expression turned suddenly to elation.

"Dutch!"

He lunged out, embracing Mr. Brink, and Karl watched his father blush.

"How're you, John?"

"Come in, come in," he said, waving. "And who's this handsome young man?"

"John, meet my son Karl."

When Karl shook Hatch's hand, it was warm and weak like someone who had been sick for a long time. They came into a grand foyer and a poodle scurried down the stairs, its tail wagging. Hatch led them into the parlor and Karl and his father sat on a sofa. With its dark curtains, faded silk wallpaper and Louis XVI chairs, the home had a genteel shabbiness that reminded Karl of a manor house he once visited on a field trip. In the middle of the room was a large fireplace with a carved limestone mantel that looked like it hadn't been used in years.

Hatch took the seat across from them and crossed his legs.

"How're things in Deutschland?"

Mr. Brink glanced beside to Karl before speaking.

125

"Last week, terrible. This week, awful."

"Good, then they're improving!"

He slapped his leg and laughed aloud. With his thin neck and gaunt eyes, he bore no resemblance to the gregarious bon vivant Mr. Brink had described and Karl was baffled.

"What'll you drink? Bourbon?"

Before Mr. Brink could answer, Hatch called out and a black woman came around the corner.

"Gabby. Bring us some bourbon."

"Just water, please," Mr. Brink said and Karl asked for the same.

"Very well. Two glasses of water. I'll have their bourbon."

Hatch reached for a pack of Chesterfields and lit one.

"So, what brings you to Boston?"

"We're staying on Monk Island, actually."

"My goodness," he said with a nostalgic sigh. "Our Shangri-La."

"We've been there since July."

"And you didn't come see me 'til now?"

Gabby walked in with a tray of drinks and it saved him from having to explain. She put down the water and gave Hatch a tumbler with ice. As his shaking hand held the glass, she filled it with bourbon and set the bottle on the table, suggesting he never had just one.

"I have a favor to ask."

Hatch took a long sip and raised his eyes as if to indicate that he was listening. Mr. Brink put his briefcase on his lap, undid the brass latches and took out a manila folder.

"I'm trying to extend our visas," he said. "We want to stay in America. Germany is no longer safe."

"I can certainly see why. First Austria, then Czechoslovakia. What next?"

"Poland," Mr. Brink blurted, and Karl and Hatch were both surprised. "Tensions between the two countries are rising. If Hitler attacks Poland, Europe is at War again."

"You need my help?"

"I need a sponsor—for my family. The paperwork must be signed and notarized, posted no later than tomorrow morning. Otherwise, we are compelled to go back."

Hatch shook the ice around in his glass, made a sarcastic smirk.

"And what makes you think I'll sponsor a Communist?"

The two locked eyes with a bearing that Karl almost mistook for hostile, and he was prepared to defend his father from insult.

"Perhaps because I saved your life."

The tension broke when they both smiled and Karl realized they were only joking. Hatch put down his drink, took the folder, and began to flip through the documents.

"You see," he said, glimpsing up. "Your father is right. He did save my life—indirectly. And on Monk Island, of all places."

Karl leaned forward and listened closely.

"...Esophageal varices, they called it. I was puking blood for days..." Hatch shuddered as he recalled the pain and horror. "Your father insisted I go to the hospital. If not, I would've died. I don't even remember the weekend—I was blotto the whole time."

With a hearty laugh, he took another sip and winced as it went down.

"I remember it well," Mr. Brink said. "It was the day Germany declared war on Russia."

Something rattled and everyone looked over to see the maid dusting in the hallway.

"Gabby? What time does the post office at Scollay Square open?"

"9 am, Mr. Hatch."

He turned back to Mr. Brink and Karl, tapped his fingers on the folder.

"Consider it done."

"Thank you."

"Now how 'bout a toast?"

Inside, Karl was overcome by an almost giddy relief, and when he glanced at his father, he knew he felt the same. But their ordeal was far from over and neither overreacted, other than Mr. Brink accepting the offer.

"Yes, I will have a drink with you."

"If it's with me Nik, you're bound to have more than one," Hatch said and he called out, "Gabby, a couple of glasses, with ice, if you please."

. . . . . .

It was getting dark and the last train to Boston was at 8 pm, the last ferry at 11. Karl didn't know the time because the clock on the mantel was broken, so he sat listening as his father and Hatch reminisced about their years at the University, reliving their youth through a liquor-induced haze. The ashtray on the pedestal table was full—the ice in the glasses had long since melted. The two had been drinking for hours, and although Karl had tried to join in, he was repulsed by the taste of bourbon, an 1898 Pappy Van Winkle which Hatch casually mentioned cost one hundred dollars a bottle.

Karl wasn't impressed by Hatch's fading wealth or by his tall tales, and the more he heard, the more he pitied him. He could see that his father loved him, but in the dutiful way that a caregiver might love the sick, or a man might love a troubled brother. It was obvious that Hatch had dreamed away his life, squandered all he had been given, leaving behind a heavy heart and a vacant soul. For all his family had been through, Karl found it hard to accept that their salvation depended on a man who was unable to save himself.

"Father," he said, interrupting. "We really must go."

Mr. Brink turned to him, his eyes glassy, cheeks flush.

"By all means."

Sunken in the chair, his eyes drooping, Hatch took a sip and spoke with a slurring incoherence.

"So the soirée is over?"

"For now, my friend."

As Mr. Brink reached for his cane, Karl got his briefcase and they both stood. Seeing that Hatch needed help, Karl went over and extended his hand, but Hatch just stared at it. Karl looked at his father, who gestured with his chin, and he knew what to do. He knelt down, put Hatch's arm over his shoulder and lifted him up, escorting him across the room towards the foyer, one delicate step at a time. All he could smell was cigarettes and body odor, and with Hatch's bones protruding, he felt like he was carrying a corpse.

Hatch didn't say a word as they slowly ascended the stairs, Mr. Brink close behind. Karl let Hatch lead the way, as much as he could, and when they got to the second floor, they went down a shadowy hallway and turned into a bedroom with a walnut dresser, tiffany lamps, and oil paintings. Karl could tell it had once been an exquisite chamber, but it was now cluttered with dirty clothes, food cartons, liquor bottles. They staggered towards the bed, and when Karl laid Hatch down on his back, Hatch grumbled and then passed out.

"Here."

Mr. Brink handed Karl the paperwork and he set it on the nightstand between an ashtray and a tissue box.

"Not there, he won't see it."

Karl took the folder and put it at the edge of the bed.

"Not there, it might fall."

As Hatch lay snoring, Karl lifted one arm, slid the folder under it, put the arm back. He turned to his father with an annoyed frown, humiliated to be sneaking some documents onto the body of an unconscious drunk.

"Good. Now let's go."

16

Ellie and Kate stood against the railing of the pier, sharing a lemonade in the hot sun while Mary and Junebug played below. The diesel smoke from an arriving ferry wafted towards them, but Ellie felt no less clean because she had been on the boat all morning and reeked of fish and saltwater. When she first started helping her father, it was mostly small chores, filling bait bags and fixing nets. Now she was out on the water a couple of days a week, exposed to the grueling side of the trade, and while she didn't actually pull traps—that was still left to the men—she hooked buoys, hauled rope, and packed the crates. The close quarters was as awkward for her as it was for Ben because, although it was never spoken, they both knew her father's intentions for them.

Jack and Ben had gone to Portland to sell the catch, and as Ellie looked out she could see the small sloop on the far side of the harbor, an insignificant speck in a clutter of trawlers, ferries, barges, and sailboats. She wondered if they would report all the lobster or if Jack was going to set some aside, exchanging it for cash on the black market. By now she was sure they had been shacking, but she didn't know the extent, whether it was a few hens or a whole lot more. Her father had lost his first boat through dishonesty and Ellie resented that he was putting their family at risk again. In fishing, there was as much treachery as there was tradition and she wouldn't miss the double-dealing when she and Karl moved to the mainland.

"Are you even listening?" Kate said.

"Pardon?"

"I said, *I hope you will visit me in Lewiston.*"

"Can I bring Karl?"

Kate gave her a sideways glance, a tender smile.

"Of course."

"Ellie?"

They both looked over and she was surprised to see Karl coming towards them. Right behind was his father, walking with his cane in a gray suit and hat, and Ellie assumed Karl must have just met him at the ferry. With her chipped nails and filthy clothing, she experienced a sudden, horrifying shame that gave her the urge to walk away. She had never met Karl's parents and knowing how different their families were, she had always hoped to make a good first impression. But dressed in her work clothes, sweaty and sunburned, she felt like a vagabond.

"Karl?"

"Father was in Portland," he explained, then he turned aside to let Mr. Brink in. "This is Eleanor."

Mr. Brink took a slight bow, tipped his hat.

"Eleanor? What a lovely name. I had a schoolteacher named Eleanor once."

"A pleasure to meet you."

"The pleasure is all mine."

He had a deep and dignified voice, with an accent much thicker than Karl's. Ellie had never met a university professor and she tried to curtsy because she thought it proper. As Karl went to introduce Kate, Mr. Brink was distracted by something and his expression changed.

"What are those, my Dear?"

Everyone turned and Mary and Junebug were behind them, their hair ragged and faces crisp. At first, Ellie thought Mr.

Brink meant Mary's crutches until he pointed at the binoculars. Mary gave them to him and he looked them up and down, wiping away some grime, squinting to read the faint markings.

"Why, these are German. Where'd you find them?"

Mary shrugged her shoulders, looked up at her sister, who answered for her.

"Our father is a lobsterman. They came up with a trap."

"Ah," Mr. Brink said, raising his eyes. "...*the gallant Fishers life, It is the best of any, 'Tis full of pleasure, void of strife.*"

Ellie smiled awkwardly, looked over to Karl.

"What Father means is it's an honorable profession."

"As noble as any," Mr. Brink said, handing the binoculars back. "I dare say your father has caught a piece of history."

"Is that so?"

"Quite. Those are Kriegsmarine *fernglas*. My brother was a Navy officer in the Great War. Had a similar pair. A sailor must have dropped them while on watch, or perhaps a U-boat was sunk nearby?"

"My father would know. He was in...*the Army.*"

Ellie almost said *the War* but stopped herself, worried it might make him uncomfortable. When the warning toot for the ferry sounded, Mr. Brink raised his hat, smiled politely, and walked off. Moments later, Kate said goodbye and returned to work at Lavery's. The girls, who had the attention spans of a gnat, had already scurried back down to the docks, and in an instant, Ellie found herself alone with Karl, the entire afternoon before them.

......

133

Karl and Ellie walked along the shore, the surf rolling over their feet. The sky was clear blue and after a weekend of rain, the vegetation was remarkably vibrant. People were scattered across the beach, the last of the vacation crowd, their bodies dark and towels faded from the sun and salt water. Even in bathing suits, their children playing in the sand, most families looked ready to go home, the weary decadence of too much fun and relaxation. There was something tragic about the end of the summer, Ellie watched it her whole life, the cooler nights and the slow diminishment of light, the strangulation of days. Soon the leaves would die and fall—soon the birds would disappear over the horizon. She always preferred the bleakness of winter, but something about being in love made her cling to the warmth, afraid to let it go.

"Will you travel with him to Boston tomorrow?"

"He wants to go alone," Karl said.

"And he'll get the visas?"

"I expect so."

"Then?..." Ellie said, stopping short, if only because she wanted him to lead.

"I have some money."

"You do?"

"My father doesn't know, it's a small savings. We could get a room...on the mainland...until I find work."

While physically he appeared calm, his words were breathless, his eyes flitted, and Ellie didn't know if his nervousness was from excitement or fear. Either way, she understood the feeling because she had it too and she tried to assure him any way she could.

"I've applied for some jobs...in the City."

"You don't have to—"

134

"Until we get on our feet."

"because I'll support us—"

"Are you scared?" she said.

Karl looked off in the distance, his bangs fluttering in the breeze. When he spoke, he was looking out at the water and yet his words had the intimacy of a penetrating gaze.

"I've been scared most of my life," he said then he turned to her. "But it doesn't matter because I'll do anything to be with you."

With a trembling smile, Ellie took his hand and she could feel the tension in it. She led him to the top of the beach and each time he asked where they were going, she put her finger to her lips. They climbed up a shallow embankment and went into the woods, pushing through the bush and stepping around thorns, spines, and prickles. Ellie tried to find the path, but it was covered in summer so she went by memory.

Soon they came upon a giant oak tree, nestled in the forest like a misplaced sequoia. Its branches were thick and scaly, hanging down in large arcs and creating a canopy that was like a natural atrium.

"Incredible," Karl said, as they ducked under.

"I used to take Mary here when she was little. I told her it was a cave."

"May I ask," he said, hesitantly, "how Mary came to be on crutches?"

"Polio."

Ellie sat down at the base of the tree in a bed of dry moss, and Karl came beside her.

"Was it an outbreak?"

"No. When she was three she wandered into Jacob's Pond. It was summer and the water was infested. Father was supposed to be watching her."

Karl nodded and she said no more, not wanting the indignities of the past to tarnish their time alone together. They clutched hands and Ellie put her head on his shoulder, staring out from the shade, birds chirping all around. When he surprised her with a kiss, she kissed him back and put her arms around his neck, pulling him close. The intensity of their embrace grew and she fell back against the moss, taking him with her. He squeezed her breast and she responded by rubbing his thigh, moving her hand slowly up until he groaned.

In the past, Ellie would have been more careful—she might have put it off and maybe until they married. But she was tired of waiting for the world to come to her and decided that if there was ever a time to be reckless it was now.

"Are you sure?" Karl said.

"I'm sure."

"You don't—"

"I'm sure."

Ellie pulled up her dress and slid off her underwear while Karl undid his trousers. She opened her legs and guided him in, wincing and writhing, trying to conceal the initial discomfort. As he moved inside her, she clutched his back and pulled him close, moaning unconsciously, rocking her hips. At first, it hurt, but soon an unfamiliar sensation rippled through her body, a feeling so pleasurable and so perfect that she wanted to believe they were the only two people in the world who ever experienced it.

Their breathing grew more and more erratic until, in what seemed like a single surge of electrified ecstasy, Karl convulsed and rolled off her, sweating and out of breath. It lasted only a minute, but the significance somehow felt eternal, and as they lay cradled in each other's arms, Ellie was glad to be alive.

17

Standing in the grass, Karl bent his knees and hurled the horseshoe, where it clanged against the spike and went in the weeds. For weeks, he had quietly ridiculed his father for playing the game and now he understood why he did. Since arriving at Monk Island, their lives were long stretches of monotony, punctuated by bursts of hope and disappointment, and they each found their own way to pass the time. For Karl, it was swimming and reading and Ellie—for his father it was reading and drinking and solitude. The cottage was spotless, but his mother still kept busy by cleaning, projecting on the outside world that orderliness which she struggled to maintain within.

As the weeks of waiting wore on, they had grown apart as a family, a sad irony considering they hadn't spent so much time together since Karl was a baby. They were always in different rooms—Karl in his bedroom, his father in the front parlor, Mrs. Brink in the kitchen—and the only time they spoke was at dinner. Karl hadn't seen his parents kiss in months and he sometimes wondered when they last made love. He knew his father could survive without intimacy—Mr. Brink was far more rational than emotional—but he worried what the loneliness was doing to his mother.

Karl tossed the last horseshoe and it missed. He dusted off his hands and looked over to his mother, who was on her knees beside the porch, trying to revive an old vegetable patch that was mostly weeds. In the sunlight, she was pale white, and her bony elbows moved up and down like scissors as she worked the earth. Karl couldn't remember the last time she was outside, but with their visas on the way, she had every reason to start living again. Back home she was always in her garden, pruning and trimming while she hummed a popular tune, Marlene Dietrich or Mimi Thoma. As Karl stood watching, his mother glanced over, her arms covered in dirt, and he saw a glint of youth in her expression, some faint spark of her former self. Although only a shadow, it was enough to let him know she wasn't completely lost, and when she smiled he got unexpectedly emotional.

......

It was almost dark and Mr. Brink was still not home. Karl and his mother sat silently at the table, their plates filled with roasted potatoes, glazed carrots, and pork chops with gravy, the first meat they had had in days. With their visas assured, Mr. Brink had gone to Portland earlier in the week to take out their savings and, in a small gesture of celebration, he splurged on some fresh food. The money they had remaining, he said, was enough for an apartment, a few furnishings, maybe some new clothes. Beyond that, he hadn't thought much beyond the present—none of them had—and the prospect of staying in America brought a new set of problems and uncertainties. His father mentioned working at the University of Maine, his alma mater, but Karl knew that if they didn't ask him back to teach his summer course like they had in years past, how could he expect to get hired fulltime? The Country had been in a depression for a decade and immigrants always fared worse in a bad economy.

Karl knew he would soon have to tell his parents about his plans with Ellie. But considering that she first had to break free from Jack, he thought it best to wait until they were all safely off Monk Island, lost in the anonymity of the mainland. Karl was sure his father would try to discourage him, warn him about the hazards of impulsive love, try to impress upon him the importance of sensible living. But Karl would have none of it, and his father's clinical approach to things, no matter how noble his intentions, had only brought them suffering and sadness. Even the idea of his objections made Karl angry because, for him, Ellie was the new beginning that Mr. Brink had spoken of when they departed for America.

Suddenly, the front door opened.

"Father?"

There was no answer. Karl put down his knife and fork, looked across to his mother, then got up. When he walked in the parlor, his father was sitting in the chair, facing the window. Karl couldn't see his expression, but he could sense his agitation like a slow and simmering tremor.

"Father?"

Mr. Brink took a puff of his cigar. He blew it out with a sigh and his entire body seemed to go limp.

"Pack your things. We leave tonight."

The words rang out like a death sentence and Karl was dumbfounded. He went over and knelt beside the chair, but Mr. Brink only gazed ahead and wouldn't look at him.

"Father, what are you talking about?"

"John Hatch didn't send the paperwork. Our travel visas expire in two days. We have no choice."

Karl stood up in exasperation and noticed his mother watching from the shadow of the hallway.

"Mother, tell him we can't go."

He begged for her support, but she stood silent, her vacant eyes conveying an almost fatalistic indifference to their circumstances.

"We must," Mr. Brink said, finally looking up. "Our ship has been canceled—they're canceling more sailings every day. I bought tickets for the Mauretania. It leaves tomorrow from New York."

"This is an outrage."

"I will apply again when we get home."

"What difference will it make?"

"I heard back from Simon Hastings. He's agreed to sponsor us. If we're lucky, we'll be back by Christmas."

"By then it might be too late!"

Karl threw his hands in the air and ran over to his mother, stooping down to look her directly in the face.

"Mother," he said, breathless and pleading. "Tell him we must stay."

She looked down, but otherwise didn't reply, respond or react and Karl hated what she had become. When he was a boy, she always sided with him against the harsh demands of his father and now she was under his spell, a broken woman with neither confidence nor will.

Behind Karl could hear his father get up from the chair, and it filled him with an uncontrollable rage. The floor creaked as Mr. Brink came over and Karl followed each footstep in his mind, praying his father would stop and come no further. Karl thought about all they suffered because of him, the lost friendships, the casual insults, the social condemnation, the sleepless nights, the terror. The moment his father touched his shoulder, Karl knew their relationship, if it even survived, would never be the same.

"Son—"

Karl spun around and punched him in the face and Mr. Brink stumbled back, knocking over a vase. His father charged at him, swinging his cane, and Karl ducked and shoved him into the wall. Mr. Brink lunged again and they locked arms, wrestling for a moment before Karl threw him on the ground and got on top. As his father struggled to get free, Karl dug his knee into his chest, pinned his arms against the floor. He started to gasp, so Karl let off some pressure and when he looked down, his father's face was a mash of blood and saliva, his eyes wide, squirming and helpless. All Karl's anger and bitterness turned to sadness as he watched this proud and accomplished man—his father—flailing on the floor like a caught criminal.

"No! More!"

Everything stopped. Karl glanced over his shoulder and saw his mother behind him, the mantel clock raised high above her head. In those tense seconds, he thought she might try to harm him to save her husband. But before he could reason with her, she shrieked and hurled it to the floor, where it smashed into pieces. Her head fell into her chest and she began to sob, bursts of inconsolable grief, her ribcage heaving.

"I want to go home, Karl," she moaned, and she sounded like a little girl. "Please, let's go home."

Karl down looked at his father, who even in his humiliating submission was ever defiant, the same defiance he had shown the Nazi state, the same defiance he had shown his complicit colleagues, the same defiance he had, since he was young, shown to a cruel and unforgiving world. Karl realized then that, despite their differences, they had one common goal, the protection of his mother, and he wouldn't abandon her in her condition. When he thought about Ellie, his heart melted in knowing he may never return, but he clung to the possibility they would. Maybe it was all a fantasy anyway, he thought, like the fantasy they had of starting a new life. Without the visas, they would always be suspect in America, always be foreigners, and if they had to live in exile, Karl knew that, at least in the short term, his mother would be more comfortable in Germany. But war was on the horizon, looming like a dark storm, the one wildcard in their fate, the great and terrifying *if.*

As Karl slowly let his father up, he knew he was making a choice he might forever regret.

18.

Ellie sat alone on the back porch, sunken into the Adirondack chair and staring out at the starlit sky, crickets chirping all around. The lights were all off in the house and everyone was in bed. Her mother had retired a half hour before, after dusting the kitchen and pantry, having her evening tea. On most nights, Vera was the last one awake, but tonight Ellie couldn't sleep. Her breathing was shallow and at points, she felt ready to burst out of her skin. She tried going for a walk down the beach, drinking a cup of warm milk—she even said a prayer. But nothing seemed to calm her.

Kate was leaving in the morning, off to nursing school, starting a new life far from the shores of Monk Island. Ellie would meet Karl tomorrow night, where they would make their own plans for the future. For a girl who had been waiting her whole life for a chance to leave, to do something better, it was all happening much too fast. Ellie remembered something her father said years before, a rare moment of eloquence in which he described what war was like: *a whole lot of madness separated by glimpses of sanity.* And she understood that madness because she felt it now, the choices and the uncertainties, the love and the loss. For the first time, she knew what it meant to be alive.

Ellie's eyes flickered open, the sun was up, it was morning. She leaned forward groggily in the chair, her neck stiff and skin clammy, mosquito bites on her arms. Realizing she had overslept, she jumped up and rushed inside, where her mother was frying eggs on the stove.

"I was wondering where you were?" Vera said.

"What time is it?"

"A little before 7."

Without another word, Ellie dashed for the front door, her mother's voice calling out behind her, "Your father wants you at the dock by 8!"

She ran up the hill and turned onto Gull Avenue where, despite her panic, the world was remarkably tranquil, the sounds of a lazy summer morning—birds in the trees, chickens in a nearby coop, the grate of a carpenter's saw. When she came around the bend, Ellie saw a plume of smoke from the ferry, still at the terminal but ready to leave. She ran towards it with all her strength, her laces untied and shoes pounding against the hard ground. She came to the village and went down the slope to the waterfront and when she looked, her heart sank as she saw the boat pulling away.

Still, she ran, and when she approached the ferry landing, Mr. and Mrs. Mallet, Junebug and Mary were huddled by the gangway, a small farewell party. Ellie went over to the railing, as far as she could go, and Kate was waving from the top deck. She was trying to say something, but the rumble of the diesels drowned her out, and Ellie watched and waved back with both arms, her eyes teary.

"She'll be back at Christmas," Mrs. Mallet said gently.

Ellie looked at her sister, said, "C'mon, Mary," and started towards the docks, where she knew her father and Ben would be preparing for the workday.

"Ellie," Joe Mallet said. "I've something for you."

He handed her a note, which she was sure was from Kate, until he added, "It was on the shop door this morning."

Ellie looked at him and his wife confused, then to the girls, who stood ragged in their sack dresses, their faces somber.

When she saw the writing on the envelope, the words Eleanor Ames, she knew straight away that it was a man's. She was overcome by a sudden dread but nevertheless tore it open and began to read.

Dear Ellie,

I tremble as I write this, but by the time you receive this letter, I will be gone. My father's friend in Boston failed to post the letter of sponsorship in time and our visas were denied. It was never my intention to return to Germany, and I considered breaking the law in order to stay with you in America. But as you know my mother is unwell, and I was not prepared to leave her in the hands of my father, who has so far shown more interest in his own schemes than her welfare. He has promised, however, that upon return he will reapply for visas at the American consulate in Hamburg, and he has been in contact with an old colleague in California who is willing to help. I believe that we will be safe in the short-term, and my only hope is that the political crisis in Europe escalates no further.

Ellie, the idea of leaving you so abruptly hurts me like no pain I've ever known before, and I vow to return as soon as I can, with or without my parents. Until then, please keep me in your thoughts, as I will you, and stay hopeful in the plans we have made, the life we will soon have together.

With love, always,
Karl

With the letter fluttering in her hand, Ellie looked up and the ferry was now halfway across the harbor, a figment in the morning haze. It was the same boat Karl and his family were on the night before, only a few hours earlier and yet a world away. By now they would be in Boston or New York or on the train between, she thought, making the long trip back to the place they had struggled to escape.

Ellie was too stunned to even cry and inside she felt as cold and dead as a wharf piling. It wasn't Karl's choice to go that made her bitter, but the circumstances which brought them together and then tore them apart. All her life, she had watched people leave the pier and not return, and some days it felt like everything she ever loved was taken away by the ferry, whether it was Karl or Kate, family or friends. When Ellie looked out across the water, the gulf between Monk Island and the City had never seemed wider and, much like her father, she found herself hating the mainland for everything it was and represented.

The others quietly dispersed, Mr. and Mrs. Mallet back up the hill to the shop and the girls down to the docks. No one had asked about the note, but Ellie was sure they knew and she was as ashamed as she was embarrassed because soon the whole community would too. For her, Karl was the love she never knew existed, the future she never thought possible, the dream she never imagined could come true. But it wasn't over, she told herself, it was only delayed and she would wait, suffering through the hours of tedium, until he finally returned.

"Ellie!"

Startled from her thoughts, she looked over and her father was at the top of the gangway, dressed in his filthy work bib, a coil of rope around his shoulder.

"Go get me a box of tap nails."

She puckered her lips wistfully and nodded.

"Then cut up those pogies," he added. "We gotta get all these traps out."

When she nodded again, a tear rolled off her cheek, a tear of hope and not defeat. She wiped it with her hand, put the letter in her pocket, and turned to start another day.

1941

19.

Ellie sat at the counter tabulating the accounts, her chin in her hand, scribbling with an old work pencil that was cracked and covered in grease. Somewhere she felt a draft, slithering its way through the gaps in the wall, a leftover from a time when Lavery's was a horse stable. But the cold didn't bother her nearly as much as the boredom. Autumn was quiet on Monk Island, when half the fleet was grounded and many men had fled south to fish the warmer waters. The tourists were gone, the seasonal shops closed, and the rental cottages shuttered. The dazzling foliage, which only weeks before had brought out throngs of day trippers, was now gone, the trees laid bare like standing skeletons. Even the beaches seemed somehow denuded, their sand a sickly beige, their vegetation shriveled and brown. The march towards winter was like a long, slow death.

In the past, the offseason would signal a return to the routine monotony of daily life. But things were changing fast on Monk Island and, with England and Germany now at war, the military had begun construction on a base on Passamaquoddy Road, purchasing land when they could and taking it by eminent domain when they had to. Serviceman and workers came over on the ferry; equipment and materials were transported on barges. Each day at work, Ellie watched trucks and other machinery come up from the docks and roar down Gull Avenue like an advancing army. Locals were starting to grumble about their presence, but with the soldiers confined mainly to the backshore, they had yet to be a nuisance.

Suddenly, the door opened, the bell jingled. When Ellie looked up, she saw a military officer in a long coat and shiny shoes. He was a few years younger than her father, with light hair and a clean shave.

"Good afternoon," he said.

Ellie put down her pencil, slipped off the stool, and stood up straight.

"May I help you?"

He made a tight smile but didn't answer. As she waited, he took off his hat and gloves and walked slowly across the wide-plank floor, looking down the aisles with an amused smirk.

"Outside," he said, pointing back with his thumb, "it says 'delicatessen.'"

Ellie grinned—it was something she had to explain all the time.

"It used to be. Not anymore."

"I can see that. What do you sell?"

The question was strange because the answer seemed obvious. But with his out-of-state accent, he could have been from anywhere—Nebraska, North Dakota or some other landlocked state—and she sometimes forgot that not every place depended on the sea.

"Traps, netting, bait, lures. Things for angling and lobstering, mostly."

As he came towards the counter, Ellie got nervous and felt herself begin to blush.

"Tell me," the man said. "Where could I buy some lobster, say, for a few hundred men?"

"That's a lot. My father would know."

"Where's your father?"

"He's probably still out."

"Out?"

"On the boat."

"He's a fisherman?"

"A lobsterman, actually."

He sighed as if surprised to learn there was a difference.

"Have your father come see me at the base. I wanna have Thanksgiving dinner for the enlisted men…"

Ellie stared as he spoke, watching his mouth move but not listening, admiring his stern and handsome face. It was more out of curiosity than attraction because even if the man was closer to her age, she never would have considered a soldier for a suitor. She saw what the War had done to her father, and with the Army now all over Monk Island, she had the same distrust as other locals, although far less severe.

"…Would you like to write it down?"

Ellie came out of the daydream and he was looking at the pencil.

"Oh, yes, of course," she said, stumbling.

"Major Rowland."

As he spelled it out, she scribbled down his name and then looked up.

"Very well, then."

Ellie smiled as an acknowledgment while inside feeling conflicted. She didn't like getting involved in her father's business because she didn't want him to think she had any interest in it.

"I'll let the staff know he'll be coming. Mr?…"

"Ames," Ellie said. "Jack Ames."

The Major nodded, repeated the name, and put on his cap, adjusting it with both hands.

"And your name?"

"Ellie—Eleanor."

"Thank you, Eleanor."

Again the Major made a tense smile, then he turned around and walked towards the door, his back arched and arms at his side like he was in formation. Ellie watched him as he went, wondering about the life of military men. Some could be polite, kind even, but they all had the same cold demeanor and it explained, at least in part, why her father had always been so harsh.

As the Major went out, the brisk air rushed in and Ellie could hear the horn of the last ferry, signaling that it was time to close up. She swept the shop floor, shut off the lights in the storeroom, got her coat and left.

Outside the village was a ghost town. The butcher and grocery store closed every day at 5 sharp, and the tourist shops were all shuttered for winter, a long row of vacant windows and leaf-filled doorways. As Ellie locked the front door, she heard rumbling and, moments later, a pickup truck pulled to the curb. Ben waved to her through the window and she walked over and got in.

"You really shouldn't have," she said.

"I don't mind."

"I could've walked."

"I didn't want you to catch a cold."

Ellie smiled and said no more, thankful for the lift because after standing for eight hours, her feet were sore. Ever since she agreed to go to the movies with Ben two months before, he doted on her like it was a courtship. Considering she had known him all her life, it was sometimes uncomfortable but she couldn't deny she enjoyed the attention.

Ben pushed the shifter, the gears grinded, and they started to move. He was one of the few men on Monk Island to own a vehicle, a 1920s Ford that his mother bought with the money she got from the Veterans Administration after her husband's death.

"How was work?"

"Pretty quiet. A soldier came in."

"They'll be everywhere soon, once that fort is done."

"He wanted some lobster—a few hundred pounds."

Ben turned to her, his expression changing.

"A few hundred?"

"For the base, for Thanksgiving. He asked me to have Father come to see him."

She reached in her pocket and took out the note, squinting to read it in the darkness.

"Major Rowland," she added.

"A major? That's more than just a soldier. That's two ranks below a General."

Ellie shrugged her shoulders, looked out the window, about as interested in military matters as she was in fishing. They turned onto her street and even in the dusky light, she could see the white spray of the waves crashing at Drake's Cove. Ben rolled to a long stop, the brakes squeaking, and they idled in front of the house. They had only been out together a half-dozen times, but it was always awkward when they parted because Ellie knew he wanted to kiss her.

"You're still coming Saturday night, right?"

"Saturday night?"

"The party at the Legion. For Armistice Day."

"Oh right, of course," she said. "Saturday."

As she reached for the handle, she could feel his longing stare, but she didn't turn to acknowledge it because she didn't want to mislead him. The truth was, Ellie didn't know how she felt about Ben, or about men in general. He was kind and considerate, but anytime she imagined some kind of life with him, memories of Karl flooded into her mind. No one had ever made her feel like that and even after two years, she still clung to the possibility that he might return.

"Thanks, Ben."

She got out and he gave her a sour smile but didn't object. She closed the door, waved cutely, and he pulled away, chugging down the hill and disappearing around the bend. As she went into the yard, she heard voices and looked to see Mary and Kate rushing towards her up the road.

"Guess who's home?!"

The girls moved aside and there, a few yards behind them, was Kate. When she got closer, Ellie realized she was wearing a military uniform, an olive green skirt and a jacket with brass buttons.

"Kate?" was all she could say.

"Hi, Ellie. I joined the Army Nurses Corp. Can you believe it?"

Ellie forced a smile, but inside she was overcome by feelings of sadness, guilt, and even resentment. Kate had been gone for so long and seeing her reminded Ellie of how much the world had changed.

"Your father didn't tell me you were coming home."

"He didn't know. It was a surprise. We just got our leave yesterday."

"Are you still in?—"

"Lewiston," Kate said, nodding. "But in two weeks I go to Florida to work in a real Army hospital."

"An Army hospital?"

"For training."

"That sounds exciting."

"I'm just not allowed to get married or pregnant"

The mere insinuation of sex melted away any coldness and when Kate raised her eyes, Ellie couldn't help but smirk. In an instant, the time and distance that had grown between them was gone and they burst into laughter, deep and mischievous laughter like when they were young.

"I'm glad to see you, Ellie."

Ellie's mouth began to twitch—a surge of emotion welled up inside her.

"I'm glad to see you, Kate."

20

Lorient, France

Karl sat next to the window, which was fogged with condensation, glimpses of the dark town square beyond. The room was crowded, every table packed with soldiers and women, mostly local girls, drinking and talking in a thick haze of tobacco smoke that made it hard to see. Glasses clinked and laughter roared, and somewhere someone was hammering away on a parlor piano, mostly old popular songs and not just German ones.

The Café Duvall was owned by an elderly couple from Düsseldorf who had lived in France for over fifty years yet still had a romantic nostalgia for their native country. On the walls were oil paintings of quaint scenes from the German countryside, peasants and haystacks, streams and small villages. Beer was served in steins upon request and bratwurst and sauerkraut were on the menu—always. Karl wondered how the owners would fare if the war ever turned—anyone who patronized the enemy was considered a collaborator—but at the moment Germany was on top, demolishing Allied shipping in the Atlantic and overwhelming the Russians in the East. As a result, the Café was a safe place for soldiers to drink and cavort because no one would dare harass them, and even the Resistance stayed away.

Beside Karl was Reinhard Brauer, a wiry nineteen-year-old he met on his first day at the training center in Neustadt. Raised on a sheep farm in the Alps, Brauer had the same provincial accent as Mr. Brink, which endeared him to Karl, and they spent six months together in class, enduring hours of instruction on instrumentation, hydrophones, minesweepers, and escape procedures. They apprenticed on the same vessel and had been together ever since, assigned to the U-206 at the Keroman Submarine Base, a vast complex of bunkers, command offices, and storage facilities just south of town. It was defended by a battalion and Wehrmacht soldiers outnumbered sailors eight to one, patrolling the docks and manning a network of small batteries up and down the harbor.

Across from Karl sat Camille and Monika, two French girls that Brauer met at the city post office before their last mission. Camille was more glamorous, with long legs and dirty blonde hair that hung down in thick ringlets. She was loud and brash, speaking in broken German that, at times, broached the sensitive topics of politics and the occupation of France, arousing the attention of some officers at the next table. If Brauer already had three bourbons, she had five, and Karl knew she would keep drinking until he stopped paying. Nevertheless, it was the closest thing to romance in a time and place racked by war, and the two sat close, their legs touching, and flirted like teenagers.

Karl had no interest in love, but he preferred the quiet plainness of Monika, a thin brunette from the countryside who, if she didn't work with Camille, probably would have never associated with her. She sipped her wine with a timid smile, her coat still on because she said she was cold, even though the café was warm and stuffy. But Karl understood her apprehension—associating with Germans could be dangerous, and although Lorient wasn't as volatile as the larger, more cosmopolitan cities, there was always the risk of being labeled a whore or a traitor.

"You don't talk much."

Realizing he had drifted off, Karl shifted in the chair and turned to Monika.

"I prefer to listen," he said.

"You don't like French girls?"

"I don't like war."

The word war caught the attention of Brauer who, for a split second, stopped talking and glanced over. But he was too busy trying to impress Camille, waving his glass around like it was an extension of his body, recounting tales of his heroism at sea.

"Do you like wine?"

Karl looked down at his coffee cup, empty except for the dregs.

"It makes me tired."

"Do I make you tired?"

For a moment, their eyes met in the low light, and her cautious expression broke into a slight, but unmistakable smirk. It was a sarcasm that Karl could understand and relate to, realizing the absurdity of war and all the unnatural antipathies it created.

"Maybe you're in love?" she went on. "It's okay, I was once too."

Karl stared with a curious, penetrating smile that concealed the uneasiness he felt inside. The remark made him feel unmasked, like when his mother used to know that he was lying. He didn't know if Monika was right or not, only that she saw something in him that he couldn't see in himself. Before he could reply, there was a loud commotion and everyone turned.

Karl looked across the room, through the smoke and people, and saw Oberbootsmann Schmitt, their superior, sitting at a card table with several officers, all dressed in gray and with medals gleaming on their lapels. His face was bright red and he was arguing with a maître de, who held a tray of empty glasses with one hand, pleaded for calm with the other.

"It seems Schmitt is losing again," Brauer said.

"That's usually when he starts to complain about the service."

Camille laughed and Monika sat up in her chair to see.

"You know that man?" she said.

"He's an officer on our boat."

Karl watched with a mixture of amusement and disgust, knowing that Schmitt always caused a scene. He was already a crewmember on U-206 when Karl and Brauer arrived, and as the son of a former submarine Captain, he seemed to believe that his pedigree entitled him to respect. But the men were sure he was nothing like his father or if he was, as one sailor put it, it explained why Germany lost the First World War.

Schmitt was fat and balding, with a space between his teeth and rosacea on both cheeks. Up close, it was obvious that one iris was bigger than the other, giving him the impression of permanent derangement. He was more of a schoolyard bully than a tyrant, and he would discipline a sailor for not saluting, but not for being absent from his post. Karl had a few run-ins with Schmitt, and Brauer a few more, but with a crew of over forty men, it was possible to avoid him.

Karl glanced over a second time, only because Monika did, and Schmitt was standing up and shouting in the man's face. The waiter looked flustered, cowering in apology while

Schmitt berated him, and the officers at the table laughed and heckled. As Karl watched, he was quietly ashamed for being a German sailor, and he was just ready to turn away when Schmitt smacked the tray and the glasses went flying. Karl expected it only to get worse until a soldier burst in and startled everybody.

"Achtung! Es gibt einen Bericht über britische Flugzeuge. Jeder muss evakuieren!"

The room went silent—the music stopped. The manager of the café, a short man in a white tuxedo, ran out and translated, but most French speakers understood what was happening. Immediately, patrons started to get up and grab their coats and hats.

"Time to go," Brauer said.

Karl took Monika's hand, Brauer took Camille's, and they merged with the crowd as it lumbered towards the front doors with a controlled urgency. The civility didn't last long, however, because in the distance was a noise, a steady hum that grew louder each second, and people started to panic. They pushed and shoved, struggling to get out like frightened cattle, exacerbating the logjam.

"Faster!"

"Hurry!"

"Move goddammit!"

The voices were in both French and German, a moment of shared concern and mutual terror which knew no culture or nationality. All the while, the menacing drone intensified, looming above like a siren of the apocalypse.

Boom!

Karl felt the ground drop from under him, followed by a gust of scorching air—then blackness. When he awoke, his ears were ringing and he was on the floor in a pile of debris, overturned tables and shattered glass, ceiling plaster and splintered wood. Leaning up, he looked around stunned and the front wall of the café was completely gone, people running and screaming in the street.

"Karl!" he heard and it was Monika.

He got up and staggered towards the voice, finding her lying between two chairs, her dress covered in white dust, tears dripping down her face in streaks of soot and mascara. He examined her quickly, searching for injuries, somehow feeling responsible for her safety.

"Are you alright?" he said, helping her up.

"I believe so."

Just then, Brauer and Camille came through the smoke, their clothes singed and hair disheveled, but otherwise unharmed. It was a miracle they were all alive, Karl thought, and although he wanted to search for survivors, it was too dark and the building could collapse.

"That was close," Brauer said, his voice shaking.

The British had been trying to incapacitate Keroman for months, but its massive concrete U-boat berths had, so far, proven resistant to their bombs. This was the first time they attacked Lorient itself, and no one knew whether it was a warning, an error, or out of frustration for all their failed efforts to destroy the base.

A second explosion rattled the café, although it sounded like it was a few blocks away, and Karl knew they could hesitate no longer.

"Let's go!" he shouted.

Together they stepped over the wreckage and out to the street, the glow of building fires all around, air raid sirens blaring. The scene was total chaos and Karl knew they were as vulnerable to the bombs as they were to angry civilians who might use the temporary confusion to get revenge for the German occupation. As Karl stood thinking, he felt a sharp pain and realized that his right arm was soaked with blood, that his elbow throbbed.

"You're hurt," Monika said.

Karl nodded but didn't respond because there was no time to inspect the wound—they had to get out of Lorient. Taxis pulled up and sped away at a furious rate and everyone was competing to get a ride, soldiers and civilians alike. Brauer leaned into Karl, spoke in a breathless but firm voice like they were conferring about battle plans.

"What should we do?"

"A taxi. It's our only chance."

Another bomb landed somewhere in the distance, causing everyone to crouch, and Karl turned towards the girls.

"Hail a cab, please."

He grabbed Brauer's arm and they stepped back, into the debris-strewn shadow of the sidewalk, knowing that a cabbie would pick up French women before soldiers. And he was right because the moment Monika and Camille went into the street a car stopped. Karl ran over and opened the door, and although the driver looked disappointed to see two Germans, it was too late. The girls and Brauer piled in the backseat and as Karl went to get in the front, he heard shouting and looked over to see Oberbootsmann Schmitt. Stumbling drunk, he had his pistol pointed at the taxi behind them and was ordering a group of civilians out, women and children, all terrified and confused.

"Herr Oberbootsmann," Karl yelled. "We have room…"

When Schmitt turned, his fat body pivoted, and even amid all the hysteria, he still found time to make a dramatic scowl.

"Mind your business, Sailor."

As the family got out, one of the men protested and Schmitt gave him a backhand to the face. His wife screamed and Schmitt shoved her away, where she landed on the curb, her dress up, undergarments exposed. Some Frenchmen stopped, their outrage apparent, and although they didn't intervene, Karl knew the incident wouldn't go unnoticed. With the German military presence, the grievances of the local populace simmered just below the surface, masked by fake civility, restrained but never forgotten. Considering it was the second time that night Karl had witnessed Schmitt's cruelty, he understood their rage and, in those few seconds, even considered trying to help, until Brauer rolled down the window and urged him otherwise.

"Brink, you're already wounded. Let's not get court-martialed too."

There was another blast and they flinched in unison. Thick, black smoke was beginning to fill the street, people running like panicked ghosts in the dim light of the flames. A horse-drawn fire brigade had arrived, but their hand pumps were no match for the infernos that raged.

"Please," Camille said. "Let's go."

Karl watched as the car with Schmitt and the other officers drove away, leaving their victims stunned, humiliated, and unsure what to do. Karl glanced at the father, who stood with his suit disheveled, a trickle of blood on his lip, and then he got in the taxi. As they pulled out, he reached over and touched a large gash on his elbow, but his arm was too numb to feel the pain. With his heart pounding, he leaned his head back and tried to breathe, and they sped off into the night, the fires burning all around.

21

Ellie and Kate stood at the pier and looked across to the shipyards of South Portland, where the noise of cranes and riveters echoed across the harbor. The hulls of "Liberty" ships rose like industrial behemoths, and behind the dry docks was a complex of new warehouses, hangars, and offices.

"This place sure has changed," Kate said.

"Some things have."

Since going away to college, Kate had only been home a couple of times, always on holidays and only for a few days. At first, she and Ellie exchanged letters, and while Kate described all the excitement of living away—days in a hospital ward, nights out dancing—Ellie found herself talking mostly about the past. Kate tried to console her about Karl, gave her advice that was sympathetic yet sensible, but like anyone in the throes of heartbreak, Ellie didn't want to hear the truth.

As the months went by, their correspondence faded, much like their friendship, and Ellie wasn't surprised because most people who left Monk Island put it behind them. She wanted to stay in touch with Kate but finally came to accept that they had drifted apart, that their friendship would never be the same. In some ways, Ellie was ashamed that her own life was in limbo, and the letters from Kate, with all their giddy optimism, only reminded her what she was missing by waiting around for someone who probably was never coming back.

"Daddy says they're building a helluva fortress on the backshore."

"I haven't seen it yet. I just see all the trucks."

The afternoon ferry had just pulled in and was idling at the terminal while passengers got off. Interspersed throughout the crowd were soldiers in dark green fatigues, rucksacks over their shoulders and duffel bags in their hands.

"I'm sure it doesn't hurt to have all these hunks around."

While Kate stood gawking, Ellie frowned and looked the other way.

"They probably don't wanna be here—as much as we don't want them."

"Junebug said you and Ben are steady?" Kate said, still staring over at the Ferry.

"I wouldn't say *steady*. We've been out a few times. We're going to the Legion tonight."

"Did you ever imagine yourself with Ben Frazier?"

Kate turned to her and Ellie felt slightly embarrassed because it did seem strange.

"I had never given it much thought either way."

They had both known Ben their whole lives and in some ways, he was more like an older brother. But on such a small island, where the choices for a mate were limited, young people couldn't be too picky.

"Would you ever marry him?"

"Kate, I really don't wanna—"

"He might make a good husband."

"I'm sure he would."

Ellie expected that, after two years of college, Kate would be more worldly but she was nosier than ever. The topic of marriage, family, and the future made Ellie uneasy so she started to walk along the pier, almost subconsciously, and Kate followed.

As they got near the dockyard, Ellie noticed her father's boat approaching, its green hull bouncing in the midday chop. She turned around to avoid seeing him, and not because she worried he would ask her to do something. Now that she was seeing Ben and had a job at Lavery's, Jack seemed satisfied that his daughter was meeting all the practical expectations of young womanhood, and he had stopped bothering her altogether. But she could never face him without feeling a tremendous resentment, the lingering anger over how he treated Karl. Jack was hardly the only person on Monk Island to scorn the Brink family—by the end of that summer, everyone seemed wary of *the Germans*. But he could have put his prejudices aside and he didn't and for that, she would never forgive him.

"You still think about him, don't you?"

Surprised by the question, Ellie winced at Kate.

"What? Who?" she said, but she knew it sounded ridiculous.

"Don't take me for a fool, Ellie."

They stopped on the boardwalk and Ellie turned to her.

"Sometimes," she mumbled.

"Sometimes?"

"Always."

......

Ellie stood by the door in her coat, her pocketbook tucked under her arm, a wool hat on her head. She had put on perfume earlier, but the smoke from the fireplace had rendered it dull.

At exactly seven o'clock, headlights cut through the darkness of the street and, moments later, Ben's truck pulled up. Ellie was just about to go when Jack came down the stairs, his bootlaces untied and suspenders hanging. He came towards her without a word and she watched as he reached in his pocket for his wallet. He took out a few crinkled dollars and handed them to her.

"Enjoy yourself."

"Thanks," she said.

Ellie took the money with a poignant smile and the small gesture warmed her heart. As she put the bills in her bag, she saw the note from Major Rowland. She could have told him she forgot, but the truth was she had been reluctant to give it to him.

"Oh, a soldier came in the shop Wednesday," she said, "asking where he could buy some lobster."

As she pressed it into his hand, she realized that they hadn't touched in ages, neither a hug nor a handshake. Jack nodded and put the note in his pocket, then turned to go back upstairs. Ellie called goodbye to her mother and walked out into the crisp evening air. She went across the lawn to the pickup and Ben was standing at the passenger-side door, holding it open. As ambivalent as she was about him, she appreciated the courtesy and liked being treated like a lady.

"Brrr," he said, rubbing his hands as he got back behind the wheel.

They drove to the top of the street and turned onto Gull Avenue, winding around to the waterfront, the lights of Portland shining in the distance. When they hit a pothole, something in the back bounced with a thud and Ellie turned to see but the bed was covered with a tarp.

"What was that?" she said.

"Just some empty crates."

"They don't sound empty."

As they came into the village, shops and lampposts were festooned with American flags for Armistice Day. There weren't as many as years past, however, and with the prospect of a new war, people were no longer so eager to honor the last one. Monk Island lost more men in the First World War than any other place in Maine, a dubious statistic that the newspapers lauded, but that Jack said was like bragging that you hauled in so much fish your boat sank.

They turned up the dirt road and parked in front of the Legion. When Ben got the door for her, Ellie was flattered; when he offered her his arm, she pretended not to notice. They walked over to the entrance and the moment they stepped inside, Ellie was blinded by cigarette smoke. When she opened her eyes, the room was crowded and she knew at least half the crowd, if not by name then by face. Swing music blared from the speakers and couples danced across the wide-plank floors. There was laughter, toasts, and cheers, and it had the festive atmosphere of a New Year's celebration.

"Can I take that?"

"Thank you."

Ellie took off her coat and handed it to Ben.

"How 'bout a drink?"

"Sure."

He turned and went over to the bar, a long counter that ran along one side of the room and had enough stools for a battalion. Two giant flags, one American and the other the State of Maine, hung from the rafters and the walls were adorned with pictures of former commanders, past members. Jack had been on the original organizing committee before

Mary got sick but after he quit drinking he saw no reason to still go. For years, the Legion didn't even allow women and they only changed the policy because the veteran population was declining.

"Here you go," Ben said and Ellie startled. "Daydreaming again?"

"I'm sorry. I'm just tired."

"Then this should pick you up."

He handed her a glass of pale yellow liquid and she stared down at it.

"Gin Rickey," he said before she could ask.

"What's in it?"

"Gin and...rickey?"

Ellie giggled and Ben smiled bashfully. He could always make her laugh—that wasn't the problem—but she never got that deeper spark, and some days she wished she did because he was awfully nice.

She took a sip and felt a warm, bitter tingle go down her throat.

"Frazier?!"

Ellie swallowed quickly and turned to see two men coming towards them. With their beards, flannel shirts, and winter tans, they looked like typical fishermen or dockworkers. She could tell they were from the north side of the Island, and not because she knew them or because they were friends with Ben. To her, people there always looked different, their eyes were hollow and skin more sallow, the result of harder living, a consequence of their poverty.

Moments later, two more men came over, forming a small circle, and Ben introduced everyone to Ellie.

"Jack Ames' daughter?" one of them asked.

"That's right."

"A fine fisherman."

"Thank you."

As they all talked, Ellie had a few more sips and soon she felt a funny sensation which was like elation without the dizziness. She had only been drunk once before when she and Kate were fourteen and they stole some parsnip wine at Christmas. She woke up the next day not remembering anything and swore she would never do it again.

The opening trumpet blast of Boogie Woogie Bugle Boy came over the speakers, riling the crowd and filling the air with patriotic energy. Men pulled their girlfriends out to the dance floor—people raised their glasses and cheered.

"The Germans are only 11 miles from Moscow," one of Ben's friends said.

"They woke a sleeping giant," another remarked.

"More like the Russian winter. The cold is deadlier than the Cossacks."

"True. Napoleon tried it in 1812 and the same thing happened."

The comments came one after another, a barrage of small quips and speculations, some insightful and some not, the musings of young men who could end up in combat if America entered the War. Ellie finished her drink and was starting to feel unsteady, the lights of the room spinning, the music and voices blending together in a haze of commotion.

"What about you, Ben. Think you'll enlist if it comes to it?"

He shook his glass around, thought to himself.

"Aw, I don't know. I'm happy to be minding the home front. Plus, I don't want my ma to be twice grieved."

Despite the noise, the space around them got quiet and they all stared down, their faces somber. Ellie looked at Ben with a tender smile, thinking about how his father had died in the Great War before he was even born.

"Goddamn Krauts."

But her sympathy turned suddenly to shock. She didn't know which one said it, but something about the voice, the tone or the inflection, was hauntingly familiar and all at once she recalled the night Karl was attacked at the Bowladrome.

"I think it's something about German people," another one remarked.

"They're barbarians."

"If I get the chance, I'll shoot one of the bastards right through the eye."

As they ranted on, Ellie listened for other hints, but she couldn't be sure it was them—the fight that summer had happened too fast, the room was too dark, boys from the north side all looked alike. Nevertheless, memories of Karl raced through her mind like hot flashes, and she got a surge of heartache that left her shaken and gasping for air.

"Where's the lavatory?" she asked quietly.

Ben pointed towards the back wall and she slipped away. The combination of alcohol and anguish made her woozy and she swayed as she walked, bumping into chairs, and people moved out of her way as she approached. Noticing an exit sign, Ellie put her glass on a table and went towards it, bursting out the door and into the cold night, leaving her coat behind.

Tears rolled down her cheeks—she sobbed openly. Stumbling across the grounds of the Legion, she came out to the street where hearing a soft voice, she had to stop before realizing it was her own, mumbling his name, over and over. She had done everything to forget him and all that they had shared, the fantasy that became a nightmare, the summer before the cataclysm, the storm which, she worried, was always lurking just beyond the tides.

Wiping her eyes, Ellie came out to Gull Avenue and some soldiers were standing in front of the Inn, slouched against the fence and smoking. They fanned out as she came down the sidewalk and blocked her way, so she went around them.

"Hey, Darling—"

Before the young man could finish, Ellie clenched her fists and turned back.

"Go to hell!"

Stunned, they all put up their hands to apologize, but she broke into a full sprint and was gone. By the time she reached the beach, she was shivering yet didn't feel cold, a consequence of the alcohol. Ellie took off her shoes and the cool sand soothed her feet, which hurt from running. She walked along the dark and empty shore, calm but feeling guilty for leaving Ben, knowing he could be sensitive.

With her arms crossed, Ellie stopped and stared out to sea, knowing that somewhere out there, miles away and in the throes of a horrific war, was Karl. The night breeze lulled her into a quiet meditation and she thought back to those magical weeks. She remembered their days together in the water, on the beach, in the woods, at the village, here and there, those small but sacred moments scattered like paint strokes across the canvas of her life. Closing her eyes, Ellie turned her ear towards the water and listened to the steady rush of the surf, hoping that maybe she could hear his voice again.

"Ellie?"

A chill went through her body—she spun around. A figure came towards her, a silhouette she knew and recognized.

"Ben?"

"I've been looking everywhere for you. Are you alright?"

"Yes," she said, nodding. "I'm alright."

22.

Trains ran only at night to avoid bombardment. The railway carried armaments as well as civilians, and Allied warplanes made no distinction between the two. As they crossed into Germany, Karl looked out and the countryside was a vast desert of darkness where, occasionally, a light would flicker through the woods; the gas lamp of a farmhouse or a Wehrmacht checkpoint on some suburban road.

With all the connections and layovers, Karl's journey from Lorient to Hamburg took over 24-hours and he was exhausted. At one time in his life, the thump of the wheels would have lulled him to sleep, but now it only reminded him of patrols, the ominous creak of the submarine hull, the rumble of the twin turbines, sounds that made him always alert and afraid. He stayed awake on the overnight trip home because he had no choice, gazing out the window into the blackness, thinking of a similar journey which, although only two years earlier, seemed like another lifetime.

When Karl and his family left America in the summer of '39, they were halfway across the Atlantic before learning that the Allies had declared war on Germany. Suddenly they found themselves enemy aliens and didn't know if they would be detained or deported once they got to England. Beyond the diplomatic uncertainties, there was also the threat of U-boats and at night they cruised at full speed with all the lights off. The ship reached Southampton without incident, however, and to everyone's relief, foreign nationals were given safe passage to France. Using the last of their money, Mr. Brink bought tickets from Normandy to Hamburg on an overcrowded train of fleeing German citizens, piled into the seats and cramped in the carriage vestibules, luggage, crates, and possessions scattered everywhere. It was so early in the conflict that hostilities hadn't even begun, but the stations in Germany were filled with young soldiers headed for deployment and Karl never imagined that he would one day be among them.

"Hauptbahnhof!"

The conductor's voice shook Karl from his drowsy contemplation, and he looked out to see only the dark outlines of buildings, realizing he had never before seen a city without lights. When they came to a stop, he got his bag from the overhead and put on his coat, draping it over the sling of his injured arm. He followed a line of weary passengers out to the platform, where steam from the idling locomotive rose into the crisp, windless air. The station was busy for the middle of the night, but there was an eerie silence and people walked with their heads down and didn't make eye contact.

Karl came out the front doors and saw a row of taxis, all running but with their headlights off. He walked over to the first one and knocked on the window.

"Wilhelminenstrasse," he said.

The driver nodded and Karl got in. The man looked before pulling out, but it seemed more out of habit than necessity because there were no cars in the streets. They drove south for a couple of blocks and crossed over the canal, cruising through a desolate city, the only activity a few bars and nightclubs whose windows were covered with blackout shades.

"Are you a soldier?"

Startled, Karl glanced up and the driver was watching in the rearview. His eyes had a sickly hue, the kind that was more from stress than fatigue, and Karl knew that the War was starting to wear on people.

"Um, yes. Navy."

As he talked, he realized that, with the exception of a ticket clerk and a train stewardess, he hadn't spoken to anyone since the previous morning and it was strange to hear his own voice.

"My son, he's in the Wehrmacht," the man said.

Karl thought for a moment because he wanted to give the proper response, whether he believed it or not.

"Everyone must do his part for the Fatherland."

The driver smiled, a vague but courteous smile which indicated neither agreement nor dissent. Slogans about duty and honor and loyalty had become cliché in Nazi Germany. But Karl knew that not everyone supported the Party or the War, and beneath all the patriotic pretense was a skepticism that he sometimes shared, although he never could say it.

They came to the next intersection and slowed almost to a stop.

"How does one drive in such darkness?"

"Very carefully," the man said with a grin. "More people have been killed by automobiles than bombs."

Just as he said it, Karl saw the burnt out remains of a five-story building emerge from the shadows of a city block. In letters from his mother, Karl learned that British air raids had been light so far, mostly aimed at the oil refineries along the docks, but there were always mistakes and miscalculations and he worried constantly for his parents' safety.

"That looks like more than a car accident."

"That was arson," the driver said and when Karl squinted, he explained. "Brownshirts, back in '38. The building was owned by Jews so they torched it."

They came to the Moenckebergstrasse, a wide boulevard lined with department stores, cafés, and businesses, and Karl recalled afternoons spent there as a boy, shopping with his mother and aunt, going to the cinema, eating ice cream by the Mönckeberg fountain. Staring out, he could hardly make the connection between then and now, and he looked away so he wouldn't be tempted to try.

Soon they turned on to a dark, tree-lined street of apartment buildings, most owned by the University, and all with the sterile look of government housing.

"What number?"

Karl sat stumped, trying to think—his parents had only moved there a year before. Mr. Brink said he needed to be closer to work, but Karl was sure that, after several demotions and a reduced schedule, he was struggling to pay the mortgage on their house in the country.

"42," he said finally.

The driver stopped and Karl handed him a few Reichsmarks and got out. The taxi drove off and Karl stood in the dark on the sidewalk, his bag at his feet, the only sound birds rustling from their slumber, the first indications of the coming dawn. He hadn't been alone in so long that the feeling was unfamiliar, and he used those few minutes to collect himself before he went in.

In his eighteen months in the Kriegsmarine, Karl had only been home three times. His last visit was after a three-week operation in the North Atlantic where, while hunting a convoy 300 miles southeast of Iceland, they were spotted by a British cruiser. Captain Westhoff ordered an emergency dive, but the ballast pumps failed at 30 meters, leaving them stranded and floating helplessly for over twelve hours. By the time the engineers fixed the problem, they were almost out of oxygen. For Karl, it was hard to face his parents after coming so close to death and, in some ways, he dreaded coming home, knowing that each time could be his last. Nevertheless, he took a deep breath and walked up the front steps, scanning the directory for his mother's maiden name, Fischer, which they used because Mr. Brink received so many death threats.

Karl pressed the bell and, moments later, the door buzzed. He came into a small foyer and as he started up the stairs, a door opened above, a hall light flickered on. He had only reached the third landing when his mother peered over the railing and spoke with an almost hysterical whisper.

"Karl?"

He hurried up the last two flights, as fast as he could go on his tired legs, and met her at the top. She went to throw her arms around him but stopped when she saw the sling.

"My God, you're hurt!"

"No, Mother, it's just a sprain."

The concern she had was mutual because Karl was stunned by her appearance. His mother had on an old nightgown, stained and torn at the seams, and shoes without laces, her legs pale and feeble. Combined with her straggly hair and yellow teeth, she looked like a bagwoman and Karl was beside himself.

"Where is Father?"

Mrs. Brink immediately looked down at the floor.

"Not here," she mumbled.

"Not here? What do you mean not here?" he said, and when she didn't answer, he began to panic.

"What is it, Mother? Speak!"

She startled like a frightened cat and he regretted raising his voice. He looked up and down the hallway, then took her gently by the arm.

"Come. Let's talk inside."

They stepped into the small flat, a three-room apartment that overlooked a University park. The only light was a small candle flickering on the table, but it was bright enough for Karl to see that she was living in squalor. The kitchenette was cluttered with dishes, there were piles of trash everywhere, and the stench of garbage, mold, and urine was overwhelming. He left his bag by the door and led her over to the couch, where they sat close together and he held her hand.

"Where's Father?" he asked again, this time softly.

"Gone."

"Gone? What do you mean gone?"

Mrs. Brink stared ahead with glassy eyes, speaking in a sluggish incoherence which Karl knew was not normal.

"They came to his office."

"Who, Mother?"

"Police," she muttered.

Karl turned away and sighed, restraining any rage for his mother's sake. Although surprised by the news, he wasn't shocked because his father had long been a target of the State. But Mr. Brink had survived a decade of harassment and intimidation and with a war on two fronts, Karl always hoped the government had bigger concerns than a minor political dissident.

He stood up and began to pace the room.

"I called the University," Mrs. Brink went on. "They didn't know anything."

"When was the last time you spoke with him?"

"Two Mondays ago. I made his lunch, he left for work. That night, Professor Muller came by and told me."

Karl walked over to the window and peered out the curtains, feeling suddenly vulnerable like he too was being watched.

"Told you what exactly?"

"That he was taken to a work camp, that it was for his own safety, that he would be looked after, that—"

"Dammit, Mother!" he said. "Do you have to be so gullible?"

Mrs. Brink put her hands over her face and began to cry, the long and hushed sobs of a woman who had wept enough for a lifetime. Just as he went to console her, there was a noise, a sinister sound that grew louder and more intense, and he recognized it at once.

"We have to go, it's a raid!"

Dabbing her eyes with a tissue, Mrs. Brink looked up calmly.

"It's only a test."

"A test?"

"They test the sirens every Wednesday before sunrise. It's too clear for an air attack."

Karl glanced out the window again and she was right. No sooner had the sirens started than they began to wind down, and even with the glow of dawn hovering at the horizon, he looked up to see the most magnificent starlit sky.

"There hasn't been much trouble for a while," she continued, her voice dry from crying. "They bombed the railway station in September, but it didn't do much damage."

Karl thought about the suffering of civilians and realized that, despite his sacrifices, his parents were fighting the War too.

"I'm sorry I've made you upset."

"Who has time to be upset?" she said, waving her hand whimsically. "I'm just happy you're home."

Karl looked over with a tender smile.

"As am I, Mother."

. . . . . .

Somewhere Karl could hear a woman, a soft but confident voice, feminine and lisping, much like Ellie's only speaking German. Lying on the couch, the sun peeking through the drapes, he opened his eyes and listened, thinking back to Monk Island and those frantic weeks of love and uncertainty. He realized how naïve he had been to think it could last, and the impermanence of that summer made it somehow more precious. Of all the memories, his most vivid was the morning they left, when he watched from the ferry as the village and waterfront faded behind the pre-dawn mist. Right before it vanished, Karl felt a great tremor, as if the gravity of world events had come crashing down between them, concluding their story, separating them forever.

Karl got up from the couch, his neck stiff and arm sore. He adjusted his sling and went over to the window, where he looked out to see kindergarteners in the playground below, climbing ladders and going down slides, running, jumping and giggling, oblivious to the despair of war. Seated on a bench was a young woman, their teacher, the voice of Ellie and with a similar profile, dark hair and a slight figure. With her back to him, Karl couldn't see her face and he preferred it that way because he wanted to imagine it was her, if only for a moment.

The front door opened and Karl turned around.

"Mother? I thought you were still sleeping."

Mrs. Brink walked in carrying groceries and he rushed over to help.

"Did I scare you?" she said. "It's almost 10 am."

Karl took the bag from her and put it on the counter. As he looked around, he realized that she had tidied up—the garbage was gone and the dishes were washed. Even her personal appearance had improved since the night before and she had on a clean dress, fresh makeup.

"I'm glad you're getting out," he said.

"It's quite convenient living here," she said, handing him things to put in the cabinet. "A grocer across the street, a butcher next door. Who would've thought city life was so easy?"

"Does Father like it?"

"Hated it," she said, and Karl was struck that she used the past tense. "There are no birds in Hamburg. You know how much he loved birds."

He made a vague smile, thinking about his father's fascination with nature, perhaps their one shared interest, and all the camping trips to the Black Forest when he was a boy. Karl laughed to himself, recalling a day they scaled a 500-foot ridge in the rain because his father thought he spotted a Lämmergeier, only to discover that it was a vulture. He admired his father's passion for the wild and often wondered why he didn't study botany or orthography rather than economics.

"Karl?"

He came out of a daydream and his mother was holding out the last can of beans. He took it and put it away, closing the cabinet like he was shutting the door on the past. Karl knew there was no time for sentimentality because, with only two weeks of leave, he had to focus on caring for his mother and finding his father.

"Mother, I have to go out today. Will you be okay?"

She gave him a stern look as if offended.

"I've made it this far alone."

"Of course," he said, averting his eyes. "You've done well."

While Mrs. Brink made cucumber sandwiches, Karl went into the bathroom to get ready. He peeled back the bandage on his elbow and the wound was swollen but not infected. He washed his face, brushed his teeth, and ran some water through his hair. He had brought civilian clothes from Lorient but decided to wear his uniform because, on city streets, a soldier had more status than a civilian.

"Karl," his mother called.

"Be right there."

Before he finished, he opened the medicine cabinet, which had ointments and aspirin—a jar of petroleum jelly and a tube of Biox toothpaste. Noticing a bottle without a label, he looked inside and saw a couple of dozen white pills. Karl tried to shake out a few, but in his rush, they all came out and he shoved them in his pocket.

When he came out, his mother turned to him.

"You look so...dignified," she said with a proud smile.

"Not always. You should see me after two weeks at sea."

186

She made a playful smirk and he sat down beside her at the table.

"Have you seen terrible things?"

He took a sandwich and began to eat.

"No," he scoffed. "It's been mostly exercises and patrols. Not much of a war, really."

They both knew it was a lie and Mrs. Brink seemed content to believe it. After they finished, she made tea and Karl declined, having been told since training that it was an "English" drink and that German sailors drank coffee.

Finally, he got his coat and kissed his mother on the cheek.

"Will you be home…?" she said, stopping short, and the slip was as troubling as it was obvious. "…*When* will you be home, I mean?"

"By dinnertime."

"I'll make something you like."

……

Outside was bitter cold despite the sun and Karl walked with his collar up. He worried more about his mother than his father, which bothered his conscience because Mr. Brink might have been in greater danger. But his mother was more fragile and Karl knew it wasn't safe for her to be alone. The year before, her best friend killed herself after her Jewish husband was executed by the Gestapo for some trivial crime. Mrs. Brink started to see a psychotherapist for depression, but then he disappeared. The previous Christmas she had overdosed on her husband's blood pressure medication and survived only because he came home early. She swore it was an accident, but everyone close to her was skeptical, including the physician who saved her life.

When Karl entered the pharmacy, a dozen people were waiting but before he could get in line, an assistant called over from the counter.

"Sir," he said, waving. "Please."

Karl walked past everyone and went over, uneasy about the special treatment but too polite to decline.

"How can I be of service, Comrade?"

"Sulfonamide," he said, glancing down at his arm.

The man made a curt smile, went in the back room and, moments later, came back out.

"Here you are, Sir."

After Karl paid, he reached in his pocket and got one of his mother's pills.

"Can you tell me what this is?"

The man took the pill, examined it closely, squinting.

"Pervitin," he said, lowering his voice. "Methamphetamine."

"Thank you."

Karl turned around and walked towards the door and although he didn't look over, he could feel everyone watching. He didn't know if it was curiosity, envy, pity or resentment, but he was sure that the sight of a soldier brought out a range of emotions. Like the cab driver the night before, people everywhere looked weary, and with food shortages, air raids, and all the other pressures of war, it was no wonder.

Once outside, Karl opened the bottle of his antibiotics and swallowed a tablet dry. He had already missed two days and knew that if the wound got infected he could lose his arm. Hearing the bell of an approaching trolley, he darted into the street and all the vehicles stopped to let him cross. The train rolled up, the doors opened, and he got on.

The ride to the University of Hamburg only took a few minutes. Walking through the main gate, Karl thought of all the times he came to meet his father after school. They would take the train home together, usually after dark, Mr. Brink working with his briefcase on his lap while Karl sat quietly exhausted, his hair still wet from swim practice.

Although the Brinks lived outside the City, Karl had grown up around the college and when he was younger, his mother taught there too. But Mrs. Brink's career in academia ended with the rise of the Nazis, a party which opposed women working outside traditional roles, and rather than fight the changing norms, she left to become a housewife. At the time, Karl was a teenager, old enough to realize the gravity of her decision, the demoralization of a woman who had always been bright and independent. The worst of the family's harassment and terror had yet to begin, but Karl was sure that his mother's resignation was the start of her emotional collapse.

As he crossed the campus, it looked much the same, except for a new science center. But now the Swastika hung from every window, flew from the flagpoles, a shrine to Nazism that even as a patriot, Karl found disturbing. The trees were bare, the walkways deserted, and he made it all the way to his father's building without seeing a single person.

When Karl walked in, he peeked into a couple of classrooms and they were empty. He went up to the third floor, past a large sign that read Department of Economics, and continued to the end of the corridor, finally coming to his father's office. The plaque with Mr. Brink's name and title was gone—all that remained was a faint outline from the adhesive. When Karl turned the knob and it was locked, he got so frustrated he tried to force it open.

"May I help you?"

He spun around startled and standing behind him was an older gentleman with glasses and a tweed coat.

"I...I..." Karl said, stumbling, "am looking for my father."

"Niklaus Brink?"

"Yes."

"Professor Klug," the man said, extending his hand. "Rudolph Klug."

With his right arm in a brace, Karl had to pivot and shake with the other.

"Karl Brink."

"A U-boat sailor," he remarked and Karl didn't know if it was a question.

"I am."

"I know," he said, reaching in his pockets for some keys. "Your father spoke of you often."

Professor Klug unlocked the door and motioned for him to enter. Karl nodded and stepped inside, walking over to the desk and running his hand along the edge, consumed by a quiet introspection. With Klug waiting in the doorway, a minute passed before Karl spoke.

"Where did they take him?"

"We don't know."

Karl looked around the small office with the eye of a detective and everything was in perfect order—there was no sign of a struggle. Mr. Brink's typewriter was on the desk and his book collection was on the wall. Over by the window, there was a hand-carved warrior mask, a souvenir from his parents' time in Tanganyika, and next to that, an antique globe. Karl could still smell his father's cologne, a faint but familiar lavender. He was seized by an astonishment that held as much fury as it did sadness, and feeling for the first time betrayed by the Country he fought for.

"There have been others too."

"Others?" Karl said, not looking back.

"Taken away, without explanation."

Karl shook his head, clenched his fists.

"This is an outrage."

"We contacted the police, they told us to contact the Gestapo. We contacted the Gestapo and they told us to contact the police. That's how it is these days, a circle of deceit."

Finally, Karl turned around and their eyes met in a moment of silent yet mutual understanding. By now, most professors in Germany supported Hitler because those who did not had been terminated, imprisoned, or humiliated into resigning. But somehow Karl knew this man was a holdout and, even if he didn't completely agree with him, he respected his integrity.

"We hear rumors," Karl said and Professor Klug listened, "about camps."

"We hear these rumors too."

"Are they true?"

Klug paused before answering, his expression somber.

"I don't know, my dear boy."

Karl stepped over to the window and the sun was shining over the quad. A couple of students sat under a tree, but otherwise, the campus was empty.

"Where is everybody?"

191

"It's a holiday—Day of Repentance and Prayer."

They stared at each other and smiled at the irony, some small cheer in an otherwise bleak and humorless time. Karl took a final look around the office as if lingering would reveal more secrets about what had happened. He couldn't help feeling that this was the last part of his father he would ever see.

"You should take these," Professor Klug said, almost as an afterthought. He reached for a stack of mail on the desk and handed it to Karl. "They're no good unopened."

Karl looked at the letters, then glanced up.

"Thank you."

The Professor nodded and they drifted towards the door. When they came back out to the hallway, Klug stood up straight and held out his hand.

"I wish you luck."

As they shook, Karl sensed that he wanted to say more, but instead, the Professor locked the door and headed back towards his office.

"Why are you still here?" Karl said.

The old man stopped, turned around, and shrugged his shoulders.

"Who knows? I'm a decorated soldier…from the last War."

"Maybe you got a pardon," Karl joked.

"Maybe they just forgot about me."

23

Ellie crept through the woods, ducking under branches, crouched low with a basket in hand. The air was frigid but wrapped in her scarf and wool hat she was comfortable, overcome by a quiet exhilaration as she scanned the barrenness for her prey. She moved steadily like a hunter, twigs snapping under her feet, the steam rising from her breath. The only other sound was her sniffling and once or twice she stopped to wipe her nose, the nuisance of a cold that, for everyone in the Ames family, began around the first frost and ended in Spring.

"Help!"

Ellie dropped her basket and the cranberries she had been collecting for the past hour went everywhere. She ran towards the voice, pushing through the dense vegetation, her heart pounding. She came over a shallow hill and saw her sister standing in a thicket down below, the colors of her dress clear against the gray and lifeless autumn landscape.

"Didn't I tell you not to go far?!" Ellie shouted.

"I'm stuck!"

Mary was standing upright with only one crutch and as Ellie got closer, she saw that she had fallen through some rotted plywood. Ellie told her not to move and then knelt down, reaching into the crack and guiding her sister's foot out, careful not to let it touch the rough edges. Mary's ankle was already scraped and bleeding from trying to get free, but instead of complaining, she stared down curiously at the snare which had beset her.

"What is it?"

Ellie cleared away some dirt and looked in but it was too dark to see.

"Probably for the hunters."

"A secret hideaway?"

"No secret if you found it," Ellie said, getting back up, dusting off her hands.

She picked up Mary's other crutch, handed it to her, and looked around. They were at the foot of a shallow ravine, an area where the forest tapered off into swampland, low-lying and desolate and without a cranberry bush in sight.

"What were you doing over here?"

"I wanted to see the fort."

Ellie followed her gaze and saw, through the grass and scrub brush, a massive concrete structure in the distance. For a moment, she was mesmerized, struck by the same fascination as seeing the pyramids of Giza or the Great Wall of China. And it was no less impressive, rising like a megalith from the earth. Ellie realized then that the base would be more than just a few barracks and some barbed wire fencing.

Suddenly, a gunshot.

"What the hell was that?!"

Ellie circled around panicked and through the trees, she saw two soldiers, dressed in full fatigues and carrying rifles. When the men saw them too, they immediately veered and came down the hill.

"Girls," one of them said. "This area is restricted."

Ellie arched her back and faced them with a cold indignation—she didn't like being called a girl and she didn't like being barred from the woods she had frequented her entire life.

"We weren't aware of that."

"There're signs all around."

"Well, you didn't have to shoot."

The men glanced at each other, chuckling with boyish sarcasm. And they looked no older than boys, Ellie thought, with pimples on their cheeks and stubble on their chins.

"That wasn't for you, Miss," the first man said, his politeness putting her slightly more at ease.

"We're hunting Adolph," his partner said.

"Adolph?"

"Adolph's a big turkey. We're hoping to get a bullet between his eyes…like we'll do to Hitler."

Ellie responded with a sour smirk and glanced at Mary, who stood stiff, too awestruck to speak. After a short pause, the first soldier gave Ellie an awkward smile, his eyes half-hidden beneath the rim of his helmet. She recognized that look, the leer of young desire but she wasn't offended. She smiled back in sympathy, knowing it must have been difficult to be so far from home.

"Well, ladies, have a nice Thanksgiving."

The young man then nodded to his partner and they turned to go.

"Pardon," Ellie said and they stopped. "What's that building over there?"

"That's no building, Miss. It's one of the biggest gun batteries in North America."

. . . . . .

Monk Island was peaceful on Thanksgiving morning. As Ellie and Mary walked home, the only sounds were the rustle of leaves, creatures in the woods. Smoke rose from the chimneys of all the homes, filling the air with the smell of roasting meats, and by the time they reached their street, they were both ravenous.

They walked past Ben's parked truck and up the front steps. When they came into the front parlor, they peeled off their coats, hats, and mittens, and their mother walked in stirring something in a bowl.

"What took you so long?"

"I found a secret hideout," Mary said, leaning her crutches against the wall.

"A secret hideout?"

Ellie rolled her eyes and handed her mother the basket of cranberries.

"She fell through some old plywood is all."

"You girls go get dressed. We'll be eating soon."

The family never used the dining room, except for holidays and other special occasions, and when Ellie came downstairs for dinner, the table was set with linen and silk napkins. Vera had also put out their best silverware, a handmade set she inherited from her grandmother, who had, in turn, inherited it from her grandmother.

Jack and Ben were already seated, dressed in suits, and aside from Christmas, it was the only time Ellie saw her father in a tie. Vera was finishing up in the kitchen, but most of the serving trays were out and there was more food than Ellie had seen in months—turkey and stuffing, peas and sweet potatoes, cabbage and carrots, cornbread and quahogs. She took a seat across from Ben, smoothing out her dress, and acknowledged him with a faint smile. Although they had been out together a few times since, she was still embarrassed about the incident at the Legion.

"Hello, Ellie," he said.

"Hi, Ben."

Mary came in wearing a white dress, her hair in a bow— and no shoes.

"Look at all the food," she said, beaming.

"Thank goodness for high lobster prices," Ben said.

Ben and Jack glanced at each other, but Ellie thought nothing of it because she always stayed out of their business. Vera walked with a gravy bowl, stopping when she saw Mary's bare feet.

"Girl, get some shoes on!"

Mary hobbled out, returning a few minutes later, and with everyone finally seated and ready, they bowed their heads for grace. Jack mumbled a few words about family and love and bounty, but it was more of a commentary than a prayer, and when Ellie looked over, Mary's cheeks were swelled like a blowfish, struggling not to laugh. Everyone said Amen and they all started to fill their plates. For the first few minutes, no one spoke, the only sound the rattle of utensils, the wind chimes on the back porch.

"How long is Kate back for?" Vera asked Ellie, breaking the silence.

"Um, two and a half weeks."

"She's in the Army," Mary said.

"Nurses Corp," Ellie corrected. "But, yes, the Army."

The conversation continued in fits and starts, but no matter what the topic, it always drifted back to war and the preparations for war.

"Mr. Brackett said there's red tide on the backshore."

"It don't matter much," Ben said. "the Army won't let anyone fish there 'til the construction is done."

"Mrs. Brackett said the base is enormous," Vera said.

"We could see it from the woods this morning," Ellie said.

"It's like a castle," Mary added.

Ben reached for more stuffing, carrots, and peas, topped it with gravy and mixed it all together.

"Gotta be over a thousand troops," he said.

"This certainly doesn't feel like neutrality," Vera said.

"They must think something's coming."

"Would the Germans really attack Monk Island?" Mary asked.

Everyone stopped and turned to Jack, who peered up for the first time. With the looming conflict, people looked to him for answers he didn't have as if his experience in combat made him an expert on all wars. He didn't speak, but Ellie could tell the question troubled him, especially because it came from Mary. Above all, he felt obligated to protect her from the harshness of the world.

"What do you think, Jack?" Vera asked.

He paused for a moment and then reached over the table.

"I think I'll have more turkey."

. . . . . .

Ellie and Kate waddled down the hill, their stomachs full and eyes watery from the wind. Behind them were Jack, Vera, and Ben; up ahead, Junebug and Mary, who stopped every couple of minutes to look at something with the binoculars. They must have looked like a procession of pioneers, Ellie thought, her father in his dark suit and suspenders and Ben wearing his father's felt derby, which had been out of fashion for decades.

As they came through the tall grass, Jack and Ben each took one of Vera's arms, helping her over the dunes, and they came out to the cold, flat sand. While the men stood talking about fishing, Vera hobbled down to dip her feet in the shallows, the salt water soothing to her swollen ankles.

"She's so grown up," Kate said, and Ellie looked over at the girls.

"Junebug as well."

Even with their bulky coats, the curves of their budding figures were apparent, and Ellie had to face that her sister was fast becoming a young woman.

"Has she had her period?"

"Kate?" Ellie moaned, more appalled than embarrassed.

"A periscope!"

Everyone turned and Mary was pointing towards the mouth of Taylor Passage, where the shallow harbor waters merged with the wide open sea, emptier than Ellie had ever seen it. Fears of U-boats lurking offshore which had started during the Great War were now back and the Army even issued a notice asking residents to be on alert. Some people dismissed the threat, others even joked about it, but it was real enough that, after hearing Mary yell, Jack and Ben came over to see.

She gave the binoculars to Ben first and he put them to his eyes, adjusted the wheel.

"Maybe it's an egret?"

"You wouldn't know an egret from an eider duck," Jack said, tearing them from his hands.

When Kate glanced over, Ellie shook her head, ashamed at how Ben was treated by her father and sometimes wishing he would fight back. But he ignored the insult and stood beside Jack, who scanned the horizon with dramatic concentration, heightening the suspense and making Ellie think something might actually be out there.

"U-boats have two periscopes," Mary announced. "One for attacking and one for just looking out."

Vera looked down with a proud smile, but everyone else was too distracted.

"Well," Jack said, finally. "This one evidently has none."

He gave Mary the binoculars, turned around, and whisked by Ellie so fast that she had to move to avoid him. Ben followed him back up the beach, Vera continued soaking her feet, and the girls walked over to explore the rocks. With everyone now occupied, Ellie nodded to Kate and they moved down the shore for some privacy.

"Ben looks nice in his outfit. Have you two made it?"

"Kate," she said, rolling her eyes. "We haven't even kissed."

"Why not?"

"I don't think of him like that."

"He's the best you're gonna do here."

"Is that so," Ellie said, mildly offended, both for herself and for Ben.

"Sorry," she said. "I didn't mean it that way. But there're lots of fish in the sea. You gotta get out of here and see things. You never realize how small this island is until you leave it."

"And where would I go?"

"To Portland, Bangor, Boston, anywhere. Factories and shipyards are booming. I hear Bath Iron Works is paying a dollar an hour. You can't wait for the world to come to you."

Ellie looked dreamily out to the sandbar, half-submerged by the incoming tide, and remembered the day Karl taught her to swim.

"He came to me," she said.

Kate went to speak, but stopped, taking a deep breath like she was preparing to dive.

"Ellie," she said, her voice low, quaking. "I'm your best friend and I care about you." She didn't often get emotional, but when she did it was obvious. "But Karl is gone. You can't put your life on hold forever—"

"Would you look at that?!"

They both turned and Ben and her father were staring towards Frazier Point, where a giant Navy ship was peeking out behind the south side of Holyhead Island. In the calm water, it moved with such imperceptible stealth that it was hard to tell if it was arriving or departing. Living in Casco Bay, with all the foundries and dockyards, they were used to big vessels, but this was on a scale Ellie had never seen before and everyone stood amazed.

Vera walked up to the men, as did the girls, and when Ben asked for the binoculars, Mary handed them to him.

"USS Yorktown," he said, looking out.

"Is that for the Battle Of Yorktown?" Mary said.

Although everyone was impressed by the question, no one knew the answer.

"Must be."

"Is it a battleship or something?"

"Aircraft carrier," Jack said.

"Of all the days to leave," his wife said.

"Wars don't take holidays, Vera."

"Say, Ellie," Ben called over, holding out the binoculars. "Won't you come have a look?"

When Ellie glanced at Kate, Kate was already looking at her. Ellie was touched by her concern and her advice, knowing that Kate wasn't telling her what to do, but rather that she had to do something. She took one last look at the sandbar, which was now covered, and then started to walk over to the others.

"Sure, Ben."

24

Karl leaned against the rusted railing of the promenade beside the river as a single patrol boat passed by. On the opposite bank, he could see the damage from aerial bombings—a collapsed hangar, a destroyed wharf, scattered piles of rubble. He wasn't sure how long he had been there—an hour, two hours, maybe more—but it was starting to get dark and the temperature had fallen. Karl wanted to get home to his mother, but he hadn't been alone in months and cherished the time of quiet reflection, of aimless anonymity, the relative peace and solitude which he knew would not last.

Karl heard rustling and saw someone hunched over a trash barrel, scrounging for scraps. The figure looked up and he was surprised to see a woman, his age or younger, with long, tangled hair and eyes that were clear but distant. Something about her reminded him of Ellie—but then all young woman reminded him of Ellie. Not a day passed when he didn't yearn for that warm femininity, that gentle touch, that soft voice which he often recited in his mind at night so he wouldn't forget it. Karl knew that, in some ways, Ellie had come to represent all they had forsaken in America, the hope and safety, the possibility of a new life. But she was more than just a symbol, and the longer he was away from her, the more he realized that that summer, however chaotic, had been the high point of his life and that she was the only girl he ever loved.

Karl resented his father as much for taking him away from Ellie as he did for bringing his mother back to Germany. Considering her mental state, Mrs. Brink needed special care and yet even with war inevitable, his father continued with his political shenanigans, speaking out at faculty meetings, distributing pamphlets, spreading his spirit of resistance anywhere and everywhere he could. The police had been to the house a dozen times to question him, and his tenure at the university was revoked, making him a low-paid adjunct. Although Mr. Brink tried to supplement his income by tutoring, it was barely enough to survive and the last time Karl visited, his father's suit had holes and he had aged a decade. He was no longer a fiery revolutionary—he was a doddering old fool.

Realizing he couldn't change history, Mr. Brink turned his frustrations inward, and his nightly bourbon became a bottle a day. He was irritable and combative, whether drunk or sober, and Karl appeased him for the sake of his mother. But Karl couldn't always restrain himself and their final blowout was worse than their fight on Monk Island, the night before they left America. He couldn't even remember how it started, but he still cringed at the thought of his father battered and bloody, pinned against the wall while his mother lay shrieking on the living room floor. When the police arrived, Mr. Brink ordered his son to leave and, with nowhere to go, Karl went to live with his uncle Walter in Bremen until he joined the Kriegsmarine.

In his youth, Karl had never considered the military, but with his dreams of swimming stardom over and with no plans of attending University, it was a logical choice to make. He was aware that, in some ways, it was a late rebellion because, throughout his teenage years, he had always been respectful, obedient, and never much trouble. But once he moved out, he no longer felt burdened by the expectations of his parents. After years of being the son of a traitor, and all the fear and shame that went along with it, he could finally prove his loyalty, a decision that was helped by the fact that his uncle had fought in the Great War. Karl never trusted the Nazis, but he believed in Germany, and when he became a sailor, it was the first time in his life that he felt important.

"Good evening comrade!"

Startled, Karl looked and three soldiers were swaggering towards him with MP-40's strapped across their chests. As he turned, he felt a tear on his cheek and quickly wiped it away before greeting them. They went by and continued along the promenade, talking loudly and smoking cigarettes, their biggest task thwarting vandals and warning teens to get home before curfew. After what he experienced in the Atlantic, Karl could have resented their easy assignment, but instead, he pitied them, knowing that life behind the lines had its own kind of terror. He had seen it in his mother, as well as other civilians, the constant fear of living while the war raged beyond, never knowing if or when the bombs were coming, the specter of that hidden enemy above.

It started to sprinkle so Karl headed back, two miles through the dark city streets, and by the time he reached the apartment, it was pouring. He stepped into the lobby, rang the buzzer and, moments later, the door clicked open. As he came up the stairs, he heard his mother come out and say, "Karl?"

Her voice was dry and feeble, and sensing that something was wrong, Karl ran up the last two flights. He came to the top landing and found her standing in a nightgown, her eyes dilated and face white, staring with the blank look of a traumatized child.

"Mother, what's wrong?"

"I'm not well."

He put his arm around her, feeling her forehead, and she was damp and shivering all over.

"My medicine," she moaned. "I've none left."

He led her back into the flat, guided her onto the couch, and then went to the stove to put on the kettle.

"I need more pills."

"Mother, you need help. This is not right."

Karl brought her over a cup of tea and she was shaking so much he had to hold it for her and urge her to drink. As she sipped, he sat close and rubbed her back, trying to soothe her. An hour passed before she stopped trembling and he knew it was more from exhaustion than because the withdrawals had subsided.

With his mother finally relaxed, Karl went over to the icebox—he hadn't eaten all day—and got a couple of pieces of cold ham and bread, made some fake coffee, the result of wartime shortages, a bitter blend of hickory and acorns. The moment he got to the couch with his dinner, all the lights flickered and then went out.

"Would you light the candle, please?"

"What's happening?"

"Power rationing," his mother said sarcastically. "Everyone must do his part for the Fatherland."

Karl snickered to himself and went over to the table, realizing that, as empty as the slogan was, he had used it often himself, the mindless utterances of Nazi propaganda. He struck a match and the room filled with a soft, yellow glow. When he came back to sit, he looked at his mother and saw that she was still feverish but calmer.

"Who gave you the Pervitin?"

She gave him a sideways glance as if surprised he knew.

"I bought it myself."

"Nonsense. They've been prescription-only since the War started."

"A friend."

"They've made you addicted."

"We're all addicted," she said, gazing at the ceiling. "This whole country is intoxicated by madness."

"Not everyone, Mother. We're merely being tested."

"That's what your father used to say."

"I went to the Gestapo to ask about him today," Karl said, between bites.

Mrs. Brink lifted her head and looked at him with a deep, almost comical frown.

"Are you crazy?"

"They don't know where he is."

"Of course they don't."

Her head dropped back to the pillow and Karl continued to eat, chewing on stale bread, sipping coffee that tasted like mud, discovering that, to his amazement, Navy rations were better than civilian food. They fell into a long silence, his mother lying still in the semi-darkness, and Karl at the edge of the couch, his back against her legs. He hadn't felt so close to her in years, and he could have stayed there all night, watching over her like she did him when he was a boy and had nightmares.

Thinking she was asleep, Karl took his plate and cup and started to get up when suddenly she spoke.

"I always admired your father's courage," she said, and Karl sat back down. "At first, I didn't want him to continue with his political work."

"At first?"

"After you left for training in Neustadt, he wanted to stop. He didn't want to embarrass you—he was so proud of your service. But I told him not to."

Karl's entire body tensed up.

"You told him not to?"

"I did," she said without the slightest remorse. "Once the War started, there was no more real resistance. The Communists were all in prison, the Socialists too. Your father wasn't a threat to anyone. But I couldn't let him give up the struggle. It was his mission."

His mission. Karl recited the phrase in his mind and it sounded almost foreign. All he ever knew about his father's work was that it caused their family problems, but he had never considered the motives.

"Of all our troubles," Mrs. Brink went on, "the hardest for him was when you didn't make the Olympic Team."

"I was outdone, Mother. That's all there is to it."

Something about the way she paused told him there was more.

"Do you remember the boy who took the Gold in the breaststroke?" she asked.

"Hans Gartner? He came in 3rd during qualifications, pushed me out."

"It's not so simple. You were tied"

"Tied?"

"People said you actually won. Your father wasn't there to see it."

"Why wasn't there a rematch?"

"The boy's father was an SS Captain," she said, her voice cracking.

"They didn't want the son of a traitor."

"They didn't say that, of course."

Karl sighed and shook his head, disgusted that even sports weren't beyond the manipulative grasp of Party favoritism. Throughout his youth, his one passion was swimming, his only solace in a world gone mad. As one of the youngest Olympic prospects in Germany, he had to work twice as hard and all he ever wanted was a chance to compete. To learn that he was cut from the team for reasons other than his own performance was more than an outrage—it was treachery, and for the first time, he felt ashamed to be a soldier.

The candle flickered out, leaving them in total darkness, the only sound his mother's gentle sobbing.

"I'm so sorry," she said.

Karl sat stunned, overcome by a feeling of numb awareness that made him wonder if that was what it felt like to be dead. Nevertheless, he didn't want to brood because he knew it would only worry her, so he forced a smile and patted her on the knee.

"That's the past. Let's concern ourselves with today."

She mumbled something he couldn't hear and minutes later was out cold. Karl knew he should get up and go to bed— tomorrow was another day and there was still much work to be done. But he stayed on the couch, almost in a trance, and gazed out into the blackness. His mind drifted back to the National Championship, many years before, when he was disqualified from the Olympic team. At the time, it was the height of his swimming achievements, a day that would prove the difference between amateur hopes and greatness.

Karl saw himself in the locker room, hunched over a bench with his eyes closed, trying to focus with the crowd roaring in the background. But he was more worried than anxious because his father hadn't come home the night before. At first, Mrs. Brink assumed he was just working late, but as the hours passed, she began to panic. When she called the University, no one answered and when she contacted the police, they were no help. In the hazy dealings of the Nazi surveillance state, people vanished all the time and considering Mr. Brink's political activities, Karl and his mother always feared it would happen to him.

By the next morning, Karl's mother was hysterical and he was faced with an impossible choice: to stay with her or to travel to the competition alone. When she insisted he go, Karl only agreed after she found a neighbor to come over. He caught the first train to Berlin, a place he had never been before, and after getting temporarily lost, arrived only minutes before the start of the meet, frustrated and exhausted.

Karl never forgot the relief he felt when Coach Lang came into the locker room to get him. His father called, he had told him, and he was safe. Karl then got up and followed the coach down a long hallway with cracked floor tiles and rusted ceiling lamps. The Aquatics Club had been around since 1882, the same year Germany formed its first swimming federation and although the building was old, it had the stately dilapidation of the Roman Coliseum or Parthenon.

They came out to a room the size of an airplane hangar, with two Olympic pools and bleachers down the length of both walls. Nazi flags hung from the rafters and there was a military brass band playing. News reporters walked around with cameras and notepads and on a podium above the stands was the announcer and several officials. As Karl squinted in the white lights, he felt all the pride of being German.

"Third place—breaststroke," he heard over the loudspeaker.

The Coach stayed close and escorted him to the edge.

"Concentrate," he whispered. "Your only threat is Hans Gartner."

Karl nodded and adjusted his cap. His body was ramped up from the adrenaline, but there was also underlying fatigue because he hadn't slept. Nevertheless, knowing that his father was alright gave him the emotional boost he needed and he felt ready to conquer the world.

"Just you and Gartner," Lang went on, patting him on the back. "There's no one else in the room."

First and second place for the 1936 Summer Olympics had already been established and Karl was vying for third. As one of the youngest prospects, he had made it farther than anybody expected and he relished the role of the underdog.

"Swimmers on your marks," a voice called out.

Karl raised his arms, bent his knees. There were eight other competitors, but he concentrated only on the lane in front of him.

"Get set."

The room went suddenly quiet.

"Go!"

He leaped forward, slipped into the pool, and swam with all his strength, battling through the water like it was an enemy. Every time he came up for air, he could hear the cheer of the crowd and it drove him on. He reached the far side in seconds and spun around with the speed and grace of a seal.

Karl had trained so hard for so long that he sometimes couldn't tell if he was exerting himself or if it was automatic.

The second lap was even faster than the first and by the time he approached the finish, he worried he might not be able to stop. In an instant, he tapped the edge, stood up, and tore off his goggles. Gasping for breath, he looked around and didn't see Coach Lang. When the results weren't announced right away, Karl sensed that something was wrong.

"You are tied," the young man beside him said, "with that guy."

Karl looked down to the first lane and it was Hans Gartner. Unlike most of the swimmers, he was short and stocky and he looked more Slavic than German. Karl had never competed with him directly, but because their best times in the 100-meter breaststroke were the same, it was his sole rival.

A small crowd formed around the judges' table, including coaches, officials, even some meddling spectators. Karl was too far away to hear, but he could tell the discussion was tense. As he watched, a man in uniform walked over and Karl realized it was an SS officer.

"That's his father," another swimmer said.

While everyone else started getting out, Karl and Gartner stayed in the pool and waited for the final results. Karl didn't like being at the center of a dispute and it made him uncomfortable. As the son of a political dissident, he had learned early on that public attention of any kind was a dangerous thing. He was relieved when the band began to play and another match started at the next pool.

After almost ten minutes, Coach Lang finally walked back over. He held his head high but Karl could tell he was upset.

"Come out, Son," he said and he gave Karl a hand. "We won the battle, but not the war."

"Pardon?"

"It's settled. Gartner has taken 3rd."

......

Karl awoke the next morning on the floor of his mother's room. Even though she stayed on the couch, he thought it somehow unseemly to violate the sacred space his parents once shared, a four-post bed that his grandfather had made for their wedding, crafted from Bavarian oak. The bedroom décor was sparse, with a dresser against the wall, a mirror in the corner, and a nightstand with a framed photograph of them all together on a ski trip to the Alps when Karl was in kindergarten. He recognized all the furniture, but the apartment was a just shadow of their former house in the country, a distillation of the life that they once had.

He sat up and stretched his arm, feeling that it was close to healed, tender at points but strong again. When he came out of the bedroom, the first thing he smelled was ammonia and he looked over to the kitchenette to see his mother dressed in her overcoat, holding a mop.

"Mother?"

She spun around, put her hand to her heart.

"You frightened me."

Karl walked over and kissed her on the cheek.

"You were out?"

"Just to the shop. I wanted to get some things before they sell out again."

She handed Karl a plate with a roll. As he buttered it, he looked around and the apartment was spotless for the first time since he arrived. The counter was washed, the furniture dusted, and all the trash had been put away.

"Looks like you've cleaned up?"

"I ought to. I have a special guest."

When she smiled, her lashes flickered and she had a strange glow which made him suspicious.

"Feeling better, I see?"

"I am, thank you."

They sat together at the small table as classical music played on the radio in the corner. While Karl ate, his mother only picked at her food, fidgety and glancing around. He was just about to remark on her mood when the music stopped and was replaced by the shrieking voice of Joseph Goebbels, the Nazi Minister of Propaganda.

"That windbag! Why must he always shout?"

Surprised by the outburst, Karl looked at her and she averted her eyes, adding, "I'm sorry."

"That okay, Mother. My allegiance is to Germany, not to Adolph Hitler."

He finished quickly and went in the bathroom to wash and change—he had been in the same uniform since Lorient and it was filthy. He turned on the faucet and then looked in the medicine cabinet to see that the vial of pills was gone. Maybe it was in her pocketbook, he thought, but it really didn't matter because he was sure she had gone out for more.

Karl shaved with cold water, combed his hair, and put on his clean service uniform, feeling truly refreshed for the first time since coming home. When he came out, his mother was in the sofa chair, one leg crossed over the other and gazing out the window, her foot swinging like a restless tic. It took her a moment to notice him, and when she did, she looked across smiling, a simmering smile that conveyed more than politeness or pleasantries, the smile of a mother's deepest pride.

"You look so...dignified."

Karl glanced down, smoothing out his jacket and fixing his tie, as sheepish as a young man on his wedding day.

"I know it's not what you and Father wanted."

"What we wanted is not important," she said, and it was the closest he ever got to an approval.

"Thank you."

"Are you often scared?"

Karl paused, thinking long before he answered, not wanting to say anything that might make her worry more.

"War is always difficult, Mother," he said. "But the men I serve with carry me through."

Suddenly, the buzzer rang.

"Are you expecting someone?"

When his mother shook her head, Karl went over to the door, and he almost pressed the switch before deciding to answer it himself. He walked down the stairwell and when he reached the bottom, he saw a figure standing behind the frosted glass. He grabbed the knob, then hesitated. Whether it was the years of his father being harassed or from the general state of German society, he had become suspicious of everyone and everything. But he shrugged off the paranoia and opened the door, and as the cold air rushed in, he was relieved to see a postman.

"Telegram for Sailor Karl Brink."

Karl nodded and signed the receipt and the man handed him a brown envelope.

"Thank you," he said.

Leaning in the doorway, Karl took out the telegram, its flimsy paper fluttering in the wind. He knew immediately that it was from the command center at Lorient. As he read, his hand trembled and, seconds later, his mouth fell open.

U-206 SUNK BY ENEMY DESTROYER

NO SURVIVORS

REPORT FOR DUTY U-130

9 DEC.

25

Ellie sat in the pew with her coat buttoned up and hat on, and it was hard to focus on the sermon because the room was so cold. She glimpsed around and everywhere were familiar faces, people she had known for so long they were like props in the stage show of her life. Kate was in the row ahead, distinguished in her ANC uniform, while Mr. Mallet had on a bowtie and his wife, a lace hat. Behind them were Mr. and Mrs. Jossip, who even as the oldest couple on Monk Island could sing louder than everyone else. There were others too, the Rankins, the Smiths, the Colliers, the Brackett's—mostly families with children or the elderly because so many from Ellie's generation had moved to the mainland. The only strangers were in the front, four military couples, the men dressed in dark suits with medals and brass buttons, their wives in white dresses.

"When we think of these difficult times, we must look to Scripture…"

The words got everyone's attention and Ellie looked up to the pulpit.

"…in Matthew 24:6, it says '*And ye shall hear of wars and rumours of wars: see that ye be not troubled: for all these things must come to pass, but the end is not yet…*'"

Parishioners shifted in their seats, looked at their loved ones, undertones of fear and worry in their eyes. People had been talking about war for years and Ellie remembered it as far back as when she was a freshman. But with England now struggling to defend herself, and the German army only a few miles from Moscow, the pressure was on America, the last bulwark against the Nazi domination of Europe. For locals, the fear was less that American boys would have to fight to preserve freedom and democracy in the West, and more about the fact that many would die doing it. Ellie dreaded the possibility as much as anyone, but her reasons were more complicated and more personal. If America entered the War, Karl and his family would officially be enemies and it would extinguish the last ember of hope she had that he was coming back.

The organ played for the parting hymn and the congregation began to file out. Ellie stepped into the aisle, followed by her sister and then her mother and finally, Jack. As a child, she would always be next to her father, whether they were working in the yard, lazing at the beach or eating at the table. But at some point, the order had changed, a sign of the growing distance between them, and now whenever they were together, he was the farthest away.

When they came outside, people gathered on the lawn like they did each Sunday, separating into groups of acquaintances, friends, and neighbors, filling the air with the polite voices of greetings and small talk. Major Rowland was standing with his wife, and when Jack saw him, he walked over and they shook hands. Ellie was surprised they knew each other and she realized that Jack must have followed up with the lobster request. The men introduced each other's wives, exchanged a few pleasantries, and then the Major looked at Ellie.

"So, how're things at the sandwich shop?"

"It's only part-time…until I find something else."

His eyes narrowed like he suddenly thought of something.

"We're looking for a secretary at the base. Can you type?"

The question caught her off-guard, but she answered without hesitation.

"I can type. Quite well."

Of all the things she was confident about typing was near the top because she had taken it her senior year and even won an award.

"It pays about 75 cents an hour. What do you think?"

Ellie was so stunned she almost couldn't speak and when she glanced at her mother, Vera responded with an encouraging smile.

"I am very interested in the position and thankful for the opportunity."

The response sounded stiff but it was exactly what a job counselor had taught her to say in high school.

"Terrific," the Major said. "Stop by tomorrow after work."

His expression went from casual to businesslike and he turned to her father.

"Stop by too, Jack. We've got some things to talk about."

The remark got everyone's interest, but Jack deflected their curiosity by ending the conversation.

"Thanks, Major. Have a fine day."

They walked away as a family but then dispersed as Vera went to talk with some women from her church group and Mary ran over to Junebug. As Ellie made her way towards the street, Kate quickly caught up to her.

"I saw you talking with the Major?"

"Yes," Ellie said, still dazed.

"Everything okay?"

They stopped at the sidewalk and Ellie finally turned to her.

"He offered me a job…at the base."

"Oh, that's terrific news!" she said.

"It pays 75 cents an hour."

They heard a rumble and looked to see Ben Frazier's pickup coming towards them from the village. He pulled up and parked across the street, stepping out and waving hello but coming no further. Religious prejudice ran deep on Monk Island and Ellie knew he was uneasy around so many Congregationalists. People from the north side were Baptist, a faith that was considered lower-class, and while many believed it, Jack said it was like trying to distinguish between redfish and pogie—in the end, they were both just bait.

Ellie glanced over at Ben, who was leaning against the truck, his arms crossed.

"We're going to see a movie," she said. "Won't you join us?"

"C'mon, Ellie. I won't be a third wheel."

"Don't say that."

"I have to pack anyway. I'm going to visit my cousins in Harpswell."

"But you're leaving next weekend?"

"I'll be back on Friday," Kate said, looking over Ellie's shoulder, distracted. "He's handsomer than he used to be."

"Stop it."

"It must be you."

"Kate!"

Ellie stood squirming, blushing, and bursting out of her skin. She knew that Ben couldn't hear them, but the conversation seemed inappropriate in front of a church and she was always uncomfortable talking about such things. Finally, their eyes met and Kate made a mischievous smile.

"Go on," she said, "have fun."

......

Ellie and Ben sat in the darkness of the State Theater in downtown Portland watching the matinee Keep 'Em Flying. The Abbott & Costello film was a slapstick comedy, but the subject of the Army Air Corps was ominous because everyone had war on their minds. Ellie couldn't help but think of Karl, which was made more awkward by the fact that she had to fend off Ben's constant attempts to snuggle and kiss. But it was more the public display that repelled her because now she probably would have let him do it.

Since her talk with Kate at the beach on Thanksgiving, Ellie had decided to give Ben a chance, or at least stop resisting him. And something about that decision made him more attractive as if romance had more to do with choice than chemistry. She didn't love Ben, but that didn't mean she never would and, like her mother always said, sometimes it was just nice having a man around.

As much as Ellie enjoyed being out on a Sunday afternoon, however, she couldn't focus. A couple of times when the whole crowd laughed, she didn't and Ben asked if there was something wrong. She smiled and said no and it wasn't a lie. She was distracted by excitement over Major Rowland's offer and the only reason she hadn't told Ben was that she still couldn't believe it happened. She thought back to her years applying for jobs in the City—the letters, the waiting, the rejections—and for the first time felt vindicated for all her efforts. Monk Island didn't have a lot to offer a young woman and she knew that working for the government could lead to bigger opportunities. After years of frustration, she might finally have a chance at a career.

Suddenly, the movie stopped and the words "Universal Newsreel" appeared. Intermissions were common, but it was too early in the show and everyone looked around confused. After some dramatic opening music, "Japs Bomb USA" flashed across the screen and there was a collective gasp from the audience.

"We interrupt this program," a voice began, "to report that at approximately 8 am this morning, Sunday, December 7th, the Empire of Japan attacked American forces at Pearl Harbor on the Hawaiian Island of Oahu…"

The announcer continued to talk, but for Ellie, the rest was a blur. Even before the lights came on, people started to get out of their seats. Ben stood up and gave Ellie his hand and she took it without hesitation. There was no panic—no alarm. Everyone filed out of the theater with a stunned calm, almost like in slow motion, and when Ellie came into the bright, sun-lit lobby, she felt like she was walking in a dream. She was terrified beyond words, and yet she got some perverse relief in knowing that, after years of anticipation, the War had finally come to America.

26.

For Karl, the Gestapo was a last and final resort. In searching for his father, he had gone to the University Chancellor's office, the local police, the Civil Administration, and even the provincial Party headquarters. None had flatly turned him away, but in most cases, he was met with polite disregard, token respect for the uniform he wore and the Country he served. There were suggestions to fill out a complaint form, promises to look into it, a feigned concern which only added to his frustration and outrage. Navigating the intricacies of the Nazi bureaucracy was like going through a maze blindfolded. At every point, Karl sensed he was being manipulated, misled, lied to, and placated.

With his time to report to duty drawing near, he came to accept that there was no more he could do to find his father, but he was determined to save his mother. Her spirits had improved since he returned, which he attributed less to his own influence than to the fact that she had some human companionship. Mrs. Brink bathed most days, went out for groceries, kept the apartment clean. But much of it was the mindless momentum of drug-fueled vigor, and Karl saw what she was like without her Pervitin, frightened and fragile, as skittish as a colt and sometimes delusional. Even on the medication, her moods were unpredictable—some days she was alert and others she seemed unaware there was even a War going on. Karl didn't know how long she could continue the habit, but with shortages in everything from socks to salt, he feared another withdrawal might kill her or make her try to take her own life again.

"What about the tea set?"

Karl looked over to his mother, who knelt beside her suitcase in the living room, surrounded by more possessions than would fit, struggling to decide what to take and what to leave.

"Just clothing," Karl said, "and anything of value—jewelry, silver, gold."

"But your father gave it to me for our anniversary."

He stopped and turned again, and when he saw her pleading eyes, his sympathy overcame his sense.

"I can take the tea set, Mother."

While she continued to pack, Karl went into the bathroom to finish getting ready. He put on his dress shirt and jacket, adjusted his cap in the mirror. His hand trembled as he brushed his teeth and he even felt short of breath. In four days, he would be back on duty and he was as anxious about getting his mother to safety as he was about returning to war.

When he came out, Mrs. Brink had made pork sandwiches with leftover meat and stale bread, and although he tried to have one, he really had no appetite.

"Shouldn't we take this? For when your father joins us?"

She held out the stack of mail Professor Klug had given him at his father's office, a day which, by now, blended in with the weeks of deceit and dead ends. Karl gave her a reassuring smile like someone would a child who talked of imaginary things, because he didn't want to stifle her optimism. Considering the brutality of the Nazi prison system, he wasn't so sure his father would return, but naïve hope was better than no hope at all.

"Of course," he said, taking them.

Mrs. Brink had one last cup of tea and Karl sat on the couch and flipped through the letters. It was mostly junk, solicitations from book publishers, academic societies—a college bulletin and something from the University of Vienna. The date stamps went back over a year as if Mr. Brink was so discouraged he stopped opening his mail altogether.

At the bottom of the pile, Karl noticed a letter with an American postmark. He looked at the return address and scribbled in small, jittery handwriting was the name, John C. Hatch.

"Would you like coffee before we go?"

"No…thank you," he said, distracted.

Karl tore open the envelope and a tingle went up his back as he began to read.

Dear Dutch,

I hope this letter finds you well. Not a day passes that I don't regret the great disappointment I have caused you. It was my true intention, both as a friend and as a patron of humanity, to submit the documents of sponsorship so that you and your family might find safe harbor from the impending calamity abroad.

It pains me to say that my wayward living has finally caught up to me, and by the time you receive this letter, if you do, I may be well on my way to meeting my maker. While a late apology is never really an apology at all, I have undertaken to make up for any harm or hardship I have caused you through my inexcusable recklessness.

I, John C. Hatch, leave to you, Niklaus Brink or immediate descendants thereof, the sum total of half of my estate and worldly belongings. A copy of this letter has been forwarded to my attorney, whose name and address is stated below, to be included with my last will and testament.

Good friend, I will always remember our time at the University, and those cherished days together on Monk Island, when the sun was bright and we were young and life seemed never-ending.

Until we meet in heaven,
John

For a moment, it seemed as if time stopped, and Karl stared at the paper with a numb bewilderment. He had always resented Hatch for letting them down, but he knew that the visas were only a bit part in a wider tragedy and that their family's troubles were far too complex to lay the blame on just one person.

"Is something wrong?"

Karl looked up and his mother was watching from the kitchen. Karl shifted nervously on the couch and shoved the letter in his pocket.

"Nothing," he said. "Nothing important."

Mrs. Brink put on her coat and took one last look around the apartment. She went from the bedroom to the bathroom to the living room, and although Karl could tell she wanted to take more, there was no room and they were only allowed one suitcase per person.

Finally, she got the note she had written to her husband, telling him where they went, instructing him to join her when he gets out. She fixed it to the cabinet with slow and solemn precision, a single piece of tape at a time, across the top and down the sides, one small attempt at permanence in a period of destruction and disintegration. As sad as it was to watch her fret, Karl admired her determination and he let her dawdle until the lights flickered, a sign that a power outage was coming.

"Come, Mother," he said firmly. "We must go."

......

The train pulled out of the station just after midnight, creaking through the suburbs of Hamburg, lights low and with no signal bell. Karl leaned against the window, the cold radiating off the glass, and looked up at the black sky. In those first few minutes, he feared an air raid more than at any time before, knowing how the universe had a strange way of thwarting the noblest intentions of humans. When his mother told him the station was bombed in September, Karl was sure it was a miscalculation because RAF planes always avoided civilian targets. And although another strike was improbable, he held his breath until they were safely out of the City.

Soon two soldiers came into the cabin, helmets shining and carbines across their chests. When Karl felt his mother tense up, he held her hand and she glanced over with a trembling smile. Neither had said it, but they both felt like fugitives, a feeling Karl was sure many passengers had because, despite the semblance of routine, anyone on the overnight train was fleeing from or to somewhere.

The soldiers walked down the aisle, scanning the rows, their expressions cold. When one of the men saw Karl's uniform, he nodded and Karl only nodded back to not seem suspicious. But in truth, he was no longer proud to be in the armed services, and he was as relieved as his mother when they passed by.

Despite their apprehension, however, Karl knew they were doing nothing wrong and the visas for Switzerland were perfectly legal, a favor from Lieutenant Gruber who had offered to help if he could. Karl remembered the morning he called him, just days after his visit to the Gestapo and after realizing he would not find his father. Gruber agreed to get the documents and didn't ask questions, passing them to Karl in a public park in an act of secrecy that, if discovered, could have gotten them both arrested. Throughout his life, Karl never recalled his father having many friends—Mr. Brink was far too serious for socializing—and he was touched by Gruber's loyalty.

The visas were only valid for sixty days, but by then Karl would be back in the thick of combat, somewhere in the North Atlantic, a thousand miles out to sea. By remaining with her sister-in-law, Mrs. Brink would eventually be in violation and that was a crime. But Karl knew it wouldn't matter because Switzerland was a neutral country and local authorities wouldn't waste time and resources tracking down a middle-aged housewife who had flouted a German travel permit.

As the train rumbled through the countryside, Karl leaned back and tried to rest. But his thoughts raced and he couldn't be still, haunted by the bitter irony that the plan he had for his mother to overstay her visa to get to safety was the same thing he had begged his father to do back in America.

......

When Karl opened his eyes, his mother was already awake, staring ahead with her hands clasped, as prim and nonchalant as if she was on a city tramcar. He sat up and looked out to see scattered homes, open fields and, in the distance, the Alps, immersed in fog from one end of the horizon to the other. Just as the conductor announced their arrival, he looked ahead and saw a sign: Basel Badischer Bahnhof.

The train stopped and they got their things, following the crowd down the platform, the smell of morning in the air. It might have even been peaceful, Karl thought, except there were SS officers everywhere. With travel between Germany and Switzerland heavily restricted, it was a sensitive route and soldiers were on the lookout for spies, deserters, criminals and enemies of the State.

Although in Swiss territory, the Basel Baden station was owned by Germany. It was in a section of Basel north of the Rhine River which, if not for the complicated history of the two nations, would have been part of the Reich. Situated at the border, it was a strategic junction, used by everyone from Jews fleeing Nazi persecution to German troops on their way to the Italian front. Because Mr. Brink was born in Switzerland, Karl had been going there his whole life to visit relatives and it never felt like a separate country. As a young boy, he would not have imagined that someday he would be escorting his mother to safety amid a devastating war.

Mrs. Brink clung to Karl's arm as they approached the station and he saw more soldiers than he could count. Passengers were ushered into a long corridor, where visas and travel permits would be inspected. There were three desks and a couple of tables for searching bags. Karl and his mother stood in line for over an hour, and their only comfort was that it was warmer than in Hamburg.

Finally, an SS officer waved them over, looking twice when he noticed Karl's uniform.

"Wrong way to the front," he joked.

"I'll be there in two days."

Karl handed him their entry visas and the man examined them.

"What's your business in neutral Switzerland?" he asked, not looking up.

"I'm taking my mother to live with my aunt."

The officer curled his lips as if it was a good first response. As Karl waited, he glanced around and there were a dozen soldiers, both Wehrmacht and SS, standing by the doors leading into the main station.

"Names of your relations?"

"Peter and Monika Brink."

The man looked at Mrs. Brink then spoke to Karl.

"Brink? So, your father's relations?"

Karl nodded once.

"And where is he?"

Karl's heart began to race—his palms got sweaty. Anticipating the question, he had rehearsed the answer for days and was still stumped. If they knew his father was accused of political crimes, he and his mother would be detained at once. Every second he stalled felt like an hour, but he finally found the courage to lie.

"He's in hospital. He was injured in an air raid."

"In Hamburg?"

"Yes, Sir."

"And which air raid was that, Sailor?"

The skies over the City had been calm for a couple of months and it was obvious the officer knew. Yet Karl remembered what his mother mentioned the night he arrived, and he had never been so thankful to be listening.

"In September—Hauptbahnhof Station."

When the officer's expression softened, Karl knew he had passed the test, and without another word, the man stamped the visas and handed them back. He glanced at the service medals on Karl's shirt—the War Badge, Wound Badge, and Combat Clasp.

"Make haste, comrade," he said. "The stakes have just been raised."

Karl looked at him confused.

"The Japanese just attacked Pearl Harbor. We'll be at war with America soon, no doubt."

27

Karl slept on and off throughout the night. In Paris, he made his connection with only seconds to spare. They were delayed for three hours outside Rennes because the Resistance left two automobiles on the tracks in a failed sabotage. Unlike the provincial route, the train to Brittany was mostly soldiers and if it weren't for a few young families with children, it could have been mistaken for a military transport line. The men were from all branches of the Wehrmacht, destined for garrisons up and down the French coast.

By the time they pulled in, it was late afternoon and Karl got a strange relief when he saw the sign for Gare de Lorient. The weather was cold and rainy and he didn't have an umbrella so he rushed down the platform and through the station. When he came out front, he stood beneath the veranda and looked around for a military shuttle.

"Taxi, Monsieur?"

Karl turned and a man was holding open the backdoor of a car.

"Keromen," he said.

The driver smiled, but Karl gave him a stern, almost threatening, look. Servicing the enemy was controversial in occupied France and many cabbies wouldn't do it. The Resistance often used taxis as a ruse to kidnap Germans traveling alone and every soldier had to be careful. When Karl got in and saw the driver's ID card on the dash, his suspicions faded.

They pulled out of the station and headed south on the outskirts of the old town, following the River Scorff towards the coast. Karl didn't have to show up until morning, but after the loss of his boat and his coincidental survival, he wanted to report on his condition and confirm his orders.

"Were you home on leave?" the drive asked and Karl looked up.

"Yes, for a few weeks."

"You heard about the Japanese?"

Karl never liked to talk about the War with French civilians, but the news was something no one could avoid.

"Quite a surprise for the Americans, I'd say."

The driver spoke in German, but Karl answered in French, as much as a gesture of goodwill as because the man's language skills were poor.

"My son went to Heidelberg University," he said, smiling in the rear-view. "My daughter-in-law is from Mannheim."

Karl gazed out the window thinking. Somedays it seemed everyone he met had some connection to Germany. The people of Europe had lived together for millennia, mixing and migrating, and the lines between nations were as absurd as they were arbitrary.

"Perhaps we are cousins," he said and the man grinned.

They passed through an area of warehouses and abandoned factories and beyond Karl could see the giant bunkers of the U-boat pens. He forgot how impressive they were and, despite his ambivalence towards the War, he felt a surge of national pride.

The road ran along a wide, open expanse that was mostly cement lots and grass fields. They approached the guard post and slowed to a stop. Three soldiers stood at the barricade, dressed in heavy parkas, machine guns at their waists. They looked no happier to be out in the rainstorm than Karl was to be back on duty. One of them walked over and Karl rolled down his window.

"Identifizieren Sie sich!" the guard barked.

When Karl held out his identification card, the man glanced at it coolly and then waved them through. Karl pointed towards an administrative building in the distance and the driver went towards it. He paid with his last remaining Francs, grabbed his duffle bag and ran for the entrance, coming into a small lobby that was warm and stuffy.

"May I help you, Sailor?"

Seated behind a desk was a staff officer.

"Reporting for duty," Karl said with a delayed salute. "After injury."

The man reached for a large binder and opened it.

"2nd U-boat Flotilla," Karl said before the man could ask.

"Boat?"

"U-206."

The officer stopped and looked up and their eyes met. In the ethos of war, there was little tolerance for sympathy, but his surprise was consolation enough.

"I was injured in a raid...off-duty," Karl explained.

The man went back to the binder and spoke under his breath.

"And lucky for that."

He ran his finger up and down, flipping through the pages, and Karl looked around the room while he waited. The walls were exposed brick and heating pipes ran across the ceiling. The offices had been converted from an old factory and, like everything else on the base, were in a constant state of repair.

The moment the officer found the assignment, Karl heard footsteps in the hallway.

"You're on U-130."

"Brink!" someone growled and they both turned.

When Karl looked over, he almost couldn't believe his eyes. Standing in the doorway was Schmitt, the overweight bully from his old boat. His beard was thicker, but he still had the same crooked jaw, the same snide expression.

"Herr Oberbootsmann," Karl said, stumbling. "You are…here?"

It was the first time he was ever disappointed to find out someone had lived. Nevertheless, he faced the officer and gave him an earnest salute.

"Providence has saved us both for other things," Schmitt said.

When he came closer, his eyes were glassy and there was booze on his breath.

"We all have our time."

The staff officer listened, but he didn't really seem interested in hearing two sailors philosophize about their fates.

"And it seems we shall hunt together again"

He gave Karl a wink that was meant to be chummy but was somehow hostile. Then he reached in his pocket, pulled out a flask and took a swig.

"U-130?"

"An iron beast," Schmitt said, wiping his mouth on his sleeve. "Class IXC. 15,000 miles. Could sail from here to New Zealand."

"Although they would seem an unlikely enemy," Karl said and even the staff officer chuckled. "Have we our orders yet, Herr Oberbootsmann?"

It was a bold question and Karl only dared ask because Schmitt was drunk. Patrols were highly classified, but in the close quarters of Kriegsmarine comradery, there were always leaks and rumors.

"Orders?"

He gave Karl a sharp, suspicious look and then broke into laughter.

"Bring your galoshes, Sailor."

Karl frowned in confusion, but he didn't press him, knowing that someone as arrogant as Schmitt would talk willingly.

"We're going across the pond. To America."

......

Karl swam furiously through the morning surf. The waves were gentle, but the water was close to freezing and he had to move fast to keep his body temperature up. As a young boy, he was introduced to ice swimming by an uncle in Bavaria and it gave him a tolerance for the cold that his competitors didn't have. The first few minutes were always excruciating, but once the chill subsided it was bliss.

Karl stopped for a moment and waded in the water. With his eyes at the surface, he looked and saw a U-boat steaming out from the mouth of Blavet River. Soon it would open its ballasts and slip beneath the sea. In the morning, he would be out there too, on a patrol that would take him three thousand miles across the ocean. Germany wasn't at war with America yet, but everyone expected a declaration soon because Hitler never wasted any time going on the offensive.

Karl turned and headed in, the tide carrying him the last stretch to the shore. He tore off his goggles and ran to get a blanket. Once he was warm and dry, he sat in the sand with his arms around his knees and gazed out. It was the last time he would be alone for weeks and he used it to reflect. He thought about how everything he had ever loved was somehow connected to the water, whether it was Ellie or swimming or those summers spent on the beaches of Lübeck as a child. He decided then that his life would either be saved by or end with the sea.

Karl's first thoughts of deserting the Kriegsmarine were never even clear to him. They started out like daydreams, small flashes of speculation, hypothetical musings. But the worse things got, the more real the fantasy became and it soon took on a life of its own. Karl's father had been humiliated and was now imprisoned; his mother had been driven to insanity by the years of stress and harassment. Even Karl, just a boy when the Nazis came to power, had his dreams of making the Olympic swim team stolen because of who his father was. In the sum total of all these injustices, Karl came to a grave conclusion: he wasn't abandoning his country—his country had abandoned him.

Karl changed behind the rocks and put his swim gear in a bag. The cold did strange things to the body and he shivered more with clothing on than he did without it. He crawled over the sand dunes to a small road that ran along the coast, through the village of Larmor-Plage and on to Lorient. As he walked, he held out his thumb for a ride, but not a single car went by.

By the time he got back to town, it was late morning and he went straight to the Hotel Beau Sejour, a 40-room building that had been commandeered for enlisted men after the base was finished. As he approached his room, the hallway was cluttered with helmets, boots, towels, and rations boxes. He stepped over a case of empty wine bottles and opened the door. Exhausted, he wanted to lie down for a nap, but roll call was at 5 am and there was much work to do. He reached in his storage trunk for a notebook and pen and sat at the edge of the bed.

Almost as a last will and testament, Karl wrote three letters. The first was to his mother in Switzerland, telling her how much he loved her and promising to come back after the War. The second was to his uncle in Bremen, explaining what he knew about his father's situation and asking him to continue the search.

Lastly, Karl wrote to Eleanor Ames and it was as much a prayer as it was a letter because he wasn't sure she would even receive it. It could have taken longer, but he had been thinking of what to say for weeks and the words flowed as easily as if he was talking right to her. Thinking back, that summer on Monk Island was the happiest time in his life and if he had any reason to persevere, it was for that vague hope that they might someday be together again. When Karl licked the glue and shut the envelope, he had sealed his fate and knew there was no going back.

......

The streets of Lorient stank of cordite and ash. Unable to destroy the U-Boat bunkers along the river, British warplanes focused on the town itself and in the time Karl was away, it had been bombed six times. He saw demolished buildings everywhere, collapsed in on themselves in piles of blackened rubble. The resentment of the local population had turned to rage and Karl could sense people glaring as he went by. He was ashamed at all the devastation and he no longer supported the War, but for now, he was still the enemy. His heart pounded and he grew paranoid, walking faster and looking constantly over his shoulder. Finally, he cut through a park and when he came out the other side, he saw a sign: La Poste.

He walked in and a bell above the door jingled. A woman looked up from the counter and her expression soured when she realized it was a German sailor.

"Bonjour," she said halfheartedly.

"Bonjour."

Karl looked around and the room was cluttered with boxes, packages, bins of mail. It was too small to be the only post office in Lorient and he hoped it was the right one.

"I'm looking for a young woman," he said.

The clerk rolled her eyes.

"Aren't you all?" she said bitterly and Karl understood why. Since the invasion, German soldiers were notorious for their mistreatment of French girls and it was a national outrage.

"It's not like that. We're merely friends."

Karl gave her a pleading smile and her attitude softened.

"Lots of girls work here."

"About this tall," he said, holding up his hand. "Dark hair, very dark."

It had only been a month since the bombing at the Café Duvall, but much had happened and he couldn't remember her name.

"Monika?"

"Yes, Monika!" he said and the clerk seemed amused by his reaction. "That's her."

"She's at lunch."

"When is she due back?"

The woman glanced at the wall clock.

"40 minutes or so."

"Thank you."

Karl left the post office and went to sit on a park bench. At a nearby café, he saw a group of Wehrmacht soldiers laughing and drinking wine. It was a lovely late-fall afternoon, the trees bare but the air cool and invigorating. With people out shopping, it reminded Karl of weekends in Hamburg, long before the War, when he was a boy and life was simpler.

If he had closed his eyes for a second, he might have missed her, but when he peered across the street, he noticed a young woman coming down the sidewalk. He waited until she was closer and realized that it was Monika. Karl got up and crossed the street diagonally to head her off, moving just fast enough to get to her without drawing attention—the War made everyone suspicious. As he approached, she must have heard his footsteps because she turned around.

"Monika?"

She stopped on the curb and squinted.

"It's Karl," he said in French, "from Café Duvall."

"Karl?" she said and quickly came over. "Oh, my God, Karl."

"How are you?"

She was just like he remembered, with black hair and small lips. For him, there weren't many women as beautiful as Ellie, but Monika was a close second.

"I thought—"

"I know. I was spared."

"You were still in the hospital?"

"No, home in Germany. I was notified by telegram."

"I see," she said, looking down sadly.

"How is your friend?"

"Camille was upset about Reinhard, of course. But they didn't know each other very long."

"I'd say they would have made a fine couple."

Monika's lips tightened, but she held back her emotion and Karl understood why. Sentiment was so rare in wartime that, like all the necessities of life, it had to be rationed and conserved.

"I need a favor," Karl said and she listened. "I'm leaving tomorrow on patrol—a long patrol. I need to send a letter to America."

Monika glanced up and down the sidewalk and then stepped forward, lowering her voice.

"That's impossible."

"We're not at war."

"Yet."

"Yet."

She thought for a moment, made a cute smirk.

"Is it for a girl?"

Something about her warmth and sincerity made him want to explain everything. Karl had gone years without having someone to confide in and his life was like a great secret unshared. But he knew the relief would have been temporary and it was safer for them both if he didn't.

"Yes," was all he said.

"I've heard that post is still going out of Vichy through Portugal. I'm going to Limoges tomorrow for training. I could mail it."

"What about censors?"

"Is this espionage?"

He started to laugh until he realized she wasn't joking.

"No, no," he said. "Just personal."

"I can't promise, but it might get through."

Karl looked around and then reached in his coat. He handed her the letter and she put it in her purse. Any excitement was tempered by caution, however, because he knew that the delivery could be hampered for a thousand reasons, including a declaration of war between America and Germany. But his entire plan was a longshot and all he could do was try.

"Thank you," Karl said humbly.

"Now I must go."

Monika leaned in and they exchanged kisses on the cheeks. She backed away with a pretty smile and he got sad as he watched her go, knowing they would never see each other again. They locked eyes for as long as possible, then she turned around and was gone.

28

War changed everything on Monk Island. The backshore was abruptly closed, guarded by soldiers with machine guns, and residents could no longer use Passamaquoddy Road unless they lived there. Patrol boats cruised up and down the coast and one was stationed at the mouth of Taylor Passage. The military dock beside the ferry terminal was hastily completed, the volume of men and equipment growing each day. Trucks drove from the waterfront to the base with increasing fury, putting a strain on roads that were built for horse-and-carriage. The harbor was now cluttered with Liberty ships, fresh off the production line and ready to bring soldiers and supplies to England. For children, all the commotion was exciting and for adults, it could be disturbing. But regardless of how people felt, there was no doubt that the days of quiet island life were over.

Aside from the sheer shock, the period following Pearl Harbor was a confusing time, especially for those who lived through the Great War. Germans were a familiar enemy, but the Japanese were so exotic that no one really knew how to hate them, and even Jack lacked a suitable slur, referring to them simply as "Oriental bastards." But if locals didn't know how to react, they certainly knew how to prepare, hoarding food and supplies like it was the End Times. The butcher and grocer struggled to keep up with demand and Lavery's was sold out of rifle ammo. Posters appeared around the village to be on the lookout for suspicious activity, and residents were advised not to be out late. They were mainly suggestions, but people treated them like official decrees and the streets were desolate after dark.

For Ellie, the timing of her new job couldn't have been worse because things were in chaos as the coastal outpost transitioned into a full-on operations center. But she knew she wouldn't have been hired if there wasn't a base and there wouldn't have been a base if the American government didn't expect a war. So, in some ways, all was going according to plan. Pearl Harbor also settled any qualms Ellie had before, the stigma of working at a place which many residents opposed. After the attack, however, attitudes changed and it would have been hard to find someone who didn't feel safer with the Army around.

Although it had only been three days, Ellie loved the work and her salary was more than she would make in Portland or Boston. The hardest part about taking the job was quitting Lavery's, but when she told Mr. Mallet, he reacted with his typical good faith, congratulating her and even giving her the last day off with pay.

There were two other secretaries in the office; Lydia was from Massachusetts and Jane, as the wife of a Captain, was from everywhere. Other civilians worked on the base too, but Ellie felt like the only local and she had yet to recognize anyone else from Monk Island. She worked quietly throughout the day, typing out memoranda, requisitions, announcements, and all the other communications of military administration. It was entirely operational and she wasn't exposed to any tactics or intelligence, which were done at command headquarters inside the fortress. Somedays it was more excitement than Ellie could handle and her life had gone from monotonous to meaningful overnight.

"How're you managing, Eleanor?"

When she looked up, Major Rowland was standing in his overcoat and hat as if getting ready to leave. Aside from an aunt in Freeport, he was the only person who called her Eleanor, the name she had introduced herself as when he first walked into the shop.

"The typewriter keeps jamming," she said, adjusting the tape, "but otherwise well."

"Those came up from Fort Devens. I'll see if I can get you one of the new Remingtons."

She looked up with a businesslike smile—no one had told her who her boss was so she always assumed it was him.

"Thank you."

Rowland made a curt smile, walked out the side door, and Ellie watched through the window as he went down the back stairs. When he reached the driveway, he turned to greet someone and Ellie was surprised to see Ben, dressed in his work clothes and boots.

"Ellie?"

Interrupted, she looked and saw Jane coming towards her.

"Could you make copies of these press releases?" she said.

"Of course."

Jane put them on her desk, walked away, and when Ellie looked back out the window, Ben and the Major were gone. She finished her work and, with some time still remaining, she tidied up her desk. Ellie wasn't used to a fixed schedule and there was something comforting in the regimentation. When she worked with her father, the hours fluctuated according to the day and season, and even at Lavery's, she never knew when she was getting out. But things were different as a secretary and, for the first time in her life, she felt like a respectable adult.

At precisely 5 pm, Ellie got her coat, hat, and pocketbook, and said goodbye to her colleagues. She walked out of the building, a newly constructed one-story structure whose corrugated roof reminded her of the fish warehouses in the City. Out front, there was a large unpaved lot, with row after row of Army trucks, utility vehicles, and staff cars. She waited in the cold but didn't mind because she had been indoors all day. A couple of minutes later, Ben's pickup pulled up. When she got in, the cabin reeked of fish and saltwater, and she realized she was losing her resistance to the smell.

"Chilly out there."

"It's good for the circulation," Ellie said, repeating what her mother always said.

"How was work?"

"A dream. The staff are lovely."

They pulled out of the lot and followed a long access road that had been cut through the woods and marsh. When Ben slowed down at the first checkpoint, a soldier waved him through and they came out to the backshore, where the ocean was a haze of gray and tumultuous chop. They turned right onto Passamaquoddy Road and continued along the coast, the wind so strong that the glass was soon covered in sea spray.

"I saw you talking with Major Rowland," Ellie said.

Ben's expression changed and he seemed almost flustered.

"Right,' he said. "Um, Coast Guard's dropping U-boat nets. Jack wanted me to ask if we can still use Taylor Passage."

"U-boat nets?"

"That's right. Big steel nets to keep them out of the harbor. The Army's putting them between all the islands."

Ellie glanced out to the horizon, dark and getting darker in the early dusk.

"Do you really think they're out there?" she mused.

"Maybe not now, but they will be soon."

They went through a second guard post, came around the bend at Drake's Cove, and went up the hill, stopping in front of the Ames' house. As Ellie reached for her pocketbook, she knew Ben was watching her and the tension of his yearning made her feel womanly and wanted.

"Well, then," he said.

They faced each other in a moment of awkward silence and Ellie got a subtle thrill in not knowing what was to come. But before Ben could say or do anything, she leaned forward and pressed her lips to his. He was so excited that he accidentally let his foot off the brake and they rolled back a few feet before he caught it.

"See you tomorrow?"

"Yeah," he said, breathless, nodding. "Tomorrow."

She got out, gently closed the door, and waved with a pretty smile. Ben drove off and Ellie stood thinking long after he was gone. It was the first time they kissed and although she didn't see stars, she certainly felt the vastness of the universe and all its possibilities. With a new job and someone who doted on her, she was reinvigorated by life, and although she didn't know what her future was, she felt like she had one again.

As Ellie passed the letterbox, she opened it out of habit and not because she expected anything. Living on Monk Island was like being in the outback and they went weeks without mail. But when she looked in, she was surprised to see a letter. She took it out and the moment she saw the markings, she got dizzy. Stamped across the front were the words *Par Avion*, followed by the handwriting of a man and she had no doubt that it was from Karl. As she walked up to the porch, she tried to peel open the seal, but her hands and fingers trembled out of control.

"Ellie?"

She looked up and her mother was standing in the doorway.

"Dinner's almost ready. Have you seen your father?"

"I haven't," she said, tucking the letter under her arm.

"You're pale as a sheet. Is something wrong?"

"Just tired, Mother."

Ellie edged by her and into the parlor, and she could feel her mother watching as she went up the stairs. When she got to the bedroom, she closed the door and locked it. She dropped her pocketbook, sat on her bed and stared at the letter, as frightened of its content as she was of how she would react to it. Ellie had waited months and years for Karl to come back, and when he didn't, she continued to wait some more. She discovered then a strange irony of fate: the moment hope was abandoned was the moment it was restored. She thought back to all those dreams of moving to the mainland, of getting married, of having a family, of forging a new life together, far from the trappings of their troubled pasts. At the time it seemed like a fairytale, and it was because it never happened. Now she had finally reached a place where she was content to be ordinary and by opening the letter, she somehow knew that would all change in an instant.

Ellie tore apart the envelope, unfolded the note, and even before she read the first sentence, tears were streaming down her cheeks.

My Dear Ellie,

Much has happened since our cherished time together. After we arrived home, the grand course of events made it impossible to return to you. I thought often of writing but feared that it would only create the illusion of hope where there was none.

Not a day passes that I don't think of you. I cannot tell you where I am, only to say that I am doing important business. And although I am safe for the moment, the same is not true for my family. Things here are difficult, as you may well imagine, and the world has been turned upside down.

Soon I will be embarking on a long journey that will bring me close. I could not bear the regret of being so near and not seeing you, so I have decided to come back. I don't know precisely when, but it may be sooner than you think.

If providence sees fit that you receive this letter, know that I am out there and watch for me always. I am, at last, returning.

With Love,
K.

Ellie sat in a cold sweat, the letter tight to her chest, her heart pounding. To finally hear from Karl after all this time was the most terrible joy she had ever known. His words were vague, but the sentiments were clear, and like a person trapped behind a wall, he was trying to communicate something without saying it. She read the note over and over again, searching for a clue, trying to understand what he meant in saying he had *decided to come back*.

"Ellie?" her mother yelled up. "Dinner!"

She jumped up, wiped her eyes, and shoved the letter in her jewelry box.

"Be right down."

When Ellie came into the kitchen, Mary was at the table fidgeting with her binoculars and Vera was taking a meatloaf out of the oven. She sat down carefully, so dazed that she was afraid she might knock something over. A few minutes later, Jack walked in with a newspaper under his arm, his beard full and trimmed. He smiled at Mary and nodded to Ellie, the most attention he had given her in days. Like everyone in the family, she never asked him about business, but she knew that lobster prices were up and it seemed to lighten his mood.

Vera cut the meatloaf and put it on the table beside the green beans and carrots. She sat down, they filled their plates, and everyone bowed their heads for grace. They could go weeks without praying, but with America now mobilizing and Christmas approaching, it seemed proper in every way.

"Germany and Italy declared war on us," Jack said and his wife glanced up.

"Wasn't that expected?"

"Hitler and Mussolini are friends," Mary said and Vera smiled.

"It's more complicated than that, Dear."

The conversation ended with the first bite. They always ate quietly but tonight Ellie found the silence unbearable. Her mind raced with thoughts of Karl and the letter which expressed so much but told so little. A range of emotions, some tender and some tormenting, filled her soul and although she wanted to shout out the news to everyone, she was forced to keep it all in.

"Are you alright?" her mother said, but Ellie deflected her attention.

"I saw Ben talking to Major Rowland at the base today."

Jack stopped chewing and looked up.

"Probably about the Civil Defense unit we're forming."

Ellie cleared her throat and spoke plainly, realizing she had caught him in a lie.

"He said you told him to ask about the U-boat nets."

"Civil Defense?" Vera said.

When Jack rushed to explain, Ellie could tell he wanted to change the subject.

"That's right. Any able-bodied man can join. We got our first meeting tonight."

"What's a *Civil Defense*?" Mary said, her lisp mangling the words.

"We walk around and keep an eye on things. Make sure everyone's safe."

"Why wouldn't we be safe?" Mary said.

Ellie looked at her mother, who looked at Jack, who averted his eyes. However fractured they were as a family, they were united in their determination to protect Mary from the harsher realities of life and for Jack, it was almost a mission. So he was stumped by the question, more than the others, and behind his wrinkled and wind-chapped face, Ellie could sense a deeper distress. When he finally went to answer, Vera saved him by speaking first.

251

"Never mind," she said to Mary. "Just finish your carrots."

After dinner, Jack walked upstairs and Mary went into the parlor to do her homework. Ellie and her mother washed the dishes, wrapped the leftovers and wiped down the table and counter. The movement kept Ellie distracted, but as they got close to finishing, the panic over Karl's letter gradually returned. She was only spared the tyranny of her thoughts when her father came into the kitchen and surprised them both.

"Jack?" Vera said, turning around, aghast.

On his head was a white helmet—around his sleeve, an armband with a circle and a lightning bolt. He also had something in his hand that looked like rolled-up tar paper. He tossed it on the table and Ellie and her mother both flinched.

"What's this?"

"Blackout shades."

Vera wiped her hands on her apron, spoke in a soft and worried tone.

"Blackout shades? Now, why on earth would we need those?"

"Enemy planes, submarines," Jack said, adjusting the strap on his helmet. "This is a real war now, Vera."

29

"Prepare to surface!"

Karl startled awake—the voice tube was right over his head. Crouched in the tiny bunk, he threw off the moldy blanket and climbed out. Men moved groggily between the compartments and many were still in their bunks. On his last boat, there was never time to sleep because they were always on the attack. But things were different now and, with their first trip across the Atlantic, all anyone could do was hunker down and wait.

They hadn't been officially told they were going to America, but by now everyone knew it. There was so much food that the floor was covered in tins and the crew had to put planks across them to walk. Blocks of cheese and sacks of potatoes hung from the ceiling—bags of flour were stuffed between the torpedoes. They had only been out for four days and would never have stopped for fuel if it was a routine patrol.

Karl put on his coat and hat and stood to attention as Oberbootsmann Schmitt came down the aisle.

"One hour on deck," he shouted, "while we refuel."

As he walked through, he looked every sailor in the eye.

"Excuse me, Herr Oberbootsmann," someone said. "Where are we?"

Schmitt spun around.

"Somewhere in the Atlantic."

Another man said, "When do we depart?"

Schmitt turned again, but it didn't matter who asked because he spoke to everybody.

"When the Captain says so. Now, any more questions?"

The men all shook their heads and got back to work. Ten minutes later, the engines went into low idle and the boat stopped moving. The main hatch was opened, sending a cool gust through the entire cabin, and Karl walked wearily towards the conning tower to get in line. He had been cooped up for four days, deprived of sunlight and clean air, trapped in a netherworld of darkness and diesel fumes, unaware of time and space. The brackish water gave him heartburn—the combination of protein-rich food and no movement made him so constipated his back hurt. Karl was relieved to be getting out, but any excitement was tempered in knowing that it wouldn't be for very long.

He reached the front of the queue and Schmitt was standing at the ladder, directing the exit. When the last man reached the top of the tower, he looked at Karl.

"Out!" he barked.

Karl grabbed the rails and started to ascend, as curious as he was enthralled to see the sky. He knew they weren't anywhere near America—it would take two weeks to get there—and they had gone too far for it to be the refueling stations in Spain.

"Welcome to the Azores, Sailor," an officer said, giving him a hand out.

Karl squinted in the sun and looked around to see white-washed homes with red-tiled roofs, rolling green mountains. The Captain was standing at the bridge with the Oberleutnant and Watch Officer and they passed binoculars among them. Karl went down a small ladder and onto the deck, where the men were tying off the boat. Below on the pier, dockworkers helped the Engineer connect the fuel hose and over at a promenade, some local girls were sitting on a bench, smiling and waving flirtatiously. After four days of undersea isolation, the scene was heavenly and Karl stretched his arms with a deep yawn.

"Reminds me of the Caribbean," he heard and when he turned around it was one of the officers.

"You've been?"

The man took a haul of his cigarette, blew it out and nodded.

"Barbados. My grandmother owned a farm there."

"It reminds me of Maine," Karl said.

"You've been?"

Karl rubbed the stubble on his chin and looked out dreamily.

"I knew a girl there once."

"A long way to travel for love, Sailor. And no less risky."

Karl chuckled to himself, his eyes fixated on some hill in the distance.

"My father taught a course at the University of Maine. We spent a summer there…before the War."

The officer lit another cigarette, his third in as many minutes. With smoking prohibited inside, crewmembers used the opportunity to get as much nicotine as they could.

"You're a regular American then," he said playfully. "I'll call you Amerikaner."

"I should think the crew won't like it."

They heard a scuffle and looked over. Someone had crafted a football from a canvas sack and towels and the men were kicking it across the narrow deck. The ball suddenly came at Karl and he lunged to stop it from going over. If there were teams, he couldn't distinguish them so he just aimed with his foot and sent the ball flying to someone at the farthest point of the bow.

"Nice pass, Amerikaner!" the Officer said.

Everyone seemed impressed and even Karl was surprised by his accuracy. Swimming had always been his best sport, but football wasn't far behind and he had played for six years in school.

"Obersteuermann Vogel?!"

Karl and the Officer turned and when they saw Captain Dietz calling them, they immediately went up the ladder to the bridge.

"Herr Kapitän," the Officer said, standing up straight.

"What's this 'Amerikaner?'"

Everyone on the bridge grinned, including Karl, who was more nervous than amused.

"The name I have Christened my comrade," the Officer said, glancing over at Karl.

"And tell me why that is, Herr Obersteuermann."

With his thick beard and intense eyes, the Captain always seemed stern, but Karl could tell by his subtle smirk that he also had a sense of humor.

"Because he's spent much time in America."

Karl cringed. His time on Monk Island was barely two months, but he was too junior to contradict what the Officer said.

"Where in America?" the Captain asked.

"The State of Maine, Herr Kapitän," Karl said, "for my father's work."

Dietz looked at his Lieutenants and they acknowledged the fact with mild interest.

"What's your name, Sailor?"

"Brink, Sir. Karl Brink."

"Well, tell me something, Herr Brink," the Captain said. He took Karl by the arm, guided him to the edge of the bridge, and gave him the binoculars. "Is this a familiar sight?"

Karl held them up and looked out. At first, he saw only the other piers of the crowded seaport, lined with trawlers, cargo boats, a ferry. But as he adjusted the knob, he noticed a ship a quarter of a mile down the coast. Obscured by a warehouse, its gray stern stuck out and when Karl saw anti-aircraft guns, he froze.

Seeing his reaction, the Captain and the other Officers laughed.

"British?"

Captain Dietz shook his head.

"American. Destroyer," he said, "and we don't expect they are alone."

Karl handed him back the binoculars back and stood stunned.

"Don't worry, Sailor," Dietz said and he patted Karl's shoulder. "Portugal is neutral, the Americans won't attack. They're just here to get fuel too. Think of it like we are sharing the same woman—"

"Herr Kapitän," they heard and Schmitt was calling from the deck. "Water holds replenished, fuel tanks full."

As he spoke, he saw Karl and his expression soured.

"Assemble the crew for boarding," Dietz ordered.

Karl and the Officer were already beside the hatch, but they had to return to the deck for a formal roll call. As Karl stepped down the ladder, the Captain said, "Amerikaner..." and he turned around. "Your experience may come in handy."

"I should hope to be of service, Herr Kapitän," Karl said.
Dietz made a big, satisfied smile.
"As you shall, Sailor."

30

Standing at the sink, Ellie looked out the window and down the hill, where she saw the light on in Kate's bedroom and knew she was back from visiting relatives in Harpswell. She finished cleaning the last pan and quickly wiped her hands. As she rushed go, her mother came out of the pantry holding Scuttles.

"Where're you off to?"

"Kate," was all Ellie could say.

She came into the parlor and Jack was putting more logs on the fire. He had been out on the water all day and was still in his work clothes. With the weather expected to get worse, he and Ben had to haul all the traps, whether they were full or not. As she put on her coat, she saw his helmet and armband on the table and knew he was getting ready to go out on patrol. Tonight was the first blackout drill on Monk Island, an order that not everyone was happy about, but with which all residents were expected to comply.

Her father glanced over like he was going to say something and when he didn't Ellie attributed it to a protective reflex from when she was younger. For the most part, he no longer interfered in her affairs, and although they still didn't speak much, she knew he was content that she had a job and was dating Ben.

Ellie mumbled goodbye and walked out. With the overcast sky, there were no stars and the shore was a stretch of impenetrable blackness, broken only by the occasional sliver of light through a curtain or shade. More than dark, it was eerily quiet, quieter than Ellie had ever heard it before. She picked up the pace, eager to talk to Kate because the past five days she had lived with the secret of Karl's letter.

Ellie turned into the Mallet's yard and tiptoed down the side of the house. She tapped on the glass and moments later, Kate opened the window.

"You scared the Dicken's out of me!" she whispered.

"You gotta have the shade down. It's a blackout."

"What do I care? I'm gone tomorrow. What are you doing?"

Ellie peered up, her eyes wide and lips pressed together, as serious as she could be.

"I got a letter."

"A letter?"

"From him."

"Meet me in back."

Ellie walked to the rear door and Kate opened it and waved her in.

"Kate, is that you?" Joe Mallet called from upstairs.

"Just getting some biscuits, Daddy."

They went into the bedroom and Ellie reached in her coat and gave Kate the letter. They sat on the bed and she read it by candlelight. As Ellie waited for her to finish, she looked around and saw Kate's suitcase against the wall, open and fully packed, her Army uniform on top.

"Unreal," Kate said. "When did it come?"

"Monday."

She turned to Ellie, grabbed her by the arm.

"You can't show this to anybody. He's German and we're at war."

"You don't think I know that?" she snapped.

Kate made an apologetic smile, looked at the letter again, and as she read the words aloud, they were as jarring as when Ellie first saw them.

"What could he mean *I am, at last, returning?*"

Their eyes locked and Ellie shook her head with a slow intensity.

"I can't even imagine."

But she had imagined and all the scenarios she came up with were farfetched. Maybe Karl and his family never went back to Germany and were living somewhere on the mainland. But that wouldn't explain the foreign airmail stamp or the fact that he didn't contact her until now. She wondered too if he had escaped to unoccupied France and was trying to get to England for asylum. If that was true, however, there was no reason for him to think the British government would send him to America. She even considered that he had been hired before the War by some international firm, perhaps in Latin America, and that his work would bring him to Boston or New York. But that was the most implausible of all because Karl had no experience or interest in business.

Suddenly, there was a knock at the window.

"Who the hell is that?!"

Kate handed Ellie the letter and went over to open it.

"Ben?"

"You need to have your shades down."

Benjamin Frazier stood in the darkness in his Civil Defense helmet and armband, a flashlight in one hand and a whistle around his neck.

"Sorry, I—"

"There's a blackout in effect," he interrupted.

He spoke like he was giving an order and Ellie could see that Kate was offended. He had only been with the Civil Defense for a week but seemed to delight in his authority in a way that Ellie had never seen before. Before it got heated, she rushed over and knelt in the window, keeping Karl's letter hidden behind her back.

"Hello, Ben."

"Ellie?" he said, and instantly his tone softened.

"Kate's leaving in the morning."

"She needs to have her shade down."

"She knows that," Ellie said, with a firm but friendly smile.

She heard voices on the hillside, but when she looked she couldn't see anyone. Nevertheless, she knew her father was out there among them, enforcing the blackout in the cold, surveilling the shore for anything suspicious.

"Ellie?" Ben said, and she looked back down. "There's Christmas dance at Recreation Hall tomorrow night. It's for enlisted men, but they invited the CD…"

She nodded as she listened and it took her a moment to realize that he meant the Civil Defense.

"…Would you go?"

Ellie had been seeing him for a couple of months, a relationship that had gone from nothing to something, and a dance at the Army base seemed like a public acknowledgment, especially because people from work would be there. But Karl's letter changed everything, and regardless of what it meant, it made her realize that her time with Ben was motived more by sympathy and loneliness than by any true feelings of attraction. She was ashamed to have been so dishonest, both to him and to herself, but she didn't have the strength to say it.

262

"Of course I'll go."

......

Ellie and Kate stood on the pier at dawn, the frigid wind in their faces. Through the gray haze of morning, they watched as the ferry came slowly towards them from Portland. The sky was overcast all the way to the horizon and the smell of snow was in the air. In the distance, smoke rose from the shipyards of South Portland, and throughout the harbor, new Liberty ships were stacked side to side in a clutter of military mass production.

"I bet you don't miss that," Kate said, nodding.

When Ellie looked over at the docks, her father and Ben were covering the traps and securing the lines and bumpers, preparing for the first storm of winter.

"It's honorable work," Ellie said, feeling unusually protective about her father's profession. "It's just not for me."

"Daddy says prices are up."

Ellie turned back to Kate, spoke with the swiftness of a sudden confession.

"I think they've been shacking."

"Doesn't everybody?"

"This is different. I saw Ben talking with the Major at the base."

"If he's in cahoots with the Army, it can't be all that bad."

"It still isn't right."

Suddenly, the ferry horn blew, shattering the quiet of the morning and sending gulls squawking into the air. Ellie and Kate started down the boardwalk towards the terminal, where Junebug and Kate's parents were standing with her luggage.

"So what happens now?" Ellie asked.

"No idea. I'll probably get assigned overseas somewhere. Probably England." They stopped short of the ramp and waited while deckhands wheeled off crates and other supplies. "What about you? What if he comes back?"

Ellie stared out at the gray water thinking. It was a question she had so far avoided but knew she would have to face. Just when her life seemed on track, the letter arrived and sent everything spiraling into maddening uncertainty. In a few hours, she would be at the Army dance with Ben, socializing with men who would murder Karl if given the chance. When he left in '39, there was no base and no war, and she feared that, in his naivety, he was returning to a hostile place.

"Then I'll be here to greet him."

The first flakes began to fall, just a few, circling around like white mosquitos. When Ellie and Kate got to the terminal, the Mallets were huddled together under the veranda, dressed in long coats, scarfs around their necks. The Captain called out to board and a small group of early-morning passengers formed a line. Kate lifted up Junebug, squeezed her tight and whispered something in her ear. She grabbed her suitcase and kissed her parents. Finally, she turned to Ellie, her lashes flickering and cheeks red, as much from the flurries as from emotion.

"I guess this is farewell," Ellie said.

"This is farewell *for now*."

"Take care of yourself, Katherine Mallet."

"Likewise, Eleanor Ames."

Ellie never cried easily, but the moment they hugged, she welled up. Kate let her go, waved to everyone at once, and then walked down the gangway, the last in line. Ellie stood beside the others and they watched solemnly as she got on. Minutes later, the engines rumbled and the boat pulled away from the dock. Ellie tried to look for Kate, but she was inside and the windows were fogged. With the snow increasing, the boat soon vanished and Ellie felt her heart sink in knowing that her best friend, once again, was gone.

31

Ellie sat in front of the mirror in the blue dress her mother bought at a flea market in Portland a week before her senior prom. She didn't get it brand new, but it wasn't handmade either, and it was the nicest article of clothing she had. For as long as Ellie could remember, everything she owned was either loaned, donated, inherited or handed-down, and she decided that once Christmas was over, she would take some of her earnings and go shopping for a new wardrobe in Portland. She knew her parents would scoff, saying it was frivolous or prideful, but she was tired of dressing like a maid.

As Ellie put on lipstick, snowflakes rapped against the bedroom window behind her and the house creaked in the wind. Knowing that Ben would arrive soon, she put on the pearl necklace she borrowed from her mother, sprayed some perfume on her neck, and was done. Staring at herself in the glass, she looked for signs of age around her eyes, at the corners of her mouth, knowing how the harsh coastal climate could make a woman old before her time. She wondered too what Karl would think if he came back and whether he would find her beautiful still.

Ellie reached in the jewelry box and took out his letter, skimming it mostly because, by now, she knew it by heart. Nevertheless, she gazed down in the dim light, running her fingers along the words, entranced by the mystery they contained, the tantalizing prospect of hope.

"Ellie?"

She looked over and Mary was standing in the doorway, her binoculars around her neck. Ellie stuffed the letter in her pocketbook and quickly got up.

"You shouldn't sneak up on people," she said.

"I called for you."

"I didn't hear. I was getting ready."

"Where're you going?"

"I told you, a Christmas party."

"I need help with my science project?"

Suddenly, there was a horn out front—Ben had arrived.

"I have to go."

As Ellie went towards the door, Mary moved aside, her lips pursed and pouting. But she looked more hurt than angry and Ellie realized that, with her new job, she hadn't been spending as much time with her as she used to.

"I can help with your project tomorrow," she said. "Okay?"

Mary nodded and Ellie walked over to the stairs, her heels clicking on the old floorboards.

"But don't you wanna know what it's about?"

Ellie stopped and turned around. Facing her sister across the dark hallway, she recalled being young and having no one to help with her with schoolwork or to nurture her interests. Neither of their parents had gone beyond 8th grade and, as the first child, Ellie's education suffered because of it. She never blamed them because they were wise in other ways, but she didn't want Mary to be similarly stifled.

Ben beeped again, but Ellie knew he would wait.

"Of course," she said with a tender smile. "Tell me what it's about."

"U-boats."

......

The storm which started that morning had finally passed, leaving four inches of powder on Monk Island, the kind of snow that was easy to shovel but hard to move around in. Ben drove cautiously down the hill, the wipers clicking and the windshield thick with condensation. With another blackout drill in effect, all the homes were dark and the roads were barren. As they went by Drake's Cove, Ellie noticed a light on the ocean, a tiny flicker that stopped and started at regular intervals. They saw it every night from the kitchen window, and although Mary was convinced it was an enemy submarine, Jack said it was Morse code from a patrol boat.

"You smell nice," Ben said, staring ahead, both hands on the wheel.

"Thank you."

"Did Kate get out okay this morning?"

"Yes."

Leaning against the door, her pocketbook snugly on her lap, Ellie replied to his remarks with vague smiles and one-word answers. From the moment Karl's letter arrived, her feelings toward Ben had changed and she realized she had been fooling herself all along.

They came around to The Pass and saw the dim glow of the Army checkpoint, its lights positioned such that they were visible from the road and hidden from the sea. For most people, the area beyond was forbidden and the military's closure of the backshore was a source of resentment for residents who didn't like being told where they could and couldn't go.

Ben rolled down the window as they approached and a soldier walked over.

"Evenin'," he said.

The man ignored his greeting and pointed a flashlight inside.

"What's your business, Sir?"

"Going to the dance at Recreation Hall."

"Are you a civilian?"

"I'm with the Civil Defense. Major Rowland invited us."

The soldier made a curt nod and then proceeded to circle the vehicle, inspecting underneath and peering into the bed. Satisfied there was no contraband, he said, "Carry on."

Ben put the truck in gear and they continued down Passamaquoddy Road, the headlamps cutting through the long and lonely darkness. A mile later, they turned into the base, bouncing over the rugged dirt surface, and a sentry at the next guard post waved them through. They drove past Ellie's office, deeper into the complex, and everywhere she looked she saw new structures, some completed and some under construction.

"It just keeps growing," she said.

"They're building another battery at the end of The Pass."

They came to a lot with rows of parked vehicles and Ben found a spot. They trudged over to a building that looked like barracks and Ellie could hear the thump of music within. As they approached the front door, two servicemen burst out, one of them was stumbling drunk, and the moment he saw Ellie, he straightened up and made an exaggerated bow.

"Your Highness," he said.

Ben just shook his head and ushered her inside. They walked over to the coat rack and when Ben took his off, Ellie noticed he was wearing his Civil Defense armband. They gave their coats to the attendant, got a ticket and Ben said, "How about a drink?"

"Sure. Something lighter than last time."

He made a cringing smile and went over to the bar.

Ellie looked around and the hall was packed, with a brass band on one side and a bar at the other. Most of the men were in uniform—and even some women—but there were lots of civilian girls so she didn't feel out-of-place. In the center of the room, everyone was doing the swing and the floor was a sea of swaying bodies and kicking legs. Green and red streamers hung from the ceiling for Christmas and against the wall was a long buffet, where pans of potatoes au gratin, glazed carrots, and string beans sat steaming over Bunsen burners.

At the end of the table was a pile of lobsters three feet high, more hens than a good week's catch, and Ellie wondered where they got them. Over the years, she worried that her father was shacking—the hidden crates, the extra money—and considering his past, it would have been an outrage. Seeing Ben talking to the Major had renewed her suspicions and selling to the Army without the boat owner knowing would have been a new level of audacity.

"Ellie?"

Ellie looked and her coworker was coming towards her.

"Lydia," she said. "Fancy seeing you here."

Lydia was in her late thirties, but she had the figure of a much younger woman and Ellie always wondered why she was single.

"Are you alone?"

Before Ellie could say no, Ben walked backed with two glasses of eggnog and handed her one.

"Ben, this is Lydia. We work together."

"Pleased to meet you."

Lydia gave him a curious look and was ready to say something when the band broke into a fast number and interrupted her. Then a soldier came up from behind, put his arm around her, and she waved goodbye cutely as he dragged her off to the dance floor.

The hall was full and people were still pouring in. Details about the base were classified, but Ellie guessed the population was approaching that of the Island itself. It was so busy they were getting knocked into from all sides and finally Ben leaned into her ear.

"Let's find a better spot."

When he gave her his hand, she hesitated at first. But she took it and they weaved through the crowd, Ben glancing back every few seconds. Not watching where he was going, he bumped into someone and spilled his drink.

"Watch it, buddy!"

The man was with a group of GI's and they all looked drunk.

"Sorry," Ben said.

As he started to walk away, the soldier looked at his armband and frowned.

"You in the Boy Scouts or something?"

When the others laughed, Ben stopped and turned around.

"Civil Defense."

"The Civil Defense? Ain't that an oxymoron."

The soldier was short, but scrappy looking, with dark eyes and an underbite.

"And wouldn't you know about morons?" Ben said.

The man handed his drink to a friend and stepped up to Ben, his arms flared and jaw clenched. Ben had outwitted him and he didn't like it.

"What are you gonna do if the Krauts come? Make a citizen's arrest?"

"Whatever I have to do."

"You can't protect America with flashlights and dog whistles."

Ellie stood at Ben's side. After years of watching him get ridiculed by her father, she was glad to see him stick up for himself.

"I'm not protecting America," he said. "I'm protecting Monk Island."

"Gentlemen?"

Everyone turned to see Major Rowland, his bars and medals gleaming on his uniform lapel, his dark hair slicked back.

"I see you've met Sergeant Pelletier?"

Ben and the soldier locked eyes, but neither one spoke. The Major put his arm around Ben and looked at the other soldiers.

"This man was one of the first volunteers for the CD," he said, then he looked at Ellie. "Your father was the first."

The Sergeant stood with his arms at his side, as focused as a new recruit before a drill instructor.

"That's swell, Sir."

"Swell, indeed," the Major said. "We need the cooperation of the community. They're as critical to the war effort as anyone…"

The soldier looked like he wanted to smirk but he didn't.

"…they enforce the blackout," Rowland went on. "They patrol the shore, they train civilians, they do first aid. These men do all the grunt work, Sergeant, so you can spend your nights playing cribbage."

Everyone laughed and even the Pelletier couldn't help but grin. Ellie was relieved and Ben, despite his agitation, seemed to appreciate the praise. Rowland circled around, giving them all a stern but friendly look.

"Merry Christmas, Gentlemen. Now go enjoy yourselves."

He walked off and the soldiers turned away and returned to their banter. Ben and Ellie tried to wander around and mingle, but there was no room to move, and Ellie was starting to get queasy from the heat, smoke, and noise.

"Whaddaya say we get out of here?" Ben said.

She blinked in surprise—she didn't know what he meant.

"Where?"

"The new lookout tower on Passamaquoddy Road. The view is amazing."

"Can you see very far?"

"Straight to Beacon Light."

She thought for a moment and as she looked around, she realized that, as much as she loved her job at the base, she never felt comfortable around military people.

"Sure," she said, with a mischievous smile, "let's go."

. . . . . .

Ben pulled over and turned off the engine. Although the snow had ceased, flurries still whipped against the glass, whirling like manic dust devils in the aftermath of the storm. Passamaquoddy Road was a sheet of white, disturbed only by the tire tracks of a patrol vehicle, half-filled and soon to be expunged by the wind. Before them stood the lookout tower, built into the sandy ground amid the dunes and dead grass, as gray and plain as a megalith.

"You sure this is okay?" Ellie asked.

"It's not manned yet. They just finished it."

She left her pocketbook on the seat and they got out. She followed Ben up a shallow embankment where the snow, at times, was up to her calves. They made their way around to the back of the structure and he reached in his pocket for a set of keys.

"Where'd you get those?"

"Don't worry," he said.

Ben opened the door and they ducked under the threshold and went in. It was pitch black and the air was even colder than outside. He found the handrail and they started up the stairs together, the smell of fresh paint and wet cement all around. They climbed two flights and came to an observation room with a long but narrow opening that faced the sea. Ellie peered out and the coastline was darker than she had ever seen it.

"What do they do here?" she said, whispering even though they were alone.

Ben came up from behind and looked out too.

"Watch for enemy planes, ships, U-boats," he said softly.

At that moment, Ellie tried to imagine a great armada coming over the horizon. She always felt safe living on the coast but looking out at the vast expanse of water, she realized how vulnerable they were and it made her afraid.

"Ellie…"

When she glanced behind, Ben was only inches away and she could feel his breath on her neck. Suddenly, his fingers touched her back and she got goosebumps.

"Ben, no."

She spun around and moved away from him.

"What's wrong?"

"Nothing is wrong."

"Is there someone else?"

Considering he worked for her father, and that they lived in a place where a person couldn't get tick bite without the whole community finding out, it was an odd question. But she answered him anyway if only to settle his conscience.

"There's no one else."

"Then why?"

"I don't think of you like that."

In the darkness, his face was a blur, but she could hear the frustration in his voice.

"You don't think of me like that? We've been out a bunch of times—to the Bowladrome, to get ice cream, to the Legion. We hugged and kissed."

Ellie looked down nodding, overcome by guilt for misleading him.

"I was wrong to," she said, "and I'm sorry. But this isn't right for either of us. This is my father's making."

"Not true! I always wanted to be with you."

It wasn't the best place to clarify their relationship, but Ellie felt more pity than awkwardness. Ben had grown up poor on the north side of the island, without a father and with a mother who was mentally ill. Some of her earliest memories were of him wandering barefoot and dirty along the waterfront, an image that, even by Down East standards, was heartbreaking.

"Ben, I'm so sorry," she said, as much for her own actions as for his misfortunes.

They stood in the silence of the tower, only feet apart but separated by so much more. When Ben finally went to speak, Ellie was sure the matter was settled.

"Ellie Ames," he said bitterly. "The only girl on Monk Island who would go with a Kraut, but not a local."

Her face dropped, her temper flared.

"How dare you!"

She went to slap him and he caught her arm. When she tried to use the other hand, he grabbed that arm too.

"Ain't it true?!" Ben shouted back. "And those Huns will be killing our boys!"

She twisted and squirmed, trying to get free, but he was much stronger.

"Stop," she moaned. "That hurts."

Instantly, Ben let go and she fell backward. She caught herself before hitting the wall, then turned and flew down the stairs. She went out the small door and down the embankment and by the time she got to the bottom, her shoes were filled with sand and snow and three coat buttons were missing. With tears pouring down her cheeks, Ellie stumbled out onto Passamaquoddy Road and ran all the way home.

32

Ellie had never meant to reject Ben, knowing it was hard for men, but what he said and did in the tower was unforgivable. She saw a side of him she had never seen before, a coldness made crueler by the fact that he insulted Karl without ever having met him. From the moment Ben joined the Civil Defense, something in him changed and he was puffed up with the arrogance of his newfound authority. She could see it in his posture and hear it in his voice, remembering how he spoke to Kate in the window before she left.

The incident should have ended at the watchtower. By the time Ellie got home that night, she had walked over two miles in the snow and her parents and sister were asleep. Although angry and appalled, she was also relieved that their relationship was over. She decided to spare Ben any humiliation by not telling her father, knowing he would lose his job and probably a few teeth too. But any advantage she had in the situation was quickly lost when she discovered, to her horror, she had left her pocketbook in his pickup truck— and Karl's letter was in it.

"Someone dropped this off for you."

Ellie had just gotten to her desk Monday morning when Lydia came over.

"Thank you," Ellie said, taking the pocketbook.

"Did you have fun at the dance?"

"Yes, fun," she said.

Lydia walked away and Ellie finished taking off her coat, containing her panic with a stiff smile. She sat down and tried to work, but her heart raced and she couldn't focus. All weekend she had worried about the letter and she even thought about going to Ben's house but was afraid it would make him suspicious. With Germany and America at war, the note could be considered contraband and Ellie's only hope was that he hadn't looked inside.

Across the room, Jane was typing and Lydia was busy at the file cabinet. Ellie reached for her pocketbook and unzipped it. She took a deep breath, glanced in, and cringed when she realized the letter was gone.

"Ellie?"

She shut the bag and looked up.

"Jane?"

"These need to go out today," she said, handing Ellie some checks. "There's one you can probably take—looks like it might be a family member."

Ellie flipped through the bunch and they were all for various businesses in the region. Most were posted to the mainland, but a few had local addresses, including a dredging company owned by Kate's uncle and two brothers who were painters. In the middle of the pile, Ellie found a check made out to Jack Ames and when she saw it was for $236, she froze. She had long suspected her father was shacking, and the fact that it was made out to him and not the boat company seemed a strong implication. Nevertheless, she returned to her work and was content to live with some doubt until she knew for sure.

Then shortly after lunch, Ellie heard something outside and got up to look. In the driveway, she saw Ben's truck backing up towards the mess hall. She was tempted to confront him about the letter, but the risks of bringing it up were worse than saying nothing at all. And it would have been a big mistake because the moment he got out, her father did too. They pulled a tarp off the pickup bed to reveal stacks of damp crates, freshly hauled and full of hens. Two kitchen workers came out the side door, dressed in shirtsleeves and white smocks, and together the four men unloaded the catch and brought it in. The entire transaction only took a few minutes, but Ellie stood at the window long after they left, overcome by a sickening feeling, a bitter blend of disbelief, disappointment, and disgust.

. . . . . .

It was the winter solstice—the shortest day of the year— and by the time Ellie got out of work the sun was almost down. Passamaquoddy Road had been plowed, but the wind was so strong it almost knocked her over, and although an Army truck stopped to offer her a ride, she declined as much out of stubbornness as because she needed time to think. With the incident at the tower and Jack's double-dealing, she was in a state of suspended panic. Her father had lost his boat once before for criminal activity and she worried what would happen if he got caught again. As for Karl's letter, she knew Ben could blackmail her, but she didn't know why or how, and she was determined not to be bullied if he tried.

At the end of The Pass, Ellie reached the main checkpoint and a sentry waved her through. She came around Drake's Cove where, in the distance, she saw the Mallet's house and the window to Kate's bedroom, now dark and vacant. She plodded up the hill and when she finally got to the yard, her fingers were numb, her eyelashes covered in ice crystals. She walked in the front door and her mother was there to meet her.

"My goodness," she said. "Your face is as red as a beet. Didn't Ben drive you?"

"Not today, Mother."

"Get those shoes off."

Ellie untied her laces, kicked off her snowy shoes and went wearily up the stairs. Ten minutes later, she came down for dinner, her mind in a fog and still shivering. She walked into the kitchen and Mary and her father were already seated, Jack hunched over the newspaper, his hands filthy from work. While Mary looked up with a smile, he ignored Ellie altogether, which no longer offended her because she was used to it.

Vera brought over a pot of stew and everyone sat down. Jack said grace, they filled their bowls, and the silence was replaced by a slow and steady slurping.

"How's the new job?" Vera said.

"It doesn't pay what lobstering does."

It was a provocative response, but she meant it that way because she could no longer hide her anger.

"Nor should it," her father muttered.

"Right, because your business has made such an incredible comeback."

He put down his spoon and finally looked up, his eyes fierce, expression cold.

"At 20 cents a pound, I'd say it has."

"Tell me then," Ellie said, her temper rising. "Why are you selling directly to the Army? I didn't know you own a boat?"

When her father frowned, Ellie reached under to her lap, where she had been hiding the check. She stood up, slapped it on the table, and it landed in such a way that all the print was clear—from "U.S. Army" to "Jack Ames." Vera turned to him, as if for an explanation, and he seemed like he wanted to snatch it up, which would have only proven his guilt.

"Jack? Is this true?" she said.

Ignoring the question, he calmly got up and the floor creaked beneath him. He looked across to his daughter with a long and intimidating glare, but Ellie stood firm and didn't cower.

"Where did you get this?"

"At work," she said, tears forming in her eyes. "Didn't you learn your lesson once?"

The remark stung and she could see it.

"You listen here…"

Before he could finish, Ellie ran for the doorway, but Jack got there first and blocked her.

"…That money is for our family!" he shouted.

"It's blood money!"

When Ellie tried to slide by him, Jack grabbed her by the arms and spun her around.

"Let me go!"

Vera got up and rushed over, as fast as she could with her arthritis.

"Jack!" she said. "Please let her go!"

"Think you know anything about life?" he said, his teeth gritted. "I work my fingers to the bone…"

Ellie groaned, struggling to get free, but her father had twice the strength of Ben. When they knocked into the cupboard, dishes fell over and several broke. Mary began to cry and Scuttles ran out of the kitchen.

"You wanna hurt me?" Ellie screamed. "Hurt me like Ben did?"

Suddenly, everything stopped. Jack let go of her and his face dropped.

"What did you say?"

She pulled up her sleeve, exposing the bruises on her forearm. Ben had been rough, but she never meant to tell anyone, knowing how people scorned snitching on Monk Island. But he had stolen Karl's letter and, in the heat of the moment, it seemed the only way to counteract any harm he might do.

"That's right," Ellie said, "the boy you want me to marry is a brute, but the one I loved you wouldn't even look at."

Jack stepped back, blinked in exasperation.

"That boy was a goddamn Nazi."

Ellie shook her head and tears went flying.

"He was anything but," she said, stomping her foot. "His father fought against the Nazis. That's why they were trying to escape to America."

Jack wilted like a man who had the life sucked out of him. The defiance in his eyes melted away to a vacant remorse and he just stared at the floor, heaving and speechless. For Ellie, he had always been hard to read because he never showed much emotion, but when he turned aside to let her pass, it was like asking for forgiveness.

33.

The men sat on the deck in the cold wind, their bodies pale from a week at sea. A storm had lashed the boat for two days straight and many were sick, but the moment it was clear enough to surface, the Captain let the crew out to stretch and get fresh air. The water was calm and the clouds were low enough to provide cover from enemy planes. Everyone came out in shifts, twenty sailors at a time, and they were required to keep moving, they couldn't sit down.

Karl circled the deck with the other men while Schmitt and the Second Watch Officer stood with the Captain at the bridge. Even though it was overcast, the light hurt Karl's eyes and he was weak from the scant rations. When he reached the bow, he gazed ahead and got some small joy in knowing that Ellie was out there somewhere. There was a thousand miles of water between them and that distance was shrinking each day.

Karl didn't know the exact course of their mission—no one did, including Captain Dietz. The chart in the control room was covered in pencil marks and redrawn lines, the frantic musings of a crew on a blind patrol. After Pearl Harbor, Hitler had jumped on the offensive and their orders were simply to go to America and attack enemy ships. About the only thing certain was that they would be cruising along the Eastern Seaboard and Karl knew he had to be ready to escape at the first sight of land.

As he stood thinking, he noticed in the dull haze, an object above the horizon. It was barely visible, just a speck in the sky, and it could have been birds if it was closer. He went over to the bridge and Schmitt and the Officer turned around.

"Herr Oberbootsmann, I think there's a plane," Karl said, nodding because he didn't want to point and alarm the men.

At first, Schmitt scoffed, but the risk was real enough that he and the Captain looked out their binoculars. Dietz passed his pair to the Second Watch Officer, who also scanned the sky, and the three men quietly conferred while Karl waited by the ladder.

"No plane, Sailor," Schmitt finally said. "You're delirious. Get back in line."

Karl saluted and returned to the crew, accepting the ridicule because he had no choice. He continued around the boat with the others, moving together in rhythmic harmony, as slow and steady as a chain gang. And some days Karl felt like he was in prison, trapped in a steel cage many meters below the sea, confined to an artificial world of dim lamps and fumes. As he walked, he took in as much clean air and sunlight as he could, knowing it might be the last he would have for days, maybe longer.

"Back in the boat, back in the boat!"

Karl turned and the Officers were screaming and waving their arms. Instantly, the diesel engines started and they began to move. Everyone ran towards the bridge, squeezing up the narrow ladder in groups of twos and threes, as panicked as a crowd fleeing a building fire. Karl got caught somewhere in the middle and as he waited to go down the hatch, he looked west and saw a low-flying plane. It might have been five miles away—it could have been fifteen. He was always a bad judge of distance, but he had no doubt it was coming for them.

"Move, move, move!" the Officers shrieked as sailors jumped in the hole.

As Karl crouched to go in, he glanced at Schmitt, looking for some credit for his earlier warning. Instead, Schmitt stepped towards him and pushed his shoulder.

"Down, Sailor," he growled.

The rush to descend the conning tower was frantic and Karl got kicked in the head more than once. Someone below him slipped and tumbled to the floor, hitting several men along the way.

"Battle stations!" the Captain shouted.

Karl got to the bottom and sailors were running in every direction. He squatted low and hurried through the cabin.

"Emergency dive! 20 seconds and counting."

Suddenly, the ballasts opened, seawater flooded in, and the boat began to drop. He grabbed the nearest overhead pipe and hung on tight.

"Boom!"

When Karl opened his eyes, he was lying on the floor in total darkness. All around him men were yelling out commands, calling for help, and giving status updates, the ordered chaos and confusion of combat.

"You okay, Comrade?" he heard and two crewmembers picked him up.

The lights flickered on and the boat was still descending, the walls creaking eerily from the pressure. Karl's forehead throbbed and when he touched it, there was blood on his fingers.

"Boom!"

A second blast knocked him into some equipment and by some miracle he didn't fall over. He looked down the aisle and everywhere he saw his comrades crouched and holding on in terror. In those moments, Karl thought of Ellie and it tormented him to imagine dying without her knowing he tried to come back.

......

The depth bombs from the plane did some damage, but in the end, they escaped. With his shift over, Karl walked wearily back to his bunk. The floor was covered in oily water and the cabin stank of sewage. As he passed the mess, Schmitt and three other men were seated around a small table beside a torpedo tube.

"Brink," Schmitt said and Karl was surprised to hear him use his name. "Have a drink with us, for Christmas."

He looked at the others and then to Schmitt.

"Christmas is Thursday."

"Then for Winter Solstice," he said and he burst into laughter.

Karl wanted to decline, but Schmitt was drunk and would only persist. So he squeezed in and sat between a pipe and circuit box. Aside from Schmitt, he knew two of the men by name and the other by sight. Kiessling was a torpedo mechanic from Berlin and Peters was an assistant radio operator with the German Cross tattooed on his chest. The third man was the tallest, but he was so young his beard didn't fill in completely.

Kiessling poured something into a canteen cup and handed it to Karl. It smelled awful and tasted worse, but he drank as a courtesy and as a show of camaraderie. Schmitt had the only chair—a small metal stool that was probably an extra from the radio room—and the other sailors squatted on things ranging from an egg crate to a toolbox. Life on a U-boat was a world of gritty improvisation and somedays Karl thought he would have been more comfortable on the front line in the Russian winter.

"Is it true," Peters asked, "that you both served on U-206?"

Everyone went quiet and Karl looked up. In moments like this, he felt the loss of the men he served with and he saw the mischievous grin of Reinhard Brauer. He promised himself that, once the War was over, he would write to Reinhard's mother and father, perhaps even visit. But he knew it was both dangerous and arrogant to assume that he would survive.

"Got a hunk of shrapnel in my thigh," Schmitt said and he took a big sip, "beside the balls. Another half inch I'd be a eunuch."

Schmitt cringed and no one knew whether to laugh or not. As Karl listened to him brag, he forced down the alcohol with the hope that it might soothe his nerves and help him sleep. He never liked the feeling of intoxication, but he saw its purpose and realized why his father had brandy every night.

"I got it in the arm," Karl said and everyone turned. "Right here."

He pulled up his sleeve and showed them the scar on his elbow, which somehow looked more grotesque in the dim light.

"We were in the same café," Schmitt explained. "During the air raid."

While Kiessling and Peters seemed impressed, the other man just sat with a tense smile, making Karl wonder if it was his first patrol.

"Was it fate or coincidence?" Kiessling said.

Schmitt frowned and banged his cup down for a refill.

"Fate?" he said. "Nonsense. We were there, the bombs hit, that's the end of it."

"Do you remember it?" Peters said.

Whether it was from the liquor or exhaustion, everyone was starting to look blurry and Karl couldn't tell who he was asking. So when Schmitt didn't answer, he said, "There was a great bang. Every table fell over. All the glass broke. We didn't even hear the planes."

"Did you know you were injured?"

Karl shook his head.

"Not 'til we got outside."

Schmitt took another sip and snickered.

"Sailor Brink was the first one out," he said. "Like a little frightened rabbit."

As he motioned with his hand, the other men laughed until they saw Karl's face. Karl looked across to Schmitt with a cold and bitter stare, no longer willing to take his taunts, prepared to risk punishment for insubordination.

"At least I wasn't pulling children out of taxis," he said.

All at once, there was a tense and hostile silence. Schmitt's face went purple, his mouth formed a nasty underbite. Knowing he had crossed a line, Karl shifted his balance and got ready in case Schmitt lunged at him.

"Amerikaner!"

Everyone turned and Vogel was coming towards them.

"Herr Obersteuermann," Schmitt said, but Vogel ignored him.

"What's this, a card game without cards?"

As the men all made guilty grins, Vogel reached for one of the cups and smelled it.

"Ich!" he said, wincing. "I wouldn't clean the sump with this." He looked at Karl and said, "Come with me, Herr Brink. You're needed."

Karl went to get up and Schmitt became suddenly indignant.

"What's this about?"

Vogel stopped and looked back with a dismissive frown. He may have tolerated Schmitt as a fellow officer, but it was clear that he didn't respect him.

"A private matter," he said. "Get back to your peasant grog."

Karl didn't look to see Schmitt's face, but he knew he was humiliated. He followed Vogel through the compartments, where men halfheartedly saluted and stood to attention. Much of it was out of habit, however, because after two weeks at sea no one took the conventions of military etiquette too seriously.

When they reached the control room, Vogel went in but Karl lingered at the bulkhead.

"Come," Vogel said and Karl obeyed.

Inside, Captain Dietz was standing with the Engineer and two Officers. Karl could tell that one had just come off the watch because his face was red and he was covered in white specks from the sea spray. To make up for lost time from the storm and the air strike, they had been cruising at full speed for over ten hours and the boat swayed in the harsh North Atlantic waters. In the engine room next door, the twin diesels vibrated throughout the hull, creating a constant and menacing drone.

"Amerikaner," the Captain said.

Either they all knew about the joke or they didn't care, Karl thought, because no one reacted.

"Herr Kapitän."

Although woozy, he stood up straight and tried to be alert. On a table attached to the wall was the plotting map and the men moved aside to let Karl in.

"You're familiar with the State of Maine?" the First Watch Officer asked.

Karl nodded, glimpsed up to the others.

"I spent a summer there. My father taught at the University."

"Your father is a professor?" the Captain asked warmly.

"Yes, Herr Kapitän. Economics, University of Hamburg."

"He must be quite proud of you."

Karl responded with a nervous smile—the irony was poignant.

"I should hope so."

Captain Dietz looked at the Officers and then to Karl.

"Tell me," he said, "what do you know about the waterways in those parts?"

In an instant, Karl's drowsiness went away and he was razor sharp. He realized at that moment that the Captain was asking his advice about where to hunt and if he hesitated they might not trust him.

"Casco Bay," he blurted out and Dietz and the Officers listened, "has deep channels, lots of shipping…"

In his vague plan to flee the boat and get back to Ellie, he had only hoped they would pass near Monk Island, but he never imagined having the chance to ensure it.

"A fuel depot, as well," the Captain said, pointing to the map.

The light was too low for Karl to see, but he nodded anyway. Vogel looked at Dietz and said, "We've had reports that convoys leave from there."

"It's the most navigable inlet," Karl went on, "farther north is perilous."

The men all acknowledged the remark and looked at each other. Even in the intimacy of the small room, they spoke differently with each other than they did to Karl and his heart pounded as he waited to see how they would respond. Finally, the Captain patted his arm and made a cordial smile.

"That'll be all, Sailor."

As Karl turned to leave, the Officers thanked him with a nod and Vogel even winked. He crept down the aisle in the cramped semi-darkness. In the radio room, the operator looked up with tired eyes, his headphones around his shoulders. Karl continued past the galley and through the Officers' Room, guided by the eerie blue lights that were always on during 'silent running.'

He was as excited as he was guilt-ridden, worrying that maybe he was putting the crew at risk for his own selfish plot. Yet nothing he told the Captain was untrue and he was satisfied in knowing that, had he been the commander, he would have targeted Casco Bay too.

U-130 had never been so quiet. In their final run to reach the American coast, there wasn't much to do but wait. Watch Officers worked in shifts on the bridge and technicians looked after the engines, torpedoes, and hydraulics. The rest of the men were either asleep or lounging around the many nooks and recesses of the interior.

As Karl approached the crew's quarters, he stopped in the shadow of a supply locker. Up ahead, the walls were lined with snoring sailors, their bodies squeezed into the narrow bunks like sacks of wheat. Karl glanced around and, when he was sure no one was looking, he opened it and inside was a stack of yellow inflatable life jackets. With a trembling hand, he reached for one, knowing that in the minds of his comrades, it was an act of treason. He gently shut the door and walked away.

When Karl got to his bed, he shoved the contraband in his duffle bag and crawled onto the mattress. Someone above grumbled and turned over, but no one else noticed. He was relieved, if only temporarily, and the life jacket was one more hurdle in the long race to reunite with Ellie. He knew that, in good weather, he could swim for miles unaided, but he had no idea where he would find himself once he escaped and the device could mean the difference between living or drowning.

Karl lay on his back and pulled the dirty blanket over him. The smell of body odor and urine reminded him that he had to piss, but he was too tired to use the latrine. Closing his eyes, he listened to the rumble of the engines and dreamt of Monk Island.

34

Ellie hadn't seen Ben since her father walked into the Legion and punched him clear off his barstool. According to witnesses, he hit him so hard that Ben fell to the floor, bounced back, and then somehow landed upright again. But locals had a tendency to exaggerate, especially when it came to personal disputes and other matters of honor, and so Ellie wasn't surprised when she heard five different versions of the story. Regardless of the exact details, Jack had "set him straight," the phrase he used when his wife confronted him about the incident. Ellie knew her father would have probably tried to deny the whole thing, but by dinnertime that day everyone on Monk Island knew that Jack Ames had knocked out Benjamin Frazier.

Ellie felt awful about what happened, knowing she could have prevented it, but any sympathy was complicated by the fact that Ben still had Karl's letter. Vera tried to get Jack to apologize, saying that all young men make mistakes and that Christmas was a season of forgiveness. But his stubbornness was absolute and any attempt to change his thinking would only make things worse. In Jack's mind, he had given Ben clemency by not killing him, and he said that if anyone ever laid a hand on his daughter again, he would break his neck.

"Ellie?"

When she looked up, Major Rowland was in front of her desk.

"Good morning, Major," she said.

"Come with me, please."

He was always reserved, but his voice was particularly curt and it made Ellie uneasy. As she rose from her chair, she looked over to Lydia and Jane, who glimpsed up before quickly looking away. Ellie grabbed her sweater and followed the Major out of the office, down a long hallway, and into the stairwell. He walked like he was marching, arms at his side, his polished shoes clapping on the plywood steps, and she had the strange sensation that she was being led off to the gallows. They came out to the second floor, the offices for senior staff members, and Rowland glanced back with a tight semi-smile, lessening her panic but in no way relieving it.

They turned into a doorway and Ellie saw two men sitting at a long table, both in their thirties and wearing neatly pressed officers' uniforms. The office had the look of an interrogation room, the walls bare and a single lamp hanging from above.

"Eleanor," the Major said, motioning for her to sit. "This is Captain Breen and Lieutenant Rogers, Military Intelligence."

She swallowed nervously and tried to smile, but her lips were stiff and the most she could do was utter, "Hello."

Ellie didn't know why she was there and she could only guess it had something to do with her father assaulting Ben or the fact that they were illegally selling lobster to the Army. But as little as she understood about military jurisdiction, it seemed farfetched that Military Intelligence would intervene in civilian affairs.

"Would you like some coffee, maybe a glass of water?"

When Ellie shook her head, Rowland took a seat at the end of the table, clasped his hands, and looked at the men to begin. Breen opened up a briefcase, took out a folder, and pulled out a single document.

"We've come into possession of something," he said, his voice cold and matter-of-fact, "which may or may not be of significant strategic interest…"

Ellie's skin started to tingle—she got butterflies in her stomach.

"…It's addressed to an 'Ellie,'" he added and then he looked up. "Is that you?"

"Yes, no…I mean, maybe," she said, stumbling. "There are other Eleanor's on Monk Island."

"Well, maybe this will help clarify," he said, leaning forward, handing her the document. "It's a copy, of course."

She could feel them all watching as her eyes descended on the text and the moment she saw Karl's handwriting, she was filled with a warm elation. She had memorized not only the words but their forms too, the flair of his e's and the grace of his l's, always looking beyond their surface meaning to get at what he was trying to communicate. Ellie could have recited the letter a hundred times with no mistake, but she read it again to satisfy them and then looked up.

"We've had the original analyzed," Lieutenant Rogers said, speaking for the first time. "It's German."

"Hahnemühle Paper Mill, to be precise," Breen said.

They gave her a few seconds to respond or react and when she didn't, Breen was more direct.

"Do you know who wrote this?"

She knew she could have lied, but it would have been pointless because everyone on Monk Island remembered when Ellie Ames fell in love with a German. And considering Ben's treachery in turning the letter over to the Army, she had no doubt he told them everything and possibly more. Her only defense was honesty and there was nothing about

295

the time she spent with Karl that she was ashamed of or regretted.

"We met in the summer of '39," she said. "He was here with his family. They left at the end of August. He said he would return in the fall but never did."

"And what was the purpose of their visit?"

"They were trying to immigrate to America. His father had been against the Nazis and they were in danger."

"And you believed him?"

"Of course, why would he lie?"

Breen glanced once over at his colleague before continuing.

"How long have you two been corresponding?"

"That was the first letter, the only letter."

"You sure about that?"

Something in his voice had the tone of accusation and Ellie was more forceful in her reply.

"I'm sure—"

"Because abetting the enemy is a federal crime."

Ellie startled and looked across to Major Rowland, who even with his stony expression seemed an encouraging presence, her only ally. She shrank in the chair and tried to maintain her composure, while under the table her legs were trembling.

"What does he mean by *important business?*" Rogers asked.

She thought about Karl's cryptic words like she had so many times before. The conversation between her and the officials had all the tension of a standoff, but in this one question, they were all united.

"I wish I knew," she said, shrugging her shoulders, knowing it was vulgar. "I haven't seen him in over two years."

"You must have some idea," Breen said.

"I don't."

"But—"

"That's all I know," she interrupted, her impatience getting the best of her discretion. She softened her tone and said, "I was as confused by the letter as you."

Breen tapped his pencil on the table, chewing his lip, absorbed in thought while the others sat still. Being there horrified Ellie more than almost anything she could imagine, as much because it was her employer as because they were with Military Intelligence. But she hadn't done anything wrong and in some ways, she was more concerned about Karl than herself.

When Breen finally sighed and looked over to his partner, Ellie took it as a sign that the meeting was over and despite her distress, it was some vindication to know they believed her.

"Thank you for your time, Miss Ames," he said, packing up his briefcase.

As they got up to leave, Major Rowland, who had so far been silent said, "Gentlemen, let me know if you need anything else."

The agents thanked him, put on their hats, and headed for the door.

"Pardon?" Ellie said and they turned around. "May I have my letter back?"

Rogers and Breen looked at each other, a hint of sarcasm in their expressions. Ellie knew it was a bold question but she had to ask.

"Unfortunately no, Miss," Breen said. "It's contraband."

They walked out and the room went quiet, leaving Ellie both stunned and confused. With Major Rowland still sitting at the other end of the table, she didn't know if she should get up and go back to work or wait until he ordered her to. She tried to avert her eyes, but the power of his gaze was unavoidable and, as the seconds passed, she started to feel self-conscious.

"Eleanor," he said, gently. "I'm afraid I have some bad news."

When she looked across to him, he seemed almost troubled, his forehead strained, his eyes bleary. Behind his formal exterior, she had always sensed some deeper compassion, but this was the most emotion he had ever shown.

"We have to terminate you."

35.

Getting fired a few days before Christmas was harsh, even for the Army, and the only upside was that it would delay, at least for a while, the humiliation of the community finding out. If anyone asked, Ellie said she was off until the new year and it was perfectly plausible because most businesses closed for the last two weeks in December and even Joe Mallet was only in the shop occasionally.

As it turned out, Jack was taking time off too, which surprised everyone because he had never done it before. He said that, with the military scrambling to secure the waterways of Casco Bay, it was impossible to get around and that he would wait until they had their system down before dropping any more traps. It was a good enough reason—the Army presence was inconveniencing people in all sorts of ways— but Ellie suspected that her father's hiatus had more to do with the fact that Ben was gone and he was now left without a helper. She hadn't seen Ben in over a week, the longest ever, and although feuds on Monk Island always healed eventually, she knew that he and her father would never work together again.

Despite all their problems, the family was spending more time together than they had in years. Something in Jack had changed and Ellie couldn't tell if he had softened or had just become more resigned to the whims and woes of life. He was reflective in a way she had never seen before, as if he suddenly realized what was important and why, but regretted having learned it so late. After years of estrangement, Ellie could tolerate being around him again and at times she even enjoyed it. He still had trouble making eye contact and when he spoke to her, it was mostly offhanded comments, fractured remarks, and small utterances. But she had no doubt he was making an effort and that was why when he asked her to go hunting with him and Mary, she didn't say no.

"Crack!"

The shot echoed through the woods and birds scattered in the trees. Jack raised the rifle and ran forward, Ellie and Mary close behind. When they reached the far side of the clearing they saw a giant turkey lying on its side, its neck long and fleshy, its body covered in dark feathers. As Jack knelt to get it, Ellie stared at its open eyes and experienced that visceral grief which comes from slaying another living thing. The feeling was fleeting, however, because growing up on Monk Island she learned early on about the delicate and sometimes cruel balance between man and nature.

"Is he?" Mary asked

"Right in the heart," their father said proudly.

"No blood?"

"Gobblers don't bleed much. They ain't like people."

He put the bird over one shoulder, the rifle over the other, and they started back through the forest. Much of the first snow had melted away from the sun, but the ground was frozen and leaves and branches crackled under their feet. When they came to the top of a ridge, Jack stopped and Ellie could see that he was winded.

"Shall I carry the rifle?" she asked.

"I'd carry ten times this in the Army," he said, then he walked off.

Mary looked up to Ellie, who smiled back wistfully, and they followed him down the hill. Her father had mentioned the War more times in the last week than in all the years previous, as if, with all the disappointments in adulthood, he found a special solace in the achievements and heroism of his past. But it went beyond combat and to his youth in general, small anecdotes about how in those days there was no electricity, no automobiles, no telephone, no icebox; how locals still lived then as they had for centuries, raising livestock, tending gardens, fishing the sea; how children were born at home and how the dead were buried by hand in one of the four cemeteries. In some ways, Jack had become a walking testament to an era gone by, the embodiment of the spirit of Monk Island itself. Ellie didn't know the reason for his sudden nostalgia, but she loved to hear him reminisce.

"When I was a boy. We'd hunt every day."

"Even when it was snowing?" Mary asked.

"Of course. Else we wouldn't eat."

"Couldn't you fish?"

"If the seas were calm," Jack said. "But we didn't have modern boats like today. If men went out in rough weather, they didn't always come back."

The conversation continued until they reached the house, fading out, like all things, with matters of the present. When they walked in, the parlor smelled of pine from the Christmas tree that Jack had cut down a few days earlier, a lanky spruce decorated with red glass balls and a tin star at the top. Handmade stockings hung above the fireplace and there were candles in the front windows, which were lit for a few hours every night.

As Ellie and her sister peeled off their coats and hats, Vera came out of the kitchen with a baking pan and Jack rested the bird on it.

"Did you girls have fun?"

"Turkeys don't bleed," Mary said and everyone smiled.

He checked the chamber to make sure it was clear, then he raised it up, looked down the barrel.

"That sure came in handy," she said. "I didn't think you still had it."

"You never know when you might need one."

......

After dinner, they sat around the table in a drowsy stupor. Ellie looked over to the chair beside her father, which was strangely vacant without Ben. Despite still being angry about what happened, she felt a sense of loss in knowing he would never be part of their family again. She told him that night that there wasn't anyone else, which wasn't a lie, but the irony of him finding Karl's letter left her with a simmering guilt that she couldn't quite shake.

While Jack finished his coffee, Ellie helped her mother gather the dishes and bring them into the kitchen. On the counter, a pumpkin and apple pie were waiting, but it wasn't time for dessert because they had to open gifts first. Vera called everyone into the parlor and they sat on the old couch, which creaked under their weight. Jack knelt next to the tree and sifted through the gifts, all wrapped in newsprint, adorned with homemade bows which Mary helped make. A log crackled in the fireplace and Scuttles lay purring in the corner.

"This is for you," Jack said, handing Mary the first gift. "From Santa Claus."

Mary frowned as she took it.

"I haven't believed in Santa Claus since I was eleven."

She tore off the wrapping and her face beamed when she saw that it was a chemistry set.

"Papa!"

As they opened the rest of the presents, Scuttles came over and rolled around in the newsprint. Ellie got a charm necklace and Vera gave her husband a wool sweater she had knitted herself. Mary made her mother a bouquet of dried wildflowers and Ellie gave her sister three pairs of colored socks, which she bought at the PX on base.

Once the small gifts were exchanged, Jack put a box on his wife's lap and the room went silent. Vera looked up with a nervous smile and then proceeded to open it, her arthritic hands fumbling with the flimsy paper. Ellie was tempted to help, but she knew her mother would be offended.

"A radio!" Mary shouted.

"Oh, my," Vera said.

Jack lifted it out of the box and set it down on the side table beside her, plugging it into the only electrical outlet in the room. When he turned the knob, they at first heard only static, but he slowly moved the dial and suddenly there was music, an old but familiar symphony. Vera was so excited she got teary and she turned to her husband with a warm smile.

"Jack, it's gorgeous."

He averted his eyes as if embarrassed by the attention, and Ellie was touched by his humility. But with new radios costing up to $30, she couldn't help thinking about how he got the money. She had exposed him in front of the whole family, throwing down the Army check on the table, and yet no one had mentioned it since. Whether it was out of fear or habit, her mother never questioned Jack about his business practices and, considering her own father had been a

303

fisherman, she was probably sympathetic. Ellie could only hope that he had given up shacking altogether and that his change of mood lately was some form of repentance. But the fact that she didn't know for sure left her skeptical.

While everyone huddled around the radio, she got up from the couch.

"Ellie?" Vera said. "Won't you come and listen?"

"I'm gonna go cut the pies."

36

Ellie walked headlong into the wind, down Gull Avenue, her collar upturned and her hands in her pockets even though she had on gloves. The temperature was well below freezing and the sky was so gray it seemed to yearn for the sun. It was the first week of January, the start of a new year, ushered in without any of the pageantry because the military had prohibited fireworks over the harbor. The streets were quiet and empty, the only signs of life an occasional passing Army truck, smoke rising from the chimneys. The winter on Monk Island was the bleakest season, two or more months of harsh cold and brutal weather, and while the rest of the world returned to work, locals were preparing for the long hibernation.

Mary was finally back to school, but Jack hadn't gone out to fish since before Christmas. With the holidays now over, Ellie could no longer pretend she was employed, and before anyone found out, she decided to go see Joe Mallet. Asking for her old job back would be embarrassing, but working as a lowly clerk was better than no job at all, and she took some comfort in knowing that she hadn't been at the base long enough for most people to know. Nevertheless, her time there had been like a dream, and although Major Rowland was kind in letting her go, she would never forgive the Army for giving her a chance at a career and then snatching it away.

Beyond her termination, Ellie couldn't understand why they were so interested in Karl's letter and she wondered if the investigation was standard procedure during wartime or if they knew something more. The question haunted her, as did Karl's whereabouts, and she got an eerie sensation that he was nearby, maybe somewhere on the mainland, living incognito or hiding in plain sight. Whenever she went into Portland, she would scan the faces of the crowd, searching for him always. She checked the postbox every day, sometimes twice, desperate for more news and yet knowing that the military was probably monitoring their mail.

Ellie walked into Lavery's and the bell over the door rang. The air inside was warm and she loosened her scarf as she walked over to the counter. Moments later, Joe Mallet appeared from the back room, dressed in suspenders and a bowtie, cheerful as always.

"Ellie," he said.

"Hello, Mr. Mallet."

"How's the new job?"

She cringed, not expecting it to be the first question.

"Actually…" she said, hesitating. "I'm not working at the base anymore."

He crossed his arms and looked at her with a warm and fatherly sympathy.

"Well, I'm sorry to hear that," he said. Ellie was about to ask about work when he saved her the humiliation by bringing it up. "I still need help. I had the youngest Fallon boy, but he enlisted last week. He leaves for boot camp Monday."

She nodded quickly, smiling and eager.

"As you know, it's pretty quiet this time of year," he went on. "It'll be mostly ordering, some restocking."

"I'd be delighted."

"You can start Monday if you'd like."

"I'll see you Monday then."

Mr. Mallet reached over the counter and they shook hands, which was as official as a hiring contract got on Monk Island.

"Say, is Jack getting bait somewhere else?"

"Not that I know of."

"He hasn't been in for a while."

"He said it's been hard getting around Taylor Passage with all the restrictions. I know he said he was gonna take a couple of weeks off."

Joe Mallet pursed his lips, squinting and perplexed.

"Funny, I haven't heard that from anyone. Boats have been going out all week."

Ellie responded with a long nod and a tingle went up her back. She thanked him and walked out, relieved to have her old job back but uneasy about what he said.

As she crossed the intersection, she looked towards the pier and saw Mary, Junebug, and some other girls. They stood in a circle with their book bags, engaged in the secretive gossip of adolescence. Noticing that Mary was underdressed, Ellie stormed down the hill.

"Mary!" she said sharply. "Where's your hat?"

"I left it at school."

"You need to go home and get another."

Before she could continue, a single lobster boat in the distance caught her eye, the only one in the immediate harbor.

"May I see those?"

Mary handed her the binoculars and Ellie looked through them. When the boat came into focus, it was her father's and she was surprised because when she left the house he was working on the shed. Moreover, someone she didn't recognize was at the stern hauling a trap. Inside Ellie got a

307

sick feeling, an amplified version of what she experienced when Joe Mallet said Jack hadn't been in to buy bait. She waited for the boat to drift some and when it did, she looked under the wheelhouse and Ben Frazier was at the helm.

She gasped and put down the binoculars.

"What is it?" Mary asked.

Ellie turned to her, still distracted.

"You need a hat."

......

When Ellie came into the kitchen, her mother was putting vegetables in a pot for stew. The potatoes and mushrooms were fresh, but the peas and carrots were canned, which was common in winter. With the War underway, however, even dry goods were starting to be in short supply and the local shop had been out of sugar for two weeks. No one was panicking, but rumors of government rationing made people leery, especially those who had lived through it in the last war. And for old-timers who had long grumbled that the modern economy was making them dependent, the mere prospect of shortages was proof enough.

But Islanders were resourceful and even Jack had been hunting for the family's food, which Ellie found odd because he hadn't used his rifle in years. Nevertheless, when she walked over to the counter she saw a big bird, headless, de-feathered, and ready to be cooked.

"Waterfowl again?" she asked, more an observation than a complaint.

"Your father caught it this morning."

"He didn't go out on the boat?"

Vera turned momentarily in her direction but didn't look her in the eye.

"Not today. It's been difficult, with the weather and all."

She spoke plainly, but Ellie could detect a slight hesitation, a faint guilt like she was making excuses and knew it. But Ellie let it go, knowing there was enough deceit to go around, and she decided to go upstairs.

"Ellie," her mother said and she stopped. "A storm's coming. I took the wind chimes down. Could you bring them inside?"

"Of course, Mother."

Ellie walked out the back door, flinching in the cold wind. She heard the sound of a hammer and peered around the side of the house to see her father still working on the shed. He looked up suddenly as if he knew she was watching, and she quickly turned away.

As she knelt to get the box of wind chimes, she noticed someone in the far distance, a figure in dark clothes on the path that went over the hill to the beach. In that instant, she was seized by an uncontrollable curiosity and she had to find out who it was. With her father now out-of-view, she left the box and went down the back stairs, rushing out of the yard and to the bottom of the road. She turned onto the trail behind the Mallet's house and scurried up the ridge. When she got to the top, she put her hands on her hips and gazed out across Taylor Passage.

Something moved behind her and Ellie spun around, startled but not frightened. Whoever it was she saw, she thought, she couldn't have passed them because there was only one path. So she assumed it was her imagination and continued down the other side of the hill, where she spotted a person in the tall grass ahead. Afraid she might lose him, she went faster, pushing through the dead vegetation and scrambling over gaps, her ankles buckling with each frantic step. Suddenly, the trail ended and she spilled out onto the shore, almost losing her balance.

"In a hurry?"

When Ellie looked up, it was a young soldier. She experienced a vague, but foolish disappointment, realizing that some part of her had hoped it was Karl.

"Oh, hello," she said.

He stood beside a small wooden structure that reminded her of the shelters French-Canadian clammers used during the winters when she was a girl.

"I...I saw someone walk over the hill," Ellie said, pointing back.

"That was me. You think I was a Kraut or something?"

She let out a nervous laugh, but the irony was unsettling.

"Is this a lookout post?"

"This?" he said, walking over to the structure. "Naw, it's for the sub nets..."

He took out some keys and opened the door and inside Ellie could see a large winch with a hand crank.

"...we usually only raise them at night," he explained, "but a U-boat was sighted off Newfoundland. We laid a couple eggs on it, but it got away."

Ellie maintained a calm and courteous smile, but something in her stirred, something that went beyond the fear of an enemy attack.

"U-boat?" she said, her voice quivering.

"That's right. And it's headed our way."

37

By the end of the week, everyone was talking about the storm. What started out as rumors of flurries had turned into a full-blown blizzard alert. There were whiteout conditions in Chicago and Cleveland and it was fast coming East. In the dockyards of Portland, owners were hauling out small craft and securing larger vessels with extra bumpers and lines. The Army had issued a warning across Casco Bay and people on Monk Island were stocking up on coal, firewood, and food. The snow was still two days away, but school had been canceled for most counties in Maine.

When Ellie walked into the kitchen, Mary was having breakfast, buttered toast and hot milk, and her mother was moving around hysterically and making preparations. In the icebox, there was frozen cod and a side of bacon; in the pantry, biscuits, flour, and turnips. She had covered the porch furniture with a tarp and taken down the bird feeder. For a woman who some days couldn't sit without wincing in pain, she was remarkably agile when she had to be.

"I need kindling!"

"I'll get some, Mother," Ellie said.

"Make sure it's dry," she said, handing Ellie the log carrier. "Small pieces—pine if you can."

Ellie couldn't tell pine from poplar, but she nodded anyway and went in the parlor. She put on her coat, hat and gloves and was just ready to leave when her father came in, bringing a gust of cold air with him.

"Where're you off to?" he said, and it sounded like an accusation.

"To get firewood."

He stared at her with dark, suspicious eyes, the most attention he had given her in days, and she would have been offended if she wasn't so mystified. She could never tell what her father was thinking, only that he was, and he was the type of man whose emotions had to be deduced by pauses, glances, sighs. If he had something to say, she thought, she wished for once that he would just say it. But the awkward encounter ended when Vera called for him and he walked away.

Ellie left and went to the bottom of the road, turning onto the path behind the Mallet's and following it over the hill. When she got to the beach, she climbed the bluff and walked across the clearing, the same route she and Karl had taken years before when they wandered hand-in-hand in the rain, made love beneath the tree canopy. She stepped into the woods, crouching to pick up twigs and bark, filling the carrier within minutes. As she reached for some pine needles, something moved behind the trees and she got up. She looked around but didn't see anyone and assumed it was chipmunk or a mink.

Ellie headed back and she was almost at the bluff when she was startled by the crack of a branch. She stopped to listen, her heart pounding, but heard only the wind and the rush of the waves in the background. She hurried down the path, glancing behind as she went, more curious than paranoid because she always had a good sense of her surroundings. And her instincts were right because the third time she looked she saw a person moving through the grass. She didn't know if she was being followed, but she was determined not to be outmaneuvered if she was.

Ellie leaped suddenly off the trail and ducked behind a dune and, seconds later, someone walked by. Knowing she could cut him off, she crawled down through the brush and came out to the beach. She looked ahead and saw a man in the distance, walking with his back to her. The moment she realized who it was, she stormed over in a rage.

"Why are you following me?!"

Jack turned around.

"I ain't following you."

"Yes you were!" she said. "You were following me the other day too."

"You left your mother's wind chimes and ran to the beach."

"I saw a soldier."

"There're soldiers everywhere."

"He was alone. I thought it was strange."

Jack looked away, chewing his gums, his frustration obvious.

"Why didn't you tell me about the letter?" he said.

"Why didn't you tell me you lost your boat?"

He finally looked at her, his expression sharp.

"How'd you know that?"

"I saw Ben at the wheel, someone else was pulling traps."

Jack shook his head, made a dismissive frown, and Ellie wasn't sure if he was denying the fact or just downplaying its significance. Either way, he looked as stunned as a film star who, after being shot, teeters too long before collapsing. After years of living with his lies and avoidance, Ellie got some satisfaction in seeing him fret, but when he started to blink compulsively, she realized she had gone too far.

"Daddy, I'm sorry."

She hadn't called him that since she was a little girl and she surprised herself as much as she did him.

As she came forward to console him, Jack put out his hand and she stopped. He looked out to Taylor Passage and the sea beyond, his one refuge in times of distress, and his face twitched in the harsh winter light. When he pretended to scratch his eye, Ellie knew that there was no itch.

"That was my fault," he said, his voice breaking up.

"I didn't mean to say it."

"No. You've every right to," he said, pausing to regain his composure. "Ben told the owner what we were doing. He said it was my idea."

"And was it?"

His hesitation was affirmation enough, but Ellie needed to hear it from him.

"I'd say it was."

For someone as reserved as Jack, those few words were like an outpouring. Ellie knew she had every right to berate him because he had put them all at risk by breaking the law. With his reputation ruined, he would be lucky to get a job as a deckhand, but it was the dead of winter and no one was looking for help. Still, she felt more compassion than she did anger, knowing that he had experienced enough hardship and regret for a lifetime. Without his earnings, the family would surely suffer but they would survive—Monk Islanders always did.

Minutes passed before Jack was calm enough to speak and when he did, Ellie heard a humility in his voice that she had never heard before.

"Tell me about the letter," he said.

"It came in the mail…about a month ago."

"You kept in touch with that boy?"

"No, it was the first time he wrote. How did you know?"

"The Army questioned me. They said to keep an eye on you."

As Jack stood thinking, she came closer and he didn't resist.

"They questioned me too. What made them so interested in the letter?"

"They thought the Germans might be trying to land a spy."

Ellie laughed because it seemed preposterous, but also because it was the only emotion she had left. As the accusation sank in, however, the humor was replaced by bitterness in knowing that, after all this time, Karl was still an object of scorn and suspicion.

"And do you think he's a spy?"

Jack squinted, his deep wrinkles clear in the fading sun. Ellie thought back to when he would carry her on his shoulders down the beach and she wondered how he ever got so old.

"I think I was wrong about that boy."

He walked off and Ellie smiled to herself. She wiped her tears, picked up the bag of kindling and followed after him. They continued down the beach together, the cold water rolling over their shoes. It was the most time they spent alone in years and Ellie remembered all the attention she used to get when she was young, before Mary got sick and before her father got busted.

"You know," he said. "I never meant it to happen."

Ellie didn't have to ask because she knew exactly what he was talking about.

"Of course you didn't."

"If I could—"

"I know."

Jack stopped, put his hands on his hips. He looked out, somewhere between the sky and the horizon, as if asking the Lord himself for forgiveness.

"It's followed me like a damn curse."

Ellie nodded because she understood—the resentment she had towards him was never about the circumstances which led to her sister's condition and always about how he dealt with it. Mary was too little to remember, but Ellie was ten at the time, and what she didn't know her mother told her when she turned sixteen, like some initiation into the secret of the family disgrace. It was the only time Vera ever spoke of the incident, and although Ellie appreciated learning all the details, she didn't like that they continued to pretend it never happened.

When Jack returned home from the War, the economy was booming. So many men were dead or dislocated that the fishing industry was desperate for help and jobs were as easy to come by as business loans. Jack got his own boat, a white Hampton sloop that he bought off Clifford Collier, who he had been working for since he was a teenager.

When Prohibition arrived less than a year later, it was received as enthusiastically by churchgoers as it was by fishermen, but for entirely different reasons. The devout saw it a solution to the wickedness of alcohol—the not-so-devout saw it as an opportunity to make money. Situated offshore, between the inner harbor and coastal waterways, Monk Island was primed for bootlegging and few could resist the temptation to get rich.

The day Jack got arrested, Ellie had gone into Portland with her mother and he said he was going to take Mary with him to collect blueberries. The truth was, however, that he and his cohorts had rendezvoused with a Canadian boat the night before and they needed to stash the liquor. Whenever they got a shipment, they would store it in the woods in a makeshift dugout covered in plywood, safe until they could transport it to buyers on the mainland.

As Jack and the others unloaded the supply from a horse-drawn wagon, Mary had asked to go over to a nearby pond. It was the middle of August and with temperatures in the high nineties, he couldn't say no. Once the men finished burying the crates, they opened a couple of bottles and toasted to another successful run. What started as a celebratory drink turned into an afternoon binge and by the time the police sneaked up from all sides, Jack could barely stand let alone run. Along with the others, he was marched off towards the road in handcuffs, but not before pleading with the agents to get his daughter, and when they found her, she was wading half-dressed in infested water. Only days later, she got a fever. Then, paralysis.

As a veteran, Jack was given a plea deal that kept him out of jail but made him forfeit his boat. He never drank again, a token penance for the crime of his neglect, but it didn't make much difference because thereafter he lived with the soul-crushing weight of an alcoholic's guilt.

38

There was a cheer throughout the cabin when the Captain announced they had entered American waters. It had been five days since they were sighted by the reconnaissance plane and, with no sign of enemy ships, everyone was satisfied that they weren't being tracked. The seas stayed quiet and the skies had a convenient cloud cover that allowed them to surface a couple of times each day. By all measures, the operation was going according to plan and morale was high.

After spending the last six hours scrubbing and oiling the torpedo tubes, Karl was too achy to eat and he went straight to his bunk. Lying on his side, he read The Birds Of Maine, a book his father had given him the Christmas before he joined the Kriegsmarine. He had no interest in ornithology, but Mr. Brink was the kind of person who pushed all his quirky interests on other people.

As Karl flipped through the pages, he touched the illustrations and repeated the names—the Northern Fulmar, Cory's Shearwater, White-Chinned Petrel. The figures looked comical in the murky blue light and he didn't know whether to laugh or cry. There were moments when he thought that, if he didn't escape to America, he would take his own life. The world he knew back in Germany had been obliterated and he didn't believe he would ever see his father again. His mother was safe for the time, but even if they did reunite after the War, she was a different woman than the one who raised him.

"Breakfast!"

Karl awoke with the book on his chest and everywhere around him, men were hopping out of their bunks, pulling on boots and caps. He quickly did the same and got behind the line of sailors crowding into the galley. As with every other activity, they ate in shifts and there still wasn't enough room to sit. He got some biscuits and black coffee and squatted by a wall beside the radio operator, who looked strange without headphones on.

"Where are we?" Karl asked between bites.

"Ninety kilometers east of America."

Karl nodded and continued to eat his stale biscuit, ignoring the spots of mold. After three weeks at sea, they were down to canned meats, powdered milk, and stale coffee that tasted similar to the fake stuff his mother had back in Hamburg.

"Sailors?!"

He glimpsed up and Oberbootsmann Schmitt was looming over them. He looked at Karl but spoke to the whole torpedo crew.

"Check the batteries on numbers three and four. After you're done—"

"Brink," they heard and everyone turned.

Obersteuermann Vogel barged into the galley, men darting out of the way, and his powerful presence changed the mood of the room.

"Herr Obersteuermann," Karl said, getting up.

If it weren't for the pipes overhead, he would have stood up straighter.

"Report to the control room…once you've eaten."

Karl looked at Vogel, then to Schmitt, who was quietly incensed that his own orders were being overruled. He swallowed and nodded nervously.

"Yes, yes, Herr Obersteuermann," he said.

"Very well then, carry on."

Vogel pushed past Schmitt and once he was gone, all the men looked over to Karl and he got self-conscious. Schmitt didn't move and the sweat on his forehead was as much from the heat of the cabin as it was from rage. The moment Karl went to sit again, he said, "The Captain's pet now, are you?"

"With respect, Sir, this doesn't concern—"

"Of course it concerns me!" he barked. He stepped closer to Karl until their faces were just inches apart. "I'm an Officer of the Kriegsmarine."

Karl averted his eyes, but it was impossible to avoid a confrontation.

"I am familiar with the American coastline," he explained. "They've asked my opinion."

"Opinion of what? The best places to dine?"

A couple of sailors chuckled, but Karl refused to react to his intimidation, standing to attention with his arms tight to his side, his chin up. The respect he displayed was for the rank of Oberbootsmann and not for the man who occupied it.

"Amerikaner," Schmitt said, shaking his head in disgust.

He stared into Karl's eyes and when Karl wouldn't flinch, he hissed and walked away.

......

When Karl came in the control room, the Watch Officers and Vogel were standing beside the chart table with the Captain. Unlike the crew, who walked around in a weary stupor, the men all looked focused and alert. The journey across the Atlantic had been agonizing monotony, punctuated by some bad weather and an air attack, and now they were eager to do what they had been sent to do.

"Brink," Captain Dietz said, waving him over.

"Herr Kapitän."

"We are close," he said, leaning over the table. "Our last read puts us here."

Like most nautical maps, it was covered with numbers and notes, indicating coordinates, water depths, weather patterns, and enemy convoy routes. The Captain put his finger on the spot and Karl glanced down. At first, he saw only a shapeless landmass, but the longer he stared, the more familiar it became and soon he recognized the coast of Maine. A chill went up his back and he couldn't believe they were almost there.

"Welcome home, Amerikaner," Vogel said and the others laughed.

Karl might have been offended, but it was only friendly taunt.

"As you can see," Dietz said, "We're less than a hundred kilometers from Portland..."

He slid the map away to reveal another one that was a close-up of Casco Bay and the Islands. It had some land markings and Karl could see Cape Elizabeth, Freeport, Boothbay. He was overcome by a warm nostalgia, remembering the day trips he used to take with his family years before.

"...We will be within sight of land in a couple of hours," the Captain went on.

"We believe there's a storm approaching from the West," the Watch Officer said. "We intercepted some radio transmissions earlier."

The Captain turned to Karl and spoke directly.

"Visibility will be low, which could work in our favor. What do you know about the shipping lanes?"

At that moment, Karl realized it was his one chance to influence their course and, as a consequence, his destiny. He stepped forward with a sudden enthusiasm and leaned over the chart, taking control with the confidence of an expert.

"Big ships pass south of here," he said, pointing to Holyhead Island. "But it is narrow and affected by the tides. There's another commercial channel to the North." Karl put his finger above Monk Island and slid it along the map. "But it's longer, not as deep. Good for light cruisers and frigates, bad for destroyers and battleships."

The men listened intently, their arms crossed, lips pressed together. It wasn't often that senior command sought advice from a sailor, but this was no routine patrol and Karl could tell they valued his knowledge.

As the men stood thinking, the Engineer stepped out of the shadows, his shirt unbuttoned and cap tipped to one side.

"Tell me," he said. "How do you know so much about shipping?"

When the Officers looked at Karl, he turned to the man and spoke without the slightest hesitation.

"I am a swimmer," he explained. "When I spent the summer in Maine before the War, I would swim among those islands. I grew to understand the boat traffic."

The Captain looked at the Engineer, who nodded as if satisfied by the answer.

"A swimmer?" the Captain remarked. "Then you're at home among the seas?"

Karl smiled nervously and found it difficult to make eye contact with any of the Officers. Instead, he gazed at the map

322

and examined the crooked coastline of Monk Island, knowing that, after all this time, he might finally be returning to Ellie.

"Very much so," he said.

39

Ellie sat at the counter while Mr. Mallet worked in the storeroom. He could have closed for the whole month of January, but even with half the fleet grounded, there was always work to do. The walls were lined with broken traps and torn nets and in the corner was an engine from a small sloop, propped up on blocks and covered in barnacles. Someone had dropped off a cracked winch, but the only welder on Monk Island had gone to Florida for the winter so they would have to send it to Portland to be repaired. Much like the ocean, the business of fishing was never-ending.

"Ellie?"

She turned around and Joe Mallet was in the doorway.

"Mr. Mallet," she said, slightly startled.

"Did the night crawlers arrive?"

"Yes. They're in the cooler."

"The nails and clamps?"

"In the cabinet. I sorted them by size."

He rubbed his chin and gazed down in thought, the crown of his head thinning, his hairline damp. He always seemed to be sweating, even in winter, and he worked six days a week whether he had to or not. Mr. Mallet had all the determination of her father, Ellie thought, with none of the demons, and she understood where Kate got her drive. She always assumed he regretted not serving in the Great War, but now she was not so sure. For many local veterans, the experience of combat was more a crutch than a distinction, and it seemed to justify all their petty grievances against the world. Joe Mallet may not have had their prestige, but he also didn't suffer their malaise. And although he wasn't a hero in the conventional sense, he was a good father and a good man, and he taught Ellie that there was honor in just being ordinary.

"Did you hear me?"

Ellie came out of a daydream.

"Pardon?"

"I said, you should go home before it starts snowing."

"Okay," she said, getting off the stool. "Thank you, Mr. Mallet."

As she went to get her things, he stopped and turned around.

"Say, Ellie? Is everything alright?"

Putting on her coat, she looked over with a vague smile and nodded.

"Yes, of course."

Ellie stepped outside into the cold and windless afternoon, the air filled with a staticky exuberance, that peculiar atmospheric lull which always comes before a storm. She moved fast to stay warm, thinking about Mr. Mallet's remark and embarrassed that he knew something was wrong. She could always restrain her emotions, but she could never hide them and, even as a little girl, strangers could tell when she was sad or upset.

For weeks, Ellie had been walking around in a fog, her mood as gray and sullen as the winter landscape. Life seemed random, aimless, devoid of any meaning. She got a letter from Karl and it was stolen; she got a job at the base and was fired; finally, she discovered that Ben had betrayed her and her father and that Jack lost his boat because of it. Only a month before, the future seemed bright all around and now it was dismal. If Ellie learned anything from the attack on Pearl Harbor, it was that the world could change in an instant.

When she came into the house, Vera was cooking and Mary was doing her homework at the table. With Scuttles purring in the corner, soft music playing on the radio, it was almost tranquil.

"Home already?"

"I got out early because of the storm."

"It's no storm. It's a blizzard."

Moments later, the front door opened and it was Jack. He stomped his boots on the mat and came into the kitchen with a newspaper under one arm.

"Our boys are taking a beating in Bataan," he muttered.

"Where is Bataan?" Vera asked.

"Philippines," Mary said and Ellie smiled.

Everyone sat down and Vera brought over a pot of soup and homemade bread. Jack said a quick prayer and they filled their bowls and began to eat.

"How was work?" Vera said to Jack.

With the spoon at her mouth, Ellie glimpsed up, but her father wouldn't look back.

"Quiet day," he said, "dropped a couple dozen pots."

Ellie cringed at the lie because it somehow implicated her own dishonesty. Since their reconciliation on the beach, neither of them had said anything to Vera, worried it would only upset her. Jack didn't tell her that Ellie got let go from the base and Ellie didn't tell her that Jack lost his boat. Considering Karl's letter and the Army's investigation into it, the two lived under a ticking time-bomb of revelations which was bound to detonate at some point. But Ellie knew they were only trying to protect her mother and Mary and she found some warm kinship in the secrets she shared with her father.

The window rattled and everyone looked over to see flakes. After a week of news reports, rumors and preparation, the snow had finally arrived.

Jack finished eating, wiped his chin, and got up.

"Are you going on patrol tonight?"

"To hell with all that," he said. "Let the Army guard the Island. That's what they're here for."

He turned and walked out of the kitchen. While Mary looked confused, Vera seemed shaken and when she got up to clear the table, Ellie insisted on helping. They washed the dishes together in silence, her mother scrubbing them with her gnarled hands and Ellie drying them with an old rag. It was barely dusk, but outside the sky was almost dark and the hillside was blanketed in white.

They heard footsteps and looked behind to see Jack standing in the doorway, dressed in a wool coat and trapper hat, clutching his rifle like he was going on a game hunt.

"Where are you going?" Vera remarked.

"I gotta tie the tarp down over the traps behind the shed. Then I'm gonna see if I can't catch some waterfowl fleeing this storm."

"Well, you'd better hurry. The storm is here."

Without another word, he left and the front door slammed shut. Once the dishes were done, Vera turned on the kettle for tea and Ellie finished sweeping the floor. They were just ready to sit down to relax when something thumped above and they both looked up.

"Will you go see what your sister is up to?"

"Of course, Mother."

Ellie walked up the stairs, the house creaking in the wind, and when she reached the landing, the bedroom door was open but the light wasn't on. As she approached, she felt a cold breeze that was more than a draft.

"What are you doing?"

Mary flinched and turned, her face aghast, binoculars in hand. The window was wide open and snow was pouring in.

"I see one."

"See what?"

As Ellie rushed over to close the sash, Mary mumbled, "U-boat," and she stopped.

They faced each other in the shadowy light and Ellie could tell that her sister was truly stunned.

"A U-boat?" she said, with more doubt than dread.

Nevertheless, she grabbed the binoculars and looked out, blinking in the gusty wind. Parts of the coast were still visible, the strange effect of snow at twilight, and she could see buoys bouncing in the surf. But when she scanned the water from Drake's Cove to Taylor Passage, she didn't notice anything unusual.

"Nonsense," Ellie said.

Mary adjusted her crutches and came closer, putting her hand on Ellie's shoulder, pointing.

"Start at the cliffs," she said. "Go left, probably a mile. It's there."

Despite her skepticism, Ellie tried again. She squinted through the lenses, turned the focus wheel, and followed Mary's directions. She started at the tip of Holyhead Island and moved north towards Beacon Light, expecting to see nothing and proceeding like she would not. But after a few seconds, a strange shape caught her eye and she froze.

"Do you see it?"

"Shush."

The longer Ellie stared, the clearer it became and she couldn't deny there was something out there. Then in one instant, the entire form coalesced and she observed the outline of a hull and a tower. She put down the binoculars and gasped.

"You saw it, didn't you?"

Ellie's heart pounded and she felt dizzy. She looked at her sister and they shared a moment of mutual and bone-chilling astonishment.

"Is it a U-boat?" Mary said.

Ellie shook her head because she didn't know and she would have looked again if she wasn't so frightened.

"It's…something…I…can't be sure," she said, her words breathless, scattered.

"Maybe it's Karl?"

Ellie's face dropped and, in one unexpected burst, she flew into a rage. She grabbed Mary by the wrist and spoke in an angry whisper.

"Why would you say that?!"

"That hurts," Mary said, squirming.

"Tell me why you said that!"

When she released some pressure, Mary's head sank and she stood whimpering. Mary hesitated a few seconds and then looked up with a remorseful pout.

"I read the letter."

Like coming out of a spell, Ellie realized the horror of what she was doing and let go. She stepped back in disgust and put her hands over her face. Her cheeks were wet, but she didn't know if it was from tears or from the snow. With the window still open, things fluttered in the bedroom, snow accumulated on the sill and floor. Ellie looked at her little sister with a trembling smile.

"I'm so sorry," she said and Mary just stared at her.

Mary had thought of something she never did and now it all made sense. Ellie leaned forward and kissed her on the forehead, soft and gently, like when she was a baby.

Then she ran out of the room and went to get her coat.

40

"Prepare to reach trim depth!"

The voice that came over the sound tube was calm so there was no reason to worry. Still, there was nervous anticipation all around because they were now in hostile waters. The ballast pumps started and the cabin lights flickered. The entire boat shuddered and slowly began to rise, surfacing to flush the air and recharge the batteries, maybe conduct some surveillance.

Walking through the cabin, Karl was overcome by a slight nausea and he couldn't look anyone in the eye. He was terrified in knowing that he would have to act at the first chance. He approached the control room and ducked to see two of the Watch Officers and the Captain. They were standing at the base of the conning tower, looking up. A gust of crisp air came into the cabin and Karl knew the hatch had been opened.

"Amerikaner!"

Karl looked and Vogel was waving from the ladder.

The Captain and his Officers glanced over, but they were busy with other things.

"Herr Obersteuermann."

"Come see your homeland," Vogel said with a quiet chuckle.

Karl nodded nervously, knowing they must have been within sight of land. Now that the time had come, he was paralyzed by fear and wasn't sure he could do it. He didn't have the inflatable life jacket and they might have been too far away from shore for him to swim without it. Or perhaps, he thought, they had surfaced somewhere else, in an area he wasn't familiar with, where the currents were deadly.

"Come see," Vogel said. "It's like Christmas."

In those few seconds, Karl remembered a technique his swim coach taught him. He closed his eyes, breathed deep and imagined the goal he wanted to achieve. As he did, he saw the water, the shoreline, the beach, the birds, the cliffs, the trawlers. In one single flash, the tranquility of Monk Island came into his mind and it was so real he could smell it. He realized then that, since leaving Ellie, everything that happened in his life had prepared him for this exact moment.

Crouched at the bulkhead, Karl looked at Vogel, who was talking with one of the Officers.

"I need my coat," he said, but they didn't answer.

He turned around and headed towards the sleeping quarters. Fellow sailors nodded as he passed and he had the strange sensation of trying to leave a party without saying goodbye. The only difference was that if he got caught he would be executed—there was no mercy for deserters.

Karl squeezed through the last bulkhead and saw his bunk in the shadows. Now that they were in enemy territory, the entire crew was on-duty and no one was sleeping. The first thing he did was grab his coat and put it on. Next, he pulled out his duffle bag and opened the side pouch. Inside was his military identification card, carefully wrapped in plastic, the only verification of his true identify if he got caught by the Americans. In most wars, spies were shot on sight and it might be his only chance to prove he was a regular soldier, that he had abandoned his ship.

Crouched at his bunk, Karl carefully untied the top flap on his bag. He closed his eyes, said a silent prayer, and reached inside. His heart dropped when he realized that the life jacket was gone.

"Sailor?"

He slowly glanced back and Schmitt was hovering over him.

"Herr Oberbootsmann," he said, standing up.

"Looking for something?"

"Nothing of importance, Sir."

Schmitt stepped forward and brought his face to within an inch of Karl's.

"Planning on going somewhere?"

Karl filled with a violent rage that took all his strength to control. He had come halfway across the world for love and freedom and nothing would stop him short of a bullet. He glanced past Schmitt and the closest sailors were two compartments away in the galley. Karl pivoted his eyes until they met Schmitt's and, for a brief moment, he actually felt pity for the man. Then he lunged and grabbed him by the throat.

Schmitt tried to resist, but Karl was too quick. He dug his thumbs into his trachea and squeezed so hard Schmitt's eyes bulged. Seconds later, his body went limp and he collapsed on the floor with a thud.

"What's the problem?!"

Karl looked and some sailors were rushing towards him.

"Oberbootsmann has taken ill, I believe."

Karl heard gargling and knew that Schmitt still alive. As the crewmembers approached, he went by them and they were confused. Whether they were suspicious or not, he couldn't tell but when he hopped through the bulkhead, he slammed the door and locked it.

Karl went quickly through the cabin but didn't run because he didn't want to draw attention. When he finally got to the Control Room, the Captain and his Officers were standing around the chart table.

"Stop him!" someone shouted from behind and Karl panicked.

It took the men a moment to realize something was wrong and by the time they did, Karl had gotten to the ladder. As he scrambled up there was a series of sharp dings—someone was shooting—but he made it to the top and burst out of the hatch. Outside it was snowing intensely and the bridge was covered. The Watch Officer and Vogel turned around at the same time.

"Amerikaner," Vogel said, surprised.

Before they knew what was happening, Karl leaped over the railing and lingered at the edge for an instant, gazing at the white, frothy turbulence below. Then he jumped head first into it.

When he hit the water, his entire body tensed up from the shock of the cold. He rolled and flailed and thrashed, but each time he tried to come up for air, waves knocked him back. He was just ready to give up when the seas around him subsided and he was able to stabilize. He got above the surface long enough to see and somehow the snow made it easier to tell where land was.

Karl turned towards the coast and swam as hard as he could. Even in a storm, there is a tide and by some miracle, it was moving in his direction. Years of ice swimming had conditioned him for this, but he knew it wouldn't be long before hypothermia set in.

Karl continued for what felt like forever and he was starting to get weak. When he looked ahead, he saw a dark landmass and went towards it for half a mile. He raised his head to look again and was so astonished he thought that he was hallucinating. To his left were some large cliffs—to his right, an island whose shape was instantly familiar.

Karl was at the mouth of Taylor Passage.

As he swam towards the beach, he noticed flickers, almost like fireflies, and when he got closer, he realized they were flashlights—dozens of them. He didn't know if they were looking for him, but he wasn't going to take a chance. So he turned and swam up the coast, staying low in the water, breathing only when he had to. His vision was blurred and he had a paralyzing headache. He stuck out his tongue to hydrate himself with snowflakes, but it wasn't enough. He was beginning to lose consciousness and, even if he made land, he wasn't sure he would survive.

Karl came around a bend and saw a dark cove. In one final burst of exertion, he went towards it and it was mostly instinct because he had lost all will to keep going. But soon his feet touched bottom and he waded through the shallows as patches of snow floated around him.

He crawled the last few yards to the shore. The air was colder than the water and when he finally got on land, he thought he would freeze like a dead seal. But he kept moving, knowing that his only chance was to get to the woods and bury himself in dirt to stay warm.

"Don't move!"

Collapsed on the rocky ground, he glimpsed up and saw a man. He wasn't a soldier because he wore civilian clothing, but he had on a white helmet, a whistle around his neck. In the snowy darkness of the storm, their eyes met for a telling half-second and Karl knew that he was hostile. But there was some peace in knowing he was caught because it meant his suffering was over. Shivering and weak, Karl rolled on his back, thought of Ellie, and shut his eyes.

41

Ellie ran frantically up the narrow trail, her arms flailing, slipping on the snow-covered rocks. When she reached the top, she looked out and Taylor Passage was a haze of white fury. She waited a few seconds to catch her breath, then continued down the other side, navigating by memory because the world was an indistinguishable blur.

In all her torment to understand Karl's letter, Ellie had considered many things, but never this. The idea that he would return on a German warship was as audacious as it was farfetched, and she felt crazy for even thinking it could be true. But she trudged on towards the shore because she had to find out.

Suddenly, there were voices, the bark of dogs.

She stooped in the weeds and squinted ahead, but the flurries made it impossible to see. She got back up and went quickly in another direction. The snow enveloped her body, seeping into her boots and crawling up her sleeves, and she knew that if she didn't keep moving, she could die of exposure. When she came to another path, she heard more voices and they were closer.

"Hey, you! Stop!"

Ellie felt a sweep of light and turned around in a panic. She ran with all her remaining strength, pushing through the dead grass, following the sound of the waves. When she finally burst out onto the beach, she looked up and her heart sank.

"Don't move!"

Standing around her was a half dozen soldiers, their rifles pointed, flashlights aimed. Blinded by the glare, she couldn't see any of their faces, but she saw three German Shepherds.

They lunged and they snarled, their jaws snapping. Ellie raised her arms and one of the men stepped forward.

"Miss," he said, shouting over the wind. "You need to come with us."

He motioned for her to move and she obeyed. She didn't know if she was being detained or under arrest, but she was adamant she had done nothing wrong. Three soldiers escorted her up to the bluff, while the rest continued their search and the fact that the Army was scouring the beach confirmed for her that something had, in fact, happened.

"Am I in trouble?

When the soldier turned to her, it was the young man she met who was raising the submarine nets on the beach.

"No one said you're in trouble, Miss."

"Are you looking for someone?"

"Should we be looking for someone?"

Before she could answer, a gunshot rang out in the distance. Clutching their rifles, the men all stopped and listened.

"What the hell was that?!"

"Maybe they got the goddamn Kraut," someone said.

"I sure hope so."

42

Ellie lay curled up on the hard wooden bench. A single light hung from the ceiling, casting a sterile glow across the small and barren room. She was wrapped in a coarse wool blanket, given to her by some staff member, but it wasn't enough to relieve the chill and she shivered uncontrollably.

Ellie didn't know how long she had been there—the seconds blended into minutes into hours—but she knew what it felt like to be in prison. Outside, people moved about in the hallway, their voices muffled, their words indistinguishable. She wanted to get up, pound on the door, demand to know why she was there. But she was weighed down by a deep lethargy that made her think she was either delirious or seriously ill. Either way, she was tired of resisting fate and decided that regardless of what had happened and what was to come, she would accept the consequences.

Sometime later, the door opened and Ellie's eyes flickered open. The first person she saw was Colonel Rowland, who made a comforting smile and stepped in. When her father walked in behind him, all her despondency turned to elation and she leaned up. He was wet all over, from his hat down to his boots, and he looked like he had been outside for hours. He came over and sat beside her, the closest they had been in years, and she finally felt safe.

"What happened?".

"Let's go," was all he said.

She stood up groggily and Jack helped her on with her coat. He put his arm around her, escorting her like an invalid, and the Major held open the door. They went slowly down the corridor, passing officers, soldiers, and civilian staff, most of whom were too busy to notice them. They turned into a stairwell and went down one flight, a cold draft seeping through the newly constructed walls. The building was similar to the one she had worked in, except twice the size, and she assumed it was the operations center.

When they came out the front door, Ellie realized that she couldn't have been detained for too long because it was still snowing, although the storm was tapering off. In the parking lot, some soldiers stood huddled in a circle, smoking cigarettes, rifles over their shoulders. Major Rowland called to them and a young man ran over.

"Sir," he said.

"Sergeant Pelletier. Take these folks home."

Pelletier saluted and Ellie and her father followed him over to a truck that was idling. The Sergeant helped her up onto the running board and she climbed in the back and sat on a bench. Jack took the front seat and they drove off, out of the lot and through the backroads of the base. Equipment rattled as they fishtailed around corners and the canvas top flapped in the wind. Ellie had never been in a military vehicle before and its cold austerity gave her some sense of the bleakness of War.

"Any sign of him?" Ellie heard her father say.

"Naw," the soldier replied. "But they'll catch the Kraut. If you want my opinion, he's probably on the mainland by now."

Nothing more was said about the incident, but when they came out to The Pass, Ellie could see twinkles of light on the shoreline and knew the Army was still searching. On the backshore, the wind off the water created snowdrifts which were two and three feet in places. The Sergeant had to stop a couple of times to clear the windshield and it took them twenty minutes to go two miles.

When they came around the bend to Drake's Cove, the homes were all dark. With no blackout scheduled, it was obvious that the power was out. They rumbled up the hill, the tires slipping, and when Jack pointed out their house, the Sergeant stopped and kept his foot on the brake. Jack helped Ellie out of the back and then thanked the man, who gave a curt wave, revved the engine and drove away.

Ellie and her father trudged across the front yard like weary travelers after a long journey. The wind had finally died down, the flakes dispersing, and in the distance, the flash from Beacon Light cut clear across the water in wide, circular sweeps. Slowly the fury was replaced by silence, the only sound the whisper of the breeze, the crack of branches under the weight of the new-fallen snow. There was a strange calm in the air, like the euphoria experienced when a fever breaks. In a place where the climate was a metaphor for life, every storm was another hurdle in the great struggle of mankind and Ellie never felt so grateful to be alive.

"Why'd they let me out?" she said, as they went up the front steps.

"There was no reason to keep you."

"But they surrounded me at the beach...like I did something wrong."

Jack stopped on the porch and turned to her, his face obscured in the darkness.

"I told them you went out looking for me."

At first, she was uneasy, but in the scope of all the secrets, lies and half-truths, one more wouldn't make a difference.

She didn't have time to fret about it anyway because the moment they reached the door, it swung open.

"My God, Ellie?!" her mother said, taking her by the arm and bringing her inside. "You had me worried half to death."

"I'm sorry."

"You should not have been out there!"

"I know, Mother."

"The Army said a U-boat landed a spy. They're looking everywhere."

It was well past midnight, but embers were still smoldering in the fireplace, filling the parlor with a smoky warmth. With the power out, Vera had lit a candle and in the shadowy light, Ellie could see her sister crouched at the bottom of the stairs, watching.

Since the summer she got the binoculars, Mary had been searching for U-boats, and while everyone found it cute, no one took it seriously. By the time she spotted the submarine, the military already knew and had launched a manhunt. For Ellie, the sighting brought more hope than terror, and she was redeemed by the possibility that Karl had finally come back. Whether or not it was him, she didn't know, but in those short minutes of running to the shore, she remembered what it felt like to love him and for that she would be forever grateful. As she took off her things, she smiled at Mary, both an apology and an acknowledgment—she had never been more proud of her.

Vera put Ellie's coat by the fire to dry and Jack roused his youngest daughter, picking her up because she didn't have her crutches. Mary embraced him like a child, limp and half-sleeping, but she looked too big in his arms, and Ellie realized that, in some ways, they were all clinging to parts of their pasts that they had outgrown.

Without a word, Jack started up the stairs, one hand on the banister, his large hulk wavering. It was an abrupt ending to a long and tumultuous night, and although Ellie knew there was still more to say, it would have to wait until morning because everyone was exhausted.

While Vera stirred the fading ashes, Scuttles walked in the room, his tail up and purring.

"What made you go down to the beach in this weather anyway?"

"I went to look for Father…"

43

The next morning the sun was out and the sky was clear for the first time in months. The blizzard had passed as quickly as it arrived, leaving the world covered under a layer of pure, crystalline white. Ellie leaned up in the bed, rubbed her eyes, and looked over to see Mary sleeping. For a moment, she thought it might have all been a dream—or a nightmare—but when she saw that she was still dressed in her clothes from the night before, she knew it wasn't.

Ellie got up quietly and tiptoed out of the room. As she came down the stairs, she heard whimpering and walked in the kitchen to find her mother crying at the table.

"Mother?"

"I have awful news," she said, her cheeks red, eyes swollen. "Mrs. Halstead called. Ben Frazier was killed last night."

"Killed?"

"He was shot, near Drake's Cove."

"But how?"

"The German spy, they think. Ben was out on patrol."

Ellie swallowed once and sat down, too stunned for tears. She didn't know if it was Karl on that submarine, but she couldn't believe that he would ever harm someone. She thought about Ben and everything that happened and, in that instant, she forgave him. She had known him since she was a child and despite their falling out, it hurt to think that she would never see him again.

Except for the old and the infirm, no one seemed to die on Monk Island, and the last murder was before Ellie was born when a man from the north side killed his wife for burning a steak. But even they were elderly so it somehow didn't count against the community's reputation as a place where bad things didn't happen. The only time a young person passed away was in combat, something which hadn't happened in twenty years, and Ellie found it easier to accept that Ben was a casualty of War.

"What's wrong?"

They both turned and Mary was standing in the doorway in her nightgown. When Vera hesitated, Ellie answered for her.

"Ben Frazier was killed last night.".

Her mouth dropped open—her face went white.

"Who?..." she said, unable to finish the sentence.

Ellie glanced at her mother, whose only response was a sigh.

"We don't know yet," Ellie said.

When Mary's bottom lip started to quiver, Vera got up and went over to her. The sight of them embraced, a cripple and an invalid, was more touching than tragic but it reminded Ellie just how hard their lives were. She felt saddest for her sister who, no longer shielded by the innocence of childhood, now sobbed like a woman.

. . . . . .

After breakfast, the girls bundled up and went outside to help their father clear the snow. With the manhunt still underway, the Army trucks had given everyone a head start by plowing the main roads, and if residents didn't feel under siege before, they did now because troops were everywhere. Patrol boats circled the Bay, going between Holyhead Island and Beacon Light, and a search plane passed overhead. Rumors were that the spy had made it to the mainland, but until it was announced, people remained on alert, keeping doors and windows locked, firearms close by.

Ellie offered a small spade to Mary, who even with crutches had the dexterity to shovel and always liked to. But when she shook her head and turned away, Ellie realized she was too upset to do anything. The news of Ben's death left them all in a quiet state of shock and the only one who seemed unaffected was Jack. Vera thought it was because Ben had betrayed him, but Ellie knew her father wasn't that callous and she attributed his indifference to the fact that men grieved in other ways.

While Mary went to play in the snow, Ellie shoveled her way towards her father, knowing he was more receptive when approached gradually. He hadn't said a word all morning, but she could tell he was agitated by the way he worked, digging through the berm left by the plow with the same fierce intensity that he chopped firewood or pulled traps. Physical movement for Jack had always been a remedy for living and she worried how long he could go without a boat or other employment. But above all, he was a survivor, the quality she most admired about him, and when it came to the big questions, she still looked to him for the answers.

"Was it him?"

Bent over, he glanced back with a frown.

"What?"

"Was it Karl. Did he kill Ben?"

Jack stopped what he was doing and turned around, winded from exertion, his forehead glistening. He rested both hands on the shovel handle and thought for a moment.

"Doubt it."

"But you can't be sure," she said, her voice breaking.

"Didn't you say his father was against Hitler?"

When Ellie nodded, it was enough to unleash the emotion she had been holding back and tears began streaming down her face.

"Impossible," he said. "They'd never let someone like that in the German Navy."

1945

44

The shop door opened and Ellie glimpsed up from the counter to see a lobsterman. With his dark scruff and crisp face, he looked no different than the dozens of others who came into Lavery's every day for bait and supplies. As he walked over, however, Ellie realized it was her father and it frightened her that she sometimes didn't recognize him. After four years, the strain of war was starting to show on people but Jack had aged a decade. His once speckled hair was now full gray and his face had a permanent wince from back pain and other injuries.

"Hello, Father."

"Ellie," he said.

In his shabby smock and work boots, Jack had a defeated dignity. After losing his boat for shacking, his reputation was ruined and he was never hired by another firm. The family nearly ended up destitute until Joe Mallet came to their aid, giving Jack a small dory that had been sitting in his yard since Ellie could remember. It was dilapidated but intact and he restored it with an artisan's pride, resealing the boards, sanding the hull, putting on a new keel, and staining it with linseed oil. Propelled by oars and a single sail, the vessel was a remnant from the past, but it could hold a dozen pots and was seaworthy enough to get around the bay when the winds were low.

"Forty pounds of herring."

As Ellie turned to get it, Mr. Mallet walked in with the mail.

"Jack," he said and they shook. "How's the catch?"

"Army's finally letting us around Holyhead, but there're a thousand traps there now."

"Have you tried farther North? Harspwell? Mouth of the Kennebec?"

"I'm gonna drop a few out by the Shoals."

Mallet raised his eyes and even Ellie was concerned enough to stop.

"I dunno, Jack. It's still pretty rough out there this time of year."

With his arms crossed, Jack acknowledged him with a wry grin—he didn't like being told how to do his work. If it was anyone else, he might have been offended, but Joe Mallet had done more to help them than anyone. He had given Ellie a job and Jack a boat. He had even written letters of recommendation for Mary, who was applying for college in the fall, the first one in their family to do so. Although Mr. Mallet never went himself, he was more literate than anyone they knew, having a brother who graduated from the University of Maine and a cousin who went to Harvard.

By the time Ellie came back from the freezer, the conversation had moved on to the War, which was developing so fast that people were losing track. In the Pacific, the Americans had invaded Okinawa and in Europe, they had crossed the Rhine into Germany. With the Russians closing in from the East, the Third Reich was collapsing from all sides. Considering that an Allied victory was in sight, there was finally something more important to talk about than fishing.

Ellie put the bait on the counter and Joe Mallet walked away. Jack scribbled his name on the invoice and grabbed the box, lingering long enough to get his daughter's attention. When she peered up from the ledger, he stood with an expression that was flat but not entirely vacant. For much of her life, she couldn't read him, but time had worn away the armor of his stoicism and even if she didn't know what he was thinking, she knew what he felt.

"Let's go into Portland this weekend," he said. "Maybe see a movie."

The offer warmed her heart and she nodded with a smile.

"I'd like that."

"See you later then?"

"Okay, sure," Ellie said. "See you later."

He turned around and headed for the door, his boots plodding across the wide-plank floor. The box was heavy, but not enough to explain why he hobbled and he carried the weight of a lifetime of regret and disappointments. Whenever Ellie saw him struggling, she got the urge to cry and she only didn't because she knew how much he scorned sympathy. Jack had always been a hard man to understand and an easy man to dislike and now those things were reversed. He may not have achieved all he wanted, but with his own boat, a family that loved him, and place where he was known and respected, he was living his best life.

"Great news!"

When Ellie turned, Mr. Mallet came out from the storeroom waving a letter.

"News?" she said.

"Kate's getting married."

Ellie acted surprised even though she wasn't, and if she noticed anything about getting older it was the gradual loss of easy excitement, giddy enthusiasm. It wasn't just about age, however, because the War had left everyone a little more cynical.

Kate hadn't been home since she left the week after Pearl Harbor. Reading about the U-boat sighting in the news, she had written to Ellie but once the manhunt ended, their correspondence faded like it did the first time she went away. The Army announced that the search was only a precaution and that it was determined that the Germans had not, in fact, landed a spy. Throughout Casco Bay, people were relieved, but on Monk Island, they maintained a quiet skepticism because no one trusted the military.

"Isn't that terrific," Ellie said. "Who's the lucky man?"

"A Captain in the R.A.F."

With the start of the War, Kate's assignment in Florida had been cut short and her last letter to Ellie said her Army Nurses Corp unit was shipping out for England. Even then, Ellie knew she was gone forever because anyone who experienced the wider world had no business returning to the provincial ways of coastal Maine.

"They're gonna settle in Coventry," Mr. Mallet went on. "Can you believe it?"

"As a matter of fact, I can."

......

By the time Ellie got out of work, the winds had picked up and it looked like rain. She crossed through the village and some soldiers were sitting on the bench by the ice cream parlor. There was a jeep idling in front of the Inn and a military boat down at the dock. By now, the Army was a natural part of the landscape and there were days Ellie wondered what life would be like without them.

The War was coming to a close—at least in Europe—but the signs of its consequences were everywhere. On her way to work each morning, Ellie saw in the windows of homes the Blue Star Flag of families who had loved ones fighting overseas. There were gold flags too, less common but far more chilling, indicating that a service member had been killed in action. Much like in the First World War, Monk Island had sacrificed more than its share for the cause of freedom. Joe Mallet's nephew—Junebug's cousin—was killed at Guadalcanal. One of the Fallon boys died in Palermo on his birthday. D-day was the worst in recent memory and three locals lost their lives on the beaches of Normandy, including Harold Simms, a classmate of Ellie's. Even with hostilities winding down, everyone was prepared for more and the cemetery had gone so far as to reserve space.

As Ellie came around the bend on Gull Avenue, the woods were starting to fill in with leaves, but she could still see the water beyond. She could never look at Taylor Passage without thinking of Karl and that long, lost and forgotten summer which, considering all that had happened since, seemed like another century. In some strange way, she felt closer to him now than she did before as if the whims of girlhood romance had matured into something deeper and more significant. She hoped Karl had survived the War, but after seeing the photographs of Germany, where cities were leveled and entire populations wiped out, she couldn't be sure.

Ellie turned onto her street and in the distance, the sky over the ocean was dark and turbulent, the rumblings of a spring rainstorm. She got to the porch just before it started to pour and when she walked inside her mother called to her before she even had time to put her things down. Thinking that something was wrong, Ellie ran straight to the kitchen.

"I got in!"

Mary looked up from the table, an acceptance letter to college in hand, and beside her, Vera sat choked with emotion.

"Our baby," she said. "Can you believe it?"

When Ellie rushed over to hug her sister, Vera put her arms around both of them and, for the next few minutes, the three women of the Ames family silently embraced.

"I'm so proud of you," Ellie said, wiping her eyes.

She thought back to when the War started and Mary was just a tomboy with tangled hair and freckles. She wore sack dresses and walked around barefoot, more interested in the mysteries of nature than of boys, bras or Bachelor's Degrees. Now she was a young lady and Ellie couldn't help but feel that some sacred duty had been fulfilled, some obligation met. Although she would always credit her mother for raising Mary, she took satisfaction in knowing that she was there too.

"You're not angry?"

"Don't be silly," Ellie said and she glanced down at the letter.

On behalf of the faculty and staff at the University of Maine, I am pleased to extend an offer of admission for the fall 1945 semester...

As she read the words, a tear rolled down her face and she reached for a napkin.

"They gave her a $1000 scholarship too," Vera said and it was more money than anybody could imagine.

Ellie squeezed her sister one more time and then got up to make dinner.

"I already diced the turnips," Vera said. "The turkey legs are in the icebox."

While Ellie prepared the food, her mother sat at the table and directed, telling her where to cut and what to add. Vera's arthritis had reached a point where it hurt to even stand and Ellie hated seeing her suffer. For a woman who had been self-sufficient all her life, it was a particularly humiliating decline and the only upside was that everyone rallied around her, assisting in ways that eased her burden without compromising her dignity. Ellie did a lot of the cooking and Mary helped with the chores. Even Jack put aside his prejudices about tradition and marital roles and some days Ellie would come home to find him hanging the laundry on the line, dusting the hallway.

"When's Papa coming home?" Mary wondered and they were all eager for him to learn the news.

"Lord knows," Vera said. "A lobsterman's life is unpredictable."

. . . . . .

Jack didn't come home that night. When he wasn't there for dinner, no one was surprised because it was the spring season. With longer daylight hours, many men worked late to get a head start on the tourists, who always arrived en masse and got in the way. Evening turned into night, but still they didn't panic, knowing that after a long day at sea Jack sometimes slept in the boathouse or stayed out fishing with friends. Although not everyone on Monk Island had a telephone, Vera called around to those who did and no one had seen Jack since morning.

By midnight, Mary had gone to bed and their mother lay on the couch in the parlor with her swollen feet up. She told Ellie how when Jack used to drink, he was sometimes gone for days. Her friends would urge her to go look for him at the Legion or down the docks, but Vera let him be, knowing how a dog that left and came back was more faithful than a dog that never went away. Her parents never wanted her to marry him but Vera knew he was the one because, unlike the more responsible men she met, he always returned.

Recollections of his wayward past were poignant, but they did nothing to comfort Ellie and she paced the room, worried and half-listening. As the hours passed, Vera eventually dozed off, leaving Ellie alone in the chair and struggling to stay awake. She resisted the fatigue with all her might, but the low lighting and patter of the rain were too much and, at some point, she drifted off too.

Suddenly, a loud knock.

Startled awake, Ellie opened her eyes and her mother was already up and going for the front door. In an instant, the fog of sleep vanished and she was seized by an unbearable dread that left her tearing up before she understood why. She wanted to beg her mother not to answer as if it would somehow forestall fate, but Vera did and Ellie saw several men, including some soldiers and Joe Mallet. As she slowly approached, she could tell something was wrong by their soft voices, somber faces. But before she could ask, Vera let out a terrifying scream and collapsed on the floor.

45

Jack Ames died as he had lived—trying to tame the wildness around him. For a man who never ventured far, he was always pushing the boundaries of his own narrow domain. Except for eighteen months in the War, he spent his entire life on Monk Island and he knew the land and waters of Casco Bay like Magellan knew the Pacific. And although the scale was different, the passion was very much the same.

Ellie was told that a patrol boat had spotted the wreckage of Jack's dory in the rough chop just after dark. The Army suspected that the hull had been smashed apart because the stern was floating off Beacon light and the bow was nowhere to be found. They combed the area for him, but with the danger of enemy surveillance, they couldn't use searchlights and had to wait again until morning. By that time, the debris had scattered and Jack's body was discovered two days later near the south side of Holyhead Island.

Most locals knew enough to stay away from the Shoals, a rocky outcropping that was teeming with lobster because it was so seldom fished. The currents were treacherous and, much like the myth of El Dorado, it threatened to destroy anyone who sought it. When Jack decided to drop traps there, it was as heroic as it was foolish and might have been his one last chance to thumb his nose at the world.

......

Ellie stood in the pew with her arm around her sister, who trembled in her Sunday whites. On her other side was her mother, a pocketbook draped over her arm and a tissue in hand, shaken and yet composed. The fact that she had on a light-colored dress too made Ellie wonder if widows wore black anymore. The War had changed everything, customs and fashion included, and while women's skirts were higher than ever before, young men were starting to forego hats. Such mundane thoughts whirled through Ellie's mind and she couldn't focus. All around them were people they had known their whole lives, their hearts heavy and faces somber, but inside she felt numb and detached, like an impartial observer at a stranger's funeral.

"Go in peace, my friends…"

Ellie was relieved to hear the Pastor's words because it meant the service was over. The entire congregation turned to the Ames', waiting for them to lead the procession out, and there was no casket because it was already at the graveyard off Passamaquoddy Road. On an Island that didn't see its first automobile until the Twenties, rituals had to form around logistics and no one wanted to carry a body a mile and a half.

Mary adjusted her crutches, Ellie and her mother standing on either side of her, and they went slowly down the aisle as hundreds of eyes looked on. It was the same aisle Ellie always imagined herself walking down at her wedding but like all the dreams of youthful innocence, fate had different plans.

They came out front and people gathered on the lawn along Gull Avenue. The breeze was warm and in the distance, the harbor was a perfect reflection of the blue, cloudless sky. As the family stood around thanking people, Major Rowland stepped over with his wife. His military suit was perfectly pressed—his bars and medals glistened.

"I am more sorry than I can express," he said to Ellie, his voice low and sincere.

360

He turned to Vera and Mary and offered similar condolences.

"Thank you for everything," Ellie said.

"If I can be of any help, please come see me."

Ellie nodded, as well as her mother, whose face was red from sobbing. She had only said a couple of words all morning and, for the first time in her life, Ellie worried more about her than Mary.

The Pastor called to everyone and it was time to go to the burial. In one great show of community support, a parade of cars had lined up on Gull Avenue to take people to the cemetery. There were even a few horse buggies, owned mostly by old men who preferred the simple ways of the past. In Jack's youth, they were the only transportation and Ellie knew he would have appreciated them carrying on the tradition.

Ellie thanked the Major again and then turned to leave.

"Oh, Eleanor," he said.

While she stopped, her mother and sister kept going.

"We got some intel," he said, almost in a whisper. "A U-boat was sighted near Beacon Light the night your father disappeared."

If Ellie had any more emotion left, she might have gasped. But she was drained by life and nothing surprised her anymore.

"He was attacked?"

Rowland shook his head.

"Unlikely, but—"

"Because I should like to believe he went down fighting."

The Major stopped, his expression changing from solemn to sympathetic. Squinting in the sun, he responded with a tender smile and said no more. Ellie smiled back and, without another word, walked away, across the grass and towards the cars.

46

Karl Brink sat at the small café like he did each morning. As he sipped his coffee, he stared at the front page of the Boston Globe:

WAR IS OVER IN EUROPE

He read it over and over, reciting the words in his mind, stunned to the point of ecstasy, a joy that was almost too much to bear. For three long years, he felt like he had been holding his breath and now he could finally exhale. But it wasn't just his relief and the excitement everywhere was palpable. Women wept openly—as did some men—and strangers congratulated one another on the streets. Japan still fought on, but the Allies were overwhelming them and people were confident that soon they would either surrender too or be annihilated. It was a hard-fought war and everyone was thankful that the worst was over.

For Karl, however, the good news was bittersweet. As he flipped through the newspaper, something caught his eye and he stopped. It was a small article, wedged between a soap ad and a story about ballroom dancing. He read the tiny print and his hand began to shake.

Lobsterman's Death May Have Been From U-Boat
Portland, Maine – Authorities say that the death of a local fisherman last month might have been the result of a collision with a German U-Boat. John "Jack" Emory Ames died after his boat broke apart and sank in waters near Beacon Light, six miles from Portland. Coast Guard officials say the damage was not consistent

with rocks and was more likely caused by an accident with another vessel. Speaking with the Associated Press, Captain Malcolm Chapin of the Army Coast Artillery Corps stated, "Canadian Naval intelligence reported a German submarine west of Yarmouth, Nova Scotia on the day of the incident."

For a moment, Karl sat stunned, but there was no time to reflect on the irony of life. He dropped some quarters on the table, grabbed the newspaper and quickly left. The streets of Boston were busy in the morning rush and he darted between traffic to get across Cambridge Street. Before today, he did his best to live discreetly and his beard and sunglasses were part of the act. But with the War with Germany ended, he had a renewed confidence and could finally walk with his head up.

Karl turned up a side street and into the narrow cobblestone lanes of Beacon Hill. For three years, he kept the same routine: coffee in the morning, a walk through the City, lunch, more coffee, a short nap, maybe a film in the evening—then sleep. Although he was happy to be alive, the monotony was like a slow death. He could have turned himself in, but he feared the military would accuse him of espionage and he would be shot. Karl struggled with these thoughts day and night and, in the end, concluded that the only thing to do was wait until the War was over. And now it was.

He stopped at the front door and looked around before opening it. Years of living incognito made him paranoid and he always feared being caught.

"Gabby?"

"Yes, Mister Brink," she said, waddling out from the kitchen.

"I'm taking a trip. Would you help me get my things?"

Gabby stood in the hallway in her white cap and apron, smiling.

"Why, I'd be happy to."

While she turned to get the suitcase, Karl went upstairs for his clothes. Moments later, he was packed and ready to go. Before he left, Gabby made him a sandwich and tea and Karl ate quietly in the parlor. Looking around at the shabby splendor, he remembered when he and his father had come to ask John Hatch to sponsorship them. He never could have imagined that the meeting that day would set off a chain of events that included both his ruin and his redemption.

With only one bag, Karl had decided to travel lightly, even though he didn't know how long he would be away. He thanked Gabby with a hug and told her to take the week off. At one time, there was a poodle to care for, but the dog died two summers earlier.

When Karl showed up at the doorstep three winters earlier, Gabby had been maintaining an empty townhouse. She took him in without question and nursed him back to health. She knew that he was part heir to Hatch's estate and, although the property sat in probate unclaimed, she treated him like the matter was settled and he was the owner. Karl never talked about his situation and she never asked. As a black woman in a white northern city, she had her own concerns and they lived a life of quiet and mutual secrecy.

Walking into North Station, Karl felt like a child going on his first train ride. He hadn't left Boston since he arrived and he was eager to see the countryside again, to experience the openness of the New England landscape. In many ways, the urban isolation had been a sentence for a crime he didn't commit and now he was free.

Karl stood on the platform and waited to board. Years before, he and his parents stood on the exact same spot, returning to Monk Island after spending all day at the INS Office. Those were difficult times, he thought, but they were nothing compared to what followed. His small family had been uprooted, upended, traumatized and torn apart and he was left to pick up the pieces of that broken legacy.

When the announcement was made, Karl walked into the first car and found a seat. With his luggage stowed overhead, he leaned against the window and gazed out as the train pulled away. No one was beside him—the train was half empty—and he used the time to think of what he would say to Ellie.

......

The ferry was at the dock and workers were loading freight before letting passengers on. As Karl waited, he looked around and Portland was much the same. The barrooms and corner markets along Commercial Street were busy, and the wharves were lined with trawlers, ferries, cargo boats, and barges. The waterfront stank of fish from all the processing plants, but it was a poignant smell because it reminded Karl of his time there before the War.

"3 pm ferry to Monk Island."

Startled by the voice, Karl looked up and saw that an intercom had been installed since the last time he was at the terminal. He reached for his suitcase and walked steadily down the ramp. Although he had been calm for the entire train ride, he got suddenly nervous, almost panicked. Nevertheless, he made it onto the boat and climbed up to the top deck.

Minutes later, the ferry horn blared and they started to move. Karl leaned against the railing with the breeze in his face. As they pulled into the harbor, he smelled a cigar and didn't see one. A chill went up his back as he recalled how his father always smoked on the ferry ride to Monk Island. Karl wasn't superstitious, but he liked to believe it was a sign.

The trip over seemed long and he attributed it to the anticipation. For all he knew, Ellie Ames was married or had moved away. They hadn't seen each other or spoken in almost six years and that was a lifetime, especially during war.

As the ferry approached the dock, Karl's palm got sweaty and he felt short of breath. He hadn't been so anxious since the night he planned his escape from his U-boat. And much like that experience, the outcome now was terribly uncertain.

Everyone moved towards the stairways and Karl merged with the passengers, dragging his suitcase like a tourist. As he went over the gangplank, he looked down and the dock pilings were covered in algae and barnacles, reminding him of the sea-worn exterior of U-130. He walked along the pier and when he finally stepped on land, he got slightly dizzy. He hadn't been on the water in a long time and had lost his sea legs.

He continued up the slope with all the other visitors. With his beard, hat, and sunglasses, he didn't think anyone would recognize him, but he felt safer among the crowd. It was only early May and Monk Island was already preparing for summer. Young boys hawked trinkets on the sidewalk—an old Ford pickup with wooden bed rails had a sign for Island

Tours. Families and couples browsed the shops and the ice cream parlor had a line out the door. Karl could have closed his eyes and opened them and the village would have looked no different than it did in 1939. Considering the obliteration of Europe, he was happy to know that some places never changed.

He walked up to the intersection and stopped at the corner. It was the same corner where he first asked Ellie for directions to the cottage—the same corner where she asked him to teach her how to swim. Standing there, he gazed out over the waterfront—at the clear blue sky, the boats in the harbor, the City in the distance—and felt like he was finally home.

47.

Ellie sat at the counter and flipped through the order slips. Knowing what was in stock, she had to figure out what they could fulfill and what they needed to send to Portland for. There was always plenty of herring, but they usually ran low on rockfish and pogies. They had no more 3/8 inch rope and hog rings were on backorder from the foundry in Lewiston.

As she took notes and tallied invoices, she kept making mistakes and the eraser was wearing out. Her father had only been gone for three weeks and she was still in a daze. Mr. Mallet said she could take the month off—the entire summer if needed. But Ellie knew the best remedy for grief was work and she only missed one day for his funeral. In a rare moment of candor, Jack once mentioned to her that he was able to get past the trauma of war by keeping busy and she cherished the lesson.

After misspelling mackerel, Ellie tried to erase it and the pencil broke. She threw it on the floor and got up to get another one in the cabinet. The bell above the door jingled and someone stepped in, but she was too frustrated to look back.

"Pardon me, do you sell sandwiches?..."

She went to say no, then stopped. There were only two times before in her life when she was awake and felt like she was dreaming. The first was when she got pneumonia as a young girl; the second was at her father's burial. Now hearing the voice, she got the same sensation.

"...because I should love a ham with cheese."

Facing the cabinet, Ellie bowed her head and pressed her eyes together, thinking the unthinkable, and yet knowing it couldn't be true.

"And would you be kind enough to tell me where Thrush Lane is?"

A storm of emotion welled up inside and tears rolled down her cheeks. She heard footsteps come towards her across the floor and was filled with a wonderful dread. When she took a deep breath and turned around, it was the bravest thing she ever did.

Ellie stood frozen for almost a minute, her mouth agape and struggling to make sense of the vision that lay before her.

"Karl?"

The word felt as strange to say as it was to hear.

"I said I'd come back—"

Without warning, she lunged over the counter, almost knocking him over, and Karl caught her in his arms. The embrace was clumsy but no less heartfelt and she sobbed into his shoulder like a child. Of all the possibilities, of all the outcomes, of all the endings, Ellie never would have imagined this. A few weeks before she had cursed God and she now found herself thanking him. Someone had been taken from her, but someone was returned and in an instant, her faith in the world was restored.

"Ellie?" Mr. Mallet said, coming out from the back. When he saw her balancing on the counter, legs in the air and arms around Karl, he muttered, "Oh, my," and turned right around.

It was moment worthy of hilarity, but they were both too emotional and Ellie knew there would be time for laughter later. When she finally pulled away, she slid back and came around the counter. She took Karl by the waist and looked up at him amazed.

"You have a beard," she said, touching it.

"Do I look older?"

Staring into his eyes, she swallowed her tears, nodded.

"We all look older."

48

It was the warmest night yet, almost summerlike, as Karl and Ellie sat on the beach and looked out across Taylor Passage. The Army patrol boat that had been there every day for three and a half years was gone and civilians were once again allowed to sail through the strait. With Japan still fighting, the War wasn't completely over, but on Monk Island and throughout Casco Bay, people had moved on.

"When I looked up, there was a man standing over me," Karl said. "He had on a white helmet. He shouted not to move. I thought I was caught. Then I heard another voice. It said to let me go…"

Ellie slid closer to him on the blanket while he ate. He had, in fact, wanted a ham sandwich and they brought a picnic basket full of food.

"…They started to argue—I couldn't understand what they were saying. Then the voice said don't blow that whistle…don't blow that whistle. Suddenly, there was a gunshot. I thought for sure I was hit but I wasn't. Then someone picked me up, put me over his shoulder…"

Ellie smiled to herself, realizing that, despite his war injuries and back pain, her father was an incredibly strong man.

"…We went through the snow…we walked and walked…it seemed like hours. I was in an out of consciousness. I had hypothermia…"

"Did he say anything?"

Karl shook his head and took another bite. With all that he was telling her, she couldn't believe he still had an appetite but she knew men were different that way.

"...He said *don't move, boy. Keep quiet, boy.* I didn't even know who it was until the next day. When I woke up, it was dark, I thought I was dead. Then the top opened, the sun was out, there were trees." He turned to Ellie and their eyes met. "It was your father—I couldn't believe it. He put me in an underground hideout."

She thought back to the day Mary fell through the plywood in the woods, never imagining it would someday become Karl's refuge.

"He came every day," Karl went on, "and told me to stay put, that soldiers were looking for me. I would have gone crazy down there, but I was used to small spaces, being on a U-boat—"

"Why didn't he tell me?" she interrupted, but there was no bitterness.

"Perhaps he was afraid," he said, then he continued. "After a while, a week or so, he came and told me the search was off. He brought more bread, some clothes, then left. Just like that. I knew then it was time to go. I waited until late, then found my way out of the woods. I got to the shore, stole a skiff, and made it across the harbor. I walked for miles in the snow, slept in barns, sheds, wherever I could stay warm. Eventually, I got to Boston. When I showed up at John Hatch's house, I weighed one hundred and twenty pounds."

Ellie pulled her knees to her chest and gazed out at the water, breathing the salt air, entranced by it all. Reflecting on Karl's ordeal, she felt some vague guilt over not being with him throughout it. Until that moment, she never thought much about fate or destiny, but the miracle of his survival was evidence enough for both. She had always known her father was a good man at heart and saving Karl was as much a gift to her as it was payback for all he had done to discourage them from being together. Whether or not he ever knew it, Ellie had forgiven him then and she forgave him now.

"How's little Mary?"

She blinked and her attention shifted. With the past explained, she knew it was time to move on to the present, and maybe the future.

"No longer little. She goes off to college in September."

"She'll make a fine student."

Ellie was pleased because, as the son of two professors, he understood such things. Karl had a worldliness she always admired and a gentleness that made it sincere.

"And your mother?"

"She manages, but her arthritis is bad. Somedays she has trouble getting out of bed."

"Then we shall be there to help her," Karl said.

"We will?"

"We will."

Ellie took his hand and squeezed it like a lifeline. She rested her head on his shoulder and together they gazed out over Taylor Passage and the unending sea beyond. The sky was now dark and the only sounds were the wind, the waves, the distant clang of a buoy. Something flickered at the horizon and Ellie thought it was a ship. But when she looked closer, it was a star.

ACKNOWLEDGMENTS

Like any work of fiction, this book would not have been possible without the support of some select friends and colleagues. First, I want to thank my wife Heidi, who continues to believe in my work. Next, I'd like to thank fellow author Chris Mooney for helping me develop the story to its fullest. For their kind endorsements of the novel, I am indebted to William Martin and Eoin Dempsey. I am grateful to Jak Showell for his expertise on German submarine warfare and to Jon March for his knowledge of Maine life and the culture of lobstering.

Lastly, it is my hope that this book can honor, in some small way, the struggles and sacrifices of Maine coastal communities during the War years.

ABOUT THE AUTHOR

Jonathan Cullen grew up in Boston and attended public schools. After a brief career as a bicycle messenger, he attended Boston College and graduated with a B.A. in English Literature (1995). During his twenties, he wrote two unpublished novels, taught high-school in Ireland, lived in Mexico, worked as a prison librarian and spent a month in Kenya, Africa before finally settling down three blocks from where he grew up.

He currently lives in Boston (West Roxbury) with his wife Heidi and daughter Maeve.